THE NAVIGATION LOG

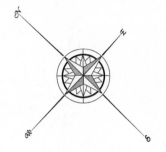

THE

NAVIGATION

LOG

A NOVEL

MARTIN CORRICK

RANDOM HOUSE
New York

All rights reserved under International and Pan-American Copyright Conventions.
Published in the United States by Random House, Inc., New York, and
simultaneously in Canada by Random House of Canada Limited, Toronto.

RANDOM HOUSE and colophon are registered trademarks of Random House, Inc.

This work was originally published in the United Kingdom by Scribner,
an imprint of Simon & Schuster UK Limited, London, in 2002.

Grateful acknowledgment is made to the following for permission
to reprint previously published material:
EDWARD B. MARKS MUSIC COMPANY C/O CARLIN AMERICA: Excerpt from "There'll Be Some
Changes Made" by Billy Higgins and W. Benton Overstreet. Used by permission of
Edward B. Marks Music Company.
WARNER BROS. PUBLICATIONS: Excerpt from "Blue Moon" by Lorenz Hart and Richard Rodgers.
Copyright © 1934 (renewed) Metro-Goldwyn-Mayer, Inc. All rights controlled by
EMI Robbins Catalog, Inc. All rights reserved. Used by permission.
Warner Bros. Publications U.S. Inc., Miami, FL 33014.

Library of Congress Cataloging-in-Publication Data

Corrick, Martin.
The navigation log: a novel / Martin Corrick.
p.   cm.
ISBN 0-375-50812-0
1. World War, 1939–1945—England—Fiction.   2. Pilgrims and pilgrimages—Fiction.
3. Air pilots, Military—Fiction.   4. Brothers—Fiction.   5. Teachers—Fiction.
6. England—Fiction.   7. Twins—Fiction.   8. Poets—Fiction.   I. Title.
PR6103.O77 N38 2003   823'.92—dc21   2002075197

Random House website address: www.atrandom.com

Printed in the United States of America on acid-free paper

24689753

First U.S. Edition

Book design by Jo Anne Metsch

*In memory of Denis and
Elizabeth Corrick*

ACKNOWLEDGMENTS

Hilary and our daughters, Georgia and Freya, have continued to encourage my writing despite the length of my apprenticeship; I am deeply grateful to them. My agent, Derek Johns, my editor, Tim Binding, and my tutors and fellow students at the University of East Anglia all helped to shape this book. A bursary from Southern Arts kept me from penury during some lengthy rewriting. And I must acknowledge that a sketch by an adult student of mine, the late Basil Chubb, was the original source of the character of Uncle Oscar—though Basil, who was a warm and charming man as well as a fine writer, would not have made him so vulgar.

The Navigation Log

The navigation log is a record which is kept, step by step, of the navigational work done during a flight. A log should always be kept, as the record it contains will often prove useful afterwards. No unnecessary information should appear in the log, but that which is entered must be clear and accurate: the amount of information recorded will vary with circumstances. The most important entries include courses steered, times of changes of course, changes of wind observed or calculated, fixes, ground speeds and tracks, and signals sent or received. A log should be compiled in a simple form so that it could be handed to another navigator without explanations.

Air Publication 1234
Air Ministry Manual of Air Navigation
Volume 1, 1935, Chapter IX

PART I

BETWEEN

THE

WARS

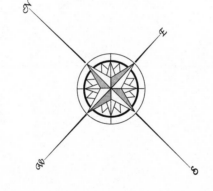

A HORSE-DRAWN cab stopped outside 27 Waterloo Crescent and a tall man stepped out. He assisted a fair-haired woman to alight, closed the door of the cab, and said something to the driver. The woman stood still and looked at the house. As the man opened the front gate, the cabdriver flicked his whip and the cab drove away.

On the first floor of number 19 Miss Betty Alcock allowed her drawing room curtain to swing back and turned to her friend Mrs. Marigold Jennings. "They've arrived," she said. "It's good to see a fair young couple moving in." Absentmindedly Miss Betty picked up her cat, carefully detaching its claws from the arm of the chair. "Do keep still, you silly creature," she said. The cat wriggled a little, but she held it securely.

The man was still holding the front gate open, and the woman was pointing up at some aspect of the house. The man, who must surely be her husband, glanced up and nodded, waiting for her to step through the gate. Eventually she did so; the couple walked up the path and disappeared from view.

"That house has been empty far too long," Miss Betty said. "Poor Mr. Winford! It was entirely unsuited to a widower living alone. I'm sure its size and draftiness were factors in his demise. All those stairs.

And the place haunted by the memory of his poor wife! What a frail shadow of herself she became, in the end." She stroked the cat firmly.

"I hope you don't mind my mentioning it, Betty," Marigold Jennings said, "but there's no need to speak quite so loudly. My hearing is not as bad as all that."

Miss Betty looked at her. "Was I speaking loudly?"

"You were. You have a tendency to boom."

"What do you mean, *boom*? I'm not sure that word isn't rather offensive."

Miss Betty twitched the curtain aside and looked again. "They've gone inside," she said. "No—wait a minute. Here they are again."

The couple had emerged from the French windows into the garden, and the tall man was standing in the center of the lawn. The woman opened the door of the summerhouse and looked inside. She turned and said something to her husband. He replied and she shook her head.

"The summerhouse is not approved," Miss Betty said. She turned from the window, and Marigold Jennings took her place.

After a few moments Marigold said, "They're a handsome couple."

Miss Betty sniffed and continued to stroke her cat. "He looks a trifle on the gaunt side."

"Perhaps he is. Personally, I don't mind a touch of gauntness in a man. Better than the other thing."

"The other thing? You should say what you mean, Marigold. Corpulence is the word you're looking for. Of course, one doesn't admire corpulence in a young man, though it may add a certain degree of presence in middle age. As for her, she's very *upright,* isn't she? Almost statuesque, one might say."

"There is nothing wrong with uprightness, Betty. It's a noble quality."

"Uprightness can easily become moral rectitude, and one can have too much of *that,* as we know only too well."

The tall man took a bunch of keys from the pocket of his overcoat. He searched through them, found a particular key, unlocked the back door of the house, and stepped aside to allow the woman to enter. As she did so, a green van marked "E. Hudson Removals" turned into Waterloo Crescent from the High Street.

AT TEN IN the morning every Sunday, Miss Betty Alcock and Mrs. Marigold Jennings foregathered at Miss Betty's and walked together down the High Street to St. Saviour's, returning after the service to imbibe a little preprandial refreshment.

"The imbibing of preprandial refreshment," Miss Betty had many times remarked to her friend, "is so much more satisfactory than mere drinking, don't you think? It's wonderful how that phrase removes all the guilt."

In winter their refreshment was dark sherry, and in summer a light Italian wine. Both were provided by Miss Betty's nephew Michael, the owner of a low-key but apparently successful import-export business in Ramsgate. Although she disliked his familiar manner and his choice of shoes, Miss Betty had learned to accommodate his gifts pragmatically. She did not question his assurance that his imported beverages were virtually free from alcohol. "My dear Aunt Betty, you can drink as much as you like, and there's plenty more where that came from."

"I daresay Michael's generosity is designed to ensure his remembrance in my will," Miss Betty told her friend. "But since the bargain is unspoken, I see no particular need to adhere to my side of it."

WITHIN TWENTY-FOUR hours of their arrival, Miss Betty and Mrs. Marigold Jennings discovered that their new neighbors were Felix Anderson and his wife, Constance, who was a painter.

"How lovely! There is a terrible shortage of artists in Finchley," Marigold said, clapping her hands.

"There is a shortage of scandal of any kind in Finchley," Miss Betty said.

As soon as they reasonably could, Miss Betty and Marigold Jennings visited 27 Waterloo Crescent and were given tea by Mrs. Anderson. Her husband, she said, was at work. They spotted an easel, a stack of blank canvases, an encrusted palette, numerous jam jars full of brushes, a wooden manikin, and two tea chests containing tubes of paint, rolls of paper, sketchbooks, and cartons of charcoal.

Marigold Jennings said, "So many paintbrushes!"

Miss Betty cried, "Oh, how urgently we require the consolation of art in the wastes of north London!"

Marigold said, "Fancy! A painter for a neighbor!"

As the friends had observed, Constance possessed a stillness that was unusual. She looked carefully at Marigold and said quietly, "I'm only an amateur."

There was the slightest of pauses. Marigold Jennings said, "Betty is so interested in art."

Constance looked at Miss Betty, nodded, and said, "Are you."

THE TWO FRIENDS agreed that the response of the artist had not been encouraging. They had worked hard at being welcoming, but she hadn't even given them a tour of the house. She had shown little interest in their intriguing stories about the previous occupants, the elusive Mr. Winford and his tragic wife. In sum, Mrs. Constance Anderson looked unlikely to become closely engaged with the established residents of Waterloo Crescent.

However, in St. Saviour's on the following Sunday, her husband, Felix Anderson, was introduced to the congregation. This development made Miss Betty and Marigold Jennings (who always sat on the aisle end of the fourth pew from the front, well clear of all the pillars) lean forward in expectation.

"Mr. Anderson," the vicar said, "is an experienced lay preacher. He will speak from time to time on matters of concern to himself, and indeed to us all. I'm sure his talks will be most instructive."

It was true that Felix Anderson looked gaunt, but his gauntness was not uninteresting; it might mean that he had endured some kind of hardship and therefore had a story to tell. When the vicar introduced him he gave a just discernible bow and a fleeting smile, but said nothing. Miss Betty and Marigold Jennings looked around for his wife, but Constance did not seem to be in church that particular day. That was a pity, for they had hoped to catch her eye and confirm their acquaintance before the assembled congregation.

"Mr. Anderson," Marigold Jennings said afterward, "looked very much the aesthete."

Miss Betty looked at her friend and raised her eyebrows. "Are you sure you mean that? An aesthete is someone who luxuriates in sensuality, like Mr. Oscar Wilde. Perhaps you mean he's an *ascetic*."

Mrs. Jennings turned pink. "Oh dear, you're quite right, of course. I was referring to his craggy appearance. I'm sure his morals are impeccable."

Miss Betty suddenly felt magnanimous toward her friend. "Craggy is an excellent word for him," she said. "I wouldn't be surprised if he had Scots ancestry. I could see him in a kilt."

LATER THAT SUMMER, Felix Anderson sat on the verandah at 27 Waterloo Crescent, developing his thoughts on a verse from Job: *Naked came I from my mother's womb, and naked shall I return thither: the Lord gave and the Lord hath taken away; blessed be the name of the Lord.*

Felix, as well as being a lay preacher, was a district manager for the post office. He was thin. His face was grooved and his hands were bony. He was thirty years old, and as a result of his hard work and his capacity to accept responsibility, he already owned a house and employed a housemaid—who, at that same moment, came in and took away his empty teacup. He did not look up.

FROM HER WINDOW Miss Betty Alcock remarked the rapid improvements that Mrs. Anderson had made in the garden. She nudged Marigold's elbow and pointed out the young woman who had emerged from the French windows to pick up Mr. Anderson's tea things and was now out on the lawn, folding the travel rug and collecting the deck chairs. Marigold Jennings said, "Oh! I wonder who she is! Perhaps Mrs. Anderson has a sister."

"Don't be daft, Marigold. She's wearing a quite horrid dress and walking about with her mouth open. She's obviously a housemaid."

"A maid! Fancy! I suppose that's because of Mrs. Anderson being an artist, and unable to put her mind to housework."

Miss Betty made a puffing noise to indicate her considerable disagreement with this notion, and pointed out that the painter herself was partly visible in a window on the first floor. She appeared to be working at her easel.

CONSTANCE ANDERSON, WHO was beginning to find her pregnancy uncomfortable, peered at one of her latest oils. It was a large picture, essentially blue. Based on a study she had made last summer, the summer of her marriage, it portrayed her husband seated on a deck chair among the pine trees that stand behind the beach at Lepe, on the shore of the Solent. She had not so far discovered more than a modest creative talent, but believed that anything could be achieved if one had the will. In the picture, her husband wore his new panama at a slight angle. The small waves of the Solent, the group of pines, and the yellow gravel of the beach were not badly represented, she felt, but somewhere in the painting there was a wrong note. With extreme concentration Constance searched for it.

Her husband nodded in his wicker chair, then sat abruptly upright, the phrase *naked shall I return thither* running in his head. Through the open French windows came a sequence of melodious chimes: it was six o'clock.

CONSTANCE HAD BEEN brought up by an aunt in Leamington Spa, her father rarely visiting. Her aunt had impressed upon her the need to behave with decorum and to cultivate artistic skills with which she might occupy the long evenings. Having taken up painting, Constance rapidly developed a strong visual curiosity. She was always on the lookout for striking compositions. There were many wounded and limbless ex-soldiers in London that year; she found their damaged bodies interesting, but one could hardly ask if one might paint them. She wondered if she might take up photography, which might be less obviously intrusive, but nothing came of that notion. As her pregnancy advanced, her interest in creative work declined. She easily became irritable. The girl Milly took an age to carry out a simple request. It was not good enough.

E ARLY THE NEXT day Felix sat at his desk, his head in one hand, his pen scratching across a sheet of bank paper, dipping into the inkpot, tapping twice on the rim. *We may take this verse to mean,* he wrote, and then stared out the window at the hurrying clouds. As a beginning, that was too stiff. He crossed it out and began again. *The word* naked *is of course used metaphorically.* That wasn't right, either, but it would have to do. *Suppose one found oneself actually walking down the street without one's clothes.*

He paused and considered the sentence. Dare he say that? It was provocative. It would make the congregation sit up. Real nakedness was a good deal more daunting than the metaphoric kind.

He dipped his pen, tapped it on the inkwell, and wrote, *Imagine how dramatic this metaphor was, when first written.* He dipped his pen again. *We have become too familiar with the language of the Bible. It has become smooth with use.* Smooth, he thought. Yes. Smooth with use. That was good. *If we uncover the truth of the metaphor, we may find its message as unsettling as sudden nakedness.*

Felix dipped his pen. *It is certainly the case that we are here being advised on the futility of material acquisition. But we must interpret these lines with care. They should not prevent us saving for our old age, or providing for ourselves and our loved ones a reasonable standard of life.*

He paused, thinking that the verse probably suggested precisely the opposite. But that was no good in Finchley in the year of our Lord 1918. One had to allow people their few possessions. Perhaps this particular verse was not such a good choice. No matter.

Even in religion, compromise and common sense are necessary. We must adhere to principles, not particulars. In the case of a text written so long ago, we need to consider the nature of the issue being debated, and translate it into the morality of our time.

He had got into his stride. The rest of it would come more easily. It was time for breakfast. Where was Milly?

A s   t h e   G r e a t   War edged uneasily into its final hours, Constance lay on her back with her legs spread, knowing that she would soon die from a pain that was unendurable. The midwives peered and prodded into the birth canal, the younger one saying, "Should we send for Doctor now, Matron?" and the older one taking no notice.

"Push, mother!" said Matron.

Constance pushed. At first there was nothing but pain, and then something gave way with a terrible tearing, the pain stopped, and the young midwife cried out, "Oh! Oh! How lovely! It's a boy!"—and blushed.

In the waiting room, Felix heard distant cries and looked across at the closed door to the ward, but nothing happened. He turned again to his copy of *The Times*. ARMISTICE SIGNATURE DELAYED, said a headline. He turned idly to the front page and looked down the personal column. It was here, he had often thought, that the real concerns of common humanity were truly displayed. *£5 reward for the discovery of a fox-terrier (bitch), white with brown patch on right side, brown spot on tail, and brown face.* No doubt there was a story of thoughtless purchase and self-indulgent tears behind that advertisement. *Answers to name of Pluto. Inscription on collar. J. R. Seward, 29 Boundary-Road NW8.* A sermon could be made of this.

A door opened and Matron strode across the room. She halted before him and said, "Congratulations, Mr. Anderson. You have a son."

Felix stood up. "A son," he said, and then again, "A son." It seemed insufficient. What else should he say? "Is my wife all right? I heard something—"

"It was not an easy birth. You may see her shortly."

Matron marched away. Felix sat down. It should be more than this, he thought. God has blessed us with a child. He unfolded the paper. PRODUCE PRICES. DISAPPOINTING CORN CROPS. LOSSES ON POTATOES. *Farmers have had a double experience of the government plan of deferring the fixing of prices for produce until the character of the harvest can be estimated, and are expressing their views freely on its operation.*

He shook his head and turned the page, wondering what would happen now that he had a son. A son!

⌒

O N THE FIRST floor of 19 Waterloo Crescent, Miss Betty said, "Something's definitely happening." She held her spectacles away from her nose for better long-range focus.

"As far as I can see, absolutely nothing is happening," Marigold Jennings said, peering over her shoulder.

"That is precisely my point. The house is empty except for Milly, who is rushing here and there with a duster. I believe Mrs. Anderson may have been transported to the maternity hospital without our knowledge."

"In that case, we should buy some flowers."

"Oh yes! That's an exceptionally good idea."

"Thank you," said Marigold Jennings with a small dip of the head.

"If you were to pop along to the florist straight away, you might get there before they close."

"I suppose I might," Mrs. Jennings said.

⌒

I T HAD GROWN dark in the hospital. A young nurse came.

"Would you like a cup of tea, Mr. Anderson?"

"What's happening? Can I see my wife?"

"I don't know. I'm sorry."

"Oh, very well. Yes, I should like some tea." He turned the page and read an article entitled ON THE CANNON: A SHOW FOR CHILDREN IN PARIS. *When the Liberation Loan was about to be launched, M. Clemenceau suggested that a show of German war trophies should be organised in Paris. He saw how direct a means this would afford of striking at the Frenchman's pocket through his heart; but he can hardly have foreseen how forcible an ally he was summoning to the aid of the loan, in the childhood of Paris.*

Felix Anderson's eyes closed. He dozed intermittently through the autumn night. Shortly before dawn Matron returned again.

"Mr. Anderson, I'm sorry to say that there is an unexpected complication. We have sent for the surgeon."

"Surgeon? What's the matter?"

"I cannot say. Professor Macmillan will let you know."

"Can I see my wife?"

"I'm afraid not."

"How long will it be?"

"A short time. I cannot say precisely."

It grew light again. A porter came around, turning off the yellow lamps. Felix rubbed his stubbled face and picked up the paper. *Holeproof Ladies' Hose. Two Months' Wear Or Another Pair! EXTRA-ORDINARY SAMPLE OFFER. 2/11d or 2 pairs for 5/6d. The London Holeproof Hosiery Co.*

CONSTANCE HAD SOME dim recognition that she had been delivered of a child, and wondered idly in her dream why it was that activity continued around her when she wished to sleep. Never mind; no doubt someone would be dealing with it.

She dozed, and a particular memory ran in a slow, repetitive loop in her head. A few weeks earlier she was on the point of making a long-considered brush stroke—just so, correcting that mistaken shadow—but had mislaid her number 8 camel-hair brush (elegantly tapered and precise, a favorite). It was nowhere in her workroom, that was certain. She glanced vaguely into the bedrooms, although there was no reason on earth why a paintbrush should be there. She looked at the attic stairs: It would not be in Milly's room. The visitors' bedroom was cold and smelled musty; it must be aired. She made a mental note to remind Milly. On the way downstairs she held the banisters firmly. It would not do to have a fall at this stage. Had Felix borrowed her number 8? Whatever for? She opened the heavy door of her husband's study. On the green leather of his desk was an inlaid box in which he kept pens and pencils. She opened it. Thin silver chains supported the lid. Her number 8 brush lay on the green velvet with six HB pencils, a pencil sharpener, a packet of steel nibs, a stick of sealing wax, a box of matches, and three letters held together with an elastic band. She took the brush, shut the box, and climbed the stairs. Her back ached. The large, round handwriting on the letters was somehow familiar; perhaps they were from a parishioner. Constance sat at her easel and moistened the brush. Probably they had something to do with the church. That night she woke before dawn and stared into the dark.

⁓

I N THE WAITING room Felix woke hearing church bells. A nurse and an elderly man in a gray suit stood before him. He could hear the wheezing of the man's breath.

"Mr. Anderson," the nurse said, "this is Professor Macmillan."

Felix stood up.

"I believe you have been told there is a difficulty," Macmillan said. He had a slow, formal manner and a burr in his voice. Perhaps he was Scottish.

"Yes," Felix said, "I have heard something."

"Yes. We are investigating the matter. We should know shortly."

"But what *is* the matter?"

"We will let you know as soon as we can."

"For God's sake—"

"We are doing what we can."

"What are those bells?"

"The Armistice. It's eleven o'clock. The war's over."

"What about my son?"

"He is small, but evidently normal."

They went away. Felix sat down. *The Times* was crumpled. He had difficulty focusing on the page. HUSH BEFORE THE DAWN. PRIMATE ON THE WORK OF PEACE. COMING UNITY OF PEOPLES. *His Grace the Archbishop of Canterbury said: "While we are saying our prayers and singing our hymns here, the sands are running out. We dare not speak yet, I mean not tonight, of definite clear-cut results; but it does seem virtually certain, and the thought uplifts us as we say the words, that the cause for which we and our allies have striven, the cause which brought England and America at least into the war, has, under God's good hand, prevailed, and that its opposite, the principle of sheer physical force and the will to power, has*

*been definitely and for ever barred from being the dominant factor in the life
of civilized man. Something higher, deeper, worthier of men with immortal
souls, has proved the conqueror, with a conquest which shall not be overset."*

Felix screwed up his eyes, unable to pin down the archbishop's
meaning. What was the time? He looked up and saw Matron and the
surgeon approaching with the air of a deputation. He could not read
their expressions. It was a bright day; they walked through bars of
sunshine and shadow. He stood up.

"Mr. Anderson. This has been an unusual case."

"What's happened?"

"Matron has told you that the birth was a difficult one. Labor was
protracted. After the birth it became apparent that your wife was becoming distressed. It was necessary to do some exploratory surgery.
There is another child. You have two boys, Mr. Anderson, not one.
Twins. Identical twins."

"Twins."

"Your wife is exhausted. We have given her something to help her
sleep. She must regain her strength. Your sons are both well."

"Twins?"

"Yes, Mr. Anderson. Twin boys. Identical."

"Twins."

Professor Macmillan and his escort walked away. Felix sat down.
Labor was protracted: The phrase meant that the man was avoiding
something unsavory. They nearly lost one of my sons. How can they
be unaware that another child is present? One day I will write a
sermon about doctors. We are grateful for their ministrations, but
they should not conceal their uncertainty by means of secrecy and
arrogance, and should not appear to claim an authority that properly belongs to our Lord. But twins! Good Lord! What would that
mean? Two cots, two chamber pots, two perambulators, two sets of
tiny trousers, two cricket bats, two beds, two rooms, two baby boys!
Identical!

The paper lay on the floor in a patch of sunlight. STILL WAITING
THE SIGNATURE. COURIER AT SPA. JOURNEY DELAYED BY ENEMY.

SEVERAL HOURS LATER, having at last glimpsed for a few moments his sleeping wife and his sleeping sons, Felix took a cab up the High Street. The cab went through crowds of revelers. It was evening, he noticed as he unlocked the front door of the house in Waterloo Crescent. He stepped inside and shut the door. The house was silent and shadowy. Felix hung up his coat. "Milly," he called. There was no reply. At the foot of the stairs he called again, "Milly?"

He went into his study, lit the lamp, took a sheet of paper from a drawer, and dipped a pen into his silver inkpot. He listened to the slow tick of the carriage clock on his desk. Outside, people were singing "Tipperary."

AH, HE'S BACK at last, Miss Betty thought, seeing the blink of a light in Felix's study and checking the time on the traveling alarm that her dear father had given her so many years ago, yes, on the occasion of her twenty-first birthday. What a lovely man he had been, and how she missed him! It was eight o'clock precisely. Felix had come home, but his wife had not, nor had the child. Let us pray that nothing is wrong.

MILLY, FELIX WROTE in his small, neat hand, *I don't know where you are. An extraordinary thing has happened. Constance has had twins, two boys, identical twins. It was a difficult birth, they say. She had to have some kind of surgery. She is weak and will require nursing in the hospital for some days. The boys are well. They shall be named Thomas and William, after my grandfather.*

I shall have to devote much time to Constance—we may have to have a nurse—there will be people in and out of the house—doctors—all that sort of thing— You'll understand— It has nothing to do with my feelings for you— It is a matter of obligations— But we could meet one evening—say next Wednesday at 8 P.M. I shall buy a bottle of Bristol Cream.

He left the sheet unsigned, placed it in an envelope, wrote "Milly" on the front, took it into the kitchen, and left it on the table beside a vase of fresh flowers that Milly must have bought: a thoughtful gesture.

He climbed the stairs to his bedroom, removed his clothes, took his blue striped pajamas from under the pillow, and put them on. He knelt by the bed for some minutes but found himself unable to collect his thoughts. Eventually he got into bed and fell into a sleep of such total unconsciousness that it was not in the least troubled by the contented chanting of the citizens of Finchley.

⁓

"I HAPPENED TO notice," said Miss Betty Alcock, sipping her midmorning tea, "that Mr. Anderson came home alone last night, quite late. The bedroom curtains are still closed."

Marigold Jennings clasped her hands together and said, "Perhaps the happy event has occurred at last! I wonder if Milly showed him our flowers."

"Something has happened, but it is not clear to me that the event will necessarily be happy," Miss Betty said.

"Betty, you're an awful pessimist," Marigold Jennings said. "A baby is always a happy event."

"A little more thought will disabuse you of that opinion, I think."

"Provided the birth occurs in wedlock, of course. And provided the dear child is healthy."

"Exactly. One can make quite a long list of provisos. Even within wedlock there are numerous circumstances unfavorable to a happy birth."

"Mr. Anderson is a man of God, Betty."

"Oh dear! I doubt there is any necessary connection between happiness and men of God. Happiness is a commonplace human emotion, not nearly grand enough for religious purposes. If one says 'God,' one feels impelled to utter large words like 'love' or 'bliss.' Possibly even 'eternal bliss.' There's nothing merely happy about God. Just imagine saying, 'I met God the other day. He seemed pretty chirpy.' "

"Betty, you do say the most provocative things."

"Isn't that why you like me?"

"Well, I suppose it might be. But you mustn't be *too* shocking. You'll get a reputation."

Miss Betty laughed and refilled her friend's cup. "I'm a proud Kentish girl and I'll say what I think. Besides, a single lady needs a reputation. It provides her acquaintances with things to whisper about. Just imagine if nobody was talking about you."

"Oh no, Betty, I don't want anybody talking about me."

"Marigold, you are surely telling a horrid untruth. One simply *must* be talked about. It confirms one's sense of self."

"I don't suppose that Mr. Anderson would like to know we were talking about him."

"Absolutely not. But that's my point: Mr. Anderson is not a happy man, not a man who enjoys company. You can't imagine him being joyful, can you?"

"I suppose not. But he may be utterly devoted to his wife."

"Devotion is no basis for a marriage. Devotion is what a brainless creature such as my cat shows towards its owner." She picked up the animal. "Don't you, dear?" She replaced the cat on the floor, and it rolled over and wriggled. "Besides," she said, "seriousness always arouses one's suspicions."

"There is surely nothing wrong with being serious, Betty."

"On the contrary. Just imagine being married to a man who never tickled you, never whispered outrageous things in your ear, never made you laugh! Oh dear, I can think of nothing worse!"

"Malcolm never tickled me."

"I don't think you should boast about that."

"Anyway," Marigold said, taking a sip of her tea and leaning toward her friend, "what sort of things have men whispered in your ear?"

                                    ⌒

AT EIGHT-THIRTY on the following Wednesday evening, Felix turned the maid, Milly, over and entered her from behind, a position he found most satisfactory. He thought, as he moved back and forward in leisurely progress toward climax, about his wife and her twins and what it might mean. Things would be different. Maybe we should have another servant, if we can find a room for her. Milly's buttocks were smooth and white. The arrangement was convenient, but things must not become too complicated.

———

TEN DAYS LATER the cabdriver passed the second baby to Constance, who passed it to Milly, who put it in the cot next to the first. "Well, that's that," Constance said. She reached up and removed a long hatpin from her wide-brimmed hat. She took the hat off and gave it to Milly, then replaced the hatpin in her sleek fair hair. Milly stood holding the hat. They looked at the pink faces of the sleeping babies. "Very nice," said the cabdriver. "Lovely babies."

"Milly," Constance said, "be so good as to pay the man."

Milly took the cabdriver downstairs into the kitchen. She put the big hat on the table and paid him from the tin on the mantelpiece. "Thank you, miss," the cabman said. "Like dancing, do you?"

"This way," Milly said, leading him to the front door. She opened it and stood aside.

"I could pick you up at six-thirty," he said, putting a hand on Milly's waist. "We could nip along to the Palais."

Milly pushed the door against him.

"Hoity-toity," the cabbie said, retreating.

Milly shut the door and returned to the nursery.

"That one's William Robert," Constance said, pointing, "and that one's Thomas Edward. At least, I think so."

Milly said nothing.

"I'm going to lie down," Constance said. "Come to my room in an hour, and I'll tell you about the arrangements for the children."

When she had gone, Milly knelt for some time beside the cot and looked closely at the babies, seeking some small distinction that would enable her to tell them apart. She could see none in their faces, though one child was perhaps more restless than the other. She reached through the bars and touched the open hand of the restless one. The tiny fingers closed about her own. After a few minutes, Milly drew her hand away and went down to the kitchen to prepare the supper. Her mistress's hat lay on the beechwood table, its feathers stirring as she passed by.

WHEN MILLY CAME to her room, Constance was sitting at her writing desk and parceling maternity clothes for dispatch to the Red Cross. "Their father chose the children's names," she said. "He wanted names without unpleasant or potentially absurd connotations, hence Thomas and William. Good English names, he calls them. As the babies are identical, you'll have to label one of them. Round the ankle, say. Perhaps you'd do that when they wake up."

"Yes, ma'am," Milly said. "What sort of label would you like?"

She looked up. "What do you mean?"

"Shall I buy a special label?"

"An ordinary label will be perfectly adequate. Here you are." Constance passed Milly one of her brown labels. "Come to think of it, I suppose they'll be frightfully messy. You'd better use my indelible ink."

THE BABIES WOKE and Milly made up their bottles as she had been instructed. She fed and changed them, then considered the question of the label. The babies lay awake in their cot. "Which of you is which?" Milly asked. Their eyes traveled absently across her face, and their hands waved jerkily.

Milly went across the landing and knocked on Constance's bedroom door.

"What is it?"

"It's me, ma'am."

"Come in."

Constance lay in bed, drawing in a sketchbook with a thin stick of charcoal.

"I'm sorry to bother you," Milly said, "but I can't tell which baby is which. For the label, I mean." She stood by the bed and saw that Constance was drawing a baby boy's penis and scrotum, which was surely not a natural thing for a mother to do, even if she was an artist.

"Neither can I," Constance said. "Put it on the first one that comes to hand."

"Very well, ma'am."

"And by the way, have you seen my hat? The one with the feathers?"

"I'll bring it up," Milly said.

"Leave it in the hall."

<hr/>

MILLY DIPPED A pen in the bottle of India ink and wrote *Tom* on the label. She looked at the babies. They moved their arms and legs and made small sounds. Quickly she reached out and tied the label around one of their ankles. The child kicked his legs jerkily, and the label fluttered. "You're Tom," Milly said. She looked at the other child. "And you're William."

The following day Tom gripped the label in his fist and tore it away, leaving the string around his ankle. Constance said it didn't matter. "The one with the string is Thomas. That's easy enough to remember."

Milly felt unhappy about the whole business, but in the end she decided it probably didn't matter all that much. Soon she was able to tell the twins apart at a glance, although for the life of her she couldn't say how she did it.

<hr/>

MRS. MARIGOLD JENNINGS said, "Well! Twins!" and Miss Betty stroked her cat and said, "Ho hum."

Mrs. Jennings responded briskly to her friend's continuing pessimism. "Two lovely boys," she said. "Two lovely healthy boys, Mr. Anderson an upright man of God, with such a useful and responsible job, and Mrs. Anderson such a handsome and talented woman, and all of them living in such a nice house with a maid and everything. I don't think there's anything whatsoever to be gloomy about, Betty."

"A useful and responsible job, did you say?"

"He works for the post office."

"I know he works for the post office."

"The post office is a useful institution."

"That doesn't make Mr. Anderson's job useful."

"Really, Betty, you're so *argumentative*. Sometimes I think you're quite horribly biased."

"I'm sorry, Marigold. I'm in a bad mood." Miss Betty topped up her friend's glass. "I feel thunderclouds gathering. I think my mood was caused by Mr. Anderson's dwelling on the word *naked* in that first sermon of his. Quite unnecessary."

"I thought you approved of nakedness."

"I used to, when I had the figure for it. But Mr. Anderson doesn't approve. He thinks nakedness is sinful and we ought to be ashamed of it. How daft! There's nothing wrong with nakedness in the right circumstances, except that it is sometimes rather chilly—and, of course, for those of us over a certain age, somewhat unbecoming."

"I think he was making a metaphorical point."

"Really, Marigold! I sometimes wonder why you remain my best friend."

Marigold Jennings's face fell, and Miss Betty reached across the table and clutched her hands. "Oh my dear, I'm so sorry! What an awful person I am! Marigold! Please believe me! You are and always will be my dearest friend! Oh, that wretched Felix Anderson has come between us!"

1921

FELIX STARED across the table. Constance looked steadily back at him.

"It cannot be true," he said.

"It is true," Constance said.

"I do not believe it, and I do not understand why you are speaking to me in this fashion."

"It is true. And you know the reason for my manner."

A silence. He looked down at the table and said, "It is quite impossible that this child of yours can be passed off as mine. People will find out."

"You'd better get used to the idea, Felix. Your name will be on her birth certificate."

"You cannot know that the baby will be a girl."

"I wish to have a daughter. I intend that she will be musical."

"This is all quite absurd. You don't even *like* children. I'll have nothing to do with it. I shall institute divorce proceedings."

"You will not, unless you want your philandering to come out."

Felix sat still, staring at his thin hands.

Constance looked at him. He was not a strong man, or a particularly intelligent one. As men went, he was no more than ordinarily sinful; they all did that sort of thing, or hoped they might.

"I do not think you will have any difficulty," she said. "Once you have thought about it, you will see that it is perfectly straight-forward. You will behave as a normal father to her."

Silence again. Felix drew in his breath and let it out again. "What about the child's natural father?"

"It was nothing to him."

And another silence. Then he said, "Why have you done this?"

Constance felt her nails digging into her palms. "You betrayed me," she said. "So I took action."

How common, Felix thought. Who does she think she is?

~⁓

CONSTANCE TOOK HER gloves, hat, and coat from the hall and went along to the kitchen. Milly had just come in. She was carrying a shopping basket. Constance said, "Milly, I shall be having another baby in the autumn."

Milly opened her mouth, but no words came out. She put the shopping basket on the kitchen table. Constance put on her coat.

"There's no need to be surprised. It's quite normal."

"Yes, ma'am," Milly said. Constance saw that her hands were trembling.

"I'll want you to help me prepare the nursery." Constance put on her hat and gloves and adjusted the belt of her coat. "When the baby comes I will see to her. You'll continue to look after the boys." She looked in the mirror over the fireplace and straightened the big cream hat with the feathers. She turned around and faced Milly. "I hope that's all right." She went out the door and shut it behind her.

After Constance had gone, Milly went upstairs to the study and knocked on the door. Felix said, "Come in," and she stood in the doorway.

"You could've said about her baby," she said. "It come as an awful shock."

"It was a shock to me, too," Felix said. He was sitting at his desk with a pen in his hand. "Shut the door."

Milly shut the door and leaned against it. The marks of tears were on her cheeks.

"I want you to understand what happened," Felix said, looking down at his desk. "Constance came to me. She was desperate. You know what she's like. Her funny moods. She said she must have a daughter. Even though we don't get on, I hadn't got any choice. I am her husband, after all."

He got up and took out his handkerchief. "There now. Wipe your face. We don't want people to see you've been crying, do we? This won't make any difference."

Milly wiped her eyes. Felix put his hands on her shoulders. "You'll see. It'll be all right. Trust me."

IN SEPTEMBER, THE daughter that Constance had decided to call Stella emerged smoothly into the world and lay there with her eyes calmly open. "Give her to me," Constance said. The midwife wrapped Stella in a woolen blanket, gave her into her mother's arms, and stood back, smiling.

"Your husband will be here soon, I expect," the young midwife said.

"He won't," Constance said. "He's away on business."

"Oh, that's such a pity!" the midwife said. "Such lovely blond hair she's got."

As soon as she was left alone, Constance unwrapped the child, inspected her all over, counted her fingers and toes, and imagined the tiny left hand lying across the strings of a cello. The genitalia appeared disproportionately large, but that was presumably normal. Her eyes had a silvery look, and the stub of the umbilical cord was quite curious. She reached for her sketchbook.

MISS BETTY WATCHED Milly hanging out the washing in number 27 and took a sip of the fresh white wine that brought vividly to mind (although she had never been outside the Home Counties) the cloud-capped profile of the Apennines. Milly had a handsome figure, although the redness of her hands could be detected even from this distance. She turned from the window and considered with satisfaction her own fine hands and neatly trimmed fingernails. "A pregnant woman ought to have the sense not to employ a pretty maid," she said.

"Betty, you can't possibly be suggesting—"

"Marigold, the world would be awfully dull without a modicum of speculation."

"Mrs. Anderson is an artist. She can't be expected to be aware of everyday matters. I'm sure she has a highly refined sensibility."

"In that case, she should know the risks of getting pregnant and employing anyone but the ugliest of maids."

"That's a silly suggestion. It's the duty of every wife to have children. Besides, they say she has money of her own."

"What a horrid word *duty* is. And I don't see what money has to do with it. She is indeed a wife, but, alas, not a warm one."

"And she's beautiful."

"I agree that she has a certain frozen elegance."

"She has beautiful hair and a lovely posture. She is always upright."

"We have discussed that word before. I would prefer the term *stiff*. Perhaps even *rigid*."

"There's no pleasing you, Betty."

Miss Betty wrinkled her brow. "I must admit I'm surprised at her being pregnant again. That's most intriguing."

"It's perfectly natural."

"Do you think so? Try to imagine Mr. and Mrs. Anderson engaged in the sexual act."

"Betty!"

"There you are. One can't conceive of it. As it were." She took another sip of the breezy Italian.

"But Mrs. Anderson is pregnant, nevertheless. That just shows that you're not always right in your horrid judgments about people."

"In this case, it seems you're correct. How odd." Miss Betty held her glass up to the light and looked deep into its transparency, her brow wrinkled.

〜〜〜

IN THEIR MOTHER'S bedroom, Tom and William stood beside the cot, gripped the bars, and stared at the new child, who lay sleeping in a close wrapping of white wool. Their mother and father came in and stood behind them.

"Come on, you two," Felix said. "Milly's waiting to read your story." He took them out. Constance sat beside the cot and took out her sketchbook. There was something vitally important about Stella's tiny, clenched face within its white hood, something she must at once record.

<hr />

KNEELING BY HIS bed later that night, Felix closed his eyes and asked for forgiveness. I know I have repeatedly sinned, he prayed, but I am torn between You and the pleasures of the body. Even as he thought this, he knew that the grand formulation rang false. The facts were far simpler and much more damning: He had betrayed his matrimonial duties and had taken up with a common servant whose body he sometimes fiercely wanted. And sometimes didn't want at all. Which was it? Did he want her or not? He pressed his bony hands together and thought of Milly's pale body, her long back, her firm thighs. The beginning of an erection disturbed the blue striped pajamas. Oh Lord, show me the way from this labyrinth, Felix prayed, knowing that the way was obvious enough, but this was not going to be the moment to take it.

1 9 2 3

THERE WAS a roar and a series of explosions in the street. Uncle Oscar entered like a whirlwind, his long coat flapping, picked up the boys, one in the crook of each elbow, and slung them round in dizzy aerobatics before hurling them onto the sofa. He tore the flying helmet from his head and strapped it on Tom's. It was much too large for him and it smelled of hot oil, as did Uncle Oscar's racy motorcycle.

"Ah, the daring aviator!" Uncle Oscar's voice boomed around the room. "And now for the goggles!" The world was abruptly framed and silenced by the thickness of the glass. Through the lenses Tom saw Uncle Oscar capering like a puppet, his teeth bright, his mustache gigantic. He balanced the boys on his knees. Their heads spun. "Listen," he shouted. He bent his head toward them and whispered, "The Bristol Fighter. That was an aeroplane! That was a beauty!" They trembled and stared at him and held tightly on to his arms. He leaned back and made a sudden roaring noise. They jumped and he laughed outrageously. "Noisy! I'll say! The old Bristol was noisy all right!"

William looked up into his uncle's face from a distance of six inches. The gigantic mustache jutted and trembled as he spoke. Stiff

bristles stuck out from his nose and ears. He squeezed the boys together, brought his face close to theirs, and made his eyes large.

"Tell you a secret," Uncle Oscar said in a growling whisper. "Met
a girl once. By God, she was a proud beauty! All the trimmings!
Parasol! Pekinese! Divine ankles! Arranged to meet her at Bournemouth. On the beach. She turned up on time, looked this way and
that, and thought I wasn't there. Aha!"

He paused and touched the boys' noses one after the other with a
colossal forefinger.

"She looked everywhere and couldn't see me. But I *was* there,
wasn't I? I was high above! Hiding in the clouds! In my Bristol
Fighter! Swooping over her! Six loops and a chandelle! Landed on the
beach and swept her off her feet!"

He let go of the boys and made a large, slow gesture, as if to en-
fold within his enormous arms the memory not only of the young
beauty and her parasol, but the beach, the sea, the sky, the calling
seagulls, and the bold airman cavorting in his Bristol Fighter. "Ah
yes," he whispered, holding the boys close and staring over their
heads, "those were the days. Those were the days."

<hr/>

STRUCK BY SOME inexplicable maternal yearning, Constance
got out of bed and moved silently through the house in the gray
dawn. As she passed his room, she could hear the slow saw of Felix's
breathing. She opened the door of the boys' bedroom. They lay together in the position they always adopted, like two spoons in a
drawer, Tom's arm flung across William's chest. She stood over them,
wondering what it was she felt for them. A distant possession, perhaps, and a kind of resignation. She stood there for several minutes,
motionless, looking down at them. Undoubtedly they were beautiful things, pure and unblemished. The texture of their skin, look at
that. They were at first glance mere creatures of nature, not yet
human, not yet marked; but closer study showed their faces to have
an oddly serious quality, something eternal and disturbing. By one
of those tricks of perception (yes, just like that drawing of a vase, the
one that turns into a pair of faces as you look at it) they might some-

times be seen as they would be in old age: two old men clasping each other. Something intriguing about that. She stepped silently away, and as she did so the boys' eyes opened. They watched her go, then turned over. William enfolded Tom in his arms and they slept.

Constance walked back across the landing to her bedroom, knelt beside the cot, and placed her cool lips on her daughter's brow.

"Five is such a nice age for a boy," Marigold Jennings said.

Her friend nodded. "At that age they're all wagging heads and clumsy feet, like wooden dolls."

"More like puppets, I think."

"You could be right." Miss Betty gazed at the boys. "What very odd things they are. When you see them sideways, the backs of their heads are just like question marks."

"Why, so they are, Betty. I'd never noticed that before."

"For a woman to bear a girl, and hence to replicate herself, is nothing much. But to bring into the world a boy, a baby man, is to engender an alien."

Mrs. Jennings stepped back from the window. "Really, Betty, that's quite silly! My Ralph certainly isn't an alien."

"Your Ralph?" She considered. "I was speaking metaphorically, of course." She let the curtain fall. It was two in the afternoon. The boys were playing in the garden of number 27. The attic curtains were closed.

"Five is the only age at which a boy is at all tolerable," Miss Betty said, sitting down with satisfaction in the reclining chair that she had recently acquired from Heal's. "Then it's all downhill until he's at least twenty-five."

"Those two little bushy-haired boys, always together. Don't you think they're enchanting?"

"Of course I do. I'm not immune to maternal yearnings. I wish to sweep them into my arms and kiss them all over. Is that maternal? Let's assume so. And one day each of them will catch the eye of a young lady with the same desire, and she will exploit their good nature dreadfully."

"I do so wish we'd had more children. But after Ralph we never found the right moment. Malcolm always said—"

"Marigold, I do believe your glass is empty."

"Why, so it is."

"Pass it over. They're attractive boys. They are affectionate with each other and with Milly. They show every sign of being perfectly normal. Quite remarkable, in the circumstances."

"What circumstances?"

"Really, Marigold, I sometimes think—oh, never mind." She filled her friend's glass. "Mind you," she said, "there is something quite unbearable about youth."

Marigold was puzzled. "I thought you liked them."

"I don't mean the boys themselves, I mean *youth*. The concept of youth. Youth in the abstract. The thing we no longer have. All that life ahead of them. All that life behind us."

There was silence, and after a few moments Betty detected that her friend was weeping. "Goodness, Marigold, what have I said?"

"I'm sorry, Betty. I was just thinking about my poor dear Malcolm, and how little time we had together."

"One must consider one's past with resolution, Marigold, since it cannot be changed. Besides, things could always have been worse."

Marigold wiped her nose on her handkerchief. "Yes, Betty," she said, "I'm sure you're right."

"As for your Malcolm . . . ," her friend began to say.

"What about him?"

Miss Betty looked at her friend's large, inquiring eyes and resolutely closed her lips. "Oh, nothing," she said.

⟜

IN THE ATTIC, Milly turned over in her squeaky bed and looked at Felix. "Now come on, lovey, give us a cuddle." She reached out and rubbed the end of Felix's nose with one finger. "Oh, you're in a gloomy mood today, aren't you? What about little Mr. Porky? Is he gloomy, too? Doesn't he want to play?"

Felix felt a kind of agony.

"I've got something for him," Milly said. "Something to cheer up

Mr. Porky." She reached out and pulled Felix's head between her breasts. "There. Isn't that nice? Ooh, Mr. Porky feels nice. Let's give him a stroke, shall we?"

Felix placed his hands on Milly's warm, familiar hips.

"Mr. Porky's taking notice. That's better, isn't it? Come along, Mr. Porky." Milly lay back on the bed. Felix rubbed his hands across her breasts and stroked her silken lips.

"Oooh! That's nice," Milly said. "What about giving my little flower a big kiss?"

Felix lowered his head.

Later Milly said, "That was nice. Give us a cuddle now." She closed her eyes. Felix looked at her and smelled her sweet breath. She opened her eyes. They were large and brown. She touched the back of his hand with one plump finger and said, "Any more in the bottle, lovey?" Felix tiptoed in his bare feet across the cold linoleum and fetched the sherry. He looked at her and wished she would not leave her mouth open so often. "I'll have to go down soon," he said.

"Oh no, lovey," Milly said, "don't go yet."

THERE WAS A period when Constance was inclined to forget the existence of the twins, such was her interest in her new child. One Sunday in late January she overslept, woke suddenly, came into the boys' room in the freezing dark, and felt a curious heat, which she realized after a moment came from the children themselves. She drew the curtains and saw the two flushed, trembling faces with their eyes staring open but unseeing. She cried out. Felix woke and came into the bedroom. She was standing over the bed with her hands to her cheeks. He removed the bedclothes, felt the boys' foreheads, and said they had high temperatures. They were sickening for something. That was all. Probably just a cold. Send for the doctor. She leaned against him and he held her elbow.

The doctor, a small Welshman, opened his bag, placed his cold stethoscope on the hot flesh, and said it was measles. Shut the curtains, he said, keep out the light. Keep them dosed with aspirin. Take this to the chemist. Good day to you. And the doctor's visit was followed by days of fever, intermittent sleep, brightly colored dreams, coughing, sudden hunger, intensifying boredom, wobbly steps, and eventually the boys' imprisonment for (as it seemed to them) no good reason whatsoever, elbows on the windowsill, chins in hands, gazing out at a damp lawn, a hedge, a blackbird, a garden, another house, a piece of unkempt ground, and the chimneys of north London.

Constance was angry with herself. Henceforth, at the least sign of a sniffle, she told Milly to administer aspirin, cod-liver oil, rose-hip syrup, and Friar's Balsam. Visits from the doctor (whose black bag with its glinting instruments the boys could recall better than his face) were preceded by a good deal of tidying up, clean pajamas, flowers in the bedroom, and laundered sheets that struck cold against the warmth of their flesh.

William was later to think of their life at that time as geometrical and precisely mapped. How slowly they grew older! How long were the days! How very ordinary their lives! Their parents came and went in the mysterious manner of parents in those days, and the boys moved regularly around the pattern of streets that joined home, school, church, park, and Allbright's General Stores: "Good morning, Mrs. Anderson, and how is the little girl? Well, I trust? And the lads? Now, let's see if I can guess which is which."

From a boy's point of view, there was little to be said about this part of London. It was gray and damp and went on, much the same, in all directions. Their primary school was around two corners and overlooked by the garden of Aunt Helen, her title being purely a courtesy since she was no relative, but an acquaintance of their mother's from the art class.

"I believe it may be a rough school," Felix said to Constance. "In due course we shall have to consider private education." New parents had just been interviewed by the headmistress, given a copy of the school rules, and lectured on the importance of reading.

At St. Edmund's Church of England Primary School, the established convention was that the boys fought among themselves while the girls played elaborate skipping games and provoked the boys with sly glances and sudden dares. Tom and William learned to exploit the freakish mystery of being twins. They developed an ability to mirror each other's movements in a most curious and upsetting manner. When the worst came to the worst, they had a back-to-back fighting technique that made them hard to overcome: They became a single boy possessed of four whirling fists and four whirling boots. They constructed unspoken alliances with others in the same social category, notably with Hans, who was not only small but had a Dutch mother, and Robin, the boy with the withered arm. At morning break their aunt Helen came down to the end of her garden in her boldly patterned red-and-yellow dress and waved to them. They pressed their faces to the wire fence and waved back, waiting for the Fox's Glacier Mints that she tossed awkwardly over the wire while laughing shrilly. At weekends they played at Robin's house. He had a Hornby model railway in the attic. When they were there his deferential, asthmatic mother came all the way upstairs, tapped on the door, and said in her whispering voice, "Hello, boys—would you like some tea and cakes?" before going all the way down again to get the tray that she had prepared. They read *The Boy's Book of Trains* and *One Hundred Models You Can Make at Home,* sailed their boat in the park, and, under Robin's somewhat pedantic instruction, nearly finished a scale model of a Sopwith Camel.

CONSTANCE SPENT A great deal of time encouraging Stella's musicality. She sat by the cot singing English traditional songs in a high, thin voice and played simple tunes upon the recorder. She bought a number of gramophone records, in the early years concentrating on songs and choral works. Visitors became used to hearing "The Ash Grove" drifting through the house, and learned to wait for silence before calling up the stairs.

ONE DAY FELIX said, "I have asked Miss Betty Alcock and her friend Mrs. Jennings to tea."

"Really, Felix, have you? It's not at all convenient. I am working up a sketch."

"They are active members of the congregation. One has to respond occasionally."

"Oh, very well."

"They have asked that Tom and William be present."

"Have they? Why?"

"I have no idea. Presumably they feel some affection for them."

"Oh."

"Where are they?"

Constance looked up. "They have gone with Milly and Stella to the park."

It was a day of brisk wind and hurrying clouds. In the park, Milly had walked ahead and the boys had been permitted to push the pram across the wide, grassy spaces. Tom shoved the pram and it rolled gently away. William ran after it and said, "You shouldn't do that."

"Why not?"

"Because she might get hurt."

"It's only a gentle slope."

Tom let the pram run again. It was a considerable vehicle, chromed and polished, its bodywork painted in cream and brown with a tawny hood in the best cotton duck. It rolled for ten yards and came to a halt, rocking a little in the wind.

"There you are. No danger."

"It's bloody."

"What do you mean, bloody?"

"It's just bloody."

"You don't say it like that. You say it's bloody stupid or whatever."

"Well, it's bloody stupid then."

"You shouldn't swear, anyway."

"Go and get Stella."

"You get her."

"Well, I'm not getting her," William said, and began to walk away.

"Neither am I," Tom said, following him. They walked a few paces, and then Tom said, "Oh, all right then," and returned to collect the pram. Together they pushed it toward Milly, who was feeding the ducks.

Halfway home their mother came striding toward them. She was irritable. "Where have you been?"

"Only to the park, ma'am."

"Why have you been so long?"

"We was just feeding the ducks, ma'am."

Constance unhooked the flap on the pram hood and looked inside. Stella stared silently up at her. "I'll take her now," Constance said, grasping the handle of the pram. Milly and the boys trailed behind her as she walked quickly home, the pram swaying on its supple springs.

THE BOOKSHELVES IN their father's study covered three walls from floor to ceiling and were enclosed by glazed doors that were kept locked. The boys could discover no reason for this. Through the glass they could see that the ordered rows were dominated by twenty-seven identical volumes. They spelled out their common title, *The Proceedings of the Anglican Church Council,* but its meaning remained opaque. Over the months and years of their childhood, the titles on many of the brown-and-green spines lodged permanently in their minds: *Dogma and the Future of Religion, Religion in a Scientific World, Accommodating Politics and the Spirit, Electricity and God,* and *Faith in the Factory.* One Sunday they heard their father refer specifically to one of the books on his shelves: "Canon Romsey's most celebrated and provocative work," he called it, and sure enough when they went hunting there it was: *The God of War.*

"THE NIGHTS ARE closing in," said Marigold Jennings.

"The long day wanes, the slow moon climbs," Miss Betty said.

"What a pretty thing to say, Betty."

"Unfortunately, not my own."

"Well, it wasn't a very *jolly* party, was it? But quite interesting. Mrs. Anderson is such an impressive woman. Such strength of mind, such dedication to her art."

"And dedication to art is so much more interesting than dedication to babies. Or, indeed, husbands."

"Really, Betty."

"You know me well enough by now."

"She was lovely with her new baby."

"Yes. That's interesting. Why should she suddenly have discovered motherhood? As far as that particular child is concerned, anyway."

"She was perfectly sociable. I think you're being rather unpleasant about her."

"Can you remember her laughing? Think carefully. Give me an instance."

"I don't believe I can."

Miss Betty picked up her cat. It attempted to escape, but Miss Betty grasped it firmly.

"Mrs. Anderson told me she dislikes cats," Miss Betty said.

"I hardly think you can hold that against her."

"It's indicative, Marigold. It is certainly indicative."

"She talked interestingly about Stella's talents and her musical prospects."

"Having shown absolutely no interest in her sons, Constance Anderson is now making the error of having ambitions for her daughter. That is an awful thing, since all children are eventually a disappointment. Mrs. Anderson ought to lower her gaze and ask herself, for example, why her husband only comes home for lunch on Tuesdays and Thursdays, when she's at her art class."

"You've made that improper suggestion before, and I've told you what I think of it. Besides, the boys would notice if there was anything going on."

"Boys never notice anything. It doesn't occur to them to look for base behavior in adults. They're too busy contemplating their own transgressions."

"Mind you," Marigold said, "I do think there's something jolly peculiar about the way they behave in that house. Civil enough, but not at all welcoming."

ONE WINTER NIGHT, Stella whimpered and Constance brought her into her own bed. The child was warm and drowsy. She fell asleep within the curve of her mother's body. She made no further sound and her breathing was almost undetectable. Constance felt an intense and secret joy. There was surely no reason why the child should not sleep with her always.

~⌒~

LATER THAT SAME night, Tom emerged from sleep, his brother whispering urgently in his ear: "Wake up! Tom, wake up!"

"What is it?"

"Come here. Look at this." William's voice was insistent.

Tom shivered. "I can't see anything. Put the light on."

"No, no," William said. "Come over here. Look out of the window."

The boys knelt on the end of the bed and pulled back the curtain. Snow was falling across the dark gardens. Huge flakes swirled through the cone of light cast by the street lamp on the corner.

"Hey," Tom said.

"Told you."

"Look at that." Miss Betty's cat stepped delicately across the lawn, lifting each foot, shaking it free of snow, leaving a steady line of prints.

"Let's get up."

"We can't. It's the middle of the night."

The boys got their dressing gowns and for an hour watched the snow going about its silent, soothing work.

1928

ON THEIR first day, Tom and William entered Avondale holding hands. The other boys eyed them with interest. Here's something! Two small pink boys, identical! And holding hands! It promised well. At the morning break, they were escorted on a tour of the grounds by two small and pleasant boys who made them feel immediately at home. Behind the cricket pavilion they found assembled a group of larger boys, perhaps twelve or thirteen years old, a group that had the air, William thought, of one of his father's church committees.

A tall boy with a shock of yellow hair said, "Are they exactly the same?" Another said, "Blimey! Which is which?" There followed a general discussion.

"Can you tell them apart?"

" 'Course."

"That one—he's taller."

"Stand them back-to-back."

"No difference."

"Which are you?"

"Tom."

"And which are you?"

"He's William."

"Do you speak for both?"

"Is he dumb?"

"Tell you what."

"What?"

"Bet they aren't *exactly* the same."

"Bet they are."

The two used their usual tactics and fought hard, but there were too many of the larger boys and they were overpowered.

"There you are. I win."

"Yeah."

"Well."

"You see. They're twins all right."

"Not natural, it isn't."

"Wait—what's that?"

"Hey—"

"That one's got string round his ankle."

"String!"

"Let's see."

"He has!"

"He's got string round his ankle."

"What for?"

"What's it for, eh?"

Tom lay curled on the grass. He said nothing.

"What about the other one?"

They looked.

"Nah. No string."

One of them poked William with his foot. "What's it for, then?"

William said, "It's just a game." The boy kicked him a little harder and he said, "It's so people can tell us apart."

The group considered this. "All right then," the tall, yellow-haired boy said, "we'll sort that out." He took out a penknife and cut the string away. "Now which are you?"

"Tom."

"No, you're not. Not anymore." He kicked Tom moderately hard.

"I'm William," Tom said.

The boys laughed. Then one of them turned to William and said, "Who are you, then?"

"Tom," William said.

"You're a bloody liar," the boy shouted, "you're bloody William." The boys laughed and kicked him again, not particularly hard.

There was a pause. "Oh, come on," one of them said.

Gradually they wandered away. The twins got dressed. William helped Tom to climb on the roof of the pavilion to get their shoes and caps. After school they walked home together, and Constance, who was sketching Stella in the conservatory, said absently, "How did our little men get on?"

Tom said, "It was fun, Mother," and they went upstairs to their room.

⌒

IN DUE COURSE Mr. Pattisson placed Tom in 1A and William in 1B to minimize confusion among the staff and opportunities for mischief making. Mr. Pattisson was the headmaster. He had been an RFC pilot in the Great War. A polished wooden propeller hung over the door of his study. He had a hooked nose and walked with two sticks. He had been shot down. Most of the flesh on his legs had burned away before the soldiers pulled him from the wreckage. At their interview, the boys told him about their uncle Oscar, who had been a cavalryman at Omdurman and later a pilot. They described their model of the Sopwith Camel. Mr. Pattisson said, "Indeed," looking at them steadily with his black and gleaming eyes.

They learned that Mr. Pattisson was particularly to be avoided in cold weather. When he beat a boy, as he did more frequently the colder it became, his wife's corgi barked a fusillade and the whole school sat still, counting the barks. At the end of Tom's first week in 1A, there was an abrupt hush when Mr. Pattisson thrust open the door and walked in like an automaton with his back rigid and his weight thrown heavily forward on his squeaking, rubber-tipped sticks. "Read this," he said, placing a book entitled *The Story of the Aeroplane* on Tom's desk. He turned and made for the door while the class and their teacher watched in silence his slow, twisting progress.

After two weeks of confusion the school provided Tom and William with cardboard badges, saying, in large letters, ANDERSON, THOMAS and ANDERSON, WILLIAM.

~⸺◦

"I F Y O U G O up into the back bedroom and squinny as far as you can to the left," Miss Betty said, "you will see Mrs. Anderson sitting in her conservatory, painting. The startlingly blond-haired child, Stella, is on her swing in the orchard. Mr. Anderson is sitting in the garden, reading *The Times*. Milly has just come out of the French windows carrying a tray of tea for him. The twins are doing something with an upside-down bicycle—failing to mend a puncture, most likely. The kitchen garden is well tended. The lawn is mown in regular stripes. I believe I can see apples on some of the orchard trees—or perhaps they're pears? I was never very good at trees. The sun gleams on the greenhouse. There are foxgloves and other colorful flowers. At the foot of the garden is a row of tall trees, perhaps poplars, gently waving. A blackbird sings. The sky is blue. It is a typical image of comfortable family life, and utterly false, of course."

"Betty, you know absolutely nothing about comfortable family life," her friend said. "And I do believe you're a little squiffy."

"Possibly so," Miss Betty said. "It may be time for my Heal's recliner."

~⸺◦

F ELIX PULLED THE window shut in order to cut down the noise of the traffic, and went back to his desk. He picked up the telephone. "Get me Jamieson," he said. He waited, tapping his fingers.

"Jamieson? Could you come up?" He put down the telephone, sat down, and flicked again through the man's file.

A tap at the door, and in came the young man Frank Jamieson, his hair flopping across his eyes as usual. He had a slight limp that Felix hadn't noticed before. "Sit down, Jamieson," Felix said. He couldn't imagine why Jamieson didn't look after himself more carefully.

"Good morning, sir," Jamieson said, sitting in the visitor's chair. He looked over Felix's head at a shelf on which there was a photo-

graph of the king, a silver candlestick, and a miniature sword em-
bedded in a block of wood on which was carved the word *Toledo.* The
shelves to Jamieson's right contained a set of *Kelly's Directories* going
back to 1904, and behind him he felt the looming presence of the
telephone directories for the whole of the United Kingdom.

That morning Frank Jamieson had told his wife, Sarah, what was
likely to happen, and she had started to cry. They had been married
for four months, she was pregnant, and she hated being in London.
Their flat was cold and dark. She knew nobody. Frank was out all day.
Seeing Sarah crying, Frank felt awkward, so he got up from the table
and put his arms around her. "It'll be all right, love," he said.

Felix saw that there was dandruff on Jamieson's shoulders. "Look,
Jamieson," he said, "we spoke last month and you agreed to make an
extra effort. Since then, the time cards show that you have arrived
late on six more mornings. In addition, Mr. Porter says you are frequently late back from luncheon. Finally, I have had a complaint
from the typing pool about an offensive comment you made to Miss
Woolley. She was most hurt."

Frank Jamieson watched Felix's mouth moving, but the words
made no sense. He looked out at the gray London sky. A pigeon
landed on the windowsill and walked back and forward, moving its
head jerkily.

Felix said, "As you know, the post office requires its staff to follow
established procedures and to carry out the tasks for which they have
been employed. It is only by following procedures strictly that we
can provide an effective national mail service."

Frank Jamieson said, "My wife had to go to hospital."

"For these reasons," Felix went on, "I regret to say that we have no
alternative but to dispense with your services with immediate effect.
Miss Clapton has your cards. You may collect them on your way out.
Your pay has been made up-to-date, with one additional week in lieu
of notice."

Felix stood up and held out his hand. He said, "I hope you succeed
in finding more suitable employment." Frank Jamieson shook his
hand. Felix saw that the man was crying. His response was unfortunate, but it simply confirmed his decision.

At lunchtime Felix opened his paper and saw an advertisement under APPLICATIONS AND SITUATIONS VACANT: *We require a Gentleman Representative in each of the South-Eastern counties and two in London. If you have courage, a mind of your own, a clean record, and a desire to earn more money per week than the average man gets per month, write to us, giving very brief details of your experience. You will handle a wonderful product with a still more wonderful future.*

Jamieson could apply for that, Felix thought, marking the advertisement with a pencil. The newspaper lay on his desk until the end of the week and was then thrown away by the office cleaner.

THE HOUSE ON the corner had no roof, stairs, or floors. Its bare brick walls were connected by a skeleton of joists and rafters. Their father said the builder had gone bankrupt. It had been like that for years. Notices said "No Entry" and "Danger." The site was a confusion of sycamore, brambles, and nettles that concealed half-dug foundations and heaps of building materials.

The boys stood outside the fence and looked at the house, as they had many times before.

"Maybe there's a loose board," Tom said, looking at the fence.

"Just keep chatting," William said, "and sort of lean on the fence as we go along."

In this way the boys duly found the loose board and got through the rotten fence and discovered a low tunnel through the brambles that they enlarged into a usable path. They explored the place and took possession. They improvised shelters from scaffold planks and sheets of iron, and constructed a platform among the rafters of the house in order to keep watch for enemy raiders. Reaching the fence at the back of the site, they found a convenient shortcut through to Stoke Lane, where the shops were.

To various features of the site they gave names that appeared suitable, such as Spion Kop (a high mound of gravel) and Mons (a boggy area). A deep trench they named the Somme, a name that had an interesting and melancholy echo. When, after an appropriate ceremony swearing them to lifelong secrecy and blood brotherhood,

Hans and Robin were admitted, they agreed that the place was highly satisfactory.

Then one day the man in the Stoke Lane news agent's shop said, "You two, come here." He had yellow teeth. "Come here," he said again. They stepped toward him. "You," he said to William, "empty your pockets."

William looked at Tom, then took a glove, a pencil, and three-pence from his raincoat pockets. "That's all I've got," he said.

The man took hold of William's shoulder and dug roughly into his pockets, finding nothing more. He looked at Tom. "And you," he said.

Tom took a *Magnet* from his pocket. "I just bought this," he said.

"I know," the man said. "I'm not bothered with that." He rummaged in Tom's pockets, then stood back, looking at him. "All right," he said, "take those boots off."

The brothers looked at each other again, and then Tom took the wellington boot off his right foot and shook a Cadbury's Flake out of it. "I suppose that's what you want," he said.

The man took hold of Tom's coat by the lapel and twisted it. He brought his face down close to Tom's. His breath smelled of bacon. "You little bastards," he said, "that's my living you're stealing. Do you know that? Eh? Do you realize that? Do you?"

"Yes," Tom said.

"So what are you going to say? Eh? Tell me that."

"Sorry," Tom said.

"And what else?" He tightened his grip. "What else are you going to say to me?"

Tom looked at his brother. "We won't do it again," William said.

"Yes," the man said. He spoke slowly, enunciating each syllable, lips pulled back from the yellow teeth. "You won't do it again. Because if you bloody do, it'll be the police. Understand? Do you?" He shook Tom's collar.

"Yes," Tom said.

"I don't know why you do it," the man said. "Boys like you, from a nice family. How old are you?"

"Ten," Tom said.

The man let go. "Ten," he said. "You wouldn't believe it, would you?" He stepped back. "All right. Get out of it."

They left the shop. Outside, Tom balanced on one leg with a hand on his brother's shoulder and replaced his wellington boot. They walked toward the back way into the corner plot. They ducked through the hedge, pushed through the bushes, and climbed into the Somme. Tom pulled the corrugated iron over the top. They sat there in the dim light, and after a while Tom said, "I've got another Flake in my other boot. Had we better take it back?"

"No."

Tom unwrapped the chocolate, took a bite, and gave it to his brother. There was a sound above and they sat still. The corrugated iron was raised and light flooded in. The man from the shop was standing there with a walking stick in his hand. "You boys," he said. "You little sods. You little bastards. I knew you had some more." They said nothing. The man stepped down into the trench. "What else have you got?"

"Nothing," Tom said. The man prodded about the trench with his stick. There was nothing but the planks and bricks they had made into seats and the remains of their candles.

"Where did you get those candles?"

"We brought them from home."

"You little bastards." The man clenched his stick. "Boys like you. You need a lesson. You need a proper lesson. I've a mind to give you a lesson you won't forget."

"We can pay you back," Tom said.

"I don't want your fucking money," the man said. "You dirty little bastards. You need a lesson, that's what you need."

They stood up and backed away from him until they reached the end of the trench. The man stepped forward and grabbed Tom's arm. "Get your trousers off," he said.

"You mustn't do that," William said. He was annoyed that his voice was unsteady. "Please leave him alone."

"You little bastards," the man said. He was trembling. With his free hand he took something from his trousers. At first William thought it was some kind of truncheon, then he realized what it was.

William grabbed Tom's arm and pulled him free of the man's grasp. They scrambled out of the trench. The man stumbled forward and grasped Tom's ankle. Tom stamped on his wrist. The man gasped and let go. The boys went away through the brambles and out toward the loose plank in the fence.

Tom said, "Is he following?"

William looked and said, "No, he's just sitting there."

At the fence they turned. They could see the man's head over the bushes. He didn't look up. They walked away up the road.

"We won't tell anyone," William said.

"No, we certainly won't," Tom said.

When they got home, Milly was on her hands and knees in their room, dusting behind the chest of drawers. She wore an apron, and a duster was knotted around her hair. She looked at the boys and said, "You've been to that old house again. You need a nice hot bath."

"Milly," William said, "how long have you worked for us?"

"Oh, a good long while. Before you two were born."

"Don't you ever want to do something else?"

"Suits me well enough."

"But don't you want a career?"

Milly laughed. "Can't say as I do."

William lay on his bed and watched her polishing the carvings on the front of the chest of drawers.

"One day you'll get married."

"Don't know as I ever will."

"But you might want a baby."

Milly picked up her bucket and stood in the doorway, looking at him.

"Who knows?" she said. "My business, that is." She went out into the corridor and shut the door behind her.

⌒

THE WOMEN WERE relieved that they had all decided to dress formally, even though it was only for twenty minutes. They sat expectantly on the benches, their backs straight and their handbags clasped on their laps. Constance sat on one end of the back row.

"I have asked our new mothers to my school," Miss Hornsey said, "in order to explain my philosophy." She wore a high-collared black dress that swept the ground. She leaned forward and drew down her eyebrows into an expression of concern.

"We live at a time when the position of women in society is under discussion. Sometimes, I am sorry to say, the discussion is less than rational. Let me make my beliefs quite clear: An education of the traditional kind is best for girls. Some of you are here because of the school's reputation in music. That is a perfect example of my philosophy. The possession of artistic skills is of immense benefit to a girl. It can only enhance her abilities as a wife and mother—and of course her position in society—if a young woman can sing and play a musical instrument. One must consider all those young men in the civil service and the professions who require their future wife to have such skills." She paused. "The discipline of art also discourages flighty tendencies."

Constance watched the rows of hats as they nodded their agreement. When she returned home she began working on a preliminary sketch. There had been some interesting tones and angles.

⌒

THE FOUR OF them were sitting on Tom's bed.

"I don't see why we can't go there anymore," Hans said. "It's the best place we've ever had."

"Unless you're afraid," Robin said.

Tom and William looked at each other.

"We can't go because we've been told not to go there anymore," Tom said.

Robin made a noise indicating disbelief. "Since when?"

"Since now."

Hans and Robin were unconvinced. There was a silence.

"Who told you not to?"

"Father."

"Bet he didn't."

"Bet he did."

"I'll ask him, then."

"Go on, then," Tom said, knowing he would not, and there the matter rested. It was deeply unfair. Something that was not their fault, and about which they could not speak, had disturbed their friendships, damaged their social position, and prevented them from reentering a world that had, until now, been entirely theirs.

SIR CHARLES CLARK, a high official of the post office, occasionally took pleasure in entertaining his subordinates. Felix grasped his second whiskey and soda at eleven-thirty on a Wednesday morning in the Royal Aero Club in Piccadilly, his reserve somewhat influenced by alcohol, uniformed servants, deep carpets, high ceilings, and the numerous photographs of aviators, mustached, helmeted, and sheepskin clad, that surrounded them.

"Felix, my dear chap," Sir Charles said, "this is Nevil Norway. Nevil, one of my senior assistants, Felix Anderson."

Felix looked away from the photographs and saw that Nevil Norway was a tall man with an air of command.

"Nevil is chief calculator for the R100," Sir Charles said.

Felix looked blank.

"Our new airship."

"Oh, of course."

"They're flying her to Canada in July."

"How interesting," Felix said. "Chief calculator! I'm afraid that I know little of engineering. But my wife's brother was in the RFC, and my sons, though they're only ten, are enthusiasts for the air."

"And so they should be," Norway said. And later, after a good lunch, he leaned across the table and said, "I say, Anderson, your little chaps must come and see our ship."

"SIT UP STRAIGHT," Milly said. "Goodness, we've left it a bit late this time, haven't we?" She wrapped a towel around Tom's shoulders and ruffled his wet hair. He looked back at her from the mirror. "Keep still," she said, and began combing.

She took up the scissors and snipped around his ears, bending down to blow away the trimmings. "Ow, that tickles," he said.

His hair was so thick, it was hard to get it even. She snipped away, leaving the fringe till last because it was the most important bit. She stooped in front of the chair, reaching out to hold his head steady with her left hand. She pursed her lips, the tip of her tongue showing, and snipped carefully across. She studied the result. "I think that's all right."

She got up and went around behind him. He grinned at her in the mirror. She bent and kissed the top of his head.

"Thank you, Milly," he said, climbing down.

"Get William out of the bath and tell him to come here. You've got to look smart. And make sure you go to the lavvy before you go."

Having been groomed to Milly's satisfaction, they ate their breakfast and climbed into their father's car. Long before the Austin arrived at Cardington, they could see the steel latticework of the mooring tower and, nuzzling the top of it, lying steadily on the wind, the airship.

"It's huge," William said.

"It's absolutely massive," Tom said.

"It's like a huge silver marrow."

"It's like Blackpool Tower being eaten by a shark."

"It's the biggest airship in the world."

"How do you know?"

"Because I do."

"Well, I bet *Graf Zeppelin* is bigger."

"Be quiet, you two," Felix said, changing gear cautiously.

Tom and William stood in the lift holding their father's hands, rose up the tower, and stepped across a gangway (for a moment poised precariously over an immense drop) into the nose of the airship, and were immediately overwhelmed by the scale of the thing, its intricacy and hollowness, the length of the swaying walkways below the swollen gasbags, the confusion of wires, winches, pipes, and valves clustered among its latticed structure, and the serious faces of the men in uniform who were going intently about their duties.

There was something lingering in the air, something that made them sniff, an odd acridity. "Hydrogen," the man called Mr. Norway said. "There are always traces of it leaking from here and there."

They passed through a door and found themselves in what looked like a restaurant. It had large windows, wicker furniture, and tables with pale green tablecloths. "Sit here," said Norway. "We'll give you a guided tour once we're airborne." The boys looked at each other. Airborne! And so casually said!

Someone called, "Up ship!" in a peremptory tone, and the cry echoed around the airship. The boys again looked at each other, knowing they should not giggle—but then, turning back to the window, they saw that the buildings on the airfield, the mooring tower, the ground-handling crew, and everything they could see from the angled windows was steadily becoming smaller.

⌒

THEY BEGAN THEIR tour by climbing steps fabricated in a light-colored metal that was cold to the touch. The steps zigzagged upward through gloomy spaces between bulging fabric gasbags. William, holding tightly to the handrails and placing his feet with care, noticed the slow swaying of the brown fabric within its enclosing framework and was reminded of the elephant house at the London Zoo. They climbed a long way. At last a hatch opened and they stepped out into the sunlight. They were at the tail of the airship. Tom and William held on firmly and looked at their feet. A walkway sloped upward. "Up you go, lads," the guiding airman said, "and hold tight." They walked upward in single file, staying close together and gripping a rope that felt not entirely secure. The walkway curved upward, leveled out, and arrived at a shallow depression, a kind of cockpit, in which two men were sitting and drinking tea from a flask. The movement of the airship created a gentle breeze.

The boys stood still, two small figures suspended a mile above Bedfordshire, gazing across the broad, silver back of the airship toward the unobstructed horizon.

⌒

HAVING CRITICALLY INSPECTED the bottle, Miss Betty emptied the dregs into Marigold's glass and went down to the pantry to get another.

Marigold nodded in her chair. It had been a quiet day. The boys were out somewhere, and there was little activity in number 27. Early on, Constance had set up her easel in the window of her studio, a room that would be a bedroom in any normal house. But that was the exciting thing about artists, Marigold thought, and indeed about her dear old friend Betty: None of them had a proper respect for normality. Such people challenged what Malcolm used to call the civilized mores of the middle classes. He would have said, "Don't they know how decent people ought to behave? As for those paintings—well, can you understand modern art? Of course not. Utter drivel, all of it. All that blue. Look around. Do you see blue everywhere? Of course you don't."

She was certain he would have disliked a female artist, if he had encountered one. He had not been affectionate toward Ralph. He had never liked Betty. He had not liked artists one little bit. Mrs. Anderson would have sent him into one of his rages. Oh dear! His rages were quite horrid.

Betty came back into the room and said, "Well, goodness, Marigold, I had to open another case. You don't think we could have miscounted the bottles, do you? We seem to have lost a couple along the way. Any movement while I was out?"

"No. Still painting."

"Golly, those artists have some patience, don't they?"

⌒

AT ONE GLANCE William knew that Mr. Harding, the tutor of 1B, would be their victim. He was a short, melancholy-looking man with narrow glasses low on his nose. His face was crinkled and his age unimaginable. He smoked a pipe. His jacket was edged with leather, and there was a brown mark over the breast pocket where (so it was said) he had once set himself on fire. He had a quiet, rhythmical voice. From the beginning the class behaved viciously toward him; after all, he was a silly little man whose pockets always bulged with books, and he walked with a curious bobbing motion.

In the last hour of a warm Friday afternoon in the first week of term, facing thirty boys, Mr. Harding looked over his glasses, pulled out a dog-eared volume, said, "Hush," to no particular effect, and then, several times, "Please be quiet." The boys continued shouting and hurling paper aeroplanes. Eventually a boy called Cedric Hole shouted, "Shut up, you filthy little bastards, the man wants to speak." Others cried out, "Let him speak! Let him speak!"

The room became still. Mr. Harding said, "Please listen to this," and in his light voice he began to read:

> On either side the river lie
> Long fields of barley and of rye,
> That clothe the wold and meet the sky;
> And through the field the road runs by
> To many-towered Camelot.

There was a silence in which William could hear distant shouts from the rugby pitch. "It's by Alfred, Lord Tennyson," Mr. Harding said. "It's a poem called 'The Lady of Shalott.' I propose to read it to you."

William put his chin in his hands, staring at this dull man reading his dull stuff. He shivered. The boys were quiet. Some had their heads resting on their arms. There was some kind of temporary truce. Mr. Harding read on into the drowsy afternoon:

> A bow-shot from her bower-eaves,
> He rode between the barley sheaves,
> The sun came dazzling through the leaves,
> And flamed upon the brazen greaves
> Of bold Sir Lancelot.

On the way home that afternoon, William said to his brother, "Listen to this. It's a bit of a poem that fool Harding read to us this afternoon." As they walked along he read aloud from his new copy of *The Selected Poems of Alfred, Lord Tennyson:*

> All in the blue unclouded weather,
> Thick-jewelled shone the saddle-leather,

The helmet and the helmet feather
Burned like one burning flame together,
As he rode down to Camelot.

" 'Lady of Shalott,' " Tom said. He was stripping the bark from a
hazel branch. "Heard it before." He looked up at the sky. " 'Blue un-
clouded weather.' A clear sky means high pressure. Did Tennyson
know that?"

" 'Thick-jewelled shone the saddle-leather,' " William repeated to
himself. " 'The helmet and the helmet feather.' "

Tom rattled his stick along the railings.

⌒

"STELLA IS A pretty child," Miss Hornsey said to Constance at
the end of the autumn term. "However, she is somewhat sulky, and
it seems that her musical talents have yet to emerge."

The gardener had suspended a swing beneath a branch of one
of the Cox's Orange Pippins. Constance placed the child on the
swing and set up her easel. There was a red ribbon in Stella's yellow
hair, and she was wearing the red-and-white gingham dress, white
socks, and sandals that constituted her summer school uniform. "Hold
tight, darling," Constance said, putting on her glasses and turning
to a new page in her sketchbook. The sequence of pictures of her
daughter was beginning, she felt, to have artistic substance; in due
course it would be a notable document.

⌒

WHEN HE DISCOVERED that they had flown in the new airship, Uncle Oscar was furious. He gave the boys a lecture on the haz-
ards and practical drawbacks of airships, balloons, and all flying
machines that were lighter than air. They were unnatural and had no
future whatsoever. "Birds had wings, did they not? Are birds full of
gas? Of course not! Airships! Absurd! Slow! Explosive! A sitting target! A traveling bonfire!"

Uncle Oscar grasped their elbows and drew the boys toward his
chair. "Let me tell you about the Bristol Fighter," he said in his re-

sounding whisper. "Now, there's an aeroplane! What power! What strength! What grace! What speed!"

He knelt between them on the carpet, his knees cracking. "Follow me," he said. "We're going to do a loop." He stretched one hand out before him. "Here we go," he said, leaning forward. "We're diving now, full throttle, and then back with the stick"—he angled his hand upward—"and up we go!" He leaned back, his hand now above his head. "Over the top," he shouted, falling backward across the carpet, and at that moment the door opened and Constance looked in. She saw Uncle Oscar lying on the floor, shut the door, and went away without saying anything. Uncle Oscar lay on the carpet, laughing, and pulled the boys down onto his huge chest. "Too slow over the top," he said. "Stalled her, didn't I? Stick hard back and bags of speed over the top, that's what you want."

I T WAS RAINING, the window was shut, and the room was dense with Golden Virginia. William stood beside the table while Mr. Harding assembled a small pile of books. "Coleridge," he said, "and, of course, Wordsworth, though you might find some of him a little . . . well . . . *mournful.* Keats, but perhaps not Byron, not just yet. Hopkins is interesting, I think you'll find. Yes, you might try Hopkins." He sat still and stared out at the rain for what seemed to William a long time, and then said, "There's a poem by Hopkins called 'Heaven-Haven.' Do you know it?"

"No," William said.

"Gerard Manley Hopkins," Mr. Harding said. "A funny chap. He thought poetry a dreadful sin." He got up and stood looking out the window for a while. Then he recited:

> I have desired to go
> Where springs not fail,
> To fields where flies no sharp and sided hail
> And a few lilies blow.

"I find that beautiful," Mr. Harding said, "though, of course, somewhat sad."

William considered what he had heard. It was disturbing, certainly, but he had an odd feeling that there might be something wrong with it. In the case of poetry, it was hard to tell the difference between what was good and what was simply too sloppy for words.

Tom, meanwhile, was lying facedown on his bed and reading *The Sky Trackers,* by Captain J. E. Gurdon, DFC.

TOM PRESSED his right index finger on the inkpad and then on the writing paper. William did the same. They studied the two prints.

"They look the same," William said. "More or less, anyway."

"If one of us committed a crime, they wouldn't know which it was."

"They'd just lock us both up."

"Would they? Is that legal?"

"Why don't we get confused ourselves?"

"Because you like poetry and I don't."

" 'I come from haunts of coot and hern, I make a sudden sally, And sparkle out among the fern, To bicker down a valley.' "

"Yes, but it isn't only that, is it? I couldn't think I was you, because I'm always me. As soon as I wake up, I'm me. Just like that."

"It's memory that does it," Tom said. "I'm me, because I've got my own memories. If I were you, I'd have your memories."

"A lot of our memories are the same."

"Well, maybe that's true. But not all of them. And not quite the same. When we're old we'll have different memories. We'll be quite different people. Won't we?"

"Imagine us in fifty years," William said.

"I can't."

"Oh, I can. Bent and dribbling."

"I suppose so." Tom took his brother's hand and turned it palm upward. "One can't imagine death. Just as well, I suppose. You've got the same lifeline as me. It goes right round the back of your thumb. That should be enough."

William looked at their two right hands. "Do you think," he said, "when one of us dies the other will know straight away?"

"I should think so," Tom said. "Wouldn't you?"

"I don't know," William said. "Do you know, I've just realized there's no such thing as God?"

"Have you."

"Yes. It's all made up. The whole of it. It's just a story."

"I knew that years ago."

"You did not."

"I did."

"You didn't."

"I bloody well did, so there."

MISS BETTY ALCOCK leaned forward and lifted her opera glasses.

"Betty, dear," Marigold Jennings said, "I really don't think you should use those things."

"Why on earth not?"

"Well—it seems like spying."

"They're growing quite tall, those boys. And sturdy."

"Please don't change the subject, Betty."

"It's got nothing to do with spying, Marigold. I'm simply taking a healthy interest in our fellow human beings. It's perfectly natural. I suspect it's mankind's oldest pastime. Well, one of the oldest."

"Yes, but those binoculars are surely—"

"They are not binoculars. They're opera glasses. Not the same thing at all. They merely offer to my fading sight a small improvement in clarity."

Marigold sniffed.

"For instance, they enable me to see through the steam on the bathroom window and discover that Stella is in the bath, reading what looks like one of the more popular weekly magazines."

"Betty! Really!"

"Here comes her mother."

"I CAN WASH myself perfectly well," Stella said, dropping *Picture Post* on the floor and sliding down in the bath until the water came over her face.

"No, you can't, darling," her mother said, picking up the soap.

THAT EVENING FELIX made a number of financial calculations on a piece of foolscap, considered them for some time, and then took the paper into his wife's studio.

"Since I cannot afford a public school," he said, "the boys will have to make do with a grammar." He looked over her shoulder at the rural scene that she was painting. "They will have to go to St. Mark's."

"Whatever you say," Constance said, wondering whether those roof tiles were quite dark enough or whether they needed a little more umber. Perhaps they should echo the tones of the shire horse that she had placed in the left foreground. Yes, that was it.

"WHO GAVE IT to you?"

"Uncle Oscar, of course."

"Wait till Mother hears it. Then there'll be trouble."

William wound the gramophone and took the gleaming disk from its cover. "Don't touch the surface," he said. "You'll spoil it."

"I'm not touching anything, stupid."

"Well, you might, if I didn't tell you."

"I know just as much as you about records."

William placed the record on the turntable and pushed the lever to Play. He blew imaginary fluff from the needle and lowered it delicately. "You can scratch them, you know, if you're not careful."

"Just play the thing."

A gentle crackle came from the speaker. "Perhaps it's a blank one," Tom said.

"Shut up," William said, and out of the horn, as from an alien world, came the voice of Victoria Spivey singing "Blood Hound Blues."

ON THE FAR side of the gardens, Marigold Jennings cocked her head and pushed the upper sash a little higher. "Music from across the way," she said.

Miss Betty yawned and turned another page of *The Good Companions*. "Probably 'Greensleeves,' " she said, "or 'Nymphs and Shepherds Come Away.' "

Marigold looked doubtful. "I don't think it is, you know." She leaned farther from the window.

Miss Betty looked up and cried, "Marigold! Do take care!"

Her friend, withdrawing abruptly into the room, struck her head sharply on the lower edge of the sash. "There's no need whatsoever to shout," she said, rubbing the top of her head.

Miss Betty put down the book. "I simply thought there was more than a little risk of your falling," she said. "You could say that my cry was an involuntary expression of my affection for you."

Mrs. Jennings gave her friend a long look. Miss Betty blushed and said, "So it isn't an English song?"

"It's an American song. It's some kind of jazz."

"It can't be," Miss Betty said, and then, seeing her friend's lips pressed firmly together, "Or rather, it seems unlikely."

Marigold stepped forward and grasped Miss Betty's elbow. "Come this way," she said with unusual force. Together they leaned across the sill and turned their good ears toward the house opposite.

"Good God," Miss Betty said.

"BLOODHOUNDS, BLOODHOUNDS," TOM sang, and began to dance in a clumsy manner.

> I done it in a passion, I thought it was the fashion—
> I know I've done wrong, but he kicked me and blacked my eye,
> But if the bloodhounds ever catch me, in the Memphis jail I'll die. . . .

The record hissed into silence. William lifted the arm of the gramophone. "Well," he said, "what do you think?"

"Play it again," Tom said. "For God's sake, just play it again. Did she really sing, 'I done it in a passion, I thought it was the fashion'?"

"What about Mother?"

"The hell with Mother."

"Isn't it good when she doesn't finish a line—"

"And leaves it hanging. Yes. It's good, that."

"IT MUST BE the boys," Miss Betty said. "Only the twins could be playing that sort of music. Everybody else must be out."

THE BOYS PLAYED the record again, and then Milly came in and said, "Your mother's home."

"Once more," William said.

"Milly," Tom said, grasping her hands, "you can dance, can't you?"

"Oh, Tom," Milly said, laughing, and William put the record on again.

"Oh no, I can't dance like that," Milly said. "If you're going to dance, you have to do it properly." She took Tom's right hand and put it on her waist. "I put one hand on your shoulder and hold your other hand, like this."

William put the record on again. Awkwardly, because Milly was laughing and because Tom was not yet a good dancer, the two of them began. When the record stopped, Tom hugged Milly, whereupon Constance opened the door and stood looking at them.

"It's all right, Mother," William said. "We've just finished."

MISS BETTY HELD her glass up to the light and admired the deep color of her nephew's latest gift.

Marigold rubbed the top of her head. "Well, I was right about the music."

"You were absolutely right, dear Marigold."

"I knew it wasn't 'Greensleeves,' or anything like that."

"Perfectly correct."

"It was jazz, after all."

"Indeed it was jazz. And jazz," Miss Betty said, waving her glass, "is simply magnificent. It's sublime and yet human, regular yet subversive. Above all, jazz is the only music capable of irony."

"I don't see how that can be," Marigold said, "since it's only a noise. And while we're about it, since when did you know anything whatsoever about music, Betty?"

1932

EXACTLY WHAT their father did at the post office was never clear. Presumably it was something reasonably important. However, it was the church that mattered. Their mother and sister had some kind of dispensation, but as soon as they were old enough to sit still, Felix took the boys with him. "Our Father, Who art in Heaven," the congregation mumbled. William and Tom sat on the hard, slippery oak with their legs swinging and looked up at Felix's hands gripping the pulpit rail. When he leaned forward they saw their father's angular face, and his voice rang out above them. He was a confidant of God, and his power held and swayed the large crowd in this enormous room. The twins sometimes felt proud and sometimes afraid and sometimes bored. They began to notice something stifling about the church. Time passed and the church became ordinary and tedious, as happens to many aspects of life in even the best-regulated circles. They began to ask each other to what purpose the church continued to mouth the same wearisome assertions. What had God to do with jazz and aeroplanes and poetry? These were modern times.

Felix saw the boys' gaze beginning to wander. Eventually he stopped insisting that they should attend. However, they always felt uneasy when he left for evensong alone.

⌒

Four of them, fourteen-year-olds, were leaning on the wall at morning break, hands in pockets. The stranger parked his Morris 8 in the quadrangle, stepped out, and placed a bowler hat centrally on his head. He was a short, plump man with a mustache. He wore a dark suit. He reached into the car, took out a long black box, locked the car, and walked in a busy fashion toward the headmaster's study. Rainbow, a tall, thoughtful boy with a small head on a long neck, suggested the visitor was the school's bank manager.

"The Morris 8," Rainbow said, combing his shining black hair with his long fingers, "is conclusive proof. The Morris 8 is only driven by bank managers. It epitomizes their station in life."

"Bloody nonsense," William said.

"You and your bloody brother, Anderson, know absolutely bloody nothing about cars."

"My brother knows quite a lot about them, actually."

"But you don't."

William said it was obvious that the man was not a bank manager. "Why should a bank manager carry a bloody box like that? Bloody great box of fivers, I suppose."

Watkins said, "Maybe it's a man delivering canes."

It was a plausible notion, but Corbett said, "That idea, Watkins, has come straight out of your arsehole, like all the shit you talk." He took every opportunity to enhance his reputation for filth.

"Well, it could be," Watkins said. "You could get two bloody dozen canes in that box. It must be five feet long, after all."

"Wait," Corbett said. "Fuck off, the lot of you. It has come to me. It's his weekly consignment of French letters. We all know the head's shagging the bloody cook." This suggestion, too obviously coarse, created a silence.

"I'll tell you what that fellow makes me think of," William said. "It's something to do with the mustache and the bowler. He's a hangman."

There was another silence. There had indeed been an air of the unmentionable about the man.

"Well, you're all wrong," Rainbow said. "The answer has come to me. I bet you half a crown he's the sex man."

He was called Mr. Glossop. Fifty boys at a time were herded into the gymnasium. Six prefects had been stationed around the walls. The boys were told to sit on the floor. The long box contained a wooden easel and a rolled-up set of colored diagrams on oilcloth. After an initial address that established the subject in the context of marriage, Christianity, and a healthy life, the headmaster introduced Mr. Glossop and left him to his lecture. Mr. Glossop wasted no time. "This," he said, hanging his first diagram on the easel and whacking it with something that might have been a snooker cue, "is a diagram of the female reproductive organs."

Around the gymnasium, a good many penises stirred at the thought. However, the diagram did not display anything recognizable as a girl, or any part of one. If anything, it resembled a map of some obscure corner of the empire. Mr. Glossop summarized the reproductive process rapidly, using precise medical terms and frequently slapping the diagrams with his stick. After talking for eight minutes, he said, "All right, lads. Any questions?"

The boys were silent. They found his tone inappropriate, and it was obvious to all but a bloody half-wit that nobody was going to admit to ignorance in a gathering of this kind.

"If you have any difficulty," Mr. Glossop said, "I'm sure you will talk to your housemaster."

Not bloody likely, the boys thought.

"I will conclude by referring to self-abuse," Mr. Glossop said. "Self-abuse isn't wholesome. It isn't godly. Self-abuse is what it says. Abusing yourself. Harming yourself."

"Oh, God," William whispered to Rainbow, who was sitting next to him.

"If you participate in such practices," Mr. Glossop went on, "it is abusing a function given to you by God for use within the holy state of matrimony."

"That's a good one," William said.

"The holy state of bollocks," Rainbow said out of the corner of his mouth. "How much do you think he gets paid for all this bosh?"

Mr. Glossop pointed his cue at him. "Did you have a question, lad?"

"No, I did not," Rainbow said.

"If you are troubled in your spirit, your chaplain can help you," Mr. Glossop said. Everyone turned to look at Rainbow, who blushed deeply.

"Given the rumors about the chaplain," Rainbow protested afterward, "Glossop's bloody silly suggestion was bloody absurd and absolutely typical of the whole bloody shambolic thing." But they still kept on laughing at him for a long time.

WHILE THE CHOIRMASTER was talking, Tom nudged his brother's elbow. William saw that from the cuff of Watkins's shorts was emerging—what was it? For a moment he was puzzled, then he realized. "Look," he whispered to his brother, "Watkins's dick."

They leaned forward and looked along the pew. Watkins licked his finger and stroked his dick until the choirmaster, noticing a slight disturbance, tapped his baton and told them to continue from letter D.

"That thing with Watkins," Tom said later.

"Yes," William said.

"What did you think?"

"I thought it was an animal at first. Some kind of pet, pushing its way out, a tortoise or a poor blind mole."

Tom laughed. "A one-eyed blind mole."

"He's not shy, Watkins, is he?"

"No."

"Would you do that?"

"Of course not. Not in public."

"In private, then."

"Well, you've got to find out how it works."

"Have you?"

"Have I what?"

"Found out how it works?"

"It must have happened to you, too."

"Well, yes."

"They don't tell you what it feels like, do they? In those talks."

"No."

"Corbett gave me a dirty photo."

"What of?"

"A girl. Well, a woman, I suppose."

"Let's have a look."

William had been fairly sure that his penis had developed some kind of disease, stiffening not only at erotic thoughts but at any time and for no obvious reason. It could happen while walking down the street, requiring him to discover a sudden interest in something low down in a shop window. The wretched thing squirted in dreams and daydreams, and it made any kind of proximity to a live girl, such as occasionally occurred in dancing lessons, extremely hazardous. He was intensely relieved to discover that something similar was happening to his brother. It was perhaps not abnormal, after all. All that blindness stuff, he knew from Watkins, was absolute bloody tosh, and he was glad that Tom completely agreed about that.

⌒

"I wouldn't say they were *handsome*, exactly," Mrs. Marigold Jennings said, "but I'd agree that they have become very nice-looking boys."

"Really, Marigold, your language is sometimes so *imprecise*," Miss Betty said. "The term *very nice-looking boys* doesn't distinguish those lads from a bowl of petunias. The Anderson boys have always been perfectly formed. In their youth I believe I described them as 'sturdy,' and suggested that they generated a good deal of maternal feeling. Now I believe we can say with some confidence that they are handsome and well proportioned and open faced and generally desirable in a way that I no longer consider maternal. They are not sophisticated, not elegant in the least degree; but elegance is not what one wants, is it? Elegance and sophistication in a young man only puts doubts in one's mind. A certain *honest roughness* is much to be preferred, a hint of muscularity, such as one observes in a young oak tree."

"Surely that's a silly metaphor," Mrs. Jennings said. "I think you're getting carried away."

"You're absolutely right, Marigold. But the contemplation of those boys is such a delightful pastime that I hope to be carried away a good many more times in the future. They are a great comfort in my declining years." Miss Betty shut her eyes, smiled to herself, and sighed a long sigh.

As for Father . . . ," Tom said as they walked to school.
"What?"

"Do you think he's all right?"

"All right? Meaning all right in the head, or what?"

"Meaning, is he *not* quite right? Is he ill?"

"I don't know what he thinks."

"I wasn't talking about thinking. I said, is he ill?"

"It isn't right if you don't know what he thinks."

"Nonsense. You can't know what another person thinks."

"I know what you think."

"That's different."

"Maybe."

"Oh, for God's sake!"

"And anyway . . ."

"What?"

"Mother isn't exactly easy."

At the school gate they went different ways. St. Mark's had begun to suspect them of providing their own society, of not requiring the institution, and even of illuminating (in a quite unnecessary and provocative way) its absurdities; hence they should be kept apart as much as possible. Naturally, they found ways to avoid this constraint.

⟋⟍

INSIDE THE ROOF of the squash court, a half-inch hole had been bored by a previous occupant through the floor, and by pressing an eye to the hole, they could follow the play of the foreshortened figures who ran in urgent patterns below. Wickford, the head boy, was playing the PT master, Mr. Thompson.

"Thompson is a vicious fellow," Tom said.

"He dislikes you," William said. Light emerging from the hole in the floor illuminated the blue iris of his left eye.

"Us."

"He considers us to be idlers."

"Yes."

They listened to the squeaking of gym shoes on wood blocks, the grunts of the players, and the whip and thrash of the rackets.

"Teachers. Odd people," Tom said.

"Yes. Lots of other jobs someone like that could choose."

"Prison guard."

"Torturer in chief."

"Teachers have a particular lumpen quality. It is the suffocating weight of his dullness that makes a teacher fearsome."

"That's a bloody silly thing to say. Would you rather your sadists were bright?"

"Can sadists be bright?"

"Hangman. Thompson could do that."

"Dentist."

"Nightwatchman."

"A nightwatchman isn't cruel. Just some nodding old chap with a dog and a brazier."

"Brassiere."

"A silly idea. Childish."

They changed places and Tom peered through the hole.

"Wickford's losing."

"Good."

"How many more years have we got?"

"Depends. One or two. Three."

"Three! God!"

"Yes."

"Pray for a catastrophe."

"It's a good word," William said. "*Catastrophe.* It's Greek, you know."

"Have you got those new pictures on you? The ones from Corbett?"

"Yes."

"Let's see." Tom looked at the photographs. "That's not very rude, is it? She's still got her bathers on."

"How rude did you expect it to be?"

"Ruder than that."

"Oh."

"Mind you, she's a big girl, isn't she? Blimey."

~

"No, I can't," Felix said.

"It's all right," Milly said.

"I seem to have—"

"That's all right, lovey. Just you lie back."

"No, I mean, it's—"

"What?"

"It feels wrong."

"What do you mean, wrong?"

Felix hesitated for some seconds and then said, "Sinful."

"Oh," Milly said. After a long moment she said, "You used not to think that. You used to want to do it a lot."

"I know I did," Felix said. "I know I did."

"I expect you need a nice rest."

Felix gazed at the ceiling. There was a silence. Then Milly said, "Is it my fault?"

"Of course not."

"Would you like a cup of tea?"

Felix turned over and pushed his face into the pillow.

"There, there," Milly said, stroking his bottom and feeling afraid.

THE TWINS WERE fifteen when the new science teacher arrived. Major Cunningham had been in the artillery and had a considerable interest in ballistics. It was, he said in his first lesson, inordinately intriguing. He was a small man whose voice was pitched a trifle too high for effective command, and the left sleeve of his jacket was pinned back, empty.

"Did you say ballistics was inordinately intriguing, sir?"

"Are you being cheeky, boy?"

"Certainly not, sir."

"What is your name?"

"Thomas Anderson, sir."

"It was your brother that I was teaching before lunch."

"Not much gets past you, sir."

The class held its breath.

"Watch it, Anderson."

The class sat back.

"TODAY CUNNINGHAM WAS talking about flight," Tom said.

"Was he," William said, reading.

"How an aeroplane flies. Equal and opposite reactions. Push the air down and you get an upward force. That's what keeps it up. You need a cambered wing section, so the air above the wing is sucked downwards. He showed us by blowing on a piece of paper."

"Did he," William said. "Listen to this." He sat up, holding the book out before him, and declaimed:

> I cannot rest from travel: I will drink
> Life to the lees: all times I have enjoyed
> Greatly, have suffered greatly, both with those
> That loved me, and alone; on shore, and when
> Through scudding drifts the rainy Hyades
> Vext the dim sea—

"I suppose that's bloody Tennyson again."

"Of course it's Tennyson."

"Aren't there other poets?"

William waved his arm in a dismissive gesture. "The thing about Tennyson is his incredible *grandeur,*" he said. "You can't doubt him." He turned the page and went on:

> Much have I seen and known; cities of men
> And manners, climates, councils, governments,
> Myself not least, but honoured of them all:
> And drunk delight of battle with my peers
> Far on the ringing plains of windy Troy.

"Good stuff," Tom said. "If you like that sort of thing."

" 'Through scudding drifts the rainy Hyades.' Don't you think that's wonderful?"

"I'm thinking of building a model glider. High-aspect ratio. The latest thing. There are drawings in *Aeromodeller.* I wonder if old Cunningham would help."

" 'Far on the ringing plains of windy Troy,' " William murmured.

"For God's sake," Tom said. "Why don't you listen?"

"All right, then, just listen to this." He turned the pages. "Here we are:"

> For I dipt into the future, far as human eye could see,
> Saw the Vision of the world, and all the wonder that would be;
>
> Saw the heavens fill with commerce, argosies of magic sails,
> Pilots of the purple twilight, dropping down with costly bales;
>
> Heard the heavens fill with shouting, and there rain'd a ghastly dew
> From the nations' airy navies grappling in the central blue.

Tom looked up and said sharply, "What? What did you say?"

" 'Pilots of the purple twilight, dropping down with costly bales.' "

"Well, I'm damned," Tom said. "When did he write that?"

William considered. "Sometime in the 1830s, I should think."

"How did Tennyson know about aeroplanes all that time ago?"

"Good question."

"Read it again."

⌒

"I NEED TO speak to you about Stella," Constance said.

"I don't see why."

"There is a difficulty about her music lessons."

"You decided on her musical career."

"Felix, please—"

"The whole thing was your decision. You'll have to resolve it yourself."

⌒

"NO, NO, NO," William said, peering over his brother's shoulder at the book. "It says two steps forward and one sideways, then turn. Doesn't it?"

"It's horribly confusing."

"It's quite simple. It merely requires concentration."

"Start again. I've lost count."

William lifted the arm of the gramophone and placed it at the beginning of the record. The two boys stood in the center of their father's study, listening to the hiss of the needle and waiting for the waltz to begin. Tom was leading, his hand on his brother's waist, while William held *Teach Yourself to Dance* in his left hand. The page had a series of diagrams showing black footprints.

"Wait for it," Tom said. "*One* two three, *one* two three, *one* two three."

"You're getting quite good at this," William said.

"I have a certain natural grace," Tom said, and laughed.

⌒

WHEN THEY WERE bored with dancing, they took a kite to the park. Trees tossed, clouds raced, rain came in scattered handfuls. Several times the kite crashed heavily to the ground.

"You're not launching it right," Tom shouted. His brother took no notice, picked up the kite, and walked backward.

"Wait for a good gust," Tom shouted.

William hurled the kite into the sky. It fluttered, lifted, staggered. Tom ran backward. The wind gusted strongly. The kite leaped up, defiant of the earth. William ran back to join his brother. Together the boys held the tugging line, delighted by the power of the wind, cricking their necks upward at the crackling dragon, yellow and red, its tail thrashing, plunging and lurching on the wind and glaring down at them.

" 'And now the storm-blast came, and he,' " William shouted, " 'Was tyrannous and strong: He struck with his o'ertaking wings, And chased us south along.' " He looked up at the trembling curve of the line. "Coleridge. 'The Ancient Mariner,' in case you don't know."

T OM DELIBERATELY SAT next to the girl on the 28B and began a conversation. At first it went quite well, but then he said, "One of the odd things about women is that they don't get bored by routine."

"What utter rubbish," the girl said, sitting up. "It's just that someone has to do it, and men don't bother."

"Oh," Tom said. "Maybe you're right." He looked again at the girl. Actually, she was a good deal older than him. A young woman, nearly. She had dark hair cut in a bob. She wasn't bad looking, but she was quite cross.

"I'm sure you're right," Tom said. "Have you ever been in an aeroplane?"

"This is my stop," the girl said, standing up.

Tom walked home, stole a slice of bread and jam from the kitchen, and went up to his bedroom. He opened the window. The sky was dark, and black-headed gulls were soaring along the backs of the houses. It was obvious when you thought about it: The monoplane was inevitable. After all, there were no biplane birds. These gulls were monoplanes with long, thin wings. He threw a crust and watched a gull swerve and take the bread easily in midair. How was it that they flew with such precision, even in the gusting winds close to the houses? How was it that they could fly so slowly without stalling? Why did they never collide? Did they have to learn how to do it? Oh, to be able to fly!

At the end-of-term dance he saw the girl again. Her name was Amanda. He took her home.

"I've always liked Grieg," she said, getting up and walking across to the wireless. "Especially the A minor."

She switched the wireless off.

"Yes, it was very nice," Tom said. It was the first time he had been alone with a girl who wasn't family. Her bones were long and looked fragile. She was hollow and light, all angles and joints. Her ankles and wrists were complex, geometrical. The insides of her upper arms were fluted. Her head looked hard and bony. She sat down again at the other end of the settee, and her legs folded like a carpenter's rule. He could hear the soft sound of her breathing. When she crossed her legs there was a faint whispering sound. She smelled of Pear's Soap.

She smoothed her skirt. There was a silence, then they spoke at once. "Sorry," Amanda said, laughing. It was a high, delicate laugh. Tom looked at the sharp angularity of her kneecaps and the thin web of her stockings stretched across the hollows of her ankle. She jumped when their elbows accidentally touched.

She looked at her watch. "Thank you ever so much for bringing me home," she said. "My parents will be back soon."

"Oh," he said. "Right."

They stood up.

"Perhaps you'd like to go for a walk or something, sometime."

"Well, yes, but I don't have a lot of spare time. Such a lot of home-work." She laughed again.

"Oh. Well, I expect I'll see you another time. Maybe at the next dance."

He picked up his coat, and she showed him to the front door.

"Well, good-bye, then."

She stood half-hidden by the door. "It was a nice dance."

He walked away, his head down, pushing his hands deep into his overcoat pockets.

WHEN TOM GOT home he said to his brother, "How do you get to touch them?"

"Touch what?"

"Girls, of course."

"I don't know. Maybe you just ask."

"Ask what? 'Can I kiss you?' "

"Something like that."

"That's bold."

"Otherwise, you could just lunge."

"You're supposed to sense some kind of mutual attraction."

"I sense an attraction for *all* of them. Well, almost all of them. But are they attracted to *me*?"

"I think you're a devilish handsome fellow."

"Idiot."

"How could you detect this mutual attraction?"

"She keeps catching your eye."

"A lingering gaze . . ."

"Your eyes meet . . ."

"She smiles sweetly."

"Every time you turn around—"

"She's at your elbow."

"Exactly."

"Doesn't happen."

"No."

"Pity."

"YOU KNOW," TOM said, "when we met I didn't think you liked me at all."

Amanda shaped her mouth into an O and made a kissing sound. "Silly boy," she said. He had spent two hours kissing her, the two of

them folded awkwardly into her parents' lumpy sofa, pins and needles in his leg, and he was still struggling politely to find a way
through the smooth and apparently faultless surface of her clothing.
He lay with her in that awful chair, his left elbow screaming and his
right hand, pursued by her left hand, roaming the seamless skin that
enclosed her whole body. Her mouth was sore on his sore mouth, his
left hand clamped in the vise of her hot thighs, immobilized, his fu-
tile penis bound in some tangle of his underwear.

DEAR AMANDA, TOM wrote, *I waited for you outside the Regal
yesterday, but obviously something had happened. Maybe you thought it was
a different night. If you like, you could telephone me. Best wishes, Tom.*

Amanda did not reply, and he never saw her again. Had he done
something wrong? If so, what was it? He wished someone would tell
him the bloody rules. She was probably giggling over his letter at
this very moment with some pimply friend of hers.

THE FEROCIOUS SARCASM of Mr. Kenning always ensured silence, and hence, although it was tentative, they all heard the knock.
The door opened and a small boy came in. With a final squeal of
chalk Mr. Kenning completed the equation he was writing, turned
with a swirl of his gown, and stared at the boy.

"Please, sir," the boy said, "the headmaster wants everyone to as-
semble in the hall."

"Indeed. And when does our lord and master wish this event to
occur, Pritchard?"

"Now, sir."

"Well, well," Mr. Kenning said, "how wearisome." He ran his
hand through his dark, wavy hair. "I suppose that one or two of you
have arranged this dramatic summons on such a warm and sunny
morning specifically to avoid the next stage in our deeply fascinating
algebraic studies. The word *algebra* originating where, Rainbow?"

"Egypt, sir. Arabic word."

"Arabic word for what?"

"Er—mathematics?"

"Please, sir, the headmaster said it was urgent."

"Oh, very well, Pritchard, take them away. See if I care. If the business, whatever it is, be complete before the end of morning school, be sure to return all these boys to me at once, Pritchard. I know what you're like. Keep none of them for yourself."

"Please, sir, he wants you to come as well."

"Oh, does he? How tedious. Very well. *En avant,* Pritchard."

The headmaster was pacing the stage when they entered. There was a row of staff seated behind him, and a gray-haired policeman.

When they had settled, the headmaster said, "A serious thing has happened. Most of you will be aware that the senior run took place yesterday afternoon. At the finish line Mr. Thompson recorded the finishers as usual. Babington did not arrive, and a search party was sent out to Nightingale Park and the Caswell valley. They found nothing. His parents and the police were informed. Searches continued overnight. This morning we have received bad news."

The headmaster looked straight ahead. He was a fat windbag of a man, but he had acquired a sudden dignity. William wondered how six hundred boys could be so still, so silent.

"Chief Inspector Marshall has just informed me that Babington has been found." The headmaster paused again. It was hard to tell whether he was trying to find a nice way of saying Babington was dead or was simply seeking to squeeze the maximum of self-important drama from the moment.

"There has been a terrible accident, and Babington received wounds which proved fatal."

That silence again. It was interesting, William thought, that the boy's death was not at all sad or depressing; on the contrary, it was delicious.

"Chief Inspector Marshall wishes to say a few words."

The policeman stood up and put on a cap with a lot of silver braid on the peak. He stepped to the front. He was wearing black leather gloves and carrying something that looked like a riding crop. "We wish to establish the facts of this accident, and therefore my men"—he gestured, and they saw that there were policemen beside each door—"my men will be asking everyone in the senior school a few simple questions. There is nothing to be afraid of. We simply wish to know who saw young Jonathan Babington yesterday, and when, and where."

The policeman sat down and the headmaster spoke again. "The lower school will stay where you are. The senior school will file out of the back doors and make your way to the Easby building, where the interviews will take place. Staff will be with you at all times. Very well."

The senior school shuffled out, and the remainder began to murmur. "That's no good," Rainbow said, "not telling us what happened."

"That's because they want someone to incriminate himself," Tom said.

"Personally, I never liked Babington," Corbett said.

"Oh, shut up, Corbett, you ass," Watkins said. "You didn't even know him."

"Did you know his name was Jonathan?"

"No. Nor did you."

"In a minute they're going to tell us what happened," Tom said. "It's someone in the senior school they're after. That's why they've separated us."

The headmaster stepped forward again. "This is an extremely painful event, and shocking for us all. There will be all kinds of rumors, no doubt, so I wish to give you the facts, such as they are. Please be aware that any boy discussing this matter with any outsider will be liable to immediate expulsion."

The boys sat still and sucked in every detail.

"The facts are that Babington was found in the railway tunnel under Nightingale Park at seven this morning. He had been severely injured, presumably by a train. You will be aware that there is a school rule about trespassing on the railway. The regulations for the senior run specifically forbid a shortcut through the tunnel."

"Who was with him?" Rainbow whispered. "And what were they up to?"

"Any boy who has any information about this tragic event will immediately contact a member of staff. There will be a special service in the chapel at five this evening. That is all."

Tom said afterward, "If you'd been with him, would you own up?" They were in the library, waiting for the evening service.

"No," William said. "Probably not."

"Bet you would. Otherwise it'd be on your conscience."

"Depends what they were doing."

There was a pause. Rainbow said, "Look." They looked down into the quadrangle. The headmaster was walking beside a man in a dark suit and a woman in a large black hat.

"Babington's parents," Rainbow said.

"How do you know?"

"It could be."

They gazed searchingly at what might be a tragically bereaved couple.

"Interesting how the head told us," William said. "How he worked round to it. And then he didn't tell us much. And how those policemen magically appeared. Like a play."

Rainbow pushed his fingers through his hair and gazed at William. "He could hardly say straight off that Babington had been sliced in half by the three-fifteen in the middle of a crazy sex ritual."

"Exactly. People have to find the right words."

CONSTANCE SAID, "FELIX, ask Oscar if he would like a drink."

Felix did so.

"Of course I'd like a drink," Uncle Oscar roared, "and not one of your weeny ones, either." He laughed loudly to show it was a joke.

Felix poured him a modest glass of whiskey. "Jolly fine," Uncle Oscar said, and drank it off. "By God," he said, belching, "I bloody well needed that! Throat as dry as a camel's arsehole."

"Really, Oscar," Constance said. "You might take regard of the boys."

"Boys?" Oscar looked around, saw the twins sitting side by side, and did an elaborate double take. "By God, two of them! Seeing double! Am I pissed already?"

The twins smiled dutifully at the familiar joke.

"You've had one or two," Constance said. "Haven't you, Oscar?"

"My dear Constance, one or two would be a grotesque understatement. I have been attending jollifications all afternoon. An excellent reunion luncheon in town."

William watched, wondering how on earth his uncle could get away with such outrageous behavior in front of his parents, and Uncle Oscar farted elaborately on a descending scale: *phrrrrtttt*. As always when he did this in company, he added the exclamation, "———— that tiger!" This cry, delightful and completely mystifying as it was, had been the subject of much discussion between the boys. Did it mean that blame for the noise should be placed on some passing tiger, now invisible, or what? It was surely impossible that anyone would be deceived by that. There must be another explanation.

"Now," Uncle Oscar said, sitting on the carpet in front of the boys. "Let us consider the principles of the dogfight."

"Attack out of the sun," Tom said quickly.

"Excellent! Out of the sun!"

"Get in close."

"Get in close, boy, get in close." Uncle Oscar seemed suddenly sleepy.

"Fire in short bursts."

"Absolutely." Uncle Oscar leaned backward until he was lying flat on the carpet. Slowly he closed his eyes. "Fire in short bursts," he murmured. "Absolutely."

"Watch your tail."

"Watch your tail, oh yes, you can say that again. Watch your tail. Abso-bloody-lutely vital." Uncle Oscar's mustache lifted and fluttered as he spoke.

"Stay high," Tom said without much certainty.

There was a silence.

"Oscar," Constance said sharply. He did not respond.

Constance said, "Oh, really!" She left the room, and the boys listened to her going upstairs, calling, "Stella! Stella! Where are you?"

William got up and looked closely at Uncle Oscar, who was even more interesting lying down. "Is he all right?"

"Of course he is," Felix said. "He's just completely drunk. He'll recover soon and feel quite awful."

"Shall we get Milly?"

"Milly? Why should you want Milly?"

"Well . . . she deals with things."

"Don't be absurd. We'll just leave him to sleep it off. Come on."

Felix left the room and the boys followed, edging around the body on the carpet. They shut the door and went up to their room.

William listened. "I believe I can still hear him snoring," he said.

"It's like having a wild beast sleeping in the house," Tom said.

"He doesn't care about anything," William said.

"Except flying. He cares about that."

"He doesn't fly anymore."

"He's too old, I suppose."

"How Mother can have a brother like him . . ."

"Yes. Strange, you've got to admit."

TOM CAME down early and picked up the envelope from the doormat. The certificate was, he thought, quite imposing.

UNIVERSITY OF LONDON

GENERAL SCHOOL EXAMINATION

SCHOOL CERTIFICATE IN HONORS

I. This is to certify that *Thomas Edward Anderson,* born *11th November 1918,* has been a pupil at *St. Mark's Grammar School* (inspected by the University and the Board of Education) for a period of . . . 6 . . . years and . . . o . . . terms ending *July 1936,* and has pursued a Course of Study in the subjects set out on the back of this Certificate.

H. Baston B.A.

Head of the School

II. Also that this pupil, having been examined in the following groups of subjects:—

(i) ENGLISH SUBJECTS, (ii) LANGUAGES, (iii) MATHEMATICS AND SCIENCE, (iv) OTHER SUBJECTS,

has passed the General School Examination held at the School mentioned above in *Midsummer 1935,* with Credit in the following subjects (*4* in number):—

English, Arithmetic, Elementary Mathematics, Chemistry

and with Distinction in the following subjects (3 in number):—

French, with credit in the oral examination, Electricity and Magnetism, Drawing

Signed on behalf of the University of London,

S. H. Shurrock
Secretary for School Examinations

He slid the certificate back into its envelope. His father had simply said no to university. Tom took the certificate out again and looked at it. It was a kind of passport to whatever came next. How could it get him into the aeroplane business?

S T. SWITHIN'S TEACHER Training College sent its students immediately into the classroom at one of the nearby schools. The headmaster of Underbank, an uninspiring figure in William's view, looked down at his desk and fiddled with a pen. "Plunge straight in," he said. "Much the best thing for a young chap like you." He opened a folder and looked at a grid of names and numbers. "Teaching's just a matter of experience. Sink or swim. No point in putting things off." He ran his finger down one of the columns. "We're short of rooms, so you'll have to take IIR in a chemistry lab, but there's only a handful of them. Reading practice. Nine-fifteen, room twenty-three A."

William plunged straight in, and on that first day his intuition was insufficiently developed to detect the charged air and secret glances. It was a long time before he realized that several of the children were missing. He labored on with their reading until at last he heard faint sounds. The missing children were not missing; they were hiding in the cupboards under the demonstration bench, among the Bunsen burners and retort stands.

Two of them came out readily enough, but one girl was clinging to a cast-iron pipe. William gave her a tug, and as she emerged there was a terrible gush of water. The broken pipe was of large diameter, the water under high pressure. He sent her off to get the caretaker. Several minutes passed, and then Alan Willard pointed out, with the resigned expression of one who knows, that Bella would have gone home, wouldn't she? William sent another child, who similarly disappeared. By now the flood, dammed by a step in the doorway, was getting deep. The children became excited and began to throw one another's possessions into the water; the occasion promised to be one of the most interesting things that had ever happened at school. A thin boy with glasses stood on a desk and said he was going to hold a diving competition. William, marooned on the bench some distance away, could think of nothing but the growing nub of his own fear.

"We're all going to drown!" said a boy who had so far been silent but who was now discovering new skills of dramatic gesture and expression. "We've got to get out!" He ran up the raked seating to the back of the room, opened a window, and started to climb out. William plunged through the water, leaped up the steps, and grabbed his belt; together they stared down at the concrete of the playground, thirty feet below.

As the water started to overflow across the landing and down the stairs, the caretaker appeared. "Well," Mr. Oliphant said when he was able to speak, "well, well, well. Reminds me of Whipsnade. The concrete pond and penguins and that. Well, well, well. Wait till I tell the wife."

The headmaster ascribed William's difficulties to an obvious lack of authority. "You've got to crack down on the little bastards from the start," he said, fiddling with his pen. "Otherwise they won't give you no respect. Here, I'll give you a cane. No, take a handful, in case you break one. Make an example of somebody. Doesn't matter who. A good thrashing makes a hell of a difference."

THE BUS LURCHED to a halt. Its headlights illuminated the end of a rutted track. The conductor called to him. "Here you are, lad. On the left. Half a mile along." Tom stepped down. The conductor passed him his suitcase and slammed the door. Gears grated. The rear light of the bus swayed into the distance, and it became utterly dark. Tom felt with his foot for the edge of the track. Rain was in the air; he buttoned his raincoat, pulled up his collar, and picked up his case.

As he became accustomed to the darkness, he began to see the outline of drystone walls, a clump of trees, a hill to his right. A single yellow light glimmered into view. He passed a barn and a hedge of windblown hawthorns. Here was a square stone house with a lamp above the door and a carved sign that said "The Nest." A stream ran through the garden. He knocked and waited. The door opened and a woman stood there. "You'll be Tom," she said. "I'm Barbara Finch." She smiled at him. "Come on in."

He followed her down a narrow hall lined with watercolors and into a room with a bright fire. "Put your coat in the hall. Take a seat. You'll want some tea." She went into another room.

Tom put down his case and took off his coat. It was a small room, cluttered with furniture; he felt large and clumsy. He looked around: a framed photograph of an elderly woman, a copper pan, an earthenware pot, a china figure of a dancer, a slim vase of dried flowers, a mother-of-pearl box, a pair of tall wineglasses, a small wooden bowl filled with silver charms. He sat beside the fire, and in a few moments steam began to rise from his trousers. In the other room there was a clatter of cups and the woman was whistling. Carefully, Tom leaned back in the chair.

MISS FINCH LOOKED up from her book when he woke, smiled at him, and tapped the ash from her cigarette. "The teapot's on the hearth."

"I'm terribly sorry—"

"Drink your tea. Then you can tell me about yourself." A Labrador wandered in, wagged its tail briefly, and sat before the fire. "That's Josephine. She's somewhat overweight. Do you like dogs? You can call me Barbara." She was wearing a white shirt and dark trousers with red braces. Her hair was gray and short, and she had a direct way of looking at him.

IN THE MIDDLE of the night he got up and opened the window of his bedroom. There was nothing but darkness and the sound of running water. He felt his way to the bathroom and back. The bed was hard and slightly damp. He turned over and pulled the eiderdown close around his ears.

In the morning the sun slanted into the room. He listened to the stream for a while and then looked at his watch. It was six o'clock. He dressed and went downstairs. The dog sat in the hall, her tail thumping the floor, and she followed as he let himself out the front door. The house was set into the side of the hill; on the far side of the road the grassy slope fell smoothly away to the flat, rich plain of the Severn, four or five hundred feet below. The river looped in a great oxbow and widened away to the west. Across the valley to the north, far away, were the dark shadows of mountains. He followed a path along the edge of the hill and sat for a while on a drystone wall. The wind was fresh. The dog snuffled in a patch of brambles and squatted in the grass.

When he got back, there was a smell of bacon. Barbara Finch was sitting in the window of the front room, drinking a cup of tea. "That way," she said, pointing, "is the Bristol Channel. Over there, Wales and the Black Mountains. Upstream, Gloucester, Tewkesbury, the Vale of Evesham. It's the best view in England, and it's all mine." She looked at him, laughing. "Don't you think it's wonderful?"

"I do," he said. "It's lovely."

"Breakfast, quick, or you'll be late. When you go out of the gate, take the footpath into town. Follow the fingerposts. You'll find the Olympic works easily. And don't be late this evening. I've got a friend coming."

As he crossed the brow of the hill, the town came into sight: a dozen mills with tall chimneys along the line of a stream and houses of cream-colored stone clustered on steep, wooden slopes.

He looked at his watch. It was seven o'clock. The path dropped steeply toward the first houses. He walked faster. As he descended into the valley, the air grew colder and there were deep shadows. He followed the river. Around a bend was the first of the mills, then a church, an inn, a post office, a market square. Other men were going the same way, their boots ringing on the pavement. They arrived at a factory gate surmounted by a sign that said "Olympic Aero." At the gate was a policeman. Tom showed him the letter. The policeman read it, his lips moving. "Waiting room," he said, pointing.

There were two other young men there. They sat in silence until a man in a brown workshop coat came in. He looked at a list. "Bulstrode," he said.

One of the young men, short and stocky, said, "Yes, sir."

The man in the brown coat ticked the name. "Don't call me sir," he said. "Call me Mr. Jakes. I'm your foreman." He looked at Tom. "Who are you?"

"Tom Anderson."

Mr. Jakes ticked his name and looked at the third man. "So you're Strawson."

"Yes," said the young man. He had a long, thin neck, a big Adam's apple, and large, bony hands.

"Follow," Mr. Jakes said. He led them into a large room filled with the chatter of typewriters. "Here you are, girls," he said, "the rest of this year's crop. Take your pick."

The women stopped typing. "I'll have him," one of them called out, pointing. "The tall one." Strawson blushed.

Another woman said, "Oh, look, he's gone pink." There was laughter.

"Form an orderly queue," Mr. Jakes said. "All requests in writing."

A girl said, "Oh, Mr. Jakes, you are awful." The women laughed and their typewriters began to chatter again.

Mr. Jakes led them up and down stairs and along corridors until they reached an office, whereupon he sat down and put his feet on a desk cluttered with aluminum components, blueprints, technical journals, and files. A propeller blade stood in a corner, and on the wall was a photograph of a silver biplane above a rumpled expanse of cloud. The three young men stood in a row.

"You're mine," Mr. Jakes said, "for the next five years." He was a heavyset man with a hooked nose and a harsh voice. "You work for me. You do what I say. I'm your boss. I'm your nanny. Any troubles, tell me. There are thirty apprentices, and you three are my special ones. My little flock. Understood?"

He took his feet from the desk and consulted a file. "Later there'll be a meeting. You'll get your timetables. It's a month in the works, a month in the school. You rotate. Try everything, see? You rotate. All right? Rotate." Mr. Jakes wrinkled his face: It was a smile. "You rotate from the machine shop to the stores, then the DO, inspection, assembly, and finally you rotate to admin."

Bulstrode asked, "What's the DO?"

"The DO, Bulstrode, is the drawing office. What are you grinning for, Anderson? You knew that, did you?"

"Yes, sir."

"Don't call me sir."

He took them to the stores, and they were given green overalls. "Baggy," Mr. Jakes said, looking at Tom. "Never mind. Fits where it touches." His face wrinkled again. "All right. Let's get on with it."

The machine shop was loud with the slapping, syncopated rhythms of the drive belts. Mr. Jakes stopped beside one of the machines and raised his voice above the slap and whirr of the belt. "You'll know what this is, Anderson."

"It's a lathe," Tom said.

"It's a lathe. This week you'll stay here with Jack." Jack was a small man with a bald head and battered, oil-stained hands. "Watch what Jack does, do what he says. Clock in each day over there." Mr. Jakes pointed to the time clock. "You'll get a card. Seven-thirty to six P.M. Half an hour for lunch. No smoking in the shop, or in the bloody bog, neither. All right?"

⁓

THE REGULAR SLAP of the drive belt was mesmeric. Jack was humming to himself in time with it and concentrating on the length of brass bar held in the lathe. Tom picked one of the finished components from a tray. "What are they for?"

"Drawing's on the tool cupboard," Jack said, bent over the lathe. Tom looked at the greasy blueprint. It was headed "Mark 4 Wing Tank Connectors."

"How many have you got to make?"

"Twelve hundred."

"Bloody hell."

"Fifty a day."

Tom calculated. "That's five weeks. You'll go mad."

Jack laughed but did not look up. Around them the machines clamored, and amid the racket men talked, their heads close together. "Oh, that's the Mark 2. Alloy insert instead of steel." "Allow two thou for the taper." "What's the rake?" "Three-inch pitch circle." "It'll do." "Drop-forged, is it?" "Last one failed the tensile, Geoff said. Radius too small." "Two thou tolerance, that's all." "Nice bit of work."

Jack held each finished component for a few moments in his battered hands, assessing it with a micrometer taken from his top pocket, turning it over, holding it up to the light. Tom stood and watched.

After three hours a whistle blew. The slapping belts slowed. Men gathered in groups around the heating stoves. Some sat on boxes or upturned buckets. The tea trolley came around. "Oh, you're new, aren't you?" the girl said, handing Tom a mug. "Do you want sugar, dear, or are you sweet enough already?"

They listened while a man called Wimshurst, who had a white coat and clean hands, told a long story about his daughter's fiancé. "And the final straw was, the silly sod hadn't got a bloody penny."

The men grunted and nodded their heads when he had finished. Jack, Alf, Fred, Ted, Frank, Bill: They had short, blunt names—except Mr. Jakes, who was called Maurice.

"But don't tell him I told you," Jack said. "He likes everyone to call him Mr. Jakes."

After ten minutes the whistle blew again. The men dispersed, the machines restarted. Tom's back ached.

Jack walked up to his lathe and looked at it as though he'd never seen it before. "That bloke Wimshurst, he don't half go on," Jack said. "Him and his bloody daughter and her bloody men. You should see her. Bloody hell." He scratched his head and looked at Tom. "Time you had a go at the lathe, I reckon."

⌒

THEY ATE FISH pie in a smoky canteen filled with clattering plates and boisterous talk. The three young men sat together. "A whole month of this," Strawson said.

Bulstrode drew on his cigarette and said, "But only a month."

⌒

THAT AFTERNOON MR. Jakes took them to the apprentice school and they waited with a group of other young men. Eventually a thin man wearing a gray lounge suit came in. Mr. Jakes stood up and said, "Good afternoon, sir."

The man looked over his glasses and said, "Oh, hello, Jakes. How's your boy?"

"He's coming on all right, sir, thanks."

"Good." He looked around. "Another lot, eh?"

"Yes, sir. Lambs to the slaughter." He turned to the young men. "Mr. Hetherington is the chief engineer."

The chief engineer sat on the edge of a desk and looked at the rows of young men. "Hello, chaps," he said. "It's nice to see you." He nodded and smiled as though he thought them a particularly interesting group. He pushed his fingers through his hair, took off his glasses, and put them on again.

"Engineering is an art," he said. "It needs imagination. Things are made inside your head. Let's take two wheels, say. One's a cart wheel, the other is a bicycle wheel. They do the same job, but they don't do it the same way. They're completely different."

He got up, took a stub of chalk from a tray, and sketched the two kinds of wheel on the blackboard. He was good at drawing freehand circles.

"Cart wheels are quite easy to make. They need an iron band that clamps it all together, but the rest of it can be crude. Thick spokes. Thick rim. You can make a cart wheel of wood, with an ax."

At this point the chief engineer looked around the room as if to see whether anyone had brought an ax. Somebody laughed.

"Bicycle wheels are hard to make. They need machinery to make the spokes and the hubs. You can't make them with an ax, but they're elegant. A bicycle wheel holds the rider off the ground by means of very little material, used cleverly. The cyclist hangs from a few spokes in the upper part of the wheel."

As the chief engineer spoke, he imitated with his hands the pedaling feet of the cyclist. With fingers and thumbs he extruded an imaginary spoke, thin and strong, from the air.

"As the wheel turns, the tensile loads move from spoke to spoke." He turned and chalked little arrows on the spokes of his bicycle wheel, then turned back to the young men.

"The bicycle wheel is elegant because it's light." With one hand he threw an imaginary wheel into the air and watched it fly up and away through the ceiling.

"It uses materials well. The wire spokes are thin and light, but strong in tension. The wheel rim is thin, too, but it resists large forces because it's cunningly shaped. A bicycle wheel is strong and light. It encloses a lot of empty space, and empty space doesn't weigh anything." He gestured with his hands wide apart. "Think about that. It's one of the great principles of design. Simplicate and add more lightness."

He tossed the chalk ten feet into a tray, gave his performance a little clap, and sat down.

"I've been an engineer for thirty years. In England we earn our pleasures. Some of you will change your minds about engineering. If you don't want us, we don't want you. If you stay, you'll work. It's a proud trade, and a hard trade. There's no money in it. It's what the British do. We're the world's makers."

NEAR THE END of the day, Tom was bending over the lathe and Jack stood at his elbow. Gradually it had become rhythmical and automatic. Unlock the chuck, slide the bar to the stop. Tighten up. Rotate the turret. Face off. Rotate the turret. Drill out. Rotate. He was beginning to get quicker. Jack picked up his *Herald,* and leaned back against the tool cupboard, and the lathe stopped with a crash.

Jack dropped his paper. "Fuck me," he said, "you left the fucking key in the chuck. Jesus." He inspected the lathe. "You're lucky, son. No harm done."

He picked up the chuck key and weighed it in his hand. "Now look, that chuck key stays in your hand while you're using it. All right? I already fucking told you that. You don't never leave it in the chuck. You don't put it down nowhere but in the rack. Right?"

"Sorry."

"Don't be fucking sorry. Just get it fucking right. Could have killed us."

"Sorry."

"Chuck key flying across the shop. Could have killed someone."

"Sorry."

"All right. Blimey. You don't know how lucky that was. Could have killed anyone."

——⋅⋆——

"DULL TALK OF Hetherington's," Strawson said. It was six-thirty. They were in the Rose and Crown, around the corner from the works.

"Oh, I don't know," Bulstrode said. "I quite liked him. He put on a nice little show, I thought."

"Done it before, hadn't he? Fancied himself."

"Of course he had. But it doesn't matter. He did it nicely."

" 'The first principle of engineering,' " Tom said, imitating the precise voice of the chief engineer. " 'Simplicate and add more lightness.' "

Strawson sniffed. "Obvious, I'd say."

"The bit about the wheels," Tom said, "that was interesting. I thought so, anyway. It's true that those wheels are quite different, when you think about it. I hadn't thought about engineering being an art."

There was a pause. Strawson leaned back in his chair and said, "Can you define a gentleman?"

Bulstrode looked at him. "No. But I expect you can."

"A gentleman takes his weight on his elbows."

Bulstrode looked inquiringly at Tom, who shook his head.

"Don't get it," Bulstrode said.

Strawson said, "Oh, for God's sake!"

"My round," Bulstrode said, and went to the bar.

"Well, I think it's a nice idea, anyway," Tom said. "Simplicate and add more lightness."

"Don't see what it's got to do with bloody workshops," Strawson said.

Bulstrode came back. "The barmaid's called Susan," he said. "She's quite nice, don't you think?"

"Oh, God," Tom said, getting up, "I'm supposed to be back early. She'll kill me."

H E S T U M B L E D I N T O the house. Barbara Finch was sitting at the table with a woman dressed in pink. They were eating lamb chops. "Don't say it," Barbara said.

"I'm terribly sorry."

"Get a plate from the warming oven. A burnt chop under the grill. Mash in the pan. Carrots in the other one. Remains of."

He got the food and sat down.

"This is my friend Nora," said Miss Finch.

"Hello."

"Pleased to meet you."

"His name's Tom."

"He smells of factories. Not to mention beer."

"Oh dear. You'd better go and have a wash."

In his bedroom he opened the window, listened to the stream, and breathed deeply. When he got back to the supper table Nora was saying, "He's one of those people who stand with their hands in their pockets, swaying back and forward and pontificating."

"Nora has strong opinions," Barbara said to Tom. "And she doesn't like her boss."

"Oh."

"He's unfit to be an employer," Nora said.

"But does it make sense to get so annoyed about him?"

"Oh yes, Barbara. It makes me feel tons better."

"It probably isn't good for your blood pressure."

"When he's giving us one of his talks I like to think of him naked," Nora said. "The spindly legs. The jutting gut. The small dangling parts." She laughed. "I feel better already."

"Tom's looking bemused, Nora. Better change the subject." Barbara turned to Tom. "We made a discovery this afternoon. Josephine isn't overweight, she's expecting a happy event." She fitted a cigarette into a long black holder and then, noticing Tom's expression, said, "Josephine is the dog, Tom. She's pregnant."

"Oh, yes," Tom said. "The dog. I'd forgotten."

Nora watched Barbara lighting her cigarette and said, "You smoke too much, love."

"THE POINT IS," Mr. Jakes said, "the Imperial system comes natural, see? It's common sense. It's evolved. It's evolved over centuries. It all fits. Gallon of water weighs ten pounds. Pint of water weighs a pound and a quarter. Learn it by heart. Once learned, never forgotten."

Mr. Jakes took a steel rule from his top pocket. "Same thing with linear measure. An inch is as wide as your thumb. A foot is the length of your foot. A yard is a man's pace. All right?"

The young men nodded.

"All right. What about half, quarter, eighth, sixteenth, thirty-second, sixty-fourth?"

The young men were silent.

"Easy. Logical. You can do the sums in your head. What's half of three-eighths?"

"Er—"

"Three-sixteenths. Easy. What's half of a half?"

"Quarter."

"Too easy. What about three-quarters of a half?"

"Three-eighths?"

"All right. Now. You need a finer measure, so you go to thousandths of an inch. How many thou in a sixty-fourth?"

They looked at one another, but nobody spoke.

"Fifteen thou. Give or take. Your thumb's an inch wide. How thick's your thumbnail?"

"Fifty thou," Bulstrode said.

"Who told you that?"

"I just measured it. With the micrometer."

"Miked it, we say. Clever bugger, aren't you. What's the span of your hand? Nine inches? Eight? If you don't know, measure it and don't forget."

"Might come in handy."

"Always do the sum in your head, roughly. That way you know where you are. Divide twenty-nine by eleven, call it thirty by ten, that gives us somewhere about three. Actually, it's two point six summat. Bulstrode, what is it?"

Bulstrode took his new slide rule from its case. "Looks like two point six three."

"Near enough. Point is, the slide rule won't tell you if it's two point five or twenty-five or two hundred and fifty, will it? You've got to know, see. All right? You've got to be sure where you are."

TOM WAS SENT to the stores window. "Mr. Jakes wants a long weight."

"Does he. Got a chitty?"

He passed the slip that Mr. Jakes had given him. The storeman looked at it and said, "Hang on a minute."

Tom waited. After ten minutes he stuck his head through the stores window. There was nobody in sight. Eventually the storeman came back.

"Have you got it yet?"

"I told you to hang on." The storeman went away again.

He waited for another twenty minutes before he began to wonder.

In the canteen the others laughed for a long time, quite unreasonably, it seemed to him. It was a silly, pointless trick, after all.

"Would you believe it! An hour, at least, he was stood there!"

"A long weight!"

"How dim can you get!"

"Oldest one in the book."

"Except maybe a left-handed screwdriver."

Much of the work was tedious, yet the routine did not entirely prevent the development of a curious satisfaction; by such means rough stock was made precise and bright. Under Tom's hands an object was made. It became itself. Even a plain brass bush, a simple thing and one among hundreds, lay heavy and particular in the palm of his hand.

On the second Friday they queued at a table for square brown envelopes, heavy with small change. Tom took his money from the clerk and signed the book. Thirty-seven shillings and sixpence. He took it back to the Nest, went up to his room, and counted the money. He had decided he was happy here. His room was up two flights, the second steep and narrow, and the roof loomed low over the bed. In the bedside cupboard he had found a copy of *Lark Rise to Candleford;* he had dipped into it, but it wasn't his kind of book.

He washed and went downstairs. In the hall was a hatstand covered with Barbara's hats. She saw him and said, "I like hats. I've got a lot so I can match my mood precisely." She smiled at him. "Your supper's ready."

Tom gave her the pound note from the brown envelope, put the ten bob in his wallet, ate his supper, and took seven-and-six to the Rose and Crown.

He and Bulstrode met William one Saturday morning at the bus stop and took him into the pub. "Well, I'm blowed," Susan said, "two peas in a pod. One of you is our Tom, but which?"

"Me," Tom said. "This is my brother, William."

"Fancy," Susan said. "Don't you never get muddled?"

"Can we have three bitters? And would you like something?"

"Seeing as you're asking, I don't mind if I do," Susan said. "Oh, I see your brother's got nice clean hands."

"I'm not a mucky mechanic like him."

"What do you do, then, dear?"

"I'm going to be a teacher," William said.

"Oh."

"You mustn't hold it against me."

"Oh, I wouldn't, love, but it brings back nasty memories, see? I didn't get on with school. Or school didn't get on with me, more like. I was a bit of a handful."

They sat down. "She still is a bit of a handful," Bulstrode said.

"I think she's taken a fancy to you, William," Tom said. "She keeps looking across."

Bulstrode stared into his glass. "Strawson says he's leaving," he said.

"I thought he might."

"Never had his heart in it."

Tom tapped his fingernails on the table. "If you're going to be a teacher, William, you'll be stuck forever at some awful school with a bunch of horrendous dullards."

"Possibly."

Tom leaned into the corner of the alcove and spread his arms along the back of the seat. "All teachers are horrendous dullards. And those awful children sniffing and giggling. You've never shown the slightest liking for nippers, have you?" He placed his little finger in his ear and poked about in an exploratory way.

William looked at him and wrinkled his brow. "Do you have to do that?"

"Absolutely."

William looked absently at old Joe, nodding in his usual place by the fire. He took a mouthful of beer and drank it down, then said to Tom, "It's all very well for you and your aerial fantasies."

"Being a poet isn't a fantasy?"

"Never said I wanted to be a poet."

"But we know, don't we?" Tom called across to Joe. "We all know, don't we, Joe?" The old man nodded and smiled, not hearing, and turned back to the glowing coals.

William got up and went over to talk to Susan. "I came all this way to see my brother and he spouts a lot of nonsense," he said.

Susan polished a glass with her big red hands. "Never mind, love, it'll be all the same in a thousand years. Want something stronger?"

⟋⟋⟍⟍⟋◠

LATER, SUSAN SAID, "It's all right, love, they won't be back for hours," and blew gently into William's ear. They were in her room above the bar. "You're a very nice boy. A perfect sweetie. But I have to be careful. Have you got something with you, dear?"

"Yes," William said. Bulstrode had warned him about that, and he'd popped round to the barber's. She got up and put a record on the gramophone.

> Blue moon . . .
> You saw me standing alone,
> Without a dream in my heart,
> Without a love of my own.

She sat down again. William put his arms around her. It seemed a reasonable thing to do. He pressed his hand around her left breast.

"If you want any more you'll have to give me my ten bob," Susan said.

"Oh," he said. "Oh, yes."

"You are William, aren't you? Let's see your hands."

"Of course I am."

"That's all right, then."

"Has my brother—?"

"Oh no, dear. Just a thought. Have you got the ten bob?"

"Yes," William said. He had borrowed it from Tom. He crumpled the note into her hand.

"That's right, dear," she said. "Now, don't never forget, you've got to be nice to a lady. No rough stuff."

"Well, I wouldn't."

"Of course you wouldn't, dear. Nice and gentle, that's the way. Cuddles and kisses is what we like. Now you just sit here a minute," she said, getting up and leaving the room. He wondered what she was doing.

You heard me saying a prayer for,
Someone I really could care for.

She came back. Whatever she had done was not visible. She sat down. "Well, dear, here we are."

He edged toward her.

"You could take your cardy off," he said.

"That's your job," Susan said.

He undid the buttons.

"What did I say?"

"Sorry?"

"Cuddles."

"Oh. Sorry."

He fumbled a little more, then she stood up and took off her shoes, her necklace, her bracelet, her watch, her blouse, her brassiere, her skirt, her suspender belt, her nylons, her knickers (were they silk?), and sat down. She grew and spread, her body flaring smoothly in various directions, her hips widening, her breasts hanging large. He had thought he knew what to expect, but he had not foreseen such expansive curvature.

I heard somebody whisper, Please adore me,
And when I looked the moon had turned to gold.

"You could stop staring now," she said.

"You're very beautiful."

She laughed. "Now, don't fiddle. Be firm, but be gentle. And don't forget that a lady never likes a man who leaves his socks on." She reached out and undid his belt, pushed his trousers and underpants down, then knelt on the floor and took his penis in her mouth.

"Oh!" he said. "Should you do that?"

She put her arms around his legs.

"You'd better stop," William said, but she took no notice and he found himself grasping her head awkwardly and jerking against her face.

"That's got that over with, dear," she said, wiping her lips on the tail of his shirt. "Now let's get in the bed. Socks off."

Blue moon . . .
Now I'm no longer alone,
Without a dream in my heart,
Without a love of my own.

———◦———

Barbara put Tom's breakfast in front of him. "So where's your brother this morning?"

"Well—actually he went to see a friend last night."

"Oh, did he?"

"Yes."

"Unexpectedly, I presume."

"Yes."

"And he hasn't come back."

"No."

Nora looked up from her toast. "Disgusting," she said.

"Now come along, Nora, you mustn't be rude about our guest."

"Well."

"Well nothing."

Nora sniffed, cut the toast into very small pieces, and ate them one by one with considerable delicacy.

———◦———

"It's so wretchedly dull since they left home," Miss Betty said, yawning.

"There's always the daughter," Marigold Jennings said. "She's a pretty little thing."

"Utterly damning though that judgment is," Miss Betty said, "I cannot but agree. Stella has a way of flicking her hair from her eyes that I find genuinely repulsive."

"She's getting a little plump."

"Really, Marigold! Pots and kettles come to mind."

"Betty, it's fortunate for our friendship that I've learned over the years to tolerate your hurtful comments. I quite realize that you don't mean them. Malcolm sometimes made unpleasant comments of exactly that kind. I hope not to hear that sort of thing anymore."

"Oh, my dear Marigold, I'm so sorry! You know what I'm like. I just get carried away. The boys have gone for good and I need a new interest, that's the trouble. I'm bored. I know I shouldn't take it out on you, I do really."

"We've been abandoned," Marigold said.

Miss Betty turned to look out across the gardens of Finchley. "Yes," she said, "they've gone away and left us behind."

Tom slid the blueprint from the drawer and carried it to his desk. He was always intrigued by the formality of engineering drawing, the crisp authority of a sharp pencil. A drawing was an end in itself; the engineering was done, the thing almost existed.

The drawing was entitled "Type 19: General Arrangement of Undercarriage." It was surely a kind of art. There might even be a connection between aeroplanes and poetry. He would have to speak to his brother about it. He leaned his chin on his hands and studied the drawing. The way in which the oleo legs and their associated components folded into the undercarriage bay was extremely elegant.

"Wake up, Anderson," Mr. Jakes said, shaking his shoulder. "Do you want to learn to fly?"

"Sorry? What?" Tom rubbed his eyes. "Oh, Mr. Jakes."

Mr. Jakes spoke one word at a time, as to a simpleton. "I said, do you want to learn to fly?"

"Yes," Tom said, sitting up. "Yes, I certainly do."

"All right, then," Mr. Jakes said, "there's a new government scheme. The company'll sponsor you. Fill this in and bring it to my office. That is, if you don't bloody well fall asleep again." He gave Tom a form and walked briskly away.

"PARACHUTE," THE MAN called Phillips said, pulling one from the rack in the clubhouse. "Put it on."

Tom dragged the parachute across his back.

"No, no, no . . ." Phillips was impatient. "I'll show you. Bend over first. Sling it on your back. Hold the top straps with one hand. Grab the bottom straps with the other." He demonstrated. "Now try again."

Tom bent and slung the heavy thing on his back. He reached down and grasped the straps that dangled between his legs.

"Pull it up," Phillips said. "Put these straps through the loop, and back up to the buckle. That's it. Get your wedding tackle out of the way, or you'll be singing like a heavenly bloody choir on your way down."

Tom struggled with the harness.

"Come on," Phillips said. "Don't be shy. Get your bollocks out of it. That's it. Get it tighter. Now check the buckle's locked."

The parachute felt like a carapace, weighty and oppressive.

"It's too tight. I can't stand up."

" 'Course you bloody can't. You don't fly standing up, do you? You'll look bloody silly if you slip out of it. Not to mention bloody flat, when you get to the ground."

"All right. But it's bloody uncomfortable."

"When you're floating down, remember me. I'm the one that told you to do the fucker up tight, sonny."

Phillips buckled on his own parachute. Bent like two old men and further encumbered by their flying suits and heavy boots, they stumbled out to the yellow Tiger Moth that stood delicately on the grass.

"All right," Phillips said, opening the rear cockpit flap. "Here you are. Throttle on your left. Stick in the middle. Slats lock on the right. Rudder pedals down there. It's all a question of rudder, on the Tiger. You'll find out. In you get. Put your foot in the step. Up you go."

Tom climbed into the Tiger Moth, the aircraft moving under him. The parachute, clumsy and unbalanced on his back, caught on the edge of the cockpit. He lifted it free and said, "Christian's burden."

"What?"

"Nothing."

Phillips reached into the cockpit and tugged the seat straps clear of the parachute. "Now get that harness tight. In ten minutes we'll be upside down."

"God, will we?"

"No. Not this time. But get it tight anyway."

"All right."

"See that?" Phillips pointed at a large instrument with two needles. "That's the turn-and-slip. That needle there, that's the one you have to keep in the bloody middle. If you can do that with a Tiger, you can fly any bloody thing."

Tom tried to move in the seat. "Should the straps be so tight? I can hardly breathe."

"Good," Phillips said. He climbed into the front cockpit and said to Tom over his shoulder, "I'll do the takeoff. We'll climb up a bit, and then you can have a go."

⌒◞

AFTER THE DAY'S flying, Tom left the lighted bar and went into the hangar. It was a repository for their toys, high roofed, silent, as full of shadows as a church. He found his way through the maze of wings to the yellow Moth and ran his hand along its fuselage.

⌒◞

"I'M FLYING ALMOST every weekend," Tom said.

William was chewing a grass stem and gazing upward, hands behind his head. He rolled onto his elbow and looked at his brother. "I knew you'd been up to something."

"There's a new scheme. The government pays. You join a flying club and they teach you to fly."

"Bully for you."

"Flight. What else is there?" Tom said, making an expansive gesture with his arms.

"It's good, then."

"It's like nothing else," Tom said. "The aeroplane is so fragile and so powerful all at once. The engine roars and the whole thing trembles with its own fury. When you're flying, the aeroplane dances along the contours of the air."

William said nothing. He looked steadily at his brother and chewed on the grass stem. Each looked at the other as if in a mirror.

"It trembles," Tom said. "All of it. When the engine starts it all begins to tremble. The needles on the instruments are blurred, the stick vibrates in your hands, it's like flying a great cage of wires, it's like—what do they call it—a harp worked by the wind—"

"An aeolian harp?"

"Yes, it's like that, it sighs and sings as you fly. It's like having something live and fierce in your hands—no, not in your hands, you're on its back and inside it at the same time, you become it, it becomes you—"

"Fear," William said. "Fear does that."

"Yes," Tom said, "you look down and see thousands of feet of empty air, the fields and rivers and roads, tiny houses far below, a mile below, and think of falling, and think of the thin layer of fabric between yourself and all that space—"

"Flailing your arms and screaming as you fall—"

"The air howling in your ears—"

"Your clothes flapping—"

"Tumbling over and over—"

"The people and the houses getting bigger and bigger—"

"Zooming downwards and then—"

"Thudding into the ground."

They looked at each other and began to laugh.

───────

IT HAD BECOME an elaborate game. That boy Hutchings, third from the front in the right-hand row, was cheating. William knew this, and the boy knew that he knew. William walked along the back of the hall, and the boy, head in hand, turned just enough to keep an eye on him. The trick was to approach softly from behind and then veer away again, so the boy never had long enough to consult whatever crib he had concealed about his person. William looked at the clock. Another hour yet. Up one row, across, back again. The boys bent over their work, most of them with an arm flung protectively around their writing. Occasional sighs.

Poetry had drawn him into teaching; at first sight it was a worthy vocation, yet it kept coming down to things like this. This had absolutely nothing to do with poetry. It was more like being a policeman. He turned and cut diagonally across the hall toward Hutchings, who glanced up as he passed and smiled ironically.

O N SATURDAY MORNINGS all through that breezy autumn he encased himself in the sheepskin suit, the enormous boots, the flaring gauntlets, the leather helmet and its dangling tube, the goggles with their angled, glinting panes. He buckled on his parachute and walked with Phillips toward the aeroplane. Phillips told him things, but Tom's attention was diverted by the Tiger Moth's structure, by its delicate tautness, by the way it rocked gently in the wind as they approached.

"Flying wires, landing wires, ailerons, the pitot tube. On the upper wing are the patent slats that come out as the airspeed falls. . . ."

Tom tried to listen, and gradually he absorbed the curious rituals of dress, language, and behavior that were evidently essential to flying. Around him was a broad, grassy airfield, above was an open sky, yet the possession of these simple freedoms required formality and discipline of an inflexible kind.

"Place your left foot on the wing root, here on the step and nowhere else. The wings consist of wooden spars and ribs covered in doped fabric. They are designed to take flying loads, nothing else. If you stand on a wing, your foot will go straight through. If you land in a field, keep the cows away or they'll eat the fabric. Hold on here. Swing your left foot into the step. Hold on to the base of the strut with your left hand. . . ."

There was too much of this, a torrent that Tom knew he could never absorb. He spoke of this to his brother, but William simply

said, "Well, there you are." He had no understanding of its importance.

"I sometimes have a feeling," Tom said, "when I think about my
future life, of being on some kind of journey to a predetermined
place. Do you ever think that?"

"Yes," William said. "Sometimes I do. Other times I haven't a
bloody clue where I'm going." He stared into the bottom of his glass.
"People quite often have a sense of predestination, you know. I read
that somewhere."

"Life couldn't possibly be planned out beforehand. That's ridiculous. It's bound to be affected by chance and accidents and whatnot."

"The only certainty is death," William said.

"You're cheerful," Tom said. He drained his glass and began to
whistle.

" 'Be absolute for death,' " William said, " 'either death or life will
thereby be the sweeter.' "

"What's that?"

"Shakespeare."

"I know that, you clot. Which one?"

"Measure for Measure."

"A dull play."

"That's your considered judgment, is it?"

"Get knotted. How did it go again?"

"I'm thinking about giving up this teacher training, you know."

"Are you? I told you it was a leaden business, but you didn't listen."

"Sometimes it isn't."

"But mostly it is."

"But what else could I do?"

"Tell you what . . ."

"What?"

"I've been thinking about Stella."

"Stella? What for?"

"Because we've never really got on with her, have we?"

"No. But I don't see what we can do about it. That's the way
things are."

"It's something to do with Mother."

"I know that."

"Something between her and Father."

"Yes."

"Well, then. Perhaps we ought to make more of an effort with Stella."

"Maybe."

⌒

At the top of the loop the engine coughed, the controls went slack, fragments of dried mud fell in his face from the floor of the cockpit, until at last, after an unconscionable time straining his head back to catch a glimpse of it, the horizon, and then the earth itself, returned. As the aeroplane swooped back into level flight, Tom was aware for the first time of the spherical curvature of the planet, sloping away under the gigantic dome of the sky. "Fucking terrible loop," Phillips was yelling into his earphones, "too fucking *slow.* Do another, and this time give it more throttle and *get it bloody right.*"

One spring day, after Tom had done five perfect takeoffs and landings in succession and was taxiing back for another, Phillips turned his head and called out something. Tom brought the Tiger Moth to a halt, wondering if this would be the moment. Phillips climbed out of the front cockpit, tidied the straps, latched the door, and stood beside the aeroplane with his head close to Tom's, shouting against the slipstream from the propeller. "All right, you're on your own, lad. Just one circuit. When you come back, don't bloody run me over." He walked a few yards away, took off his helmet, sat on the grass, and took his cigarette case from his pocket.

Tom turned the aeroplane into the wind, looked all around, reached out his gloved left hand, and steadily opened the throttle. The aeroplane began to roll forward, bumping a little over the uneven grass. The tail came up. He concentrated on keeping straight, waiting for that instant at which the wheels would lift, skip a little sideways, touch again, hesitate, and rise cleanly away, the engine bellowing and the grass streaming below.

⌒

"I DON'T THINK there are words for it," Tom said to his brother. "But when you take off alone something happens. You leave the past behind. There's just you and the empty sky."

William raised his eyebrows a little.

"All right," Tom said. "But that's my point. It's hard to find words. That's why flying people don't talk about things like that."

"Haven't got the words."

"They just don't like bullshit."

"Maybe you need to be French. Isn't 'aeroplane' a French word?"

"It *is* amazing. You have to admit that. I looked back and there was Ted Phillips, a tiny dot on the grass."

"Well, he would be, wouldn't he? A tiny dot. From that height."

"Oh, come on, you sod."

"Well."

"Well what? Don't talk bollocks. Anyway, my landing was bloody perfect. Perfect three-pointer. Kissed the grass."

"Kissed your arse, more like."

"Solo! Now I can get in some hours. They say I can fly the Hornet Moth as well as the Tiger."

"Good for you."

"You can come and have a ride. It's cozy, the Hornet. Just like a car. A little beauty."

"No bloody fear."

———

"OFF YOU GO," Ted Phillips had said, "do what you like for an hour. Don't break it, don't get lost, and learn how to fucking fly."

How *slowly* could he fucking fly? Tom wondered, closing the throttle and easing the stick back. If a seagull could do it, then so could he. The Tiger Moth wallowed and the slats rattled out from the upper wing. He sat there as the aeroplane staggered along. He had begun to admire his skill, his light touch on the trembling controls, when a wing dropped and the Moth twirled into a spin. The earth rotated, growing rapidly more detailed. I know what to do, he thought. This is a spin. I know how to stop it. Opposite rudder. Stick forward. Oh, he thought, *come out now.* That's it. Yes, that's it.

He pulled out of the roaring dive. He would try slow flying again, soon, and with a bit more height. In the mess, the old stagers said it wasn't flying that killed you, it was the fucking ground. Keep away from the fucking ground, sonny. Stay high. They much enjoyed ironical saws of that kind. Flying is a piece of cake, old chap. Just keep clear of the ground.

In an empty space beside a towering cumulus, he climbed the Tiger Moth in steady circles until the altimeter read six thousand feet. It was an immense height: Infinity surrounded his tiny, bellowing world. The silhouette of the Moth, sharp edged and black, bounded in uneven leaps across bulging clouds that were blindingly white, fresh, and pure. He waved. The shadow pilot waved. Tom yelled into the slipstream and pushed his aeroplane into a dive, becoming Mannock, McCudden, von Richthofen. He rushed downward into a magnificent collision in which he and his aeroplane became one with the cloud and the shadow.

When he had landed he felt foolish. He put the aeroplane in the hangar and Ted Phillips came stumping across to him. "I saw you dive into that cloud," he said. "You're a bloody fool. Could tear the fucking wings off, going into cloud at that pace."

WILLIAM GOT out his notebook and switched on the wireless. The valves began to glow, and there was a humming silence. The announcer spoke, then came the dramatic series of chords that open the Schumann A Minor Piano Concerto. He listened to its gathering power, its slow summoning of the storm, emotion harnessed, then released into lyricism. The piano lifted into a high register and was joined by the clarinet. He made some notes, thinking of flight among tall clouds, and of sudden sorrow, and listened to the fragile notes of the principal theme, first glimpsed, then returning secure and strong and familiar, and the honeyed sadness of the second movement. At the end, the piano was strong and confident, leading the orchestra out among sunlit fields. He grinned to himself, tore out the page of scribbling, and screwed it up. Music was not easily done in words.

FLYING ALONE ON a cross-country exercise to Liverpool and back, Tom looked down and felt, as never before, a sudden and intense love of his shabby, muddled country, its smoky cities, its rivers, woods, and hills. As the evening advanced there was a flicker, now and again, of yellow sunlight reflected from a lake, a window, or a greenhouse. The sun went down. The sky cleared and a few stars faintly emerged. He flew onward. Pinpoints of light began to appear in the darkness below: glimmers from isolated houses, the inquiring headlamps of a car, a lighted village street. The stars gleamed coldly above the Mersey as it passed, black and forbidding, beneath his steadily roaring aeroplane. He looked ahead. Liverpool, wreathed in mist from the river, was a cascade of diamonds thrown into the night, denying in its luminous beauty everything he knew about the city. He circled once, and then again, before beginning to descend toward the lighted runway that lay beside the dark water.

WILLIAM TOOK NO notice of Reggie Basset's warning. He edged into the back of the hall and stood in a corner. A crowd of adults and children overflowed the rows of benches. Seated on stage was a plump man wearing a blue fez and a robe secured with white cord. This must be James Masterman. His robe was a reddish dun color that suggested the rolling steppes of central Asia. He was wearing open-toed sandals. The hall grew quiet. Masterman stood up and grasped the lectern with delicate hands. Gold-framed reading glasses hung on a string around his neck, and on his right wrist was a copper bangle. He spoke in a confident, high-pitched voice.

"Good people of Winchester," he said, "I am honored to be asked to talk at St. Swithin's College tonight, and perhaps to introduce our young pedagogues to one or two original ideas." He paused. "Let me first ask you this. What is a school?"

The question hung in a silence punctuated by one or two coughs. William leaned his elbow carefully on a hot radiator. In the center of the hall a man put his hand up.

"I will tell you in one word," Masterman said, leaning forward. "A school is a prison."

The man put his hand down. Masterman stepped from behind the lectern and stood on the edge of the stage. The audience looked up at him. Masterman held out his hands. He spoke in an impassioned tone, his gaze sweeping the audience.

"A school is a prison. I will confess to you that I am myself damaged. I am damaged by the schools I attended as a child. My spirit was imprisoned. My mind was imprisoned. My imagination was imprisoned. My body was imprisoned."

He paused and looked around the hall. "It is my life's work to escape from this imprisonment, and to enable others to do so."

He paused again for several seconds. William heard somebody whisper, "You'll have to wait, Maisie."

"I will state my intention quite simply," James Masterman said. He walked back to the lectern, stretched out his arms, and said loudly, "I want to set our children free!"

There was nervous applause. A woman in the front row, William noticed, was wearing a dun-colored robe like Masterman's. A child started to cry and was fiercely shushed by its mother.

Masterman took hold of his reading glasses, placed them on the end of his nose, and peered at the audience.

"Let us consider what an ordinary school does," he said in a sober tone. "An ordinary school in this fine and ancient city. Such a school takes a child from his home and community. A school divides the child's day into regular segments. A school divides the great panoply of knowledge into arbitrary and mutually exclusive domains. A school is *essentially* divisive." He paused, then repeated the sentence with a different emphasis: "A school is essentially *divisive.*"

William felt a nudge. It was the melancholy figure of Reggie Basset. "Hello, Basset," William whispered. "I thought you didn't believe in libertarianism."

Basset gritted his teeth. "I've got to get a message to the principal," he said. "Disruption has been threatened."

"Yes," said William. "You told me that before."

"Well, what have you done about it?"

"What do you mean, done about it? Nothing."

Around them, people were beginning to get restless. "I say," a woman hissed, "we can't jolly well hear, with you talking."

Basset seized William's collar and placed his mouth close to his ear. "The fascists are gathering," he whispered. "They may pounce at any time."

"You'd better squeeze through, then."

Basset pushed past William and edged his way through the audience. Masterman was talking about the spiritual needs of the growing child. Basset got to the front. The principal was sitting in the center, next to the robed woman, who was presumably Mrs. Masterman. William saw that Basset was undecided. Masterman said something about the need to sustain the child's natural curiosity. Eventually Basset stooped and shuffled toward the principal, thus attracting the attention of everyone in the hall, including Masterman, who stopped talking and watched Basset's progress with interest. One or two people at the back stood up to get a better view. Basset knelt before the principal and said something.

"What?" said the principal in his precise voice. "Fascists?"

The word whispered round the audience. "Ah, fascists! Now there'll be trouble." Several more people stood up. A man in front of William said, "All right, Maisie, we can go now."

Masterman raised his hands. "Be tranquil," he cried. "We need not fear these rabid ideologues."

William wondered how many of those present would understand the phrase. He looked around at the crowd. Probably everyone, come to think of it.

Masterman gave a large, gentle smile. "It is interesting, is it not," he said, "how fierce a response is generated in some quarters by the simple word *freedom*."

From the wings appeared a man in black, wearing a balaclava. He had an object in his hands. He tossed it toward Masterman. William saw that the object was a firework. Someone shrieked. The principal stood up and shouted, "Look out, Masterman!" There was a flash, a bang, and a cloud of smoke. Masterman fell over, hitting the stage with an enormous thump. Dust rose and mingled with the smoke. People started shouting and scrambling toward the doors at the back of the hall. One or two climbed onto the stage and ran toward the wings. William was pinned against the radiator by the crowd. There was no sign of the man who had thrown the firework. At center stage lay Masterman. The woman in the robe stretched her arms across the footlights toward him, crying, "Oh, oh, oh," in a thoroughly unsettling way.

The principal conferred with others and then climbed onto the stage. "Ladies and gentlemen," he called out, and then again, more loudly. People turned to look. The robed woman stopped her cries. "Please be seated. I am sure there is no more danger. The offender has absconded. The police have been summoned. Is there a doctor here? If so, would he please come to the front."

The crowd talked it over. Most sat down. A young woman wearing cream-colored trousers came forward. "I'm a doctor," she said to the principal.

"Are you?" he said, looking her up and down. She stepped past him, climbed on stage, and knelt beside the fallen radical.

Two policemen pushed into the hall. One of them addressed the crowd from the stage. "Now, then. No cause for alarum." William was pleased to hear this antique usage. The policeman held out his arms in a gesture akin to a blessing. "Kindly sit down. We have to take names and addresses." Several of the audience looked uneasy at this, but slowly the hall became calm.

~⸻⸺

IN THE EAGLE, William and Reggie Basset conducted a postmortem.

"I've still got a terrible ringing in my ears," Basset said.

"I'll tell you one thing, Basset," William said. "You may have been deafened, but I've horribly burned my backside on that bloody radiator."

Basset's wrinkled face was pinched into deep gloom. He stared into his empty glass. "To be honest, old chap, I've decided I'm not cut out for this teaching lark. I'm too much of an introvert."

"Oh, I don't know," William said. "It takes all sorts."

"That chap Masterman, well, he's a performer, isn't he? So is the principal, in his way. They have a certain style. They can dominate. I can't. I sometimes think I'm a total failure."

The door opened and in came the principal, escorting the lady doctor. William stood up.

"Ah," the principal said. "Anderson. And Basset also." He turned to the woman. "Two of my trainee teachers. They're interested in Masterman's opinions on progressive education."

"I'm not," Basset said, but the principal was ordering drinks.

"Do have a chair," William said to the doctor. She smiled and sat down.

"Is Mr. Masterman recovered?"

"Oh yes, he's fine. It was just shock." Her dark hair was tightly curled. "Did Mr. Troughton say your name was Anderson?"

"I'm William Anderson. This is Reggie Basset. He's having second thoughts about being a teacher."

She laughed. "I'm Polly Morris."

"Only a step from polymorphous," Basset said.

"Quite so," Polly Morris said. There was a silence. The principal returned from the bar, handed Polly a gin and tonic, and sat down with his whiskey.

"Have they captured the villain, sir?"

"No, Anderson, they haven't. And are unlikely to do so."

"A pity. Mr. Masterman was just getting into his stride. Perhaps he can visit us on another occasion."

"Perhaps."

William looked at the principal and decided not to succumb meekly to superior rank. He tried again. "I presume you're interested in progressive ideas, Dr. Morris?"

"I'm interested in institutions." She had delightful eyebrows.

"Institutions?"

"Yes. How they work. What they do to people."

The principal moved his shoulders. "Useful things, institutions."

"Of course," Polly said, "but they have unfortunate tendencies. Your college toilet paper, for example."

"Our toilet paper?" The principal sat up straight.

"Yes. It's a peculiarly harsh kind, don't you think?"

"We save our money for teaching."

"That's precisely my point. An institution has a tendency to do things for its own reasons, and ignore the needs of the individual."

"In this case, the end user," Basset said. William saw that he was quite drunk.

"Are you researching the subject?" William asked. "Institutions, I mean."

"It's just an interest. Lots of us work for institutions of some kind, don't we? It's nice to understand how they work."

"Well," said the principal, placing his hands flat on the table, "I expect you two have essays to write, eh?"

"The great panoply of knowledge," Basset said. His head fell forward until it rested on his folded arms.

Polly Morris said, "I think the excitement has been too much for your friend."

"It's his doubts. He was daunted by Masterman's command of his audience."

Basset yawned and said, "Arbitrary and mutually exclusive domains."

Polly laughed again. "At least he's been listening."

"Would you care for another drink?" William said.

"That's kind of you. Then I must be going."

The principal stood up. "I must get back to my wretched institution. We are so grateful for your help, Dr. Morris."

"Not at all."

"I take it that you'll deal with Basset, Anderson." The principal turned and strode away.

"He seems a little irritated," Polly Morris said.

"It's not been a good day for him."

"No, I suppose it hasn't."

"I don't suppose you'd care to go somewhere for some supper?"

"Well—had you somewhere in mind?"

"Gazzi's, perhaps. It's round the corner."

"What about your friend Mr. Basset?"

"He'll be fine. He always finds his way home."

"If you're sure."

They walked around the corner and up toward the High Street. It was a warm evening. A silver barrage balloon swayed beside the cathedral. High-flying aircraft had marked the sky with abstract designs.

"My brother's a pilot," William said. "We're twins."

"Are you? The identical sort?"

"Yes."

"How interesting to have a perfect copy of yourself."

"Nothing perfect about him."

She laughed. "Do you get on well?"

"Fairly."

"But he's a pilot and you're a teacher."

"Here's Gazzi's."

William held the door and she walked in. Gazzi came up with his usual eagerness. "Dear madam! Sir!" He clicked his fingers. "A table for two—the corner table—Frederico will show you—"

Frederico took their coats. They sat down, William somewhat cautiously. Polly looked at him and asked, "Are you all right?"

"Oh yes, I'm fine. I just . . . well . . . burned myself a bit on a radiator."

"Oh. I suppose your friends call you Bill, do they? Or Billy?"

"Sometimes they do, but I'd prefer them not to."

"Oh," she said again.

"It just sounds . . . well . . ."

"Not quite serious enough."

"Well, no, it's silly, of course, but . . ."

"Not at all. I'll call you William."

Frederico had begun to strum a banjo and was approaching their table. "It's a lively place," Polly said. She gave Frederico a straight look and he smoothly altered course toward another couple.

"I was going to say that my brother and I are quite different."

"No flying for William."

"No," William said. "But we're not here to talk about me."

"Oh dear—squashed."

"No, I mean—"

"It's perfectly all right. I was being nosy. I'm sorry."

"No, look—"

"It's always difficult to know what to do with one's life. I wasn't at all sure about doctoring. My parents were both doctors, you see. It seemed such a dull thing, just to do the same as them."

"I really didn't mean to squash you. I'm nervous about the subject, that's all. My brother being the heroic fighter pilot and all that, and me thinking maybe it's wrong to fight."

IN SUCH A manner, as the sun went down, the candles were lit in
Gazzi's restaurant, and Frederico plunked gently on his banjo, William Anderson and Polly Morris negotiated their careful way into
the beginning of an understanding. On the way back to his room,
having escorted Polly back to her mother's house, William whistled
as he walked and at one point he broke into a run for no reason whatsoever. He opened the gate into the basement area and nearly fell
over Reggie Basset, who was sitting on the steps and smoking a cigarette.

"A fine thing, leaving a chap like that," Basset said.

"I'm sorry, Reggie."

"You're not."

"No, you're right. I'm not."

"You went off with that doctor woman."

"Her name's Polly Morris. She's only just qualified."

"What's that got to do with it?"

"Nothing."

"How old is she?"

"Not sure."

"Older than you, though."

"Maybe."

"Bloody certain."

"Doesn't matter."

"You'll see."

"Sod off, Reggie."

"Still, we spoilt the principal's plan."

"I thought you were too sozzled to notice."

"I'm never too sozzled to notice. But seeing as you're offering, I'll
have another of the same."

"Go to bed, Reggie, you silly sod."

"How's your backside?"

"What?"

"I thought you burned your backside."

"Oh yes. So I did."

⁓

I N HER OLD bedroom in what was now her mother's house, Polly Morris lay awake. He was quite young, that was for sure. She turned over and hugged her knees. He was a serious young man, but not, she hoped, a melancholy one. No point in spending one's life cheering up a gloomy man. He was clever enough. He was youngish. He was unpretentious. He was going to be a teacher. His brother was a pilot. She got up, went to the window, pulled back the curtain, and peered into the dark street. The gleam of the river was just visible. On the roof of Barnaby & Mason's the helmets of the ARP wardens were moving against the sky. One of them threw a cigarette end down into the street, a red dot curving down and ending in a tiny burst of sparks. She laughed to herself and went back to bed.

⁓

St. Swithin's College,
Winchester,
Hants.
4th October 1939

Dear Polly,

I very much enjoyed our evening last week and I wondered if you might like another evening out before long. Perhaps we might go and see a film. Friday is a good time for me, but of course I'll fit in with your hospital duties.

> Best wishes,
> William Anderson

St. Swithin's College,
Winchester,
Hants.
4th October 1939

Dear Mr. Masterman,

I was present at your interesting talk at my college in Winchester last week, and I much regret that you were unable to finish it. I hope you have fully recovered. I am training to be a teacher, and have read something about your libertarian school. I would like an opportunity to see how theory is put into practice—I have little experience but am keen to learn. I would very much like to discuss this with you, and I could come to the school at any convenient time that you could spare me a few minutes. I don't live far away.

Yours faithfully,
William Anderson

Flat 2a
Melbourne Street
W2
10/5/39

Dear William,

Thank you for your letter. I still laugh when I think of the Masterman talk and our meeting in the Eagle—I hope your friend Reggie is feeling better. I'm afraid that I mostly have to be at the hospital at weekends and I don't often get home to Winchester, but I could probably manage an evening between Tuesday and Thursday if that was possible. Can you get up to town? Let me know.

Best wishes,
Polly

St. Swithin's College,
Winchester,
Hants.
6th October 1939

Dear Polly,

Thank you for your letter. What about next Thursday, 12th October? I could come up by train and collect you from your flat at 7:30 p.m.

Best wishes,
William

Flat 2a
Melbourne Street
W2
10/7/39

Dear William,

Thanks for your letter. Yes, that's fine. I'll expect you at 7:30.

Best wishes,
Polly

⌒

I N CONVERSATION, Polly's brown eyes flickered from one speaker to the next. Her face and body mimicked the mood of the discussion, displaying a series of transient expressions: concern, wide-eyed happiness, wrinkled puzzlement, gleeful laughter, gloomy doubt. Surely, William thought, she must be conscious, at least to some degree, of the intensity of her appeal to him, and must, in some sense, be performing for him in particular? She glanced at him and grinned, seeming to display for him alone (and surely more frequently than could occur by chance) the warm shadows between her breasts. But then he saw that she engaged eagerly with everybody. She reached toward people and often touched them, speaking fast and laughing frequently, her thoughts jumping ahead. "Oh yes, how true!" she would say, or, "But surely . . . ," or, "So that means . . . ," or, "Don't you think . . . ?" Once she paused and, with a vivid display of wide-eyed awe, said, "How absolutely wonderful!"

But later in the evening, for some puzzling reason, she became quiet and withdrawn. When they said good-bye she went away down the escalator without looking back.

⌒

St. Swithin's College,
Winchester,
Hants.
13th October 1939

Dear Polly,

I'm sorry that something went wrong between us last night and somehow we didn't get on so well at the end. I'm sure it must have been my fault and I apologize. I hope you might be prepared to have another evening out with me sometime.

Best wishes,
William

Flat 2a
Melbourne Street
W2
10/13/39

Dear William,

Well, something went wrong last night, didn't it, and we ended up gloomy. I don't know how it happened, but I think it was my fault. I was in a bad mood suddenly. Anyway I'm sorry. Don't hold it against me.

Best wishes,
Polly

Liberty Hall
Waterside
near Winchester

William my dear fellow,

Do come round any time—I'm sure we can find something for you to look at. Libertarian is a big word to live up to, but we do our best.

Regards,
James

Flat 2a
Melbourne Street
W2
10/15/39

Dear William,

Thanks for your telephone call—it must have cost you a fortune! I couldn't think who it was when the night sister said there was a call! Anyway, I'm glad we had the conversation. Funny about our letters crossing like that. I'll see you on Tuesday.

Best wishes,
Polly

⌁

"COME AND MEET my wife," Masterman said. "She's in the bath." He opened the bathroom door, and clouds of steam rolled out. "Irma, my dearest poppet," he called out, "Liberty Hall has a visitor."

William could see no more than vague shapes. "Hello!" he called out. "Nice to meet you!"

He stepped back, bumping into Masterman, who said, "Go on in. She wants to meet you."

William stepped into the mist. "I can see you," a voice trilled. "Turn left at the clothes horse." The mist cleared and William looked no farther than the face of the figure reclining in the bath. It was the robed woman who had cried so distressingly at the fascist attack.

"Hello," William said. "I'm William Anderson."

"Oh, you're a lovely boy, aren't you! I'm sure you'll have terrific fun here!" Irma was much younger than Masterman, William saw, perhaps no more than thirty. She had a little round laughing face, a big mouth like a clown's, and her long hair floated on the water. She was not entirely submerged.

"It's a very big bath," William said, a remark that he would occasionally remember, with a sharp sense of horror, for the rest of his life.

"Here, help me up," Irma said, stretching out an arm. William took her hot, soapy hand in his and pulled. She emerged from the water and stood before him.

"Now, dear boy," she said, "behind you is my towel."

"She's so utterly lovely," Masterman said from the doorway. "Don't you think so?"

"Oh, certainly," William said. "Tremendously."

"She's a complete sweetie," Masterman said, leaning on the edge of the door. "She's a hot potato all right. In fact, dear boy, perhaps you wouldn't mind leaving us alone for a few moments."

"Oh," William said. "Oh, all right."

"No need to shut the door," Masterman called after him. William walked hurriedly out into the garden. Three small girls were burrowing in a heap of earth. They were, although filthy, fully clothed.

"M Y TRAIN'S AT five-fifteen," William said.

Polly licked her ice cream, looking steadily at him. "Stop flapping," she said. "We've got all afternoon. Tell me more about Liberty Hall. I can't believe it's really called that. It's a terribly bold name."

"Masterman is a terribly bold man."

"Tell me about him. No, tell me about Irma again." There were wrinkles at the corners of her mouth.

"Are you laughing at me?"

"Of course not."

Behind her, a bronzed oarsman stroked a skiff across the Serpentine, his girl reclining in the stern seat and steadying a wide-brimmed hat with a white-gloved hand.

"I know you think Masterman's a bit of a fraud," William said, "but there really is something in what he says. You've no idea how awful ordinary schools can be. When they're little, children are wonderfully inquisitive and lively, but they gradually get bored to death by the routine of school. It affects the teachers, too. Years of time-tables! Imagine the effect of that on a person! Knowing that in five years' time you'll be sitting in the same room, teaching the same thing to another bunch of children who don't want to be there. Something drastic needs to be done."

"I believe you," Polly said. "I just don't know whether Masterman's the answer."

⁓

At the rear of Liberty Hall, the grounds sloped down to a stream. A meadow beside the house had been marked out as a football pitch. Beside the meadow lay an orchard that contained twenty or thirty children, several donkeys, a nut brown shire horse, and a gypsy caravan in poor repair. A plump, blond girl who looked about sixteen had climbed on the back of one of the donkeys and was urging it forward. The donkey stood rigid, its legs braced like those of a vaulting horse, its head hanging down. Several children chased each other up and down the steps of the caravan. The shire horse chewed lazy mouthfuls of the long, damp grass, and two of the younger boys tried to tear a branch from one of the apple trees.

William and Irma watched from a rusting garden seat as Masterman went across to the boys and suggested that their action would threaten the school's supply of cider. "Fuck off, Masterman," the bigger boy said. "What's it to you?"

Masterman came back and sat beside William. "What energy they have! What aggression! This sort of intensely physical, aggressive play must have been vital to the training of our ancestors, the hunter-gatherers."

"You've got a lot of donkeys," William said.

"A wonderful teaching aid," Masterman said. "The children keep a full record of their behavior and development week by week. It was an idea of my wife's." He blew Irma a kiss, and she leaned across William and wiggled her fingers at her husband. "We saved a pair of donkeys from the knacker," Masterman continued. "In due course more came along. We've named them after philosophers."

"Philosophers. Oh."

"Yes. We thought it would be fun," Irma said. "We intend no offense to the world of the intellect, of course. It began when one of the more observant children remarked on the donkeys' habit of standing still for hours. With his usual genius, Masterman realized they might be attempting to unravel complex abstractions."

"As they undoubtedly are, my dearest, as they undoubtedly are. They spend so long at it, one wonders whether they have approached a solution to any of the great questions."

William looked from Masterman to Irma. They giggled at each other, made kissing sounds, and then embraced across him.

William leaned back as far as he could. He said, "So they're called Plato and Socrates and whatnot."

Masterman unwrapped his arms from Irma and said, "Actually, my dear wife's interest is more eclectic than classical. The one being ridden by Belinda is indeed Plato, I believe, but the other is Marx, or possibly Wittgenstein. To be honest, I find it hard to tell them apart. One donkey, after all, is much the same as another. Unlike the cart horse. He's a magnificent specimen, don't you agree? Such musculature! There was no option but to call him Samson."

One of the donkeys took a limping step. "As a matter of fact," William said, "I think Marx has thrown a shoe."

Masterman was bored with donkeys. He took a cigar from his breast pocket, clipped the end, and lit it. He leaned back, puffing smoke upward. "What an utterly delightful autumn it's been," he said.

"Well, apart from the war," William said.

"Oh yes, the war. They're putting barbed wire along the edge of the river for some reason. I suppose we'll have to abandon midnight swimming."

The smaller of the two boys let go of his branch and walked over to the bench. He insinuated himself between Irma and William and looked closely at him. "Who are you?"

"My name's William Anderson. I'm working here for a bit."

"God, are you?"

"And who are you?"

"Ian Lambert. My mother's an actress."

"Moira Lambert?"

"Oh God, you've heard of her."

"She's very famous."

"Oh God, how tedious when people say that." He looked about seven years old.

Masterman drew on his cigar. Childish screams came from various corners of the orchard. The donkeys stood like gray statues among the trees. Samson, steadily cropping the grass, lifted one of his vast hooves and moved it forward. A light easterly breeze blew in from the river. The spire of All Saints was black against the horizon.

"Belinda," Masterman called out, "you might get off now. I suspect Plato has had enough." The blond girl climbed down from the stationary donkey, stuck her tongue out at Masterman, and walked away, moving her hips elaborately.

"There are salmon in the river, you know," Masterman said. His eyes had closed. He blew a thin stream of smoke into the calm air.

"Really?"

"They dwell in the slack pools below the shallows."

Ian Lambert got off the bench, stood beside William, and looked him up and down. He said, "Can you read?"

"Yes," William said.

"You can read to me, then."

William looked at Masterman, who appeared asleep.

"All right."

"Come on."

William followed Ian Lambert into the house. Masterman opened one eye and watched them go.

The boy went upstairs into a dormitory, kicked off his shoes, climbed onto an unmade bed, and pulled a blanket over himself.

"Shouldn't you wash first?"

"No."

"Oh. Well then. What do you want me to read?"

"Oh God, choose whatever you like."

Books were scattered here and there. William picked up the nearest and opened it. " 'For four days we have been unable to leave the tent—the gale howling about us. We are weak, writing is difficult, but for my own sake I do not regret this journey, which has shown that Englishmen can endure hardships, help one another, and meet death with as great a fortitude as ever in the past.' "

He stopped reading and looked at the boy. Ian Lambert had his thumb in his mouth and was gazing at William with large eyes.

"Go on," he said.

"It's not very cheerful."

"Oh God, I know that. I've read it a hundred times."

From outside came a noise like manic laughter. William got up and looked out the window. "What on earth's that?"

"It's the donkeys, of course," Ian Lambert said. "I would have thought you'd know that."

———

Flat 2a
Melbourne Street
W2
11/5/39

Dear William,

You're a rotten letter writer, aren't you? A week of silence. No, I don't mean that, really, but I wondered how you're grappling with Masterman the Magician. I'm pottering along as usual at Bart's. I'm on nights now. We've got some soldiers from France. Some nights it's bad and you get to thinking too much. Hard to say what you feel, isn't it? Such intense feelings when we met, but then I don't know if—oh bloody hell! Anyway, it isn't more than a couple of hours from Winchester to Waterloo, is it? Or the other way round.

My friend Ann knows someone in the Royal Philharmonic, an oboe player, and they meet in the boiler room every lunchtime.

I don't know why I said that. I do wish you were nearer. There's all kinds of bomb shelters and sandbags everywhere. We've got some boys from France, but not many. I bought a new dress yesterday, a red one, very fashionable! Ann and I went into town last night—men in uniform everywhere—they get so bossy in their caps and belts and everything—they loom out of the dark at you—I'm rambling on, sorry.

Love,
Polly

P.S.—it's firework night!

⌒

I RMA WAS CURLED up beside Masterman's chair, engrossed in a
large book.

"Rousseau," Masterman said. "Whitman, Ruskin. And of course,
the immortal William Blake." He poured himself another sherry and
caressed Irma's hair. "That is where it all begins, doesn't it, my poppet? With Blake."

"I see," William said. "You must have read an awful lot."

"I'm a fast reader," Masterman said. "I absorb ideas like lightning.
It's an invaluable skill, and, of course, a rare one."

"Yes," William said, "I suppose it is."

" 'Man was made for joy and woe, And when this we rightly know,
Thro' the world we safely go. Joy and woe are woven fine, A clothing
for the soul divine.' "

"*Songs of Innocence,*" William said.

"Excellent!" Masterman beamed.

"Well, I'm not all that familiar with—"

" 'Sooner murder an infant in its cradle than nurse unacted desires.' "

"I don't think I know that one."

" 'The road of excess leads to the palace of wisdom.' "

"Blake again?"

"Exactly!" Masterman lowered his voice. "And then along came
Carl Gustav Jung, the great master."

"Yes. I suppose he did."

"Are you familiar with his work?"

"Not exactly, no."

Masterman expanded. He slid his fingers into the top of Irma's
blouse and looked down at her fondly. She looked up and said,
" '*Alles, was wir an den Kindern ändern wollen, sollten wir zunächst wohl
aufmerksam prüfen, ob es nicht etwas sei, was besser an uns zu ändern wäre.*' "

Masterman was delighted. He leaped from his chair. "Listen
to that," he cried. "My sweetie! She's word perfect! If we want to
change something in a child, we must first see whether we shouldn't
change it in ourselves. So terribly true, don't you think?"

"Yes—I'm sure it is."

"What an utter darling she is!" Masterman knelt beside Irma and kissed her neck.

William said, "It's a bit like motes and beams, I suppose."

Masterman looked perturbed. "Not at all the same thing," he said. "That's religion. Mere superstition. This is the philosophy of the new education. I think, my dear, we will have to recommend some reading, don't you?"

"Of course, my love."

"Dear boy, you must read up on power and punishment. Neurosis. Questions of morality." Masterman looked at Irma. "For example, what do we mean by the word *naughty*?"

"Or *dirty,*" Irma said, her lips full and red.

"Psychic conflict."

"Approval."

"Creative sublimation."

"Release."

"Sexuality."

"And, of course, masturbation."

"Yes," William said. "Yes. I suppose so."

"You'll soon realize," Masterman said, looking at William with a confident smile, "that 'the tygers of wrath are wiser than the horses of instruction.' "

"Blake."

"You're one of us!"

———

Liberty Hall
Waterside
near Winchester
10th November 1939

Dear Polly,

Yes, sorry about the letters, it's all a bit disorganized here, but of course I'm thinking about you all the time. This is an odd place, and I think some of the children are in a bad way, but it's difficult to know what's what. Lots of them are from rich families—one is the son of Moira Lambert—he's seven and he hasn't seen his mother for two years—he's a nice boy, but quite demanding. There's a girl called Belinda who's a handful, too, and a lad called Todger who's got a pet ferret. It's a fashionable school for a certain kind of parent. The parents like it more than the children, I sometimes think. Some of the children don't like it at all. Most of them do, though.

There are several teachers, I think. (Everything's so vague, it would drive you crazy!) I'm told there is a Mr. Montmorency, a Miss Linnet, and someone called Bob D'Arcy. I'm not quite sure whether they actually work here, or whether they take the children to them sometimes. I seem to have got taken on, but I don't know how long for. I can't get away until the end of term, and even then Masterman wants some of us to stay here. Some parents leave their children here all the time. I can't work out whether he's a fraud or what. He's very convincing sometimes. He knows a lot. The school's got several donkeys and they've named them after philosophers, would you believe! And on the farm next door they're building an army camp. Tanks and guns on their side of the wire, donkeys and children and Carl Gustav Jung on our side. Ho hum.

Love,
William

Tom had developed an ability to exclude from conscious hearing the considerable roar of the engine, although he was alive to any change in its note. Precisely trimmed, the aeroplane appeared to lie motionless on the air; only the trembling of the controls betrayed its speed. The shimmering needles of the instruments glowed before him, a scatter of stars gleamed above; but the country below was utterly dark.

He looked toward the east. Was there the slightest dimming of the stars, the slightest lightening of the sky, a reflected glimmer from a river or lake? Yes: And as he flew north he was treated again to the slow ceremony of dawn.

⌒

THE MANAGER TOOK the money, tossed a key to William, and gave them a cold look. "Room forty-two," he said. "Fourth floor."

They climbed the shabby stairs, William carrying the virtually empty suitcase, and when they reached the room Polly drew the ring from her finger and dropped it into a glass ashtray on the dressing table. She sat on the edge of the bed and swung her legs. William looked out the window. "Not much of a view," he said. It was growing dark.

"Better draw the curtains," Polly said. He turned on the bedside lamp, pulled the curtains across, and then sat in a chair and looked at her. She looked around the room. "It's not very jolly, is it?"

"No," he said. "Not very jolly. It would have been nicer in your mother's house, you know."

"I daresay it would." She stood up. "I thought you'd brought something to drink."

"I did." He got up, opened the suitcase, and took out the whiskey. There was a tumbler on a glass shelf above the washbasin. He rinsed it under the tap, dried it with a large white towel from the suitcase, and half filled it with whiskey. Polly took a sip and laughed.

"What?"

"I was just thinking of my father."

"Is this a good time to think of him?"

"Oh yes. He was quite intrepid, but not terribly well organized. He used to get into some frightfully silly scrapes, but he was never downhearted. He'd look around, push his glasses back up his nose, and grin and say, 'Not to worry, chaps. Never say die.' "

"I wish I'd met him. He doesn't sound at all like my father."

"I wish you had, too. He died the year before last. He had a cerebrovascular accident."

"Oh," he said. "I'm sorry."

"A stroke."

"I know what it means."

"Sorry."

"It's all right."

"So there you are."

"Yes."

"You can meet my mother instead, one of these days. She's quite intrepid, too." She sat on the bed again and offered him the glass. "Do you want some of this?"

He knelt on the floor in front of her and laid his arms across her knees. "You want this to happen more than anything," he said, "and then it isn't so easy, somehow. Not in a place like this, anyway."

She placed her hand on his. "Well, I suppose we could call the whole thing off, if you like."

"Oh no, I don't think so. Not now we're here."

"I agree."

"Good."

"Some people like to keep the light on. Others turn it off," Polly said.

"Oh, do they?" William said. "All right. I can reach it." He shuffled across and switched off the lamp.

"Oh! It's very dark. I ought to put this whiskey down. Pity to spill it."

"Here—give it to me. I'll put it on the table."

"Where are you?"

"Here."

"Do you think we ought to keep talking?"

"What do you mean?"

"About what we're doing."

"I don't know."

"Well, in that case I think we should." Polly sounded quite certain.

"I don't know if I can do that," William said.

"Do what?"

"Talk about it, as well as doing it."

"I don't see why not."

"Well, it takes away the . . . well, you know."

"Romance?"

"Yes. The magic of it."

"I see."

"Don't laugh."

"Oh, I'm sorry! Let me kiss you."

"That's nice."

"Yes, it is. Really nice. Oh, that's nice, too. I think we should take more of our clothes off, don't you?"

"Yes. Maybe we should."

"Shall I take your clothes off?"

"Well, I don't know—maybe I should take yours off first."

"That would be nice."

"How does this work?"

"Like this."

"I can't really see what I'm doing."

"Maybe we ought to put the light on."

"All right."

William reached out and pushed the switch. They looked at each other, tangled on the bed in the sudden glare. Polly's blouse was undone. She said, "Perhaps we should take our own clothes off. As we know how they work. It would save time in the long run." She sounded quite businesslike.

"All right," William said.

"If you could get off me, so I can get up."

"Oh, sorry." William got off the bed, took off his trousers, and stood there in his shirttails.

"It's all right," Polly said, lifting her skirt and undoing her suspenders.

"Would you mind awfully," William said, "if we put the light off while we undressed?"

"Well, all right," Polly said, "if you like."

There were faint sounds as they undressed. William said, "Have you finished?"

"Yes. Eee, it's chilly."

William felt her bounce on the bed. "Where are you?" He reached toward her and encountered her legs, her waist, her arms, her breasts.

"Here I am," Polly said. "Goodness, your hands are cold."

"Sorry," William said.

"Don't be silly. I know about this, you know, and the first thing is not to say you're sorry."

"That's quite off-putting."

"What?"

"You knowing all about it."

"I suppose it is, come to think of it. But you must know something about it, too."

"Oh, of course. Not a lot, actually."

"Good," Polly said. "Let's get into bed."

"All right."

They did so, and Polly said, "Could we put the light on again, do you think? Now we're safely covered?"

William switched on the light. Polly had pulled the covers up to her chin. "This is nice," she said. "It was getting cold out there."

"Yes."

Polly sniffed the edge of the sheet. "Do you think this bed is damp?"

"Maybe it just needs airing." He put his arm around her.

"You're very good at cuddling," she said. "Kiss me again. That's nice. Oh, that's nice. Kiss me again."

"I have to breathe sometimes."

"I don't see why. And don't tickle!"

"I thought you liked being tickled."

"I do."

"Well, then."

"I think if I lie like this, and you got round there—"

"Oh, I don't think I'm quite—"

"That's all right. It just needs a bit of encouragement. Let's put the light off again."

"All right."

William switched off the light. Darkness again, and silence. He stroked her. Her skin felt considerably different from his own. There was something sleek about her. After a while he made some small, careful movements.

"This is nice," Polly said.

"Yes."

"I don't think I can go on much longer."

"That's all right."

There were low sounds followed by a pause. They became conscious again of the noise of traffic and the yellow light of street lamps through the curtains.

"Well, that was really nice."

"Was it?"

"Yes, it was, you silly man."

"Polly . . ."

"What?"

"Should we have worried about babies, do you think?"

"Of course we should."

"Oh."

"But it's a bit late now, isn't it?"

"I suppose so."

"It was really nice, anyway."

"Yes, it was. Really nice. And as the years roll by we'll get better and better at it."

"Good," Polly said.

⁓

THE FIRST SNOW came early in December, drifting almost undetectably down from the night sky and settling lightly on the barbed wire and raw concrete of the army's watchtowers. The guards stamped up and down and beat their gloved hands together and cursed. One night William was woken by Ian Lambert climbing into his bed.

"It's only me," the boy said. "It's cold."

"Let's go and find Matron," William said.

"Oh God, not Matron."

"Yes."

"You can't make me."

"Oh yes, I can."

"That's not fair."

"Come on. She'll probably make you some Horlicks."

"I know she will. She always does. It's quite horrible."

⁓

AT TWENTY THOUSAND feet the air was still and clear. Tom trimmed the aeroplane straight and level, and it flew itself. He slid back the hood. From this high point the world was sharply defined: He might reach out and touch those hills, brush with his fingers that clump of trees. In the Dover Strait he could see the smoke and the steady wakes of half a dozen steamers. A train ran south from Canterbury across squares of brown and green. Sunlight illuminated the South Downs, Beachy Head, the Dover cliffs.

Above the North Foreland he turned the aeroplane in a wide sweep toward the west. England, at first more water than land, began to gather under his wings. Long shoals, yellow and gray, edged with surf, emerged from the shallows. The coast was pierced by glinting rivers: the Swale, the Medway, the Crouch, and the Blackwater. Ahead, reaching into the haze of the city, was the looping signature of the Thames.

Peering downward, he followed the narrowing river past Sheerness, Tilbury, Woolwich, Millwall. As he circled above the docks, he spotted the thin line of the Grand Union Canal, climbing up from Limehouse lock by lock. He straightened the aircraft and followed the river away toward the west.

PART II

1940

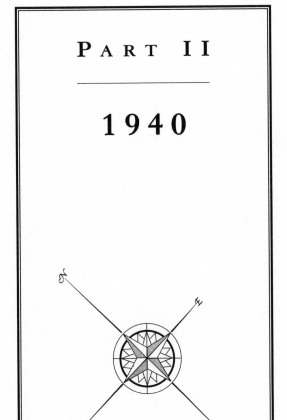

January

MANY A day with ten degrees of frost. Deep snow, fierce winds, burst pipes, blocked roads, canceled trains, closed shops and schools. Every city a coalman's paradise: yellow smoke rising from ten million chimneys and returning as sulfurous fog.

In the countryside, the spade clanged uselessly on the soil. Plowmen, elbowed from their cottages by irritable wives, nodded over the fire in the King's Arms. Rivers and ponds were bound in ice. Snow lay deep in the lanes. A bored girl found a pair of rusty skates in Grandma's tin trunk, polished them up, and put them to work; in the bronze light of a Sunday afternoon, her coat and scarf were bright against the sky. Smoke drifted through bare willows, and laughter rang across the ice.

All across the country, in the darkness of Monday morning, children dawdled back to school with brilliant cheeks and chapped legs, their gloves still soaked from snowballing.

At Boulogne the sea froze. Across the plains of northern France the waiting armies hugged themselves for warmth, and yawned, and paced about, and lit another cigarette.

TOM ANDERSON TURNED to the aircraftsman. "Let's have a look from the top." They climbed the snow-covered earth bank of the blast shelter and stood together, looking down at the aeroplane.

"What's your name?"

"LAC Willis, sir."

"I mean your first name."

"Alan, sir."

"You needn't call me sir all the time, you know. We'll be working together a lot of the time, won't we? You can use your judgment."

"All right, sir."

"My first name is Tom. I don't mind if you call me that when we're alone. Perhaps I can call you Alan."

"Very well, sir."

The Spitfire stood in its dispersal bay with that eager look, like a fellow's gundog waiting, and it was puzzling to Tom why chance had placed in his care so triumphant an example of the engineer's art as this lithe and ferocious aeroplane. What had he done to deserve it? He glanced at the aircraftsman, whose severe haircut revealed the strong curve of his neck, the twin tendons and the deep valley between. He clapped his hands. "Well, Alan," he said. "She looks all right, doesn't she?"

"Yes, sir. Very nice."

"I'm doing the Met flight tomorrow. Crack of dawn."

"Yes, sir. She'll be ready."

THE MET OFFICER said, "Horrible murk all across the south coast and out into the Channel." He pointed to a diagram he had chalked on the blackboard. "You'll find the cloud base is seven hundred, and the top's about four thousand. The Downs will be in cloud. You might get some icing. Should be clear as a bell on top." It always began, the astonishing business of flight, with these familiar and banal solemnities.

Outside it was still dark. Tom clumped across to the aeroplane. "This is a fine time to be up," he said to Alan Willis. He clambered into the cockpit. The aircraftsman reached in and tightened his straps.

The aeroplane rocked on its undercarriage as the engine started.

There was a cough of smoke, a sudden barrage of noise and vibration. The slipstream curled in through the open hood, thrashing around Tom's head. He crouched low in the seat, watching the trembling needles of the instruments and waiting for the engine temperature to rise. He looked at his gloved hand grasping the throttle and thought of the twelve great pistons hurling themselves about their cylinders, the steel crankshaft whirling in a fume of oil, the clatter of the valves, the crackling harmony of the magnetos: Never had so much power been strapped to the soft body of a man, so much fury grasped in a single hand. Tom laughed to himself, waved the chocks away, and took off in a swirl of snow.

He climbed through the cloud on an easterly course. The cloud grew slowly brighter until, at five thousand feet, the aeroplane burst out into sunlight. He noted the time and altitude on his knee pad, turned south, and went on climbing. The scene had a simple grandeur: nothing but the orange disk of the rising sun, the rippled surface of the cloud below, the azure dome above. He switched on the oxygen and after five minutes made another ninety-degree turn. At intervals of a thousand feet he noted the temperature and humidity. At twenty thousand feet he leveled out, the aeroplane suspended in the steady air, the sun projecting a thin warmth through the Perspex of the hood. He looked at his watch, turned again through ninety degrees, glimpsing the condensation trail unrolling behind, then throttled back and began to descend.

At less than four hundred feet the Spitfire came out of the cloud over the sea. Ahead were the cliffs of the Seven Sisters and the gray shadow of Brighton. It was misty and snowing lightly. The water was streaked with long lines of foam and overhung with drooping skeins of cloud. He flew parallel to the coast, past Hove and Worthing, then turned toward the gap in the Downs behind Littlehampton. On either side the hills, flecked and patched with snow, reached up into the cloud.

The rest was the familiar homeward run. He flew along the winding Arun level with the turrets of the castle, found the main road, pulled the aeroplane into a steep turn—quite unnecessarily steep, but that was how a Spitfire ought to be flown—and descended toward the aerodrome.

Alan Willis was waiting. Tom parked the aircraft, shut down the engine, and climbed out. Alan had an inquiring expression.

"Everything all right, sir?"

Tom stretched and yawned. "Fine, Alan. Like a bloody sewing machine. Terrific job. Cup of char, I think."

⁓

A T LIBERTY HALL William was on his hands and knees in one of the dormitories, looking under the beds for Todger's ferret. It was difficult to recall the number of times the wretched creature had escaped. "All right," he said to the children, "you lot can help as well. Todger, start at that end and drive it towards me."

"I don't like ferrets," Belinda Boon said. She was the girl William had first seen riding Wittgenstein—or was it Plato?—in the orchard. "I'm not helping," she said. She climbed onto one of the beds, accompanied by her friend Amy Pluck, a thin, dark-complexioned child of twelve who wrote poems and shadowed Belinda everywhere.

"I'll help," Ian Lambert said. "I'm not very frightened of ferrets."

"Good for you," William said. "Come on, Arthur, and you, Timothy."

"No," Timothy said. "I don't think I will, actually." He turned and left the room.

"What a right silly little boy he is," said Arthur Beckingsale.

William sat on the floor among the children and wondered what on earth he was doing. Could this be the best use of his talents? What were his talents, anyway?

"Hey, look," Belinda said. She opened the window and a flurry of snow blew in. William stood up. Below, in the football field, a group of children worked eagerly in the snow.

Amy put her head to one side. "What's that?"

"It's a sleeping snowman," Belinda said.

"Oh no, it isn't," Amy said. "It's Masterman. You can tell from the cigar."

The great white figure lay on its back, wooden cigar pointing at the sky. A team of children was attending to the detail of its boots while another group manufactured a coat and scarf from stolen curtains.

"Let's go down," Belinda said. She jumped from the bed and the others followed.

William called after them, "What about the ferret?"

Todger stopped as he was going out the door. "You could keep an eye on it, William," he said. "If you don't mind."

William laughed. "Go on, then."

He leaned on the windowsill and watched the group of children run from the building and across the field. As they neared the figure, they stopped to negotiate with the working party. In a few moments the newcomers were allocated tasks and the work continued. William rested his chin in his hand. It was quite true that some kind of collective organization emerged spontaneously from activity like this. Nobody in particular seemed to be in charge. It was all very flexible and efficient and good-humored. There was a continuous process of debate and remarkably little dissension. But was this a possible model for a progressive society, or was it just children playing?

He shivered and shut the window. Kneeling, he peered under the bed. The ferret crouched in the far corner of the skirting boards. William lay on his stomach, reached out, and grasped the animal with both hands. "Got you, you little bastard," he said. The ferret looked at him steadily with its small red eyes.

⁓

Liberty Hall
Waterside
near Winchester
14ᵗʰ January 1940

Dear Polly,

Today the children made a terrific snow sculpture of Masterman, and he paraded beside it, puffing his cigar like a king. What a curious man he is! I can see that he's a showman and sometimes quite absurd, but he seems to believe what he says—and despite all the bluster, what he says is interesting. Sometimes the truth of it strikes me with sudden force. He says that schools are prisons, and I know he's right about that. He says we're denying our true nature and bottling ourselves up with rules and conventions and inhibitions and all that kind of thing—and that's hard to argue with, isn't it? These children are happy and friendly—as children should be, but often aren't in ordinary schools. All those school timetables and lists and rules and punishments and examinations! How can real learning happen when children are treated like criminals? But this place is like a big family, full of all the squabbles and affections of a family, and bound together by some kind of unspoken agreement that we will all get on together—and, amazingly, we do!

Oh, how I miss you, Polly!

William

TOM GOT UP and looked out the window. It was still foggy. "Bloody English winters," he said. Dougie Wells folded the letter he had been reading, put it in his pocket, and looked at his watch. "Dark in an hour."

Tom threw another log on the fire, took off his Mae West, sat down, and pulled the chair nearer to the fireplace. He watched the red sparks crawling up the back of the chimney. Dougie turned sideways in his chair. "You could put another record on," he said.

"I could," Tom said, yawning, "but I can't be bothered."

Dougie lit a cigarette, throwing the match into the fire. He inspected the cigarette packet. "Do you know the one about the bloke who crashed in the desert and tried to crawl home? In the blazing heat? He was driven mad by a voice counting all the time. One thousand and ten, one thousand and eleven, one thousand and twelve—"

"Yes, I do, actually," Tom said. "That's the third time you've told me. He gasped his last breath, a packet of Players fell out of his pocket, and he read on the flap—"

" 'It's the tobacco that counts.' " Dougie laughed. "The old ones are the best."

"If you say so."

The door opened and the squadron leader came in. They got to their feet. "All right, chaps, at ease," he said. "Bloody awful weather.

Nil vis. Soon be dark. Time to stand down." He looked around the mess. "Where are the others?"

"Some are in the pilots' room, sir," Dougie said. "The others are in number two hangar. Playing football, I think."

The squadron leader sat down. "Good-oh," he said. "Had a dreadfully tedious day. A quick one wouldn't go amiss."

Tom looked at Dougie, who said nothing, and then said, "What would you like, sir?"

"Splendid idea, Anderson. Pint of best. And while you're about it, get Jenkins to nip over to the hangar and tell the chaps that flying's off for the day."

"And while you're buying," Dougie said, winking.

Tom went to find the mess steward. The squadron leader leaned back in his chair and eyed the smoke curling upward from Dougie's cigarette. Dougie said, "Care for a fag, sir?"

"Thanks, Wells. Don't mind if I do."

Dougie lit another cigarette, and they looked at the fire. Eventually the steward, Jenkins, came in, switched on the bar lights, and opened the shutters. After a while Dougie got up and put on a record of Don Redman's orchestra playing "Shakin' the African."

Tom came back with the drinks, and a crowd of pilots came in. Colin Frampton said to Roy Hawkins, "Care for a dance, darling?"

Hawkins fluttered his eyelashes. "Oh, darling, you are a one. I thought you'd never ask."

Several of the men formed pairs and started to dance, laughing at one another. Jenkins filled glass after glass. Behind the squadron leader's back, Dougie was bending over and Jack Horner was trying to light one of his farts.

"No, I didn't, actually," Nobby Clark was saying. "She told me she had a waterworks problem. Besides, the colonel was due back any minute."

The squadron leader stretched himself in his chair, drew on his cigarette, and watched the dancers. Tom brought his drink. "Great bunch of chaps," he said.

"Yes, sir," Tom said. "Great chaps."

February

POLLY'S VOICE was thin and distant. "They're absurdly difficult, these telephone things. I hate them."

"They generate silence," William said. "You can hear the wires sagging from their weather-beaten poles and moaning in the winter wind."

"You're being gloomy," Polly said. "Gloomy, gloomy."

"Yes, but only because you're not here. Also, it's freezing cold and raining."

"It's raining here, too."

There was a pause.

"There you are," William said. "A silence crept upon us."

"I need to speak to you," Polly said.

"I need to speak to you, too."

"No, I mean really speak to you."

For some moments William studied the rain running down the window. "Polly," he said, "I can think of several reasons why you should use exactly those words, and they're all terrifying."

"I daresay you can," Polly said. "But I'm not talking about any of them over this bloody telephone."

The wires hissed and crackled.

"I'm leaving now," William said. "I'll catch the three-twenty and I'll be there in two hours."

"But aren't you working?"

"This is a free school, don't forget. People make their own decisions. Besides, someone else can do it. Or not, of course. All right? I'm leaving now. Waterloo, under the clock."

He put down the receiver and hurried downstairs. Ian Lambert was flicking marbles across the hall floor. "Go and find Masterman, there's a good lad. Tell him I've got to go to London. He'll have to do the reading group this afternoon. Tell him it's *The Jungle Book*."

"Can't I come?" Ian asked.

"No, you can't," William said, putting on his coat. He heard Ian asking, "Why not?" but by that time he was hurrying away down the drive.

WILLIAM LOOKED EVERYWHERE among the smoke and steam and the snorting engines but couldn't find her. She wasn't under the clock. She wasn't anywhere. He hurried this way and that before discovering her in the tearoom, sitting beside a cup of cold tea while a waitress swept the floor around her. Her nose was red and she clutched a crumpled handkerchief.

He sat beside her, took hold of her hot hands, and said, "Why weren't you under the clock?"

"This is very silly," Polly said. "God knows why I should have this pathetic response."

"Your tea's cold," he said. "Do you want another cup?"

"I wasn't certain until this morning," she said.

The waitress came up and said, "Sorry, love, we're closing in a minute."

"All right, all right," William said.

"I'm only doing my job, sir," the waitress said.

"It's due in the autumn," Polly said.

"Oh," William said. "Autumn, is it? Oh." He looked at her for a long moment and said, "Are you all right? Is the baby all right? Did they tell you that?"

The waitress said, "Oh, lovey, you're having a baby!"

"Yes, she is," William said. "Or rather, we are. So it seems."

"Oh, that's so nice," the waitress said. "How lovely for you both! Would you like some more tea, dear?" She was a middle-aged woman with thin arms and an orange scarf knotted around her hair. She put her hands around Polly's cup. "This one's stone cold, love."

"Oh, yes, please," Polly said, looking up at her. "That's really kind of you."

"Won't be a minute," the waitress said, hurrying away.

"I love you," William said.

"I daresay," Polly said. "But shut up for a minute. This is all too hectic."

William stood up, took off his raincoat, and sat down again. Polly blew her nose. "I'm perfectly all right," she said. "I felt funny and now I know why."

"Well, that's lovely," William said. "Isn't it?"

"People talk such rubbish about babies. I hate people who say they want boys. I've always wanted to have a girl," Polly said.

The waitress came back. "Here you are, love," she said, putting a tray down on the table. "I hope you don't mind me asking, dear, but when's it due?"

"I don't really know yet," Polly said. "Sometime in September, I think."

"Oh, that's really lovely!" She hovered around Polly. "Would you like anything else, love?"

"No thanks."

"We've got some nice cake. The lemon sponge is very nice."

"No, thank you."

"All right, then. Don't let your tea get cold." She went away.

Polly said, "Tell me what you think."

"I think it's lovely. I do really. We'll get married."

She looked at him. "Your family. What difficult sods they are."

"All right. But we'll get married anyway."

She laughed. "Is that a proposal?"

"Sorry."

"Oh, William, really!" She sat up, blew her nose again, and lifted her teacup. "Here's to us. Do you know, I feel quite all right again now?"

"Good."

"Yes, we'll get married. God, what big words those are."

"As soon as we can."

Polly looked up. "Here she comes again."

"I thought you ought to have a little bit of cake anyway, dear," the waitress said. She held a plate on which lay a narrow wedge of yellow cake. "Feed you up. You're far too thin, you know. Just a little bit. No charge. Have it on me."

"That's really kind," Polly said, putting her hand on the waitress's arm and smiling. "Thanks so much."

"I hope it all goes well," the waitress said, putting the cake on the table. "I hope you're both very happy." She looked at Polly's ringless left hand and then at William. "And you'll look after her now, won't you."

"Yes, I certainly will," William said. "I'll look after them both very well."

"Oh, that's nice," the waitress said. "That's so nice, you wouldn't believe. I wonder if it'll be a boy or a girl."

The waitress began brushing the floor again and humming to herself. William said, "We ought to celebrate somehow."

"We'll go to the Queen's Arms on the way home. That'll have to do."

They went out into the blackout and found a bus that lurched across London in darkness and rain. Sitting on the bus, they experienced for a few minutes a fragile sense of self-importance, as if, for that moment, they represented everything that was vital in the entire world.

In the Queen's Arms the landlord was playing a Goodman record, and by a happy chance Louise Tobin was singing:

> There'll be a change in the weather,
> Change in the sea,
> Before long there'll be a change in me:
> My walk will be different,

My talk and my name,
Ain't nothing 'bout me gonna be the same.

In Polly's room they put on the gas fire, took off their wet clothes, and climbed into her narrow bed. William kissed Polly and said, " 'O Love, O fire! Once he drew with one long kiss my whole soul through my lips, as sunlight drinketh dew.' "

"Your interest in Tennyson verges on the obsessive," Polly said, kissing his ear. "Can I live with it?"

"Oh, I should think so."

"Don't you like any other poets?"

"That's what Tom always used to say."

"Why do you like Tennyson so much?"

"I don't know. I like the sound of him. That's all. He resonates."

"Hmm."

"Besides which, he says things you can't say anymore."

"You mean he wraps things up in great big poetry."

"Maybe," he said, stroking her cheek. "I know big poetry isn't everybody's cup of tea."

"No, it isn't."

"Your hair is so strong and springy."

"Don't speak of it," she said sharply.

"Oh," he said. "Why not?"

"Because I hate it."

"You hate your hair?"

"Yes."

"Well, that's really funny. I think it's lovely."

"Well, you're wrong."

They dozed, their limbs entangled. After a while William said, "We had a maid, you know. She was called Milly. She more or less brought us up, Tom and me."

"Polly, Milly, and William," Polly said, her eyes closed. "Polly, Billy, Milly. I hope you realize I'll never look after you. You can look after yourself. I dislike domestic tasks, especially, with a deep and venomous hatred, ironing."

"No housewife you."

"It's enough to marry a man, let alone a house. But you can kiss me if you like. In a humble and discreet manner."

He kissed her and said, "Despite your beauty and your great age, despite my immaturity, my ridiculous job, and my complete lack of prospects, you'll marry me. Well, I never."

"Only because I'm pregnant, of course. Polly Anderson, I'll be. Mrs. Polly Anderson. No, Mrs. William Anderson. Perhaps I'll change both my names. I'll be your chattel. Polly is an absurd name. My mother chose it to keep me in my place. She thought I wouldn't give myself airs if I was named after a parrot."

"Poor woman. Wrong again."

"Parents always are. The world moves on and every parent's left behind. You'll see."

"Say that again."

"Why?"

"There was a rhythm in what you said. 'The world moves on and every parent's left behind.' Iambic hexameter."

"Oh God. Can I live with Tennyson?" She looked up at the ceiling. "William, Polly, and Milly," she said again. "Milly and Polly and Billy. Polly and Billy and Milly and Tom."

"What's Tom got to do with it?"

"He's your brother, your romantic brother. The knight of the air."

"Don't fall in love with him."

"Perhaps I already have. How do I know you're not him?"

"Because I know your secrets."

"Do you?"

"I do."

"Save that for the registry office." Polly laughed and he reached for her. She attempted to wriggle away, but he held her legs. He saw there was a mole in the crack of her bottom. She turned her head and tried to see what he was doing. "What are you up to?"

"Kissing the mole in the crack of your bottom."

"What mole?" She jumped off the bed, opened the wardrobe, and bent over in front of the mirror. "What a day," she said. "First I'm pregnant, and now I've got a mole in the crack of my bottom."

"Told you."

"Well, I never knew that before. Would you believe it. A mole in my bottom for all these years and I never knew. And another thing, I've got this tremendous fizzing sensation in my . . ."

"Your what?"

"I was going to say breasts, but for some reason I was embarrassed to say the word."

"What, breasts?"

"Yes. Breasts."

"You can't possibly be embarrassed about things like that. You're a doctor."

"I don't see why not. Doctors are people, you know. Besides, you're embarrassed about almost everything."

"Am I?"

"Yes. You're a proper little prude."

"Which is why I'm lying here with no clothes on."

"Actually, one does have to use ordinary words for things when talking to patients." She climbed back into the bed and pulled the blankets over them.

"Oh, does one?" William said. "We're such dim creatures, I suppose." A moment later he said, "Ouch! No need for pinching."

"A tremendous fizzing sensation in my nipples."

"A tremendous fizzing sensation, you say?"

"Yes. Especially when you do that tweaking thing."

"This?"

"Yes. Like that. Let's begin again. Do you know, when you do that, I get this terrific fizzing sensation in my nipples?"

"Perhaps you ought to see a doctor. Oh no, you are a doctor. Doctor, are fizzing nipples good or bad?"

"Oh, they're good. Provided you're a girl, of course."

"Are you a girl?"

"Oh yes. Look."

"And I'm a boy."

"Oh dear, that little thing of yours has gone floppy, hasn't it? Collapse of stout party. Billy's willy is not its usual eager self. I think I shall call it Mr. Floppy. No, Mr. Button is better. He ought to have a first name, too. Something like Eric. Mr. Eric Button."

"That's not a very impressive name, is it? Eric Button. You'll give him an inferiority complex. Besides, now I come to think of it, there's a boy's book called—"

"*Eric, or Little by Little.*" Polly began to laugh, rolled over, and fell off the edge of the bed.

William looked down at her. "Serve you right," he said. She was still laughing. "It's just as well I'm not a sensitive kind of chap," he said.

She stopped laughing. "Oh, I'm so sorry," she said. "You're wounded, and I didn't notice." Then she started laughing again.

When she stopped he said, "Are you all right?"

"Of course I'm all right."

"I mean, falling off the bed, and being pregnant."

"I'm quite all right, thank you. But I'm tired and I've had a teensy bit too much to drink. In a minute I'm going to sleep. I won't wake for hours and I'll be in a bad mood. It's the privilege of pregnancy, and you'll have to put up with it for ages and ages."

She went into the bathroom, turned around, and came back in again. "Do you know," she said, "I didn't eat that cake the waitress gave me? I expect she was hurt." She stood in the doorway, holding on to the door and looking, it occurred to William, extraordinarily beautiful.

"William," she said, caressing the edge of the door, "do you think registry office, or do you think church?"

"I don't know," William said. "I was thinking that I'd better write to Tom and tell him about us."

"All right," Polly said. "And you'd better tell your parents, hadn't you?"

"Yes. I suppose I ought to."

"Really, William! You can't avoid telling your mother and father that you're getting married."

"No, I suppose not. But they don't find it easy to be enthusiastic about things."

"Ah."

"I hope they don't put you off."

"So do I."

ALAN STUCK HIS head into the cockpit and shouted in Tom's ear: "She's still running rough. If you shut her down, I'll look at the plugs on number four as well."

Tom closed the throttle, let the engine tick over, and flicked off the magnetos. The propeller slowed and stopped with a rattle. He unlatched the cockpit door and climbed out. The frosty grass crunched under his feet. "Bloody cold still," he said.

Alan had climbed onto the wing root and was wiping oily finger-marks from the windscreen with a scrap of cotton waste. "I'll get some of the lads and we'll put her back in the hangar," he said.

WHEN HE HEARD how few hours the latest recruits had flown, the CO said, "Get into those bloody aeroplanes and get flying, keep on flying, and don't come back until you can fly like the bloody birds. My God, whatever next?"

The following morning, tensing himself against the straps, Tom turned steeply toward the south and pushed the aeroplane as low as he dared, flashing twenty feet above an army convoy on the Brighton road and pulling up for the gentle climb over the back of the Downs toward Beachy Head. The shadow of the aircraft flickered across the snow in the hollows as he climbed until, abruptly, the chalk cliff fell away and there was nothing below, nothing but the gray, empty waters of the Channel.

"I LOVE DOING that," he said to Dougie Wells. "You ought to try it. Climb up the back of the Downs at full throttle and fire yourself off the top of Beachy Head into midair."

"Favorite spot for suicide, that is," Dougie said, stretching horizontal in his chair. "Beachy Head. You're always reading about nannies with prams hurling themselves over."

"Spitfire terrifies nanny into suicide leap," Colin Frampton said. "Pilot accused."

"Very droll," Tom said.

Dougie drew on his cigarette and blew a smoke ring. "Pilot accused in nanny death says, 'I was only having a bit of fun.' "

"All right, all right," Tom said, laughing.

"Come on, Tom," Dougie said, getting up and pulling on his flying jacket. "A quid says you can't catch me."

⌒⌒

EACH DAY, LIKE cubs, they fought each other. Where was Dougie? Could he be on his tail already? Tom rolled the aircraft to port and pulled it into a steep turn, feeling the airframe tensing as the load came on, the stresses building in the main spar and fuselage, the progressive flexure of the wings. No: It was all clear behind. He looked downward into a hole in the stratus. There was Dougie, the bastard, two or three thousand feet below. He rolled the aeroplane more steeply, throttled back, and dropped into a diving turn.

As Tom chased Dougie Wells among the clouds, he began to forget what he knew of aerodynamics and structures and stresses. It was best to forget all that. It was all very well to be graceful and precise, but this business required something instinctive and forceful. He grew bolder, sweating in his seat and hurling the aeroplane this way and that. Each of them, they found, could catch and kill the other; the trick was not to be caught and killed oneself. The sky was too large for looking. An enemy might be mistaken for a fly on the windscreen or a speck of dirt on the Perspex of the hood. He might be hidden by cloud, or he might lie in the impenetrable brilliance of the sun.

⌒⌒

THE NEXT MORNING Tom took his brother's letter from the rack and walked into the crew room. Dougie Wells was dozing in one of the battered leather chairs. As Tom walked past he said, "It's that fellow Anderson. Trust him to wake a chap up."

"Hello, Dougie, you sod," Tom said. He sat down and opened the letter. After a while he said, "Blimey! My brother's getting married."

"Oh God," Dougie said. He yawned. "That's a frightfully tedious thing to do, isn't it? I thought he was the same age as you."

"He is. We're twins."

"What's he doing getting married, then?"

"He says he's met this lovely girl."

"She's probably in the family way, old boy."

"Oh no," Tom said. "I don't think so. William doesn't say anything about that. Besides . . ."

"What?"

"Well, I don't think he'd do that sort of thing."

Dougie laughed. "Dear Tom," he said, "you're such a silly little boy, you really are."

Tom picked up a cushion and threw it at him. "And you're such a man of the world."

"Let me tell you," Dougie said, "when it comes to the ladies, I know a thing or two. By God, yes." He closed his eyes. "There's nothing like a popsie."

Tom looked up at the ceiling. "I haven't seen William for ages."

"Best thing, old chap. Always keep clear of your bloody relatives, I say."

~⁓

TOM AND WILLIAM stopped in the middle of Westminster Bridge and leaned on the parapet as a string of barges passed beneath. The steersman on the last barge looked up and nodded his head at them as he entered the bridge's shadow. The brothers watched the swirling brown water.

"I'm sure you'll like her," William said.

"I'm sure I will," Tom said. "Where are you going to live? At that school of yours?"

"We won't be able to live together for a while. She's got her job at the hospital, and of course we need that money, since I'm only paid a pittance."

"Oh."

"We'll be together at weekends, either in Winchester or here."

"Well, that's something."

"Yes."

Traffic roared steadily across the bridge. They looked at the river for a while and then walked on into Trafalgar Square. Polly was waiting at the Lyons' corner house behind St. Martin's. She stood up when she saw them.

William kissed her. "Are we late?"

"Not at all. I was early."

"This is Polly," William said. "Polly, this is my brother, Tom."

"Hello, Tom."

"Hello," Tom said. He shook her hand. She was wearing a dark coat and a bright red beret.

"I haven't seen that beret before," William said.

"That's because I've only just bought it," Polly said. "I thought it was quite natty, myself."

"It's very natty. It makes you look quite different."

She laughed. "Now, just stand still for a second." They did so, and she looked at them with her head to one side. "Yes," she said. "The uniform makes a difference, but otherwise I really couldn't tell which was which. You've even got your hair parted on the same side."

They sat down, and when the waitress came they ordered tea and cakes.

"We've just walked across the river," William said. "It's funny how normal London looks, except for those huge balloons hovering everywhere."

"They're not hovering," Tom said. "They're tethered to winches."

"Well, you know what I mean."

There was a pause, then Polly said, "How long have you got, Tom?"

"Oh, all afternoon. The evening, too, if you like."

"We could have supper, then."

"That would be nice."

"Unless you want to see a show, or something."

"I can't, I'm afraid. I have to get back quite early."

William was looking around the tearoom. "I hadn't realized quite how many people were in uniform these days," he said.

"There's a war on," Tom said.

"I know that, you idiot."

Polly said, "If you're going to snap at each other, I shall leave you to it."

The waitress brought their order. When she had gone Polly

laughed and said, "I thought for a moment she was going to ask about the baby."

Tom said, "What baby?"

"Our baby," Polly said. There was a pause, and she said, "I'm having a baby, Tom. Hasn't William told you?"

"No, he hasn't."

"I was just going to," William said.

"Oh, William," Polly said.

"I'm sorry. I thought it would be nicer if we told him together." Polly said nothing.

"That's jolly good," Tom said. "It's really nice. A baby! I'm so pleased."

"Thanks," Polly said.

"I'm sorry," William said. "I really should have told him before."

"Yes, you should. I can't see why you didn't, unless you're ashamed of it."

"Oh Polly, I'm not. Really I'm not."

"Well then." Polly took off her beret and looked at it. "I tell you what. Let's start again."

"I met Polly at a lecture by a man called Masterman about progressive education," William said. "It's him I'm working for now."

"Liberty Hall," Tom said.

"Yes. He's got all these radical ideas about schools. Anyway, we met at his lecture and that was the beginning of it. We're going to get married next month and Polly's having the baby sometime in the autumn."

"That's very nice. And you're going on working for this chap Masterman, are you?"

"Well, yes. For the moment, anyway."

"It's interesting, is it?"

"Oh, yes."

"Masterman's a bit of a mixture," Polly said.

"Sometimes he talks nonsense," William said. "But other times there's a funny kind of sense to it."

Tom stirred his tea and said, "Where are you going to live when the baby comes?"

William and Polly looked at each other. "We don't know," Polly said. "We've haven't got that far yet. I'll keep working as long as I can, of course."

"Oh," Tom said. He looked at his brother. "Funny, you having a baby," he said. "Being a father and all that."

"I don't see what's funny about it," William said. "It's perfectly normal."

I N FINCHLEY that spring, it was clear to Tom and William that Uncle Oscar was growing old. His face was a mass of deep wrinkles, his hair was silver and sparse, his breath wheezed in his throat, and his hands—the strong, square hands that had once displayed his Bristol Fighter for the girl on Bournemouth beach—were subject to occasional tremors. His racy Scott Squirrel was similarly tired; it spat and smoked and oozed black oil into the tawny gravel of his sister's drive. And yet, Tom thought as he watched them approach, the motorcycle and its rider still displayed considerable panache.

Seeing Tom in the garden, Uncle Oscar heaved the Scott onto its stand, tore off his helmet, and came trotting on his cavalryman's legs across the flower bed, his ancient leather coat billowing behind him. He grasped Tom's hands and said, "My dear fellow! The Spitfire! Tell me about the Spitfire! Is she as good as the old Bristol? Is she balanced? Is she sensitive?"

Tom clasped his uncle's hands. "Dear Uncle Oscar, she's a wonderful aeroplane! A thoroughbred!" He bent into a dramatic crouch. "Imagine this," he said, his hands chasing each other through the air. "The enemy's below. I'm in the sun. I pull her over on her back and into a vertical dive. I push the throttle through the gate. She's doing two hundred, three hundred, trembling in every rivet. The Messerschmitt is in my sights, getting larger by the second—"

"Wait for it, you've got to wait," Uncle Oscar cried.

"Oh yes, I wait, and then, at the last possible second, I hit the button—"

"Yes, yes," the old man said, crouching beside his nephew, "Fire! Fire!"

"Smoke bursts from the Jerry, bits fly off—"

"You've got him!"

"I've got him, and in a trice I'm past him and suddenly everyone's gone and I'm alone! It's so strange."

"The sky's empty."

"They've all gone."

"Just some wisps of smoke and the empty sky." Uncle Oscar straightened up and grasped his nephew's elbow. "Oh, my boy," he said, "it's the greatest thing, and the saddest thing, too."

Tom felt ashamed of the silly melodrama he had conspired with his uncle to create. "Uncle Oscar," he said, "come inside and have some tea. William's here with Polly."

~~~

STELLA WAS OUT with her American, as usual these days. In the kitchen, Polly considered a vase of dusty dried flowers and teasels. When she saw Tom she said, "I think these ought to be chucked out, don't you?"

"Polly," Tom said, "here's Uncle Oscar."

Uncle Oscar swirled the tails of his coat, clicked his heels, and bowed. Polly stared at him. He put a hand to the end of his mustache and said, "Enchanted, my dear Miss Morris."

"Uncle Oscar," Polly said. "Goodness me! How delightful to meet you! I've heard all about you. You're Tom and William's great hero."

Uncle Oscar stood as tall and straight as he was able.

"Come with me," Polly said, putting her arm through his. "I know it's teatime, but I've brought something stronger, specially for you. It's in the pantry." Uncle Oscar followed, gazing up at her and with his free hand inserting a twirl in his yellowing mustache.

"YOUR UNCLE OSCAR," Polly said to William, "is a lovely old chap."

"Yes, he is," William said. "He's utterly failed to grow up."

"Isn't it odd," Polly said, "when you think that your mother is . . . well, such a cool person."

"I suppose it is."

"I can't work out what to call her. I simply cannot call her 'Mother.' "

"Why not call her Constance?"

"Good morning, Constance," Polly said experimentally. "No. Absolutely not. I'll have to avoid calling her anything. But you can ask her to stop calling me Dr. Morris. That would be a start."

At tea, when Polly asked after Felix, Constance said, "Oh, he'll be working late. He always is."

"I HEAR TOM had a string on his ankle when he was a baby," Polly said.

William looked at her. "You've been talking to Milly."

"Yes. And I bet you don't realize how much that woman loves you two."

"Actually, I do."

"Oh, damn!" Polly said. "Strange, isn't it, when you encounter someone else's family? I keep thinking I've discovered something you don't know."

William kissed her and she laughed.

"Mind you," she said, "you're quite funny when you say things like 'Actually, I do.' "

"I'm so glad I make you happy."

"Oh God, so am I. But do you know . . ."

"What?"

"Your mother has never shown me a single one of her pictures. I'm not even allowed in her studio."

"That doesn't mean anything. She never shows anyone, not even me or Tom. We have to steal in and peep when she's out."

"WELL, THIS IS nice," Polly said. "Tomato's my favorite." They were sitting around the dinner table, she and William on one side, Tom and Uncle Oscar opposite, Felix and Constance at either end. Milly had brought in the soup tureen, and Constance was ladling it out. There was a pause. Polly felt William's knee pressing against hers, looked at him, and saw that he was waiting for something.

"For what we are about to receive," Felix said, "may the Lord make us truly thankful."

Serviettes were removed from their rings, unrolled, and spread across knees. Soup spoons were selected and lifted to readiness.

"Do help yourselves to water," Constance said.

Uncle Oscar looked at the jug and sniffed. Felix dipped his spoon into his soup, and they followed his lead. While smiling in a friendly fashion at Uncle Oscar, Polly lifted one foot and pressed it down upon William's.

"Of course, we haven't decided where we're going to live yet," William said.

"In fact, a lot of things aren't decided," Polly said. "We could live in my flat in London, of course, but at the moment William's still rather involved with Liberty Hall."

"Liberty Hall," Uncle Oscar said. "That's a silly name, if you ask me."

"Do have some bread," Constance said to Polly.

"Liberty Hall," Uncle Oscar said again. "That's what they say when people take things that aren't rightly theirs." He gestured with his spoon as if to a crowd. " 'What do you think this is? Liberty Hall?' "

"Yes, Oscar," Constance said. "Everybody knows that."

"That's typical of Masterman," William said. "He likes being provocative."

"Liberty Hall," Uncle Oscar said. "Humph."

"I suppose there's something in it," Tom said. "We're awfully conventional in this country, aren't we?"

"Damned right," Uncle Oscar said. "Damned po-faced lot, the English."

Polly laughed, and Uncle Oscar looked at her gleefully. "There you are," he said, "the beautiful young lady agrees entirely."

"The beautiful young lady is honored by your compliment," Polly said, dipping her head. Uncle Oscar grinned across the table at her, his spoon hovering in midair.

"When you two have finished flirting," William said.

"But you've got to have values of some sort," Felix said. "One has to have something to live by."

There was a silence.

"I think you've just got to work things out for yourself," William said.

"And what does the beautiful young lady think?"

"Oh, Oscar, really," Constance said.

"She agrees with William," Polly said. "But you can't take all day over it, that's the only thing. You've got to get on with life before it's all gone."

"Quite right," Uncle Oscar said. "Look at me. My damned joints have seized and my eyes have gone dim, but at least I've got some bloody good memories, eh? What?" He looked slowly round them all, reached for a slice of bread, and dipped it triumphantly into his soup.

Behind Uncle Oscar the door opened and Milly put her head in. When she saw that nobody had yet finished, she withdrew her head and closed the door.

A WEEK LATER the sun was shining. Milly looked out the front door of number 27 and saw that it had turned out quite nice after all, though a bit windy. She picked up the letters from the mat and put them on the hall stand. Mrs. Anderson had left her usual note about the arrangements for the day. Milly took the note and went down to the kitchen. The note said Stella would be in for supper. Smoked haddock was required, with potatoes and runner beans. Milly opened the tin on the dresser and counted the coupons. There ought to be enough for the week, if she was careful.

But at lunchtime, when she came back from the fishmonger's with a really nice piece of haddock, a letter was lying alone on the hall stand, a creamy envelope addressed to Miss Milly Budd. She picked it up and turned it over in her hands. It must have been there this morning, but she hadn't noticed it, not being in the habit of getting letters. The words *Liberty Hall* were printed on the flap, with a little picture of a house with pillars on the front of it. It was the invitation, of course. She didn't intend to go to the wedding. The thought made her feel hot and bothered. She could feel the sweat running down under her arms. People would look at her as if they knew everything. She opened the envelope and took out the big white card. *Dr. Clare Morris requests the pleasure of the company of Miss Milly Budd at the wedding of her daughter Polly to Mr. William Anderson. R.S.V.P.*

There was something else in the envelope, a letter on stiff cream paper that crackled as she unfolded it, and at the top it had the same words, *Liberty Hall,* and the same picture as the envelope. It was a letter from William. *My dearest Milly, I know you don't like big occasions, but I really do hope that you'll come to our wedding. Tom and I owe you so much for looking after us all those years, and besides, Polly wants to see you again—you got on so well together, and that was really nice. Much love and best wishes, William.*

She read the letter and stood there holding it. She rubbed her eyes and decided she would have to go to the wedding after all. She couldn't say no to William, could she? Not when he'd asked her specially.

Later that afternoon she slipped out of the house and went shopping for a nice big casserole dish, a proper one with a lid. When it came to wedding presents, you couldn't go wrong with a casserole dish, really, because everyone needed them, didn't they? It didn't matter if they got more than one. They were ever so useful. The boys had always liked shepherd's pie. Miss Polly would surely know how to make it, even if she was a doctor.

She decided on her best black dress with the red silk collar, her ordinary black shoes, a new pair of gloves, and a new hat. They were more or less her usual outdoor clothes, but she washed and ironed everything carefully and bought new gloves and the little black hat specially. She had even bought some new undies, though nobody would know about them, of course. The hat had some fine gauze netting on it, and a shiny black feather. When she looked at herself in the mirror and turned this way and that, she thought the hat looked quite nice, really. She only had one winter coat, so she'd have to wear it, even though it was brown and worn at the cuffs. She decided she would save up and have her hair done so she wouldn't disgrace William.

ON THE DAY of the wedding, catching sight of herself in the mirror on the way out the front door, Milly wondered again if she didn't look too drab. She might be going to a funeral rather than a wedding. Come on, now, don't be so daft, she said to herself, you mustn't worry. You're as smart as you can possibly be.

She put the casserole dish in her shopping bag and walked quickly down to the main road because she thought she might miss the 28B that came at half-past ten, but fortunately she didn't. The conductress said, "Hello, Milly. Oh gosh, you're looking smart! Going somewhere special?"

"Yes," Milly said, "I'm going to a wedding. One of my boys."

"You look very nice, dear," the conductress said. "Your hair does look nice."

Milly smiled at her. She had an idea her name was Daphne. After that, she felt much better.

On the way into the church, Milly bumped into Miss Alcock and Mrs. Jennings from around the corner. They said, "Good morning, Miss Budd," in a very nice way, and stopped to talk for a few minutes. That was nice of them. It was a pity they were thinking of moving away to the country. They were quite a funny pair, and they often made her laugh when she saw them squabbling. Miss Alcock complimented her on her hat, and Mrs. Jennings said her hair looked pretty. People had said that twice now, so it must be true.

She sat on the end of the last pew at the back of the church, leaning sideways from her seat and looking down the aisle at William's back. He was waiting with his hands clasped behind him, fiddling about with his fingers, and every so often he looked round and caught her eye and smiled. Oh dear, he was nervous, though. You could tell. Tom stood next to William, wearing his RAF uniform and looking ever so smart. It must be nice to have your brother as best man. Just fancy, Milly thought, all those years ago that little baby held my hand and I put that label on his ankle.

Beyond the boys was the altar and those huge stained-glass windows that showed all the disciples sitting around at the Last Supper. Milly sat on the edge of her pew and clasped her gloved hands together. She caught a glimpse of Stella and her nice American, a very polite man, even though he was so big, and then the organist began to play "Here Comes the Bride." She jumped to her feet and turned around. Miss Polly was coming into the church on the arm of her brother, a handsome man who looked ever so like her. He was wearing a morning suit and carrying a gray top hat. Polly's dress was not white, it was sort of a cream, with a veil, of course, and she had some lovely flowers. Milly dabbed her eyes. It was just as well she'd brought two big hankies. She's a vision, Polly is, she's so lovely, and William's so lucky, my little boy William is.

Milly bent her head and pretended to be praying, just in case anyone was looking at her. When it came to the hymns she just said the words to herself, in case she wasn't quite in tune. Over there was Uncle Oscar—he was singing very loudly indeed and not minding if he was in tune or not. He was a one, he was, really.

At the reception Milly started to help with the drinks, and then William and Polly came along and gave her a big hug and a kiss. William gave her a glass of sherry and said she wasn't to help because she was a guest. She went and stood at the back of the room, sipping the sherry and watching what was going on for quite a long time. Then she saw they were all getting ready to sit down and have the speeches and all that. Felix was standing by the top table, and he was going to say something. When nobody was looking Milly put down her sherry, slipped out and got her coat, and went down to the bus stop. Luckily a 28B came before very long, and thank goodness the rain had held off. All the way home she thought about them being such a lovely couple and hoped they would be very happy. Soon there would be the baby, and perhaps they would ask her to help with it sometimes.

THE RAIN cleared, the visibility improved, and the wind veered to the northwest, brisk and turbulent. Small, puffy cumulus appeared here and there, moving rapidly on the wind. By midday the clouds were aligned in streets, their undersides flat and dark and their tops, brilliantly white, surging upward. Tom, celebrating an escape from Dougie, flew two careful loops and a barrel roll between the cloud streets, the aeroplane buffeted by the rough air. He pulled out of the roll and slid along at two hundred knots close beneath the nearest cloud street, allowing the strong updrafts to draw him into the dark base of the cloud.

Bravery was an odd thing. It was quite illogical. It just put you at greater risk of losing everything. And it wasn't a matter of choice. If you weren't brave, you couldn't choose to be so, could you? The more afraid you were, the braver you could be. That was odd, but surely it was true. Its converse certainly was: If you were unafraid, you could not be brave. *Be brave, old chap.* That was what the doctor used to say. To be brave was to overcome fear. It was impossible to know how brave someone else was; you could only know how brave you were yourself.

He came out of the cloud and turned back toward the aerodrome. It was strange that being brave was almost the same as being stupid.

⌒

"R EALLY, WILLIAM," MASTERMAN said, "you ought to realize that Easter is merely an element of the culture of guilt that sus-
tains the hegemonic conspiracy of church, state, and capital."

Despite Masterman's opinion, everyone felt like celebrating the
coming of spring. Irma's drama group devised a performance using
ideas she had gleaned from *The Golden Bough.* They called it *The
Death of Winter.* It was performed in the garden at sunset. Amy Pluck
devised and recited a free-verse narrative in which an icy kingdom
was enmeshed in treachery and war, rescued by heroism, and eventually bathed in the inevitable victory of sunshine. Her recitation was
accompanied by a small band of drummers and cornet players; at
moments of crisis a large chorus added wordless cries. Summer and
Winter, portrayed by Belinda Boon and Patsy Fish, played out their
eternal battle, and the O'Leary boys intervened occasionally in the
characters of Time, Space, and Nature.

Polly watched the performance with William. The volume of the
choral accompaniment swelled throughout the piece in a way that
was subtle and menacing. Large numbers of children were employed
to represent the vast mysteries of the primeval forest. The climax,
taking place under a great oak (stolidly played by Arthur Beckingsale), saw Belinda forced into a sacrificial pot from which she emerged
in a simulacrum of birth, to be greeted with ecstatic hooting from
the whole company.

Afterward Polly said to William, "It was really rather good, you
know. Terrific energy. Raw and rough edged."

"There you are. That's exactly the kind of imaginative thing you
can do in a school like this."

"That's a different point," Polly said. "You could do it in an ordinary school just as well."

"What, and do nothing else for weeks, like they did?"

"Well, I suppose that's a valid point." She thought for a moment.
"The whole thing was so convincing that it made me uneasy, somehow. There was something primitive about it."

"Oh, come on! It was *intended* to be primitive."

"Yes, of course it was. I don't know what I'm saying, except that it was more upsetting than I thought it would be. The slow movement of the trees in the darkness. Those fearful screams when they caught Winter and clubbed her to death."

Certainly the event had been disturbing. "Does it ever occur to you," William asked Masterman, "that some of the children might be developing thoughts or behavior that might not be in their own best interests?"

Masterman laughed. "Of course not. Freedom never harmed anyone."

Polly sought out Belinda and had a talk with her. "Of course I liked doing it. I love all kinds of games," Belinda said. "I'll race you to the summerhouse."

"Well, in a minute, perhaps," Polly said. "But I think you ought to be careful about being so enthusiastic about everything. It can get people into trouble. Boldness can be misunderstood."

Belinda blinked her blue eyes. "I couldn't possibly get into trouble at Liberty Hall," she said. "Anyway, what's it got to do with you?"

FOLLOWED BY THE squadron adjutant, the CO walked briskly into the tent, stepped onto the rostrum, and said, "Good morning, everyone, good morning."

The pilots stood up and said in a ragged chorus, "Good morning, sir."

"At ease, chaps. Do sit down." The squadron leader placed his cap and gloves on the table and stepped to the front of the rostrum. "This isn't a formal lecture. It's more of a chin-wag about one or two things, so you're welcome to speak out, if you feel like it. All right?"

He stepped back and sat on a table, swinging his legs. "Oh yes," he said, "and carry on smoking, if you want to." He patted his pockets, found his pipe, and put it on the table beside him. The pilots settled in their chairs, some lighting cigarettes.

"It's a trifle ad hoc, this blessed tent," the squadron leader said, looking around. "Bloody drafty, isn't it."

"The new huts are supposed to be here next week," the adjutant said.

"As long as they're here before the Jerries are," the squadron leader said. The pilots laughed politely. "Now then. We've been getting on pretty well in the last couple of weeks. I know you've done a lot of hard work, and things haven't been easy. We've had quite a few difficulties of one sort or another. But I reckon it's time to step up a gear."

He stood up and walked to the blackboard. "Here's the jolly old V," he said, sketching three crosses to represent a section of three aircraft in formation. "We've been practicing the standard section attack, coming in from behind the target in a V, moving to line astern, echelon starboard, break away downwards, and back into line astern." The chalk scratched across the board. "We've also been practicing the beam attack."

"I hope you're taking all this in, Anderson," Dougie whispered. "You might learn something."

"Shut up, you silly bugger," Tom said.

The squadron leader turned around. "Yesterday afternoon your section, Wells, carried out several practice attacks on my section."

"Yes, sir," Dougie said, sitting up straight. "We did four altogether."

"What did you think of them?"

"Well, sir—obviously there's always room for improvement. But we're getting better. The last one wasn't too bad at all, I thought."

"I thought they were loose. Far too loose. The flying's sloppy when you get in close. You're letting the section open out. In a real combat you'd lose contact with each other. That's one thing. And the other thing is, you're breaking too early." He looked at Tom. "You're the number two, aren't you, Anderson?"

"Yes, sir."

"What's your job?"

"Sticking with Dougie, sir."

"Yes. And sticking with him doesn't mean flying a hundred yards away, does it."

"No, sir."

"Sticking with him means you get your wing in behind his and you keep it there whatever he does."

"Yes, sir."

"It isn't your job to look where you're going. You stick to Wells like bloody glue, even if he flies into the bloody deck." He looked at Dougie. "Who's your number three, Wells? Frampton, isn't it?"

"Yes, sir."

The squadron leader looked at Colin. "Same goes for you, Frampton. Too sloppy. Got to tighten up."

"Yes, sir."

"In this bloody game you won't kill anyone from five hundred yards, never mind what the books say. You've got to get inside a couple of hundred yards. That'll give you at least a chance of hitting something."

The squadron leader looked along the rows of pilots. "Don't think I'm only talking to Wells's section. The same goes for everyone. After this session we'll get airborne and we'll go on doing these attacks until we get them bloody well right. Now then. Let's go through it again, and then we'll look at the beam attack."

⁓

I N T H E M E S S that evening, Dougie placed his beer glass carefully on the bar and said, "Listen to me, chaps." He waved a finger at them. "This is what we'll do. We'll wait until we see the CO walking across the apron by number one hangar, and then we'll do a section attack on him."

"Oh, for God's sake, Dougie," Colin said. "What are you on about this time?"

"I mean we'll get into a V, come up behind him, line astern, starboard echelon, attack, then break away in line astern again." He leaned back and emptied his glass. The other two looked at him.

"You mean *walking*," Tom said. "Us three walking and him walking. Is that what you mean?"

"Exactly. But marching would be better still."

Colin began to laugh. "We march along, tucked in close together in a V—"

"Yes," Tom said, "and then we move into line astern, echelon starboard, pass a couple of feet behind him—"

"And break away to port in line astern," Dougie said. He clapped his hands. "Wonderful!"

"Wonderfully silly," Colin said. "He'd put us on a charge."

"Bet he wouldn't."

"Five bob."

"Done."

"Let's get outside and practice it."

⌒

So it was, the following morning, when the squadron leader had got out of his car and was walking toward his office, that he became conscious of three of his young men coming up behind him, marching quickly together. He stopped and turned around.

"Line astern," Dougie called out, and then, "Echelon starboard." The others moved smoothly to the right. "Wait for it," Dougie said. Five feet from the squadron leader he called, "Break," and they shaved past him, swerving away to the left and changing to line astern as they did so. It was smartly done; they stayed in step the whole time.

The squadron leader began laughing. "All right, Wells," he called out, "come back here."

They lined up in front of him. He was still laughing. "I've seen some bloody silly things in my time," he said, "but that takes the biscuit. You must have practiced that quite a lot." He put down his briefcase and looked pensive. "Actually, I suppose it might be rather a good exercise. Could you do it running, do you think?"

"Bloody hell, Dougie," Tom said, and the squadron leader laughed again.

"Come to think of it," he said, "I think we might get everyone out here and try it. At least you wouldn't forget it in a hurry."

⌒

That evening, in the mess, Nobby Clark said, "Whose bloody idea was it, anyway?"

"I cannot tell a lie," Tom said. "It was Dougie's."

"You rotten sod," Dougie said. He took a pace toward the door but was grasped by several hands before he could take another.

⌒

WILLIAM WAS READING quite an imaginative story by Ian Lambert when an odd sound, a kind of squealing and roaring, entered his consciousness. Were the donkeys fighting? He got up and looked out the window. A convoy of tanks was edging past Liberty Hall and turning into the meadow, where an energetic sergeant was marshaling them into rows. A squad of soldiers had folded up the cricket nets; as he watched, they trundled the rollers and sight screens into the bottom corner of the meadow. The tanks had already cut a pattern of curved scars through the grass of the outfield, deep into the brown earth.

Downstairs, William found Masterman waving his arms at a young army officer who was standing in the hall. "I don't care who signed your piece of paper," Masterman was saying, "you have no right to throw innocent children and their trusted guardians from their sanctuary."

The officer shuffled his feet. "I'm afraid I do, sir. It's the Emergency Powers Act."

"Besides which," Masterman said, "this is Liberty Hall. It's a free school. It's officially recognized as such. How can you and your horrid soldiers invade a place called Liberty Hall? It's a criminal act."

"Now that Britain is threatened, sir, emergency measures are required. Schools are being requisitioned," the officer said. He adopted a confidential tone; this was something he had thought about. "It's all the land they own, you see? And the buildings. They're often appropriate for military purposes. It's quite interesting, really. Schools have dormitories, storerooms, sports facilities, big halls, all the things that the army needs. I suppose the army is like a big school. Anyway, sir, it's unfortunate, but there you are."

Masterman had begun to breathe heavily. He stared at the soldier. "What's your name?"

"Major Turner, sir."

"Major Turner." Masterman walked around in a circle, one hand on the top of his head as if to prevent it from exploding. He stopped and looked at William. "How to respond to this incredible assault upon us," he said. "That's the question."

William said, "Are we being evicted?"

"Yes," Masterman said. "This buffoon says we've got two months to get out. I know what it's all about, of course. It's nothing to do with France giving up. It's just another attempt to close us down. We're a serious threat to the English ruling class. They've always been after us. Now Churchill's coming back, and they've found the perfect excuse for a head-on assault."

The major took a step forward. "If you don't mind my saying so, sir, that's got nothing to do with it," he said. "We just need more room to park our tanks and all that sort of thing. There's a war on, you know."

Masterman screwed up his eyes and seemed to swell slightly. He continued his circular walk and arrived again in front of the officer. He placed his right index finger against the man's chest. "Well, Major Tank Parker, I can give you the school's response immediately."

The major leaned backward to reduce the pressure of Masterman's finger. "Very good, sir," he said.

"We'll go," Masterman said. "We'll leave. We'll depart. We shall behave with dignity, and our principal concern shall be the safety of our youngsters in the face of brute force and the powers of darkness."

"I say, sir—" the major began to say, but Masterman interrupted him.

"We shall seize the day. We shall turn your violence into our good fortune. The children of Liberty Hall shall go on a great journey. We shall discover our destiny in another place, a place where we are welcomed."

The major stared at Masterman. "Do you mean you'll comply with the order, sir?"

"We welcome it. Thank you, Major Parker, for giving us this wonderful opportunity." Masterman turned to William. "This is something I have always longed for. Here is the perfect moment. A pilgrimage in search of peace and happiness! What is the human race but a lost tribe? What is our destiny but a journey of hope into the mystery of the future? *Solvitur ambulando.*"

Without waiting for a response, Masterman headed toward his study, shouting, "Irma! Irma! Something wonderful has happened!"

"Well, sir," the major said to William, "I think that's all, then."

"Yes," William said. He stepped to the door and opened it. The tanks growled and squealed outside. "So we've got two months."

"Yes, sir," the major said. "Two months." He paused. "I didn't quite get that last thing he said."

"*Solvitur ambulando,*" William said. "He says it will be solved by walking."

⁓

"NAME'S MASTERMAN," THE major said to his company sergeant. "Odd kind of bloke. Not sure he's all there. Says he'll go, though. So carry on, there's a good chap."

May

O N THE door, it said, "IO," standing for "Intelligence Officer." Inside, Tom Anderson was sitting beside the desk and waving his hands. "Jesus," he was saying, "a bloody great hole appeared in the starboard wing, there was suddenly smoke everywhere, and I thought the bloody thing was going to burn."

"But it didn't," the intelligence officer said. "It kept on flying, didn't it?"

"Before that, Dougie Wells went in. I saw it. He went straight in. There was no smoke or anything. Just him going straight down and a splash and in a moment, nothing. There were so bloody many of them."

"All right, lad." The IO was a gray-haired man who was making penciled notes on an official form.

"I saw Dougie go in. We never had a chance. We came on these two Jerries just stooging along a few hundred feet below like sitting ducks, and Dougie said, 'Tally-ho,' and dived away, and we followed, and I looked up and there was another lot of them, a dozen more of them, up above the first lot, and there were only the three of us against—it must have been twenty or more of them, at least—"

"Okay. I've got that."

"I heard Dougie say something on the radio, I think it was 'Stay close,' or something like that, and he just went straight on down. Jesus. He went straight in like an arrow. There was a huge spout of water and then nothing at all."

"Yes. I've got all that."

"There wasn't anything wrong with his aeroplane, or nothing you could see, anyway. Nothing fell off. No smoke. I can't work out what happened to him. It was so strange. He was talking normally and then he just flew straight into the sea. It was such a shock."

"Yes, it must have been."

"It was only ten minutes since we'd taken off. We went off at full boost and we were at about fifteen thousand when we came on them over the coast, somewhere near Rye. We were climbing like hell, but nowhere near high enough. Besides, there were so many of them. The squadron was scattered all over the place, but the three of us managed to stick together. Then Dougie went, and that just left the two of us, and straight away we had two or three of them behind us, and all the other Jerries hanging about, waiting, and Hawkins pulled round very steep and fired on the turn and hit one of them, a terrific shot it was, got it in the belly, and it lurched and smoke came out—"

"Yes, I got that before."

"Then they got him, someone got him, Roy Hawkins, I mean, I couldn't see which one of them, it was all happening so fast, a filthy great cloud of smoke and some silvery bits falling, and I looked round and there was nobody left except me. It must have been only a few seconds. And I just thought, Where is everybody? Then something put a hole through my wing."

"Yes. The starboard wing, you said."

"Neat as you like, a bloody great hole just inboard of the aileron, and then there was a bit of smoke and the engine stopped. I got the hood open and suddenly it was all quiet and I was just gliding along and there wasn't an aeroplane in sight anywhere. Nothing at all except some trails of smoke in the air. Quiet, as well. They'd all gone. Sunny day. Sun on the cliffs somewhere up towards Beachy Head. Quiet as you like. Sun shining. You wouldn't believe how quiet it was, all of a sudden."

"All right," the IO said. "I've got all that."

"It was so quick, you see."

"Yes."

"It wasn't even ten minutes from us sitting in our deck chairs until Hawkins and Dougie were gone and just me sitting there with a dead engine. I thought I was going to have to bail out."

"Yes. I'm sorry."

"Phillips."

"Pardon?"

"An instructor I had once. Ted Phillips. I suddenly remembered him. He taught me to put a parachute on properly. Ages ago."

"Oh."

"But Dougie."

"Yes. I'm sorry."

"I really thought I'd had it."

"Yes."

"You'd think there would be oil or something on the water. Some sort of mark. But nothing. Not a sign of him."

"No."

"No oil or anything."

"I see."

"I had plenty of height. I dived away and they didn't follow, God knows why not. I made it back to the coast and came down in a field. Wheels up. Made a bit of a mess of the aeroplane. I think they've written it off. But at least it didn't burn."

Tom got up and walked across the office, then sat down again. "You've never seen anything like the way Dougie went in. It was like drawing a line with a T-square. It couldn't be any neater. A tidy splash like you get when you throw a stone into the sea edgeways, then the lines of waves again. Do you know what I mean? Dougie gone. He was such a noisy bloke, you see. You expected something more than that, somehow."

WILLIAM KNOCKED ON the study door and went in. Maps had been pinned on the walls, and others were spread across the table. Masterman was pacing up and down. Irma crouched over a typewriter. "Sit down, dear boy," Masterman said, waving William toward a chair. "I've converted this room to my campaign head-quarters."

"Oh yes," William said, looking around. "Jolly good."

"Move those binoculars and sit down. We're engaged in a moment of creative inspiration."

Masterman stopped pacing, stared at the ceiling, and pressed his palms to his temples. "Now," he said to Irma, "put the date and then 'A Vital Message from the Principal.' "

Irma typed rapidly and Masterman began dictating: "My dear parent, the army has informed me of its decision to commandeer our school buildings. This gives us a wonderful opportunity to challenge our children with new experiences and radical learning opportunities."

Masterman stopped and said, "A new paragraph there, I think." He began pacing again, waving his arms as he spoke.

"The school will shortly take to the road in search of a new home. We will march eastwards along an ancient path, the Pilgrim's Way, which leads eventually, of course, to the great shrine of Sir Thomas Becket at Canterbury, a prime objective of pilgrims for centuries."

He paused and put his hand to his chin. "Do I need to say that last bit? Perhaps not. Strike out the bit about 'prime objective.' It ends more effectively on the word *Canterbury.*"

Irma worked urgently with her eraser.

"Gracious me," Masterman said, "the whole idea makes me tremble with excitement! Are you ready, Irma?"

"Ready, Masterman," Irma said, her hands poised.

"Parents, like ourselves, will welcome this exceptional opportunity to encourage independence, comradeship, and physical fitness. Should any of you feel that your child is unsuited to this experience, please collect him or her from Liberty Hall in the next two weeks. We will inform you of our new abode in due course. Yours sincerely."

Masterman sat down, blew out his cheeks, and said, "Well, then! Read it back to me, my sweet."

Irma did so with enthusiasm. Masterman clapped his hands and paused, screwing up his eyes. "One more thing. I think we need a postscript. Wait. It will come to me."

He shut his eyes and after a moment said, "P.S. Parents should provide their children with good strong boots."

"Excellent!" Irma said, typing quickly. "A practical touch of that kind is so convincing."

Masterman sat back in his chair and looked at William.

"Well," William said. "It's certainly an extraordinary idea. Do you really think it's the right thing to do?"

"Yes, it is remarkable, isn't it," Masterman said. "One of my very best ideas." He turned toward Irma. "Don't you agree, my dear?"

Irma reached up and caressed his arm. He blew her a kiss. "Get the letter duplicated, my dearest, and request Matron's assistance with the envelopes."

"I just thought that most of the children were going the other way, that's all," William said. "Evacuation and all that."

Masterman whistled a few bars of an unrecognizable tune and then said, "A procession is always a good reason to go the other way, dear boy."

Irma left the room. Masterman turned to William, gave him a straight look, and said, " 'The bat that flits at close of eve has left the brain that won't believe.' "

"Oh yes," William said after a moment. "Blake, of course."

Masterman looked up at the ceiling. "Blake and Bunyan," he said musingly. "Bunyan shall be another seminal text on our pilgrimage. There are many other possibilities."

After a moment William said, "Chaucer, of course."

"And Cobbett. A fellow radical."

"Gilbert White, perhaps."

"Yes indeed! The skills of the naturalist! Very good!"

William felt a small gush of pride that he knew to be foolish.

"Above all, we'll need Belloc's *The Old Road*," Masterman said. "It's the key text. Also Alfred Watkins. You presumably know *The Old Straight Track*."

"I don't think I do."

"Fascinating. Ley lines and so forth. You have a treat in store, dear boy. Now I really must consider what I shall say in my address to the school."

William went upstairs. In his room Polly was lying flat on the window seat with a cushion under the small of her back. She turned her head toward him and said, "What on earth are those tank things doing in the meadow?"

"I'll tell you," he said, kneeling on the floor beside her. "But you aren't going to like it."

~~~~~

"THE CO WANTS to see you right away, Tom," Nobby Clark said.

"Christ, does he? What does he want?"

"Search me, old chap."

Tom straightened his tie and went to the office. "Go straight in," the clerk said. "He's expecting you."

The squadron leader was lighting his pipe. "Oh, Anderson. Good." He puffed clouds of blue smoke and sucked his pipe until the tobacco crackled. "Bit of good news, old boy. They've found your chum."

"My chum, sir? You don't mean—"

"Dougie Wells, old chap. Bit of a special chum of yours, wasn't he?" He waved a message form. "The army says they've found Flight Lieutenant Wells hanging in a tree near Eastbourne. He's in hospital, but they say he'll live."

Tom sat down.

"Take your time, lad," the squadron leader said.

"Dougie's still alive?"

"Absolutely."

"He can't be. I saw him go straight in. That's rubbish. He couldn't possibly have survived."

The squadron leader laughed.

"I'm sorry, sir, I didn't mean—"

"I know what you meant, Anderson." He laughed again. "But here you are." He looked at the message. "An ack-ack crew saw him drift into a wood. They sent a couple of blokes in after him. His chute had hooked up on a tree and the lads cut him down. They took him to hospital in Hastings. No mistake, old chap."

Tom sat still.

"He must have bailed out long before his Spit hit the water," the squadron leader said. "His chute must have opened high up, or he wouldn't have reached land."

"But I didn't see a parachute. I saw him go in, and there wasn't a parachute. Surely I would have seen it?"

The squadron leader grinned and waved the message form again. "When it's sunk in, Anderson, round up two or three others, take a car, and pay him a visit. Then perhaps you'll believe me."

"They didn't find Roy Hawkins, I suppose."

"No, Anderson, they didn't."

THEY TELEPHONED AND discovered that Dougie had been moved from Hastings to London. Tom, Colin Frampton, and Nobby Clark drove up to see him. A nurse delivered them to a ward sister, who said severely, "You ought to have telephoned before you came." She considered the three young men. "Do you know what happened to him?"

"No," Tom said. "Except that he was shot down, of course."

"I'm afraid he was rather badly burned, especially his face and hands. We're having to give him quite a lot of morphine. He's probably asleep."

She took them down the corridor and opened a door. They followed her into a room with drawn curtains. In the dim light it could have been anyone in the bed. Dougie's arms were heavily bandaged, and there seemed to be some sort of dark dressing across his face. He did not move.

The sister looked at his notes. "He's just had another dose. He won't be awake for a good while." She replaced the clipboard. "His parents are coming this evening."

They listened to the slow whistle of Dougie's breath. There were flowers and cards on the table. "Perhaps we ought to wait until he's a bit better," Colin said.

"I think that would be sensible," the sister said.

Outside the hospital they stood together on the pavement. Nobby Clark folded his arms and said, "Oh, bloody hell."

"Yes," Tom said.

"A drink is required," Colin said.

"I still can't work out what happened," Tom said. "How did he bail out without me seeing? I was right behind him all the time."

"Come on, Tom," Nobby said, taking his elbow, "it's your bloody round."

"God, he didn't look very good, did he?" Colin said.

———

At first light, the Met officer checked his instruments and eyed the sky gloomily. Wisps of high-altitude cirrus trailed across from the west. In the morning briefing he said, "It looks all right now, but there's a front coming in. Lots of duff weather, rain and clag down to a couple of hundred feet. Be here in three or four hours. You can forget about flying today, that's my view." He sat down.

By nine o'clock low cloud covered the airfield and flying had been canceled for the day. The pilots lay in battered chairs around the fire in the pilots' room. Rain hammered on the roof of the hut.

"The adj says my new Spit's supposed to come today," Tom said.

"Just so you can break another one," Nobby Clark said. "But it won't come in this bloody murk, boy." He gestured with his thumb at the gray sky beyond the window. "Cloud base isn't four hundred feet."

"No, I suppose it won't. Sod it." Tom walked across to the window, looked out, went back to his chair.

"Poor little Tom waits for his birthday present," Colin said. "The lad broke his aeroplane, so he asked his daddy for a new one, and his daddy, being a nice friendly daddy, said, 'Of course, my dear little boy, whatever you want, my dearest boy.' "

Tom laughed. "Shut up, and stoke up the bloody fire. It's damn chilly."

There was a silence, then Colin said, "I wonder if there's anything we could do for Dougie."

"I was wondering about that," Tom said. "But I couldn't think of anything."

"No, I suppose there isn't," Colin said. "Except that we could go and see his parents, I suppose."

"I don't think that would do much good. It might make it worse for them to see us." Tom got up and stood looking at the fire.

"A hand or two of poker is called for," Nobby said. "Who's eager to lose their worldly possessions? Colin? What about you, Tom?"

"I'm broke," Tom said.

"You know me, boy. Always willing to allow credit to my friends."

They gathered around the rickety card table and by midday Tom had lost three and ninepence. "Blow this for a game of soldiers," he said, standing up and stretching. As he did so, he heard the sound of an engine overhead.

The card players looked up. "That's a Merlin," Colin Frampton said.

"My new Spit," Tom said.

"Don't be bloody daft, lad," Nobby Clark said.

They made for the door. Colin poked his head out and said, "Christ, it's bloody foul out here."

Tom peered upward, shielding his eyes from the rain. "Well, it's a Spitfire, right enough."

They watched as the aircraft, flickering through hanging veils of cloud, flew a low circuit, lowered its wheels, and turned into the final approach.

"Now just take it easy, there's a good fellow," Tom said. "Don't break it."

The aircraft touched down neatly on the rain-soaked runway, spray whirling in two great vortices behind its wings.

"Nicely done," Nobby said. "Rough old day. That lad can fly a bit."

"You know, you could be right, Tom," Colin said. "It's a very shiny one. No squadron letters, either. Could be your new one."

The Spitfire turned onto the perimeter track and taxied toward them. An aircraftsman carrying an umbrella ran out and waved the aircraft to the apron in front of the hangar. "I think that's Alan Willis," Tom said. "It must be mine. Hooray." He went inside and took his overcoat and cap from a hook.

"Don't forget you owe me eight-and-six," Nobby said.

"Three-and-nine, you bugger," Tom said, pushing past him into the rain and hurrying across the tarmac. The aircraftsman had pushed a pair of chocks in front of the wheels and the pilot was climbing out. Tom ducked under Alan's umbrella.

"Is it my new one, Alan?"

"Yes, sir," Alan said. "Looks like a nice one, too."

"Brand spanking new, eh?" Tom shivered and hopped from one foot to the other.

"Yes, sir. Very nice."

The pilot stepped down from the wing and turned toward them.

"Goodness, it's a girl," Tom said.

"You'd better come under here, miss," Alan Willis said. The three of them stood together under the umbrella.

"I'm sorry," Tom said. "I was surprised to see a lady pilot."

"People often are," she said. "I can't think why." She took off her helmet and pushed her fingers through her hair. "Do you think someone will come and get us? It's an absolutely frightful day." She seemed very small, standing beside them.

"Your van's already here, miss," Alan Willis said. "They phoned from the gate. It's on its way over."

"I could give you a lift wherever you want," Tom said. "My friend Colin's got a car and a terrific lot of petrol."

"Thanks, but there's no need."

"That was a horrible flight, I should think."

"It was all right until the estuary, then it clamped right down. I nearly went back, but it was just as bad behind, so in the end I came on."

"You put it down very nicely," Tom said. "Awkward crosswind. Terrible vis, too."

"Thanks. Is it for you?"

"Yes it is, as a matter of fact."

She smiled. "I thought it might be. It was the way you came running out." She turned to look at the Spitfire. "Well, it's all right. It's quite a pretty one, in fact."

"Oh, good."

Alan Willis said, "Have you got the paperwork, miss?"

"Yes," the girl said. "It's all here. There's nothing wrong with it. It all worked all right. Can you sign it off?"

"I'll do that," Tom said. He initialed the forms, and as he did so a green van drew up beside them. The driver wound down the window and said to the pilot, "Well, Liz, that was quite horrid, I should think."

"Hello, Mavis. Thanks for coming. Yes, it was rather dreadful. I'm all done here. If you're ready, let's get back straight away."

"Be back for tea, I should think," Mavis said.

"Thanks very much," Tom said to the pilot.

"All part of the service. Cheerio." She opened the door of the van and got in. "Toodle-oo, folks," Mavis said, winding up her window. The van drove away through the puddles.

"Well, fancy that," Tom said. "Fancy her being a girl. She was carrying a cushion. Did you see that?"

"Yes, sir."

"She must need it so she can see out properly."

"Yes, sir."

"Really, Alan, you can call me Tom, you know."

"Sorry. I'll get some blokes and put her away, shall I?"

"All right. I'll give you a hand. Maybe we can find a leather and dry her off, once she's inside."

When Alan Willis inspected the aircraft, he found a powder compact in the bottom of the pilot's seat. He showed it to Tom. "I don't rightly know what to do with this," he said.

Tom turned it over in his hands. It was silver and had the initials *EB* on the lid. Above the initials were a date and an engraving of an aircraft. "Leave it with me, Alan," he said. "I'll send it back to her."

June

SMOKE CLIMBED from fires on the beaches and among the crush of equipment packed behind them. The dark columns drifted upward past the circling squadron of Spitfires, the smoke thinning and spreading as it rose. Tom followed Nobby Clark in smooth curves among the grimy clouds, glancing downward now and again at the sparkling sea and the sands that stretched away to north and south. Thin black lines of men straggled into the water from numerous points along the beach. The harbor mole was crammed with soldiers. Offshore, ships lay waiting, sometimes obscured by the smoke of their own guns. A ragged chain of small craft moved with infinite slowness between shore and ships; from five miles above, the vessels seemed as insignificant as water boatmen on a forest pool. For thirty minutes the fighters circled; but this time the enemy did not come, and eventually the squadron leader signaled them for home.

SHORTLY AFTER THE posting of Masterman's letter to parents, the drive leading to Liberty Hall filled with shooting brakes, ancient Austins, a mud-encrusted Morris 8, a fishmonger's van, and several imperious limousines. Powerfully built mothers, their big hats fluttering with the speed of their passage, stepped urgently toward the front door. Fathers leaned on their vehicles and commiserated one with another until they were summoned to lug the dear child's suitcases down from the dormitory.

Masterman eventually locked himself in his study and refused all communications. There was a near riot when a Rolls-Royce, groaning with wicker hampers and liner trunks, stalled and blocked the drive. "I'm glad we've always had Daimlers," Mrs. Campbell-Barley was heard to say as she hustled Deborah toward her own softly purring vehicle. "I always think a Rolls is just too gaudy for words."

When all the coming and going was complete, twelve children remained in the school. William rounded them up and made a list.

Belinda Boon, plump rider of donkeys and star of *The Death of Winter,* was there with her friend Amy Pluck and the boy called Todger, the eleven-year-old who owned a nameless ferret. There had been no response from the well-known actress who was Ian Lambert's mother, so he too was counted in. As far as William could discover, the three O'Leary boys (nine-year-old Steven, ten-year-old Nigel, and Marcus, thirteen) had intercepted Masterman's letter, preventing it from reaching their parents. They told him under sworn oath that their father had telegraphed his approval from his Peruvian expedition, yet they could not produce the telegram. "Oh well," Masterman said, "in the absence of any other communication we might as well hang on to them."

Timothy Needham, a timid boy of ten who was notable mainly for his stamp collection, seemed unlikely to have the character required of a pilgrim. Arthur Beckingsale, however, the thirteen-year-old from Wigan, was the kind who could be relied upon in a tight place. Lucy Standish, a witty, amiable girl of ten, would perhaps help to maintain morale in difficult times, as would Susan Portman, a robust fifteen-year-old noted for her common sense. Patsy Fish, a muscular child of fourteen, had little ambition beyond becoming an even more successful tennis player than her mother, but her remarkable strength and athleticism might be useful.

⌒

"AIR TRANSPORT AUXILIARY," a woman's voice said.

"Oh, hello," Tom said, plaiting the phone cord with his free hand. "My name's Anderson. I'm speaking from RAF Tangmere. I'd like to know the name of one of your pilots who delivered an aircraft here the other day."

"I'm sorry, sir, we can't divulge operational details over the telephone."

"But it was my aircraft she delivered. She left something in it. It's a personal item, and valuable, I think. I need to send it back to her."

"I'm sorry, sir. I suggest you send the item to us and we'll see if we can find out whose it is."

"Could you get a message to her? Ask her to ring me?"

There was a pause. Then the voice said, "Possibly, sir, if you give me the details of the delivery."

"It was a Spitfire," Tom said. "The number's P5022. Delivered here two days ago. I'm Pilot Officer Anderson."

"All right, sir. I've made a note. I'll see what can be done."

"Thanks ever so much," Tom said. "You're a real sweetie."

"I can't guarantee anything, mind," the woman said. "But I'll try for you."

"That's lovely. I think her name was Liz something."

"Liz, did you say?"

"Yes. She's quite small and she has short brown hair. I'd like her to phone me if you can find her."

"All right. I'll do my best."

"Thanks very much. Good-bye."

"Good-bye, sir."

⌒

"MESSAGE FOR YOU, Tom," said the adjutant, passing Tom a slip of paper. He unfolded it and read that First Officer Bowman would be most obliged if PO Anderson would return her property to her at Air Transport Auxiliary HQ via the official bag.

"Damn," Tom said.

"Hard luck, old chap," the adjutant said.

"But at least I've got her name," Tom said.

"It's a start, eh?"

—⁓—

"AIR TRANSPORT AUXILIARY." It was a different telephonist, a younger, brisker voice.

"I'd like to speak to First Officer Bowman."

"Who's that speaking?"

"Urgent message from RAF Tangmere," Tom said. "Pilot Officer Anderson."

"Just a moment, sir. I'll ring the crew room."

Well, Tom thought, that was easy enough. He banged his fist against the wall and clutched the receiver tightly. The line popped and hissed as he waited. Why was it taking so long? He hopped from one foot to the other. Eventually there was a clattering sound and a voice said, "Hello?"

"Is that Miss Bowman?"

A fractional hesitation, and then she said, "This is First Officer Bowman speaking."

"It's Tom Anderson."

"I don't think I know you."

"Yes, you do. You delivered my Spitfire a couple of days ago."

"Oh, it's you."

"Yes, it's me."

"I'm sorry, I'm on duty. I can't talk to you now."

"You left your powder compact in my aeroplane."

Another hesitation. "Yes, I did. I'm sorry. Perhaps you could send it back to me. I left a message."

"I got the message, but I thought I'd bring it over myself."

"It's an awful long way. I'd much rather you sent it. You could put it in the official bag."

Pips sounded on the line. "Your time's up, dear," the operator said. "Do you want any longer?"

"Yes, I do," Tom said. He pushed coins into the box and pressed the button. "Look," he said, "I've got to do some flight tests. It's easy for me to drop in. It's only half an hour or so."

"I'd rather you just put it in the message bag."

"But if I did bring it, I could give it back to you, couldn't I?"

An even longer pause, and she said, "All right."

"I'll come this afternoon, if that's all right."

"THANKS FOR BRINGING my new aeroplane in such foul weather," Tom said.

"It's my job," Elizabeth Bowman said. Then, after a pause, she asked, "What happened to the one you had before?"

"I got shot down. It was my fault. I wasn't looking out properly. We got jumped and one of them put a hole in my wing and hit the engine. I had to put it down in a field that wasn't quite big enough. The aeroplane got a bit bent, and in the end they decided to write it off."

"Oh."

"It was a nice aeroplane, but not as nice as the one you brought. She flies beautifully. Didn't you think so?"

"She flew all right. I was only flying her for forty minutes or so, don't forget. I was mostly thinking about the frightful weather and not getting lost."

"Where did you learn to fly?"

"Oh, I belonged to a club before the war."

"You must have been terribly young then."

"Quite young. But old enough for a license."

"Yes, of course."

She looked out of the window, then turned back to him.

"Look, I ought to tell you straight away that I don't go out with fighter pilots."

"Oh," he said. "Why not?"

"Because I don't."

"Are you engaged or something?"

"That's a personal matter."

"You haven't got a ring," Tom said.

"Aren't you being a bit cheeky?"

"I'm sorry. I suppose I am. Sorry." He dug into his pocket. "Here's your compact."

She took it and looked at the inscription. "Thanks. My father gave it to me. I'm glad it isn't lost. It was stupid of me to drop it. There was a lot of rough air on the way and it must have jumped out of my pocket."

"Lucky it didn't come open."

"Yes," she said. "Actually, that happened to someone I know."

"Golly, did it?"

"It made an awful mess."

A pause.

"Your friend Mavis called you Liz," he said.

"I know. Nearly everyone does, but in fact I prefer my full name."

"Elizabeth."

"Yes."

"I saw your compact had a Tiger Moth engraved on it."

"Yes." She paused and tapped the tips of her fingers together. "Look, you ought to have some lunch before you go back. You could come over to our mess. It isn't too bad."

⌒

AFTER LUNCH ELIZABETH Bowman watched the Spitfire fly away into the distance and then walked back to the flight office. The duty officer was writing on the air crew blackboard. She said, "Give me something to do, Geoff."

He turned around. "Oh, Liz," he said. "Are you free? Good. There's an Anson to go to Ringway. They're in a terrible flap about it. Can you do it? They want it this afternoon."

"Jolly good. I'll get my kit."

⌒

"IT'S NOT JUST that she's a woman," Tom said to Colin Frampton. "She's such a little one, too. Delicate. Fancy her bringing my new Spit! I can't get over it."

"Crumpet," Colin said. "Nothing like it."

"Attaboy," Nobby Clark said. "Go get her, boy."

"I'm trying, dammit," Tom said. "I'm bloody well trying."

⌒

IN THE PROSPECT of Whitby, a soldier with a New Zealand flash on his shoulder was playing "Twelfth Street Rag." Tom sat at a table beside the dance floor. Opposite him sat Elizabeth Bowman. The pub was crowded with people in uniform.

"It's because you think we're all going to get killed," Tom said.

"Yes," she said. "That's pretty obvious, isn't it? I'm sorry."

"In a war, anyone can get killed. You could get killed yourself. You're flying, too."

"I know that."

"So, in the meantime—"

"That's a feeble argument."

"In the meantime, life has to be lived." He dipped his finger in his beer and drew a circle on the table. "Life is this moment, here and now. That's all it is. It's a whole lot of little moments like this. This empty bar, that New Zealander tinkling on the piano, us sitting here talking. Look out there." He pointed toward the river. A tug was passing, towing a lighter stacked high with timber. "Look at that. London all around us, and everybody getting on with it. Life is happening now. We shouldn't miss it."

She looked at him sitting there at the bar with his lips pushed forward. "Tom," she said, "stop it. I don't feel the least bit sorry for you, I'm not going out with you, and that's that."

"But you are here, after all's said and done, aren't you? And so am I."

"Well, yes, but—"

"There you are, then."

"Only because you tricked Mavis into saying we were coming up tonight."

"But you don't mind my being here, do you?"

She laughed. "Tom, you're so bloody persistent!" She looked across the bar at the pianist. "Can you dance?"

"It depends what it is," Tom said. "I never had much practice."

"For this, all you need is a kind of shuffle."

"I expect that'll be all right."

"Come on, then."

They went across to the tiny dance floor. The New Zealander

grinned at them through the smoke of his cigarette and began playing "Moonglow."

"I used to practice dancing with my brother," Tom said. "We had
one of those books with black footmarks in it."

"Did you? Which of you led?"

"We took it in turns."

"Well, I think you'd better be the man today, if it's all the same to
you."

"All right."

They began to dance.

"Besides," Elizabeth said, "Mavis will be here in ten minutes, and
we're going out to dinner with her parents."

"I know."

"And then we're getting the ten-thirty back to the aerodrome."

"There's probably another train."

"I'm not leaving Mavis to go home on her own."

"I could come back on the train with you both."

"No, you couldn't."

" ' 'Tis better to have loved and lost,' " Tom said, " 'than never to
have loved at all.' "

"Really, Tom," she said. She let go of him and stood still. "That's
a dreadfully corny line."

"Sorry," he said. "I suppose it is. It was just something my brother
said once. It's Tennyson, you know. He's interested in that sort of
thing, poetry and whatnot. He's a poet. Well, not a poet yet, but I
think one day he'd like to be. We're identical twins, you see. He likes
playing about with words."

She took out a handkerchief and blew her nose. "This isn't at all
fair," she said.

He took hold of her hand. "I don't know why I'm saying these
silly things. Just nerves, I suppose. Shall we go on dancing?"

"Yes," she said. "You've got seven minutes left." They began to
dance again, and after a minute she said, "And another thing—how
did you get to be such a good dancer if you only practiced with your
brother?"

"We've got a natural talent for it, I suppose. But so have you."

Over Tom's shoulder Elizabeth saw that Mavis was watching them from the edge of the dance floor.

"I'm sorry, Tom," she said. "Mavis is here. I've got to go."

"I'll see you again soon, though," Tom said.

"Honestly, Tom, I'd rather you didn't," she said.

⌒

THE SIZE OF the parental mutiny made Masterman thoughtful. Looking at the disparate group of children remaining, he fondled his chin and said, "Given the pusillanimous response of most of our pupils' families, it's hard to see why all the little poppets weren't re-claimed. I suppose it's conceivable that the parents of this motley crew, their attention distracted by the prospect of immense war prof-its, have simply forgotten they possess them."

"Twelve children isn't enough to make a viable school, let alone a pilgrimage," William said.

"On the contrary; it's a perfect number. I've always been interested in twelve. The country would have benefited greatly from adopt-ing the duodecimal system. It permits such a convenient variety of mathematical permutations."

William had often noticed that disagreement energized Master-man.

"However," Masterman went on, "given the size of the insurrec-tion, there will be severe reductions in staff."

William felt a momentary sense of relief, then realized that he didn't want to leave, at least not yet. Absurd though it might be, the adventure ought to be followed to a conclusion. Besides, Irma had, only the other day, presented him with what appeared to be a framed antimacassar upon which she had embroidered the words "Prudence is a rich, ugly old maid courted by incapacity."

"Reluctantly," Masterman said, "I think it has to be the end of the line for Mr. Montmorency, Miss Linnet, and Bob D'Arcy. Assuming you don't want to leave yourself, of course."

"No, I don't," William said, thus easily casting the die.

"But we can't do without Matron, and, of course, Irma. Will your lovely wife wish to come? A walk of a hundred and thirty miles is an ideal way for a pregnant person to keep herself in trim."

"I'll have to ask her. She's still working, so she won't be able to be with us all the time. She'll visit when she can, I expect."

"Good. The presence of a doctor could be useful. That will, I think, make a party of seventeen. Five adults and twelve children. Plus, I think, a couple of the donkeys, which can take it in turns to pull a cart with all the tents and whatnot. Not a multitude, but a respectable convoy. I shall also take my three-liter Sunbeam."

"Oh, you're going to drive, are you?"

"Certainly not. I'll walk every step of the way. But the motor will be useful for carrying stores and as an ambulance in case of emergencies. Polly can go in the car if she wishes, and Matron can drive it. That will please her. Didn't she once say she had driven at Brooklands?"

"I suppose it's possible," William said. "Anything's possible."

LATER THAT EVENING Masterman stopped massaging Irma's foot and said, "Another idea has come to me." Irma looked at him expectantly from the other end of the bath.

"Accommodation during the pilgrimage has been much on my mind. But now I realize that we can fit bunks into the old gypsy caravan, which can be drawn by—"

"Samson!"

"Of course, my dear. Two souls and but a single thought."

"The caravan!" Irma clapped her hands, spilling water over the rim of the bath. She slid down until only her face and knees projected above the water. "The romance of the road! At one with wind and the weather! Samson is so brawny, isn't he? A proper stallion. Such huge feet. So enormous in every part, Masterman."

"He is indeed," Masterman said. He looked down at himself with satisfaction. "We shall light a beacon for humanity. We shall show the way, and where we lead, the world will follow." He paused and looked thoughtful. "There is the question of what to do with the spare donkeys, of course. We don't want to upset anyone. I'll get William to arrange something. And I shall ask him to institute a program of handicraft training based on the refurbishment of the caravan."

⌐⌐

THE NUMBER RANG for a long time, and when it was answered the girl said, "I'm sorry, she's on duty at present, so she can't speak to you."

Tom kicked at the wall of the telephone box. "Can you tell her I called, please?"

"Yes, sir, I'll tell her. I told her last time, but she's very busy these days, you know."

"Do you know when she'll be free?"

"I'm sorry, sir, I don't know."

"Oh, very well. Thanks anyway."

"Thank you, sir. Good-bye."

⌐⌐

"I JUST WANTED you to clarify the exact purpose of our trip," William said. "So I can answer when people ask me."

"Purpose?" Masterman was elaborately baffled. "It's not purpose that matters, it's possibility."

"Yes," William said, "all right, then. What sort of possibilities are you talking about?"

"Dear boy," Masterman said, taking William's elbow, "I'm sure we agree about the nature of ordinary life. How do you choose what to do next?"

"Well, I'm not sure I consciously choose all the time. There's always something that needs doing, isn't there?"

Masterman beamed and capered a little on his small feet. "You don't choose at all," he cried. "You're completely at the mercy of chance!"

"Well, I suppose I choose in a general kind of way—"

"Aha!" Masterman pointed his index finger at William like a gun. "But is that enough?"

"Of course it isn't, but that's just how things are. Lots of things in life aren't quite as good as one could imagine—"

"So why not break free from convention? Why accept limitation? Why accept routine? Possibility is a doorway to a new world. It may be better or it may be worse. But one thing's for certain, there's nothing new in sticking to the same old routine, is there? If you want fulfillment in this life, you've got to break free. Roll the dice, William, roll the dice."

"Yes," William said, "I'll have to think about that."

⟨ornament⟩

"OH, HELLO," MAVIS said, looking up from her desk. "It's Tom, isn't it?"

"That's right," Tom said. "Tom Anderson. I just wondered if you knew—"

"I'm sorry," Mavis said, "she's been transferred to Aberdeen."

"Aberdeen?"

"Yes. There's a lot of ferry work needed in Scotland at the moment."

"She didn't say anything about it."

"Oh, didn't she?"

"Well, I mean I haven't seen her, but I thought she might have . . . well, said something. Left a message or something."

"I'm afraid not."

"You haven't got a number for her in Scotland, have you?"

"I'm sorry, no."

"Oh, all right, then." He turned away and then back again. "If you should speak to her, you could just say—"

"I'll tell her you've been in. That's if I see her, of course."

"Thanks." He stood looking down at the desk and then looked up at her. "Well, good-bye then."

"I'm sorry," she said.

⟨ornament⟩

WHEN TOM HAD left the office, Mavis got up and went into the crew room. "He's just been in," she said to Elizabeth. "Did you hear him? I was afraid you might walk out in the middle of the conversation."

Elizabeth stood up quickly. "What did he say?"

"He wanted to see you. I said you'd been transferred to Aberdeen."

"Oh God," Elizabeth said.

"Is that all right?"

"Of course it is, Mavis. Oh gosh, I'm sorry to make you do that."

"It's all right. I don't mind."

"I shouldn't have done it, I suppose."

"Don't worry. It'll be all right."

"Let's hope he doesn't fly up to Scotland looking for me."

July

ILLIAM, POLLY, Matron, Irma, and Masterman stood in a line and looked at the map pinned to the wall. Colored paper flags had been inserted at intervals along the line of the ancient road. Masterman turned to face them. "I've been engaged in intensive research," he said. "The Pilgrim's Way follows the North Downs from Winchester to Canterbury, but the exact route is not always clear." He waved a book. "Belloc's *The Old Road* is the definitive guide."

"Before you get going," William said, "I don't understand why we're following the path of Christian pilgrims when none of us are believers."

"Ah," Masterman said. He put on his glasses and flicked through the book in his hands. "Belloc deals with precisely that point."

"Wasn't he an ardent Catholic?"

As he turned the pages Masterman said, "Beneath his superficial religiosity lies a deeper wisdom, as I'm sure you realize. He knows that an ancient road puts us in touch with history and the deepest roots of feeling. Ah, here we are."

He held the book up with his left hand and raised his right index finger.

" 'By the recovery of the past, stuff and being are added to us; our lives which, lived in the present only, are a film or surface, take on body—are lifted into one dimension more. The soul is fed. Reverence and knowledge and security and the love of a good land—all these are increased or given by the pursuit of this kind of learning.' "

"Goodness," Polly said. "Whatever does he mean by 'stuff and being'?"

"You must recognize that he's a master of English prose, Polly. He's employing a heightened style that's entirely appropriate to his subject. It's absolutely clear." Masterman shuffled his feet. " 'By the recovery of the past, stuff and being are added to us.' Oh yes, I think that's quite clear. He means that our journey will result in spiritual growth and all that sort of thing."

"Perhaps I can borrow that book," Polly said.

"Of course, dear girl," Masterman said, putting it on the table and placing one hand upon it. "But first we must deal with the practicalities. We'll begin our journey, of course, at Winchester Cathedral."

William was about to say more, but Masterman did not look as though he would be interrupted again.

"Winchester first," he said, "and then Martyr Worthy, Itchen Abbas, Itchen Stoke, New Alresford, and Chawton, once the home of our beloved Jane Austen. St. Martha's Hill, a delightful viewpoint. The covertly subterranean river Mole. Box Hill, another celebrated point of vantage. The flags on my map indicate some of the most enchanting places in southern England."

Masterman sat down at the table. "Gather round," he said. "I've decided that the routine work, cooking and that sort of thing, will be shared by everyone, including the children, of course. Matron will keep an eye on health and welfare, referring to Polly if necessary. William will organize appropriate learning activities. Irma will be Samson's driver, since she has an instinctual bond with the animal kingdom."

William asked, "What will you be doing?"

"As principal, I shall be in overall command. My role is that of navigator and guide. I shall negotiate with officials and resolve difficulties. My main aim will be the identification of a new site for Liberty Hall, of course."

"The worst thing would be to lose somebody," Polly said. "One of the children, I mean."

"An excellent point. I'm sure you're willing to undertake the vital task of counting heads, Polly."

⌐⌐

AFTERWARD, POLLY WAS irritable. "How did I get stuck with that counting heads business? I'll be forever totting up the little darlings."

"Because, dearest Polly, we rattled him a little bit, and he saw an opportunity to pay us back." William kissed the top of her head.

"You're patronizing me," Polly said. "You'd better watch out."

"I don't think a kiss can be patronizing."

"Well, you're quite wrong there."

"Polly, Polly, Polly," William said, kissing her again.

"Humph. You can't get round me that easily. Besides, why did he have to say the river Mole was 'covertly subterranean'?"

"It goes underground sometimes."

"I know that, you idiot. But why didn't he just say it like that?"

"Because it doesn't sound so flashy."

"There you are, then."

William looked at her. "You're right, of course. The Boy Scout notion is all very well, but the whole thing is beginning to look a bit daft, even for Masterman."

"Ouch," Polly said.

"What?"

"The baby kicked."

⌐⌐

THE ORCHARD AT Liberty Hall became a tented encampment centered on the gypsy caravan. A working party consisting of Belinda Boon, Amy Pluck, and the O'Leary boys groomed the two donkeys and cleaned their cracked and moldy harness.

A pair of wooden panels were painted by Timothy Needham in the familiar security of the art room and attached to the sides of the caravan; they proclaimed THE LIBERTY HALL CHILDREN'S PILGRIMAGE, and, in smaller letters, *We welcome your support.* Additional bunks were added to the interior. "They look more like shelves," Ian Lambert said. "I'll have that top one."

"Very nice, but where's the lavatory?" Matron asked, looking around. "And how are we going to wash?"

The workers looked at one another. "We're getting to that," Todger said, and a plan for a washroom and toilet compartment was soon devised.

~

PLATO AND HEGEL were selected for the journey. Plato's age and steadiness, it was felt, would complement Hegel's energy and moderate his occasional combativeness.

"I'm terribly busy," Masterman said, lying back in his chair and blowing cigar smoke at the ceiling. "Perhaps you can negotiate with the abattoir about the other donkeys."

"Oh, very well," William said. He went to the abattoir and a deal was agreed, William insisting that the surplus donkeys must be collected in a plain van.

When William came back, Polly looked up from her book and said, "Have you read this? Alfred Watkins? *The Old Straight Track.* Ley lines and whatnot."

"No, I haven't," William said.

"It's probably quite silly," Polly said. "But he's such a nice old buffer that you end up believing it all. Everything's a matter of alignment, apparently."

"I haven't read it," William said. "And besides, I've had a difficult afternoon."

"Have you? Oh, the donkeys, of course. You must feel like a murderer."

"Well, no, I don't, actually," William said.

"I didn't mean you *were* a murderer."

"It had to be done, I suppose. Somehow or other, I drew the short straw."

"Actually, Masterman presented it to you."

"Yes, I suppose you're right. How does he get away with it?"

"He has no sense of shame."

"It's getting beyond a joke, you know."

"You're losing faith, aren't you?"

"Oh God, Polly, I don't know. But I'm beginning to wonder how much dice rolling one can actually stand."

⌒

"THIS IS MY brother, William," Tom said to Nobby Clark. William had been smuggled into the airfield in the back of Colin's car, under a blanket.

"Hello, William," Nobby Clark said. "You're the poet, I hear. Everyone calls me Nobby."

William made a face at his brother. "I wish you wouldn't tell people about the poetry."

"Sorry," Tom said, grinning.

There were deck chairs and camp beds on the grass, and young men reading or dozing in the morning sun.

"Jerry's not here yet. Too early," Tom said.

"Does he always come at the same time?"

"Usually. Depends on the weather."

It was a large grass airfield, brushed by a steady wind and scented with clover. One of the pilots, a boy who looked about seventeen, was smoking a pipe and scratching the ears of a black Labrador. Others were reading. Nearby was a wooden shack with a siren on the roof. Parachutes, flying suits, and leather helmets lay here and there on the grass. Aircraftsmen dozed in the shade under the wings of the parked aircraft. An aeroplane flew overhead and William looked up, but nobody else moved. William tapped Tom on the shoulder and pointed at the sky. "What about that?"

"It's one of ours."

"How do you know?"

"It's a Wellington. Nice and smooth. The Jerries don't bother to synchronize their engines, so they have an uneven beat. If you hear a bomber coming and the engines are synchronized, it's one of ours. If not, get under the table."

William lay back in the deck chair and listened to the young men talking. After a while he said to Tom, "I came to see you because the school's off on a bit of a jaunt in a few days, and I don't know where I'll be for a while."

"All right," Tom said. "Where are you going?"

"I'm not too sure. Towards Canterbury. We're moving the school. We're taking some children and a caravan on a little trip."

"Not far from here, then."

"No. Not far."

"I'll keep an eye out for you." Tom was fidgety. He stood up and said, "Come and look at my Spitfire. It's a new one."

They walked across the grass. William said, "What happened to the old one?"

"Oh, nothing much. I broke it, so they got me another one."

"You crashed it, did you?"

"Well, yes. More or less."

"You haven't told anyone about it. Anyone in the family, I mean."

"No. No point in worrying people, is there?"

"But you could have told me, at least."

"Sorry. Didn't seem much point."

They looked at the Spitfire. "Very nice," William said. "It's quite big, isn't it? Bigger than they look from the ground, anyway. It looks frightfully powerful."

Tom laughed. "Oh, William," he said. "My dear brother."

William was offended. "I can't help not knowing about aeroplanes." He reached out and put his hand on the wing. The aluminum was warm under his fingers.

"A girl delivered it," Tom said.

"What do you mean?"

"A girl delivered my Spitfire. A lady pilot."

"I didn't know there were any."

"Of course there are. Lots of them. They're ferry pilots. They fly aircraft all over the place. Her name's Elizabeth."

"What's she like?"

"She's lovely."

"I had a feeling you were going to say that. Do you mean—"

"No," Tom said. "Unfortunately not. She doesn't like fighter pilots."

"So you asked her, then."

"Yes. But no go. Bit of a bugger, really."

"Oh well. There are lots of women in the world."

"I know that, you clown. This one is a bit special, that's all."

"That's a pity, then."

"Yes."

○N THE DAY of their departure, the orchard was busy from dawn. The tents were folded, the groundsheets rolled up, the children's kitbags loaded into the caravan. Matron strapped a crate containing six chickens to the roof of the Sunbeam. "One can't do without fresh eggs," she said.

By noon the packing was complete. Masterman stood on the driving platform of the caravan, called everyone together, and spoke loudly, dealing the caravan a series of smart blows with his whip: "*Here* is our new home, *here* are our worldly goods, *here* is our society! We are now without fixed abode. We have become people of the road, wanderers, travelers, tramps, didicoys. Together we shall walk in sunshine and rain, together we shall sleep under the moon and stars."

Matron looked doubtful, but Masterman was not deterred. His whip waved in a bold arc across the blue sky.

"We may experience hardship, accident, or privation, yet we will gain strength from knowing that we are a company of friends, a band of brothers."

Samson shook his head, his harness jingled, and Masterman's words floated upward into the warm air.

"We shall throw off the shackles of convention, relinquish privacy, share possessions, abandon outdated scruples." He paused and lowered his voice. "We shall draw strength from traveling an age-old track. Like the pilgrims of ancient times, we seek renewal, a new beginning, new hope, and a new home."

There was a scatter of applause. Masterman stepped down from the caravan, climbed on Plato's back, and kicked at his flanks. Plato turned his head, looked at his rider, and took a few steps. Polly got into the front of the Sunbeam and the O'Leary brothers climbed into the back. Matron revved the car's engine, setting the chickens fluttering, and the Sunbeam accelerated down the drive in a spray of gravel. Irma shook the reins, and Samson leaned into his harness. William tugged at Hegel's leading rein. In the meadow the tank crews stopped work and waved. The children waved back and cheered.

"Poor dears," the company sergeant said. "It don't seem right, really, sending them away like that." He turned to the squad of soldiers waiting with ladders and paintbrushes. "All right, you lot. Let's get cracking." He took out his wire cutters, snipped through the fence, and the squad marched down the grassy slope toward Liberty Hall.

⌒⌐

Tom said, "Goodness, is that really you? Your office told me you'd gone up north. I phoned the ATA in Aberdeen a couple of times, and they said you weren't there, either. But then I thought I'd try your old office one more time."

The wires hummed.

"No, I wasn't up north, actually," Elizabeth said. "The office must have got it wrong."

"You were down here all along."

"Yes, I was. Sorry."

Tom looked down at his right hand. He had been helping Alan to fit a new seal to the starboard undercarriage leg and there was oil under his fingernails.

"Oh, all right," he said. "I just thought it would be nice to see you again if you were down this way, but obviously if you're too busy . . ."

"Tom, now look, I did say—"

"I know you did."

With his oily finger Tom drew a circle on the window of the telephone box. After a moment he drew another, intersecting the first.

"It's not personal," Elizabeth said. "Really it isn't."

"I never met a woman pilot before, you know."

"Yes. You said that before."

"Flying is all I know about, really," Tom said. "I used to work for a little company that made fuel tanks and pumps, stuff like that. Up in the Cotswolds, it was. I joined them on a training scheme when I was eighteen, and I learned to fly when I was still working for them. Then I joined the RAF last year. I quite liked the company I worked for. It was only a small place. The trainees went round all the departments, one after another. I did all sorts of things—sweeping the floor at first, of course, but later I worked in the machine shop, inspection, the drawing office. All sorts of things. I even did some bits of design and stressing. Most of them were really nice chaps. I got to know them all. It wasn't a large place. I'd quite like to stay in the aeroplane business after the war."

There was a considerable pause, then Elizabeth said, "That company you worked for, was it Olympic Aero?"

"Yes. How did you know that?"

She laughed. "There can't be many companies in the Cotswolds that make aircraft fuel systems."

"Oh, of course. You know about that sort of thing. I was forgetting."

"Yes."

"When I was there I learned to fly in a Tiger. On that government scheme."

"Tiger Moths were the first aircraft we flew on Jerry trips."

"What did you learn on?"

"A Magister."

"Oh, that's very smart, isn't it?"

"Yes. I liked it. It was easy to fly. They say the Tiger's more difficult, don't they? It floats when you're landing and it needs a firm boot on the rudder."

"Yes."

"It belonged to a friend of my father's."

"What, you mean you knew someone who had a Magister of his own?"

"Yes. We lived on a big estate. There was a little hangar, and a grass runway."

"Oh."

Again the humming of the wires, then Tom said, "Where was the estate?"

"It's in Hertfordshire."

"That's lovely countryside, isn't it?"

"Yes," she said. "It's a big estate. It's very beautiful, very grand. It wasn't ours, of course. My father worked there, and our house went with the job."

"I was brought up in the town. In London, in fact. I don't know anything about the countryside at all."

"They took our Maggie away when the war came."

"Oh, that's horrid. But I suppose they wanted it for teaching people like me."

"Yes."

"So lots of people have learned to fly it."

"I suppose they have." She paused. "Look, Tom . . ."

"What?"

"I've got to go now. I've got a delivery to do."

"Oh, all right."

"But I suppose we could . . ."

"What?"

"Well . . . meet somewhere. If you really wanted to."

"You know I do. Tell me where."

"But I never know where I'm going to be, or whether I'll have any time of my own."

"Neither do I."

They both laughed. "Bloody war," Elizabeth said.

"All right," Tom said, "I tell you what—you phone me and tell me when you're free, and I'll tell you when I'm free. Eventually we're bound to coincide."

"All right. I've got to go now. But I'll phone you. I really will."

"And I'll phone you, too."

He put the phone down. He must tell someone. Where was Nobby?

In WINCHESTER CATHEDRAL William said to Polly, "I know Masterman says we ought to throw off the shackles of convention, but I'm not all that keen. I've brought my pajamas."

"It all sounds pretty half-baked to me," Polly said, "but you never know, I suppose."

Masterman came across and said to William, "The cathedrals are the bookends of our journey. They give it a sense of weight and purpose. Winchester to Canterbury! A proper odyssey!"

"I thought you said we didn't need a sense of purpose."

"*I* don't, dear boy, but others may." He looked up and down the enormous church and clapped his hands and called out, "Gather round, all you Liberty Hall pilgrims!"

The children drifted toward him, whispering to one another and listening to the multitude of echoes that came rustling from the shadows.

"What we have here," Masterman said, "is the deliberate realization of a fiction. Take a look around you. Adopt a critical frame of mind. What do you see?"

The children obediently looked about them. "It's big," Susan Portman said. "It's very big."

"It's cold, I'll tell you that," Arthur Beckingsale said in his ponderous way.

"Never mind about the cold," Masterman said. "But it's huge, all right. Why is it so big?"

"Because it's a cathedral," Lucy Standish said. "I've seen lots of them. They're all big."

"Yes, Lucy," Masterman said, his brow wrinkling a little. "Let's put it another way. What does it make you feel?"

Susan put up her hand. "It makes us feel sort of small, doesn't it? It makes us feel kind of tiny and unimportant."

"Well done, Susan!" Masterman's smile showed all his teeth. "Yes indeed! It makes us feel sort of small. Exactly!"

"And right cold as well," Arthur Beckingsale said.

Masterman considered. "Well, I suppose you do have a point, Arthur. Now, why does someone want us to feel small and cold?"

There was a silence of the murmuring, drafty kind that cathedrals induce. Then Timothy Needham had a moment of true, if tentative, inspiration. He said in his small voice, "So we'll do what we're told?"

Masterman clapped his hands again and the echoes clattered about the building. His joy was so intense that he appeared to rise an inch or two above the ancient flagstones. "Wonderful!" he cried. "Wonderful! They built it big so we'll do what we're told!"

He hopped from one foot to the other while the children watched with interest. "All right," he said, steadying himself for the next intellectual leap, "we've got a hypothesis. It's all about power. Somebody built this place to keep us in order. Who was it?"

Susan Portman said, "God, of course." She folded her arms.

"Ah," Masterman said, "so God built it, did he, Susan?"

"Yes," she said, pursing her lips.

"It wasn't King Alfred," Masterman said, "or William the Conqueror, or Bishop William of Wykeham, or William Wynford or William Lyngwode or any of the other hundreds of gentlemen clerics, woodcarvers, stonemasons, tilers, roofers, carpenters, glassmakers, and common laborers who had a hand in it. None of them. It was God."

Susan was aggrieved. "That's not fair, Masterman," she said. "You know that isn't what I meant. I meant it was built *for* God. To show their faith."

Masterman easily evaded her point. "That's what we're supposed to think. Let's introduce some critical observation, some science," he said. "We'll gather evidence." He looked around. "Have a look at the plaques and memorials. Each of you write down the name on one of them. Then bring your notes back here. All right?"

Considering that they belonged to a free school, William thought, it was curious how amenable the children were to an unequivocal order of this kind. They wandered away and started squabbling over the brass plaques and black marble slabs.

"My pedagogic aim is the abolition of irrational belief," Masterman said.

"You've got a bit of a job on, then," William said, but Masterman wasn't listening. His attention had been caught by a monument to St. Swithin. "It's one of those things you always wonder," he said, looking at it with his head to one side. "Could I have been a saint if

I'd been born at the right moment? Do I possess the character, the discipline, the raw courage?"

When the children returned Masterman collected some of their notes and began to read them aloud. "Sir John Steven Cownas, Quarter Master General to the Forces. Lieutenant Colonel Charles Berkeley Pigott. William Hull Newbolt Clerk DD, Rector of Minstead, Vicar of Collingbourne Kingston and twenty-nine years Minor Canon of the Cathedral."

Masterman looked at the children. "What's all this? Why is this cathedral full of dead soldiers and priests? What's it got to do with God?"

William eased backward into the shadow of one of the piers. "I think I've got the drift of it," he whispered to Polly. "Let's go and look round."

"So long as I'm back in time for the next head count."

They sat on the steps in the crypt and looked at the robust Norman stonework. Polly quoted from the guidebook. "A deep-sea diver called William Walker spent five years underwater repairing the foundations and saving the cathedral from collapse."

"Well, there you are," William said. "Good for him."

"And when they cast a nice little bronze in his memory, they modeled it on the wrong chap."

William laughed and put his arm around her. "As usual, the sublime nestles close to the ridiculous," he said.

⌒

ON THAT FIRST warm evening, the travelers pitched camp on a fragment of common land beyond New Alresford. They drew straws for duty cook and William lost. After supper the children went to their tents and bunks. Their chatter died away. William lit a hurricane lamp, and he and Polly lay in their tent, listening to the prodigious grinding of Samson's molars and the jingling of his bridle.

"You'd think he'd need to sleep occasionally," Polly said.

William, writing in his notebook with Masterman's pencil, did not reply.

Polly nudged him. "What's that you're writing?"

"When I went to see Tom the other day," William said, "they were sitting about on the grass, waiting. I listened to them talking and realized there was something strange about it."

"What sort of strange?"

"All that slang, for a start."

"Wilco, chaps," Polly said. "Roger and out. Wizard prang."

"Yes, that's the sort of thing."

"What else?"

"It wasn't just the slang. They talked in a funny way. Quite odd, really. Clipped but somehow rhythmical. A couple of them were chatting about somebody they knew, a pilot called Rankin, and I realized they were talking a kind of ragged verse. So I made a note of some of it. I've been fiddling with it."

"Read it out."

"It really needs three different voices."

"Doesn't matter. Read it out."

"All right. I've topped and tailed it a bit." He read her the fragment:

> A deck chair on the yellow grass, a blue
> Enormous sky, the murmur of enclovered bees,
> And one there half asleep, who, idly in
> The morning's heat, asks after Rankin.
> —*Remember him? The chap who always flew*
> *With one wing low? He was transferred, I think.*
> —Oh yes, I know. How long ago was that?
> —*A month, six weeks.* —Cack-handed Rankin! Yes!
> I know his wife. She's in the family way.
> —*He's bought it in a Beau.* —Oh dear. Poor chap.
> —*Poor wife. Was he from Suffolk? Somewhere flat.*
> *Quite tall, and wavy hair. Obliging type.*
> —Somehow I knew you'd say he'd got the chop.
> —*It's pukka gen.* —I know, I know . . . He sucked
> His pipe. The crouching aeroplanes await.

"There you are," William said. "People talking in natural iambics. It needs a bit more work, of course."

"It's odd, isn't it? What are you going to call it?"

" 'Cack-handed Rankin,' I thought. It's a peculiar kind of elegy, I suppose."

"I like it."

"Good."

"You're right, it would be nice to hear it performed with different voices for each bit."

"Yes."

"Like a tiny play. Could you make it any longer?"

"I don't know. I don't think so. It was just a thing I happened to hear."

William turned off the lamp and lay listening for a while to Samson's rhythmical crunching.

"I managed to write it down without them noticing," William said, but there was no reply except the small, regular sound of his wife's breathing. He placed one hand carefully on her abdomen. There was detectable movement.

Polly stirred. "Just checking, are you?"

"Just checking."

"I COULD MANAGE next Sunday, if you could, too," Elizabeth Bowman said. "I'll be in London. We could meet somewhere halfway, perhaps."

"Yes, I'm due for a day off." Tom thought for a moment. "What about the seaside? Somewhere like Margate."

"That would be good."

THE SUN SHONE and Elizabeth's train lingered through the East End. At Gravesend it stopped for twenty minutes for no reason that she could see. She opened the window and looked up and down the platform, but there was nobody in sight. Eventually a whistle blew, there was a jerk, and the train started again. As it rattled across the Medway, she looked at her reflection in the window and thought how foolish she was to be doing this, and how impossible it had been to deny. The river was full of gray-painted ships. She took off her hat, fanned her face, and said to the woman sitting opposite, "Golly, it's so hot, isn't it?"

"Wonderful, I call it," the woman said. "Long may it last. Winter will come, soon enough."

At Margate Tom was pacing up and down the platform. "I'm sorry I'm late," she said. "The train stopped for ages on the way. I don't know why."

"That doesn't matter at all," he said. "I say, you do look nice."

"Thanks," she said. "It's so hot, I didn't bother with a coat."

A breeze was blowing in from the sea. Walking a yard apart, they strolled around the harbor. Angular obstructions and coils of barbed wire had been planted in the shallows, but inshore the beaches were clear. They walked across the sand and reached an ice-cream seller who put his hand on Tom's arm and said, "For a gentleman of the Royal Air Force, sir, and his young lady, we offer a special price."

Tom laughed and looked at Elizabeth. "Would you like one?"

"Oh yes," she said. "I would, actually."

They sat on a bench and licked their ice creams while the seagulls cruised above the harbor wall.

"I used to watch the gulls for hours when I was young," Tom said. "In stormy weather they came into London and soared around the gardens at the back of our house. I sat at the window and wondered how they kept going without flapping, and how they never collided in midair."

"Effortless," Elizabeth said, watching the gulls. "But their beaks are vicious."

"I haven't planned anything," Tom said. "I thought we could just explore a bit and have a talk. I'll have to go back quite early, I'm afraid. I'm on standby first thing tomorrow."

"We could have some lunch as well, couldn't we?"

"Oh yes, of course."

"Fish and chips is what everyone has at the seaside, isn't it?"

"I did wonder if you'd prefer a proper lunch."

"Fish and chips is quite all right. It's too hot to go into a restaurant, anyway. I'd rather be outside, wouldn't you?"

"Oh yes," he said. "Much." He leaned back. "It's so nice to have a day off."

They looked out to sea. After a while Elizabeth said, "I was in London for my father's birthday. He's at the Ministry of Food, working on all sorts of plans."

"Does he like that sort of thing? Farming and all that?"

"I suppose he does. He's always liked organizing things. That's what he enjoys best. He thinks he ought to do something useful for the war effort. He's good at it."

"You didn't want to be a farmer, then."

"Oh, I don't know about that. I might be, one day. Or a farmer's wife, I suppose. I don't know whether I'll want to go on flying after the war. Maybe a little, just for fun."

"I'd like to do some long flights one day. To India, say, or Australia."

"Like Amy Johnson."

"Yes. You know about her, of course."

"Oh yes. I was thirteen when she flew to Australia. That's what made me want to fly in the first place. I used to read about her under the bedclothes. I've read everything I could find about flying."

"Have you read *Wind, Sand and Stars?*"

"Oh yes. And *Southern Mail* and *Night Flight.* Saint-Exupéry is another of my heroes."

"*Wind, Sand and Stars* is a bit of a muddle, isn't it? But it's got those wonderful bits about the Andes, the high crags with scarves of snow that flutter in the wind as Mermoz tries to find his way through."

"And that lovely description of how an aeroplane's made—do you remember?"

"Doesn't he compare it with a poem?"

"Yes, he does." She laughed. "Not quite the English way, is it? He says an engineer is like a sculptor, freeing an image that's asleep in a block of marble."

"Yes," Tom said. "I'd forgotten that. So he does." He thought for a moment. "But people do get emotional about flying, even in England, don't they? We just don't say much about it."

"Oh yes, I know. I get emotional myself." She looked up at the sky. "Especially in lovely weather like this."

"*Night Flight* is his best, though."

"Well, maybe. But it's frightening in lots of ways." She put her hands to her face and said, " 'Already, beneath him, the shadowed hills had dug their furrows in the golden evening and the plains grown luminous with long-enduring light.' " She looked at him and smiled. "That's the first sentence of *Night Flight*."

"Goodness! Do you know it all by heart?"

"Only that bit. I've read it so many times before falling asleep. There's another lovely bit at dusk, when lights are beginning to flicker on the ground below and Fabien flashes his navigation lights as if to reply to them." She put her hands in her lap and looked at them. "It's a beautiful book, but it's terrifying as well."

"You mean when Fabien is lost in the mountains."

"Yes." She paused. "But also that man Rivière, and all his talk about duty."

They were both silent. Eventually she said, "It's a funny thing about flying, you know. It's so free and so confined at the same time."

"Yes," Tom said. "It certainly is." He stood up. "Shall we see if we can find a fish-and-chip shop?"

"Yes," she said, "let's do that." She shaded her eyes. "It's a pity the tide's out. It would be nice to go paddling."

When he saw that her arms had begun to redden in the sun, Tom bought her a paper parasol. As the shadows lengthened they returned to the railway station.

"Thanks for the brolly," she said, twirling it. "It's been a lovely day."

"I hope I'll see you again soon," he said.

"We'll keep phoning," she said. "You never know, do you?"

She turned away from him and stepped into the train. He closed the door and she let the window down. "I've just remembered another thing Saint-Exupéry says."

"What's that?"

"He says that altitude, as every pilot knows, is our particular store of wealth. He says that somewhere in *Night Flight*."

Tom smiled at her. "Let's hope we both stay rich, then."

"Yes," she said, holding out her hand.

Tom took it. "We'll do this again soon," he said.

"Yes," she said. "Yes, we will."

The guard blew his whistle and a crowd of pigeons fluttered into the station roof. As the train began to move, he walked beside it for a few paces. "Good-bye, then," he said. "Thanks for a lovely time."

"Good-bye," she said.

⁓

On yet another hot day, having crossed the river Wey, the gypsy caravan, the Sunbeam, and the donkeys were dispatched along the lower, easier road while Masterman led what he called a "scouting party" along the sandy track that led up through the Chantries woods to the hill and church of St. Martha's. The scouts sat down to eat their egg sandwiches in a sloping meadow on the high scarp of the North Downs.

"Ah, the Home Counties," Masterman said, shading his eyes and gazing out across the valleys, woods, and villages. "How admirably resilient is the backbone of England!"

"I don't see how you can say that," William said. "Nobody down there would agree with a single one of your ideas."

"Nevertheless, one has to admire their intransigent spirit and their absolute dedication to self-interest." He lit a cigar and waved it in the air. "I delight in their ferocious grip on what they have. Such determination, such focus, even if utterly wrongheaded, is magnificent."

"To be honest, I can't see the slightest logic in that," William said.

Masterman turned to him and said, " 'I will not reason and compare: My business is to create.' "

William scratched his head. "I know that's what Blake thought," he said, "but I'm not sure it's a practical philosophy for ordinary life."

"If you want your life to be ordinary, so be it. You're only here once, so why not have a nice dull time?" Masterman puffed his cigar triumphantly.

"Yes, I suppose that's quite a good point," William said.

"William, you really must learn to live more dangerously," Masterman said, unfolding his map with a flourish and peering at it. "I must say, it's an awful nuisance, the way they've taken down all the road signs."

There was a tug at William's shirt. He looked down and saw Ian Lambert gazing at him.

"I wondered about being carried for a bit," the boy said.

William laughed and picked him up. "I suppose it depends what you call dangerous," he said to Masterman, but their leader was already striding away down the track. William swung Ian Lambert up on his shoulders. "Hold tight," he said, "we're going to run for a bit."

At regular intervals groups of soldiers and laborers were building fortifications among the trees. An officer with "Canada" on his shoulder leaned against one of the great beeches, carving his initials into the soft gray bark with a bowie knife.

"They're to stop the panzers, if they come," he said in answer to William's question about the pillboxes.

"Do you think they actually will stop them?"

"Oh, sure. Not a doubt of it."

Ian Lambert said, "I want to carve my name, too."

"Well, you can't," William said. "We'll get left behind again."

"I'll do it for you, sonny," the officer said. "What's your name?"

"Ian Lambert."

"Consider it done, young fellow."

"Thanks frightfully," the boy said.

"Suppose the panzers just drove between the pillboxes," William said to the soldier.

He considered the remark for a moment and then grinned. "Well, shit," he said. "That's a thought, ain't it? Let's hope they don't, eh? For your sake and mine."

As he spoke, a formation of aircraft roared overhead, almost drowning his words.

A DAY LATER, toward evening, they came to the river Mole, crossed the stepping-stones, and climbed slowly to the top of Box Hill. When the Sunbeam and the caravan arrived, the pilgrims pitched their tents. Polly lay on the grassy slope, hands under her head, gazing upward.

"All that writing," she said to William. "It ought to mean something."

He looked up at the condensation trails that the afternoon's aerial combats had scrawled across the sky. "High cloud is a warning of bad weather," he said. "Tom told me that." He got to his feet and looked out across the countryside. "This is the highest point for miles, you know."

She rolled over, leaned on one elbow, and said, " 'What country, friends, is this?' "

William bowed and gestured toward Surrey. " 'This is Illyria, lady.' "

Polly looked up at him, shading her eyes. " 'And what shall I do in Illyria? My brother, he is in Elysium. Perchance he is not drowned. What think you, sailors?' "

There was a silence. "Oh God," Polly said, "I'm sorry. Not the cleverest quotation to use, in the circumstances." She got up and took William's hand.

"It's all right," he said. "We walked straight into that one."

"Yes, we did. I'm so sorry."

Masterman came bounding across to them. "Do you know," he said, "the warden tells me there's a chap buried here head down, because he felt at odds with his fellows? Asked for it in his will. What a splendid notion! One has often felt something similar."

After Masterman had trotted away, Polly said, "Sometimes I don't see why you put up with him."

"It's getting near the limit."

They looked out across the countryside.

"I was only showing off with that *Twelfth Night* stuff," Polly said.

"It's all right. It doesn't matter."

"I was in it once, when I was a student."

"Who did you play?"

"Viola, of course. I only know her part."

WILLIAM AND POLLY climbed up the steps into the caravan and sat at the table. "I phoned Tom again," William said. "He's had a letter from Father."

Polly looked at him. "Has he? That's rare, isn't it?"

"Yes. Wishing him well."

"That's good, then."

"Yes . . ."

"Has he ever written to Tom before?"

"No, I don't think so."

"Ah."

"I'm not sure he should have decided to write just now. . . . It looks as though he's . . . I don't know . . . apologizing or something."

"Oh." She thought for a moment. "What about your mother?"

"She won't write."

"Because she isn't thinking about anything except her painting?"

"Well . . . But also . . ."

"What?"

"Oh, I don't know. Something about her acceptance of things. She just lets things happen to her, somehow. It's as if all her emotions are being . . . diverted. Diverted into Stella and her painting. It's almost like absentmindedness. She can't concentrate on anything except her pictures. Sometimes when I say something to her, she looks at me and seems to be thinking, Who is this person? She doesn't get on with Father. They don't talk much. But she wouldn't do anything about it. Neither of them would. They wouldn't break the rules. That's what I think, anyway."

Polly went around the table, stood behind him, and put her arms round his neck. "Oh God," she said. "Bloody families." She rested her chin on the top of his head. "Is Tom all right?"

"He's all right," William said. "He told me that Father says he's sorry."

"Oh dear," Polly said. "That isn't very happy stuff, is it?"

"No, it isn't," William said.

"What's he sorry about, exactly?"

"He says he's let everyone down, apparently."

"Everyone?"

"That's what he says. It does sound . . . well, rather all-inclusive, doesn't it?"

There was a clatter of feet on the steps and Ian Lambert came in, followed by Lucy Standish. They were panting. William looked at their faces and stood up.

"We've found a man in the woods," the boy said. "A man with a gray beard and great big boots."

"He's dead," Lucy said.

"He's lying in the bushes," Ian said. "Lucy says he's dead, but I don't think he is."

"He *is* dead," Lucy said. "He won't wake up. We've tried."

"You'd better show us," William said.

THE PLACE WAS marked by a semicircle of children sitting at an appropriate distance. The man lay on his back in long grass beneath the dipping branch of an oak. He was thin, bearded, a man of middle age. His eyes were closed. Polly knelt beside him, opened his shirt, and put her fingers on his neck. After a moment she looked up. "He's not dead," she said. "He's got a pulse. It's weak, but he's alive." She dipped her head and sniffed at the man's face. "He's not drunk, either."

"He looks exhausted," William said. "He's frightfully thin, isn't he?"

"Lucy," Polly said, "run and get a bottle of water, a cup, and a towel."

When Lucy came back, Masterman was with her. "Well, well," he said. "What have we here, Polly?"

"It's just a man the children found," Polly said. She held the man's head up and wiped his face. "He'll be all right in a little while, I think."

Masterman squatted beside her and looked the man up and down. "Dusty boots," he said. "Worn and cracked. He's come a long way." He stood up, faced William and the children, and said, " 'Can I see another's woe and not be in sorrow too? Can I see another's grief and not seek for kind relief?' "

"This isn't the moment for Blake," William said.

"On the contrary," Masterman said. "Blake reminds us of the need for human sympathy. Chance has placed this man in our path. We shall not pass by on the other side."

"Nobody said we were going to," William said.

"We need some sort of stretcher," Polly said.

"I know how to make one from branches," Arthur Beckingsale said.

"All right," Polly said. "Get cracking, then."

They carried the man to the caravan. Matron emerged and instructed them to lay him down in the shade. After some minutes he opened his eyes, sipped some water, and looked around at the group of children and adults.

"Welcome," Masterman said, crouching before him. "We are the Liberty Hall pilgrims."

The man stared at Masterman and after a few moments said something unintelligible.

"Oh, he's a foreigner," Lucy said.

"Really, Lucy," Matron said, "that's not his fault."

Masterman stood up and called out, "Irma! Irma, we need you!"

Irma came out of one of the tents, stretching and rubbing her eyes. "I've been having an absolutely lovely snooze," she said.

"We've encountered a man in great need," Masterman said. "Evidently he isn't a native of these parts. See if you can talk to him, would you, my dearest?"

The conversation between Irma and the stranger began hesitantly but soon gathered pace. It went on for what seemed a long time. Near the beginning, Irma turned to the watchers and told them that the man was a Pole who had escaped the invasion of his country, and that his name was Janosz Pasenik. At one point in the conversation she reached out and took both his hands. Eventually they stopped talking and the man lay back.

"He's a schoolteacher from a village in Poland," Irma told them. "He escaped when the German soldiers came. He walked over the mountains and all across Europe and eventually got to France and came across in a little boat." She hesitated and then went on. "They killed everyone in his village, including his family. On the way he met some partisans, and some of them were killed, too. He thinks he'll be imprisoned if he's found."

"Janosz Pasenik," Masterman murmured. "A refugee. An alien. A man on the run. That's perfect." He turned to Irma. "Tell him he's safe now. Tell him we'll look after him. He won't be locked up if we have anything to do with it."

Irma looked a little offended. "I've already told him that."

"Good." He nodded and then looked around at the pilgrims. "Isn't it wonderful how destiny has put this man in the way of exactly the right people to give him succor?"

IN NORMANDY a German fighter pilot called Hauptmann Matthias Altenhan sat beside a table lamp in his room. He was writing to his wife, Kristel, as he had done every evening since he arrived in Normandy. He told her about the long sunny days and said he was busy but safe and well. He asked after little Hans and then, tapping his teeth with the cap of his fountain pen, he stared for some minutes at the writing paper. Eventually he folded the sheet and put it with the others; he would write more later. He stood up and walked out of the hut into the darkness. Between slow clouds the stars were bright. There was no moon. Laughter drifted from the officers' mess. He walked around the perimeter track until the laughter faded. The wind was steady and warm from the south and carried the scent of mown hay.

Matthias Altenhan breathed deeply, stretching his chin upward and turning his head to left and right. He raised both arms parallel to the ground, then swept them forward in a controlled movement: He had discovered the mesmeric, easeful properties of slow and deliberate exercise. He stood and stared up at the four bright stars of Cygnus, so simple, so calm, so elegant. He walked back to the hut past the parked 109s, and the bored sentry stared after him, sucking his cupped cigarette into a sharp point of light.

The following day, just after eight in the morning, Matthias Altenhan took off with several companions and flew northeast, climbing steadily.

⌒

ALAN WILLIS LEANED against a wing and absorbed the morning sunshine. The aircraft was still warm from the engine test he had just completed; it ticked and creaked as it cooled, smelling of hot oil and the fresh dope the armorers had put on the gun patches. He liked smells of that kind. He wondered if today he would be left alone; he had always found it hard to understand the jokes of the ground crews, and frequently suspected that they were aimed at him. His head nodded, but then Tom came up behind him and said, "Morning, Alan," and he jerked awake and said, "Good morning, sir."

⌒

SEVEN THOUSAND METERS above the Kent countryside, Hauptmann Matthias Altenhan was at peace. The ground below formed an abstract design of considerable elegance, each element having its natural and inevitable place, each leading the eye onward to the next. The Great Stour wound east through Canterbury, surrounded by acres of striated orchards and field after field of hops. North ran the Medway, cutting through the wooded, irregular hills of the North Downs toward Rochester, and in the far northwest lay the smear of smoke that was London. In every direction the subtle curve of the earth dipped away toward an indistinct horizon. Matthias circled patiently, waiting for the bombers to arrive and the English fighters to rise from their airfields into the warm summer air.

⌒

TOM ANDERSON CAME steeply out of the sun, exactly as he had been taught by his childhood reading, by the animated lectures of his uncle Oscar, by the Royal Air Force, and (most thoroughly of all) by his intensive practice with Dougie Wells. He waited until the last moment, gave the solitary Messerschmitt a long burst, and saw the aircraft jerk in its flight. Got him. Tom pulled his Spitfire savagely into a turn. God help him. The 109 straightened and slowed. Tom

checked the mirror and twisted his head: nothing above, nothing behind, nothing right, nothing left.

He came up behind the Messerschmitt again. It flew on, trailing a
thin line of smoke. With finger and thumb Tom inched the throttle
forward and sidled the Spitfire alongside. He saw the pilot unclip his
oxygen mask and stare across at him. The 109's cockpit canopy
glowed red in the sunshine: Blood, there was blood all over the inside of the Perspex. He watched as the other man turned and looked
ahead, flying steadily southeast toward the sea.

⌁

Six rounds from the Spitfire's guns had penetrated the starboard side of the cockpit and severed Matthias's right leg above the
knee. He was flung about in his straps. He saw blood pumping from
the mess of the stump and felt something like relief that the long-
imagined end was in plain sight. He eased the throttle and trimmed
the aircraft into level flight. With such a wound, I have a short time
only. His hands had become heavy. He wondered how dying should
be done. With an effort, he unclipped his oxygen mask and let it fall
clear of his face. One should surely do certain things. Movement
caught his eye: He turned his head and saw the Englishman alongside like a concerned companion. For a moment he was grateful for
the act of grace, but then he recalled his dignity: He looked ahead
and flew onward, gripping the stick firmly with both hands, straight
and level toward the coast, toward France.

Knowing the enemy pilot was lost, but unwilling to shorten
without reason the final moments of his life, the Spitfire followed.

⌁

When the last bright day of Hauptmann Matthias Altenhan
began to fade, his head drooped and his strong arms clenched the
Messerschmitt into a steeper and yet steeper dive. Sixteen thousand
feet below, the church of St. John stood foursquare in a clump of oak
and chestnut, the cross of St. George flying from its tower. South of
the church lay a village and to the north a substantial Georgian
house, its drive passing through woods and meadows and along the
shore of an ornamental lake. The aircraft, its dying pilot strapped se-

curely within, edged toward the vertical and began to tremble in the
roaring air.

⌒

TOM SAW THE man look down and watched the downward slant
of the Messerschmitt. He pulled his aircraft into a turn and com-
manded from his high vantage the long fall to earth; there was nothing above, nothing behind, nothing right, nothing left.

⌒

IN THE VICARAGE garden the Reverend John Vernon heard
gunfire. He leaned on his spade, tilted his head back, and saw the
black speck, high among the curling condensation trails. I'll watch
you die, he thought, and then was ashamed of the thought.

The guns had stopped. There was birdsong and a lazy breeze. The
speck grew larger. The vicar squinted up at it, thinking of the article entitled "Know Your Enemy" that he had cut from the *Daily
Express*. He had read it last winter at the kitchen table, the silhou-
ettes of the aircraft reminding him strongly of the frail models of
balsa and tissue that had briefly engaged his attention at the age
of thirteen. John Vernon looked up again and saw the thin line of
a fighter's wing, the narrow fuselage and distinctive tailplane of a
Messerschmitt Bf 109e. He had read that it had a V12 engine
of eleven hundred horsepower. He knew that its pilots were fond of
the 109e—they called it "Emil," in accordance with their phonetic
alphabet and the affection of men for the apparatus of war. All this
he had learned from his study of the newspaper.

This Emil is falling straight toward me, John Vernon thought;
may the Lord have mercy on me, miserable sinner that I am. He
tugged his spade from the soil and took a step toward the great
chestnut that overhung the corner of the garden. He hesitated, looked
up, and lifted his right foot to run.

⌒

SILENTLY, SINCE IT was traveling close to the speed of sound,
the Messerschmitt fell to earth, hitting the church of St. John in the
center of the nave. There was an enormous moment of destruction:

Twenty-six great oak beams, dozens of ash battens bearing Welsh slates, yards of lead flashing, careful stone moldings, painted plaster, the dry nests of swifts—all these and many other components of this sacred place, having lain undisturbed for upward of 320 years, flew into pieces. Explosive pressure burst sixteen windows in the nave, hurled a shower of stained glass across the churchyard, and tossed John Vernon like a whirling doll into the potato patch, his right arm fracturing with a crack that made him think his spine was broken. He lay on his back among dry stalks and fat white King Edwards, seeing the sky dark with dust and flying objects and reciting to himself, *O God, Who art the author of peace and lover of concord, defend us, thy humble servants, in all assaults of our enemies*— And there was a pause, it seemed to him a long silence, before a slice of the tower with its golden cockerel and flagpole and brave St. George's cross slid down into the nave and buried the aircraft and its pilot under six hundred tons of limestone.

AT MIDDAY THE church warden, Alvin Sutton, whom they called Sutty, returned from visiting John Vernon in hospital. Constable Hopper was standing guard at the church. The fire was out, the stones well soaked by the Canterbury firemen, but wisps of smoke still lingered among the rubble. Sutty assembled a gang of volunteers, six old men, and they met beside the church. Sutty asked Brian Morgan if they could borrow his crane and some lengths of timber. Brian was initially reluctant, but in the end he agreed. They brought the crane from Brian's yard and chocked it level on railway sleepers among the gravestones. After some discussion they propped the remains of the tower with six-by-fours and began to lift the largest of the fallen stones. One by one the stones swung through the air, turning slowly in the slings below the arm of the crane. The old men built a neat stack of blocks. Dust and ashes drifted in the sunshine. As the day went on, they came upon the tail of the aircraft, smashed and twisted, and the fuselage, the crumpled wings. Here the heap of stone and white dust was stained with water and oil, fuel and blood. They cut out the side of the aircraft with an ax and took the crushed thing that was the pilot, picking him up by the corners of his flying suit like a slippery sack and wrapping a tarpaulin around him. They placed the body in a coffin that had been brought by ambulance from the aerodrome.

A young RAF officer was standing there. He had arrived on a motorcycle. He stood to attention and saluted as the dead pilot was loaded into the dark green ambulance with the bold red crosses on its sides. The ambulance departed, followed by the officer on his motorcycle. The old men watched them go, then sat on the stones and lit their cigarettes.

At last, Sutty polished his head with his handkerchief, replaced his cap, and looked up at the sky. They started the engine of the crane and began lifting the stones again and swinging them up and over to the stack. After a while they came upon the gaping mouth of the tenor bell. They gathered around and wiped the dust from the inscription: *B Mumford fecit ~ Praise the Lord.* They talked some more, by which time the shadows were long and the day almost over.

TOM AND COLIN Frampton picked up Nobby Clark and carried him shoulder high and dripping into the mess, where the barman was lining up the glasses.

"Party time, chaps!" Colin shouted. "Nobby's back! Buggers tried to drown the sod, but no chance they could sink old Nobby, eh? Popped back up like the proverbial bloody cork. Drinks on Nobby, chaps!"

They wound the gramophone and played "Get Happy" over and over again, smoking and drinking. Late in the long warmth of the evening, the sirens sounded. A Junkers 88 came low across the airfield and disappeared to the south, one engine trailing smoke. They rushed out and waved their glasses after it, then went back into the bar, suddenly melancholy.

"The bastard's not going to make it," Nobby said. He had removed his wet trousers and was standing there in his shirttails. "He'll be in the drink, too."

"Cheerio, Jerry," Colin said.

"Don't be so bloody wet," Tom said. "It's only a bloody Jerry."

They laughed and put on "Get Happy" again and filled their glasses and lit their cigarettes.

Colin said, "Any joy today, Tom?"

"Yes," Tom said. "I got a 109 this morning. I saw it crash."

"Well, well," Colin said, "what a secretive bugger you are! Hey, chaps, Tommy got one! Tommy got a bloody Jerry! Drinks on good old Tommy!" He leaped onto a table. "Chaps! I say, chaps!"

"Fuck it," someone said, "Colin's at it again."

"Shut up, chaps," Colin said. "Listen. We're going to have a little song. 'When you wake up in the morning—' "

"Oh, shut up, Colin," Nobby shouted, but he went on singing. The young men began to cheer and stamp their feet as they yelled the chorus:

> *Cats on the rooftops, cats on the tiles,*
> *Cats with syphilis, cats with piles,*
> *Cats with their arseholes wreathed in smiles,*
> *As they revel in the joys of fornication.*

IN NORMANDY THE duty sergeant opened Matthias's writing case, removed his fountain pen, and was about to close the case when he noticed the letter. He unfolded the pages.

When he had finished reading, he stood holding the letter. Eventually he replaced it in the envelope, sealed it, and put it in his pocket. He closed the case. He placed Matthias's two books, his photograph of Kristel and Hans by the lake, his spare shoes, his dress uniform, his cap, his towel, his handkerchiefs, his washing kit, his shoe brushes, and his writing case in a canvas sack with a brown cardboard label. He licked the nib of Matthias's pen and wrote on the label *Matthias Altenhan, Hauptmann, Deceased* 08/09/1940. The man was a cold fish, the sergeant thought, but this is a good pen, a smooth writer. He clipped it into his top pocket and buttoned the flap. That was something. In return, he'd post the letter.

⁓

THE CONVOY MOVED slowly in order not to disturb Janosz Pasenik, who lay asleep in the caravan. It was late in the evening when Masterman found a farmer who would accommodate them. The showers had stopped and the sun cast long shadows. William unharnessed Samson and built a campfire. Irma got out her guitar and began to sing in a slow, mournful voice. The children assembled around the fire. Masterman sat in his deck chair, lit a cigar, and watched Belinda emerging from her tent wearing shorts and a shirt that was insecurely buttoned. Her legs and arms were covered with fair down that shimmered in the low-angled light; she seemed to walk in a golden haze. Her hair and skin were without blemish, and her hips flared into long, strong thighs.

"Belinda is a very willing girl, isn't she?" Masterman said. He leaned back in his deck chair and puffed a spear of smoke into the air. "She's always enormously enthusiastic."

"I daresay she is," Polly said.

William said to Irma, "What's the language you were singing in?"

"It's Hungarian," Irma said. "My mother came from Hungary. Our family is scattered all over Europe."

"I don't know anything much about Europe," William said. "My family didn't travel much beyond Finchley."

"The English are true introverts," Masterman said. "They lack awareness of the world, just as they lack passion and self-knowledge."

Polly started to say, "Well, that's simply not true—"

"In love," Masterman said, "an Englishman applies the skills he learned from his model railway. Connect up, a bit of shunting, and that's it."

"But not you, darling," Irma said.

"I hope not, Irma my love, I do hope not. I have spent a good deal of time perusing the literature and polishing my technique."

William and Polly looked at each other and started to laugh.

"I'm sorry, Masterman," William said after a few moments, "that was rather funny." He reached for Polly's hand, and they began laughing again.

Masterman puffed his cigar calmly and said, "I quite understand your attitude, dear boy. For the English, inhibition turns sexuality into a vulgar joke."

"I wouldn't say I was inhibited," William said.

"Oh, wouldn't you?" Polly said, still laughing.

"Masterman expresses himself as man is intended to express himself," Irma said. "With his penis."

"Oh," Matron said. There was a moment of silence.

"Well," William said. "Tennyson said something about that." He recited:

> Man is the hunter; woman is his game:
> The sleek and shining creatures of the chase,
> We hunt them for the beauty of their skins;
> They love us for it, and we ride them down.

"Oh no," Polly cried. "Really, William! What nonsense! What awful tosh that is! Surely you don't believe that!"

"Of course I don't believe it," William said. "I just thought it was appropriate to the conversation."

Masterman's eyes gleamed. " 'The sleek and shining creatures of the chase,' " he murmured. " 'They love us for it, and we ride them down.' " He held his hands together as if praying, and looked up at the fading clouds. "It reminds me of something Blake said: 'He who desires but acts not, breeds pestilence.' "

———

THE MAN THEY had found in the woods, Janosz Pasenik, lay dozing in one of the caravan bunks, listening to the faint sound of the guitar. He had been a schoolteacher in central Poland. His pupils were the children of farmers. When not at school they labored in fields and forests about which they knew little, and one of his aims was to inspire in them a liking for nature. His nature walks had been highly popular. A straggling crocodile of children, the youngest hand in hand, wound along behind their teacher, following him beside the stream and through the woods, in which he encouraged them to make drawings of interesting plants—*Quercus ferris,* perhaps, or *Fagus sylvatica.* The pupils gossiped and passed up and down the procession a number of amusing jokes. When Janosz Pasenik wished to draw their attention to a notable item, he raised his butterfly net and the column coiled itself into a circle that was politely attentive despite a subcurrent of giggling.

On that September day, nearly a year ago, Janosz Pasenik had turned from his bedroom window when the firing stopped and sat on a chair for several minutes. Eventually he reached down, took a pair of boots from under the bed, and pulled them on, tying the laces firmly. He opened the drawer of the bedside table and lifted out a worn leather wallet and a prismatic compass. He walked down the stairs and, in the kitchen, filled a wine bottle with water and slapped a cork into its neck. Somewhere was the canvas bag that Maria used when she went to market; she had given it a wide strap that made it comfortable to carry on the shoulder. He looked about the house and finally found it, full of toys, in Natalia's room. He tipped out the toys and took it downstairs. In the bag he placed his wallet, the compass, the bottle of water, six apples from the rack in the pantry, three tomatoes, a large slice of goat's-milk cheese, half a loaf of bread, and the remains of the smoked ham from yesterday. The ham was a sizable piece of meat, about half a kilo. Wrapped in a sheet of greaseproof paper and tied with string, it would last for several days. From the top drawer of the dresser he selected a particular kitchen knife, and from a hook under the lowest shelf he took one of the set of six cups with the blue-glazed dragon pattern. He took his hat and his heavy overcoat from the peg on the back of the door, then slung the bag on his shoulder. He picked up his walking stick from its place beside the back door and stepped out into the yard.

It was raining lightly and there was mist in the air. His dog stood beside the step, whining and pawing at the ground, her rough black coat silvered with rain. Janosz Pasenik said to her, "Be silent." She followed closely as he walked through the yard and into the meadow.

The man and the dog walked away from the house and up the gentle hill toward Karol Tazbir's birch plantation. Smoke was drifting across from the houses beyond the stream, and dark red flames fluttered from their upper windows. The soldiers were busy with their shovels and did not look up. Their sergeant puzzled over his map and shouted at his men to hurry up and get back to their vehicles; he was annoyed that his platoon was so lacking in energy and commitment. They had no sense of purpose whatsoever. There were five more of these damned villages, and the major had only given them two days. Now there was this bloody rain. Despite his incessant shouting and swearing, the soldiers did not look at him. They kept on working at the same steady pace. Some spread the earth and patted it flat with the backs of their shovels, others trailed petrol from one house to the next.

It was not quite eight o'clock in the morning. The wood was silent except for the footsteps of the man and the dog rustling through a thin layer of freshly fallen leaves. The wood had been managed with obsessive care by Karol Tazbir, a man of solitary habits. The children of the village liked to taunt him by trespassing in his plantation, climbing his trees, hiding, laughing, and running this way and that while he chased after them, red faced, waving his driving whip, but never catching anyone. The ground was flat, the pale trees stood in severe lines, and the brush underfoot was tidily trimmed. In places there were broad swathes of garlic, properly known, Janosz Pasenik recalled, as *Allium sativum.* It was easy walking except where the panzers had gashed the soft ground and smashed some of the young trees.

⌒

ON A DAY of sunshine and showers, the pilgrims reached the edge of the Downs above Snodland and stopped by a telephone box so that William could telephone his brother. The others waited in the shade. Before them a grassy track fell away toward a wide valley.

"What's that river?" Polly asked, pointing.

"It's the Medway, dear girl," Masterman said, stepping to the brink and focusing his binoculars. "It's the last great river crossing before we reach our goal."

Behind his back Polly walked in a small circle, stabbing at the turf with her umbrella.

⌒

THE TELEPHONE BOX was extremely hot and the line was bad. William jammed the door open with his foot and pressed the receiver to his ear. "Tom? Are you there? What did you say? I couldn't hear."

His brother's voice came faintly through the crackles. "I said I'd got one."

"Got one what?"

"A Jerry. A German fighter. I shot it down."

"Oh."

"Yes. It crashed on a church in Kent."

"On a church?"

"Yes. Smashed it to bits."

"Oh, did it?"

"Yes. It went straight through the roof and half the tower fell down."

"Oh. I hope there wasn't anyone inside at the time."

"There wasn't."

"Where is this church?"

"A few miles west of Canterbury. A village called Goodman St. John."

"It can't be, surely? That's not far from where we are now."

"Well, that's where it is, William. You'll know it if you see it. The church was completely wrecked."

The line hummed for several seconds.

"I'm sorry," William said, "I don't really know what else to say about it. It's very brave, of course, what you're doing. Everyone knows that. I'm glad you're still alive."

"Don't tell anyone else about it, will you?" Tom said. "I shouldn't really have told you."

"Of course I won't," William said. "I'll ring you again soon. We're supposed to be stopping when we get to Canterbury. We've picked up an extra passenger, a chap we found along the way."

"Have you? I'll tell you one thing, William," Tom said. "I'm bloody tired. We're flying all the time now. Every bloody minute."

"I thought you must be," William said. "The sky's always full of aeroplanes. They leave those squiggles high up."

"Condensation trails."

"Sometimes we can hear the guns, too. It's funny to think you're up there somewhere." He paused. "Are you all right, Tom?"

"Of course I am," Tom said. "I'm quite all right. I'm just tired, that's all. I'll be all right. Don't worry about me."

∽

WILLIAM WENT BACK to the convoy. Masterman was lying on his back on the grass verge. He had removed his shirt, and his face was covered with a straw hat.

Polly said, "Is Tom all right?"

"Yes," William said. "He's shot down a German aircraft."

"Oh," Polly said. "Goodness."

"That's what I said. I couldn't think what else to say."

"But at least he's still alive."

"I said that, too."

"Man is the hunter," Masterman said from beneath his hat.

"Yes," William said. "Come on. Let's get going."

∽

AFTER THEY HAD crossed the Medway it was Irma's turn to drive the caravan. Samson leaned into his collar, and the convoy rolled slowly eastward.

Janosz Pasenik lay in his bunk, content to be traveling among these people; they were curious, but they were of good intent. They had set a rota of children to keep an eye on him; one of them was watching him now, in between turning the pages of her book. The steady swaying of the caravan was extraordinarily comforting. The great thing is to move: An English storyteller had written that, and it was true. What had happened in his own village was now happening all across Europe. When war came, the killing and burning began. It was quite normal. People often talked of what had been done to themselves and their parents and their grandparents, and who was to blame, and the revenge they would take when the time came; and when the time did come, the only answer was to start walking.

After he had left his village, he had set off southward, realizing after two or three hours that he had escaped alive, and had done so because he did not care whether he survived or not. He had simply walked away with the dog at his heels and they had not noticed his going. Perhaps it was destined that a single life should be spared in order that he might testify not only to the events of the last hours, but also to the long history of his family and his village, their past happiness and sorrow, and all that was lost. Thus his life might, in time, be given purpose.

He did not think of what he had seen from the bedroom window. It was as if, when he laced up his boots and went down to pack his wife's market bag, he had opened the first page of a completely new story, and the old story was closed, replaced in the shelves and utterly forgotten.

Each morning he woke early and lay dozing, feeling the cold seeping up from the earth and trying to visualize the map of Europe that he had pinned up, several years ago, on the wall of class two. But he could not remember the pattern with any precision; in his half-awake mind, the countries of Europe ran one into another like a child's watercolor, their bold and separate colors merging into something dark and without form.

For several days it had been the same. He got up, drank some water, gave a cupful to the dog, and set off again. He called the dog to run ahead and then followed her, striding fast into the thin mist that covered the plain. There were frequent swampy patches containing beds of dark green *Phragmites communis,* and the grass was rough and tussocky, making for difficult walking. He pushed on as quickly as he could, the bag bumping against his hip and the heavy coat thrown across his shoulder. As the mist cleared it grew hot. At midmorning he stopped for water, and again at noon for food and more water. There was little by which to measure his progress, no distinctive feature save occasional cattle and sheep, a swamp sucking at his boots, or the black cross of a kite hanging above. Under the immense dome of the sky, the tussocky grass continued, the gentle wind blew, skylarks sang. Guided by the trembling needle of his compass, he walked onward and the far hills seemed to come no nearer.

Walking in this manner, urgently and mechanically, he did not see the girl until he was upon her: a ten-year-old, minding a tiny flock of sheep, woken from a doze in the long grass by a man almost stepping on her, a stranger with a sweating face and big hands that grasped her arm fiercely. Such was his state of mind that Janosz Pasenik thought, *I must kill her,* thinking of the knife in his bag, Maria's kitchen knife, a sharp-edged, serviceable knife with a riveted wooden handle, a knife familiar with the necks of pigs and chickens—and then checking himself at these absurd thoughts, casting the girl to one side, and walking on, calling the dog, striding onward across the uneven grass.

When he confessed it years later to the English priest, Janosz Pasenik cried out at the memory of the girl's thin, startled face, her dark skin and lank black hair, the rags of her dress, the raw stink of her. She must have been living wild with her pathetic handful of sheep out in the depths of the grassy plain, meeting nobody for weeks on end, and then there was this sudden stranger, a violent man who left bruises on her arm and was gone again.

HE OPENED HIS eyes. The caravan was still rolling steadily along, and now there was another child keeping watch over him, a boy this time, with large dark eyes.

AT THEIR NEXT stop Timothy Needham, Matron, and William helped Todger look for his ferret while Janosz Pasenik looked down from his bunk.

"There's simply got to be more to life than looking for Todger's ferret," William said from beneath the bottom bunk.

"Timothy," Matron said, sniffing. "At the next stop, a good wash and a change of clothes is required."

"I haven't got any other clothes," Timothy Needham said in his tiny voice.

"Nonsense, boy," Matron said. "What's in that suitcase of yours?"

"Nothing," Timothy said. Matron stepped forward and pulled the suitcase from beneath the bunk. She flung back the lid and there was a flicker of movement, too fast for the eye.

"Todger's damned ferret," Matron cried, striking out with a hairbrush in the general direction.

"Oh, Matron, you shouldn't swear," Patsy Fish said.

"Oh no," Timothy Needham said, putting his hands to his mouth. The suitcase contained several leather-bound albums and, in one corner, a sizable heap of finely chewed, translucent paper and several pink objects that squirmed this way and that.

"Oh look, babies," Matron said.

Timothy Needham took a pinch of the ferret's bedding and inspected it closely. He turned to Todger and his voice was stronger than usual. "Before your blasted ferret got it," he said, "that was a perfectly good set of British Honduras."

The caravan set off again, turned a corner, and began to climb a gentle slope. "William, we're coming into a village," Irma called. "We'll stop for lunch, shall we?"

The travelers moved slowly up the hill to the village square. "Oh God," Ian Lambert said, "the church has fallen down."

"Oh yes," William said, looking at the shattered church and the neat stacks of stones around the ruins. "So it has. I know what happened here. I know who did it, too."

Ian Lambert looked up at him and said, "Who was it?"

"Never you mind," William said. "One day I'll tell you."

"I absolutely hate it when people say that," Ian Lambert said.

"Yes," William said. "It's jolly annoying. But grown-ups do it all the time, don't they?"

"It's not fair," Ian Lambert said.

⁓

NOBBY CLARK SAID, "Are you going to tell that girl of yours about your Jerry?"

"She's not really my girl," Tom said. He thought for a moment and then said, "I don't think I will, actually."

"Might frighten her off?"

"Yes. She's not happy about fighter pilots, anyway."

"Funny, that. When she's a pilot herself, I mean."

"I don't think it's anything to do with flying. She's just being careful."

"Not what you want in a woman, is it? Being careful."

Tom laughed. "She's very nice."

"I daresay she is, old chap. But you know what I mean."

⌒

MASTERMAN ADDRESSED THE vicar, who had his arm in a sling. "As you can see," he said, waving his straw hat toward the caravan, "we're the Liberty Hall pilgrimage. We're looking for somewhere to house our waifs and strays for a night or two. However, I can see we've arrived at an inconvenient moment."

"Waifs and strays?" The Reverend John Vernon eyed Masterman's shorts, his sandals, and the expansive curves of his chest and was initially cautious. However, his benevolence was activated by an introduction to Polly and the children; it was obvious that a woman in her condition needed somewhere comfortable to sleep, and those children certainly looked as though they could do with a proper bath.

"As it happens," he said to Masterman, "we have a sizable vicarage that's almost empty. You're welcome to borrow a few rooms for a day or two." He pointed to the building. "Do you think that's big enough?"

Masterman turned around and looked at the vicarage for some moments. "Well now," he said, "that really is a big place, isn't it."

"Oh yes," John Vernon said. "It's got seven or eight bedrooms, I think, as well as a kitchen garden and an orchard. Of course, it's a bit of a muddle at the moment. We're still clearing up after this dreadful crash." He gestured vaguely toward the church.

"Well, well," Masterman said. "How interesting. And the vicarage is empty, you say."

"Oh yes. It's quite empty except for my own rooms and our little library. To be honest, keeping up such a large house is a bit of a worry. We get no help from the church commissioners."

"A library," Masterman said. "That's rather a useful thing to have. But I suppose a house of that size would be something of a burden."

"Other than that," John Vernon said, "I don't think we can help you much."

"It's absolutely perfect," Masterman said. He turned and clasped the vicar's left hand. "We'll be delighted to take you up on your generous offer."

"Oh, jolly good," John Vernon said.

Masterman climbed onto the bonnet of the Sunbeam, waved his hat in the air, and called the pilgrims to him. "Here we are," he said, his voice unusually calm. "Let's just park the caravan, unhitch Samson, and unload the donkeys. We're going to stay in the vicarage for a while. Get your bags. William and Matron will sort out the rooms."

Masterman jumped down from the car and seized William by the shoulder. "William, my dear boy, a powerful sense of destiny has come upon me. I believe we have discovered the new Liberty Hall."

ON THE FOLLOWING morning, the pilgrims were having breakfast when Constable Hopper knocked on the door. "I have reason to believe," he said to John Vernon, "that you are harboring an alien." After a short discussion he took Janosz Pasenik away in a police van.

"Oh dear, that's not a good start for the new Liberty Hall," Polly said.

"My dear Polly," Masterman said, "it's nothing but a momentary setback. After breakfast I will begin making plans for his immediate release." He took a large bite from a slice of the vicar's toast and marmalade and chewed it rhythmically.

IN HAMBURG, KRISTEL Altenhan read the letter again.

Do you remember that time on the platform at Hannover? Yes, you must. How often had we met then? Only twice, and always chaperoned—but meeting in the station like that—you walking out of a cloud of steam like some vision!—it was charming! You had that little round hat, the dark red one, plum-colored, and I so much liked the neatness of you. You swerved a little when you saw me, thinking for a moment that you should avoid me. But you came marching on, saying, "Good day, Herr Altenhan," in your best formal manner and stopping a clear meter away—very elegant you looked, and always with that self-possessed look. I suppose one should not say that what one likes about one's wife is her dignity, exactly, but that is what I love about you.

I went out this evening for a stroll on the airfield and there was Cygnus just above the horizon to the southwest—the constellation Cygnus, do you know that? Four stars, and when you hear they are called Cygnus, you see at once that the name is completely inevitable. Can four stars make a swan?—Yes indeed!—Look for it next time there is a clear sky. It is beautiful and dignified. After the war I will do some astronomy—I have some binoculars, but they show too much. Too many stars! It's odd that seeing more stars should be less satisfactory. But Cygnus! Cygnus is so calm, so steady, so elegant, even through my wobbling binoculars!

Kristel put the letter with the others and smiled to herself. Her husband was a clever young man and usually rather reserved, but he had moments of naive enthusiasm that were enchanting. On his next leave she would pull his leg about this business of Cygnus, the four stars that somehow looked like a swan.

T

HE CHAIRMAN straightened his tie, gazed severely at the row of children whispering on the public benches, tapped his gavel, and turned to the clerk. "I understand that Mr. Pasenik does not speak English. I have been provided with notes on his case, and I gather that a translator has kindly volunteered her services."

"Yes, sir," the clerk said, indicating Irma, who had somehow acquired a somber two-piece suit for the occasion.

"Thank you, madam," the chairman said, showing his teeth in a thin smile. "Kindly tell Mr. Pasenik that this tribunal is duly constituted under government order to determine the status of aliens, and consequently to decide on the question of his internment or otherwise."

Irma did so, and Janosz nodded.

"You claim to be Mr. Janosz Pasenik, a schoolmaster who has escaped from Poland, and you have papers in that name. Kindly tell the tribunal exactly what happened to you."

Irma again translated. When she had finished, Janosz Pasenik reached forward and picked up the pencil that lay on the desk before him. He held both ends between the tips of his large, blunt fingers, the pencil parallel with the desk, and stared at it intently. Everyone looked from the pencil to Janosz Pasenik's face and back again. The sound of traffic became audible, and somewhere high in the roof a pigeon cooed insistently. The silence continued for a considerable time.

Eventually the chairman made a sniffing noise and said, "Well, Mr. Pasenik?"

The silence continued.

"I object," said a man's voice from the public gallery. "This is a most unworthy proceeding. It is cruel and inhuman. Nobody should be treated like this. This man has obviously been traumatized by his experience and cannot answer."

"Traumatized?" The chairman considered the word for a moment, then said, "Constable Hopper, kindly escort that man from the room."

"You can't do that," said the man. He stood up: It was Masterman. His shirt was open and a gold chain glinted on his chest. "This is not a court of law," he said. "It's a Town Hall, and the tribunal is supposed to assess the status of aliens, not punish them. It's perfectly obvious that Mr. Pasenik has been through a terrible experience of which he is unable to speak." He turned and smiled brilliantly at the other spectators. "I'm quite sure we all agree, don't we?"

Constable Hopper looked at the chairman and began to get to his feet.

"I agree," a woman said. "I certainly do agree with that man, whoever he is." There was a murmur of support. Constable Hopper eased himself back into his chair. As he did so, Janosz Pasenik said something in a barely audible voice.

"What?" said the chairman. "What did he say?"

"He said that he is unable to speak of his family and what happened to them," Irma said.

There was a long pause, and the chairman made another of his puffing, sniffing noises.

Irma shut her notebook and stood up. "It is obvious, Mr. Chairman, that this man is in a distressed state. In the circumstances I am unable to continue translating."

"Good for you, love," somebody said. The spectators in the gallery turned toward the chairman.

"Constable Hopper," the chairman said after another long pause. The spectators saw from his expression that he was attempting to convey good humor and magnanimity.

"Sir," said Constable Hopper.

"Constable Hopper, I don't think the comments of the gentleman in the gallery or those of our translator need be included in the record of this hearing. I have read your report of Mr. Pasenik's arrival. I have seen Miss Irma's notes of her conversations with him. He is evidently a professional man. My decision is that Mr. Pasenik will be allocated to Category C. The tribunal stands adjourned for fifteen minutes."

Constable Hopper stood up, put on his helmet, and said, "Very good, sir. Mr. Pasenik, Category C. Tribunal adjourned until eleven-thirty."

Masterman stood up again. "That means he's free," he said loudly. "That means he can stay here." He began to clap. One or two others joined in, somewhat hesitantly at first, like spectators at a cricket match. The applause gradually swelled until it set the pigeons swirling and clattering in the high roof of the Town Hall.

Irma put her hand on Janosz Pasenik's arm and said to him in Polish, "It's finished. He says you can stay in this country. You're free to do as you wish."

Janosz replaced the pencil on the desk and put his head in his hands. Irma put her arm around his shoulders.

"Excuse me."

Irma looked up. It was the Reverend Vernon. "I don't want to intrude at this wonderful moment," he said, "but you might like to tell Mr. Pasenik that I have a job to offer him at St. John's, if he would like to consider it. Not awfully well paid, I'm sorry to say, but it includes full board."

WILLIAM HAD BEEN trying to phone Tom for some time. When he eventually got through, there was a lot of noise on the line.

"We've got a crossed line," he said. "There's a funny singing noise."

Tom laughed. "There's a bit of a party going on, that's all. The boys are celebrating."

"Celebrating what?"

"Oh, we had a bit of luck today. Nobby Clark got a couple of Huns."

"Oh, I see." William hesitated. "Well, I was only ringing to say that we'd got to your church. I'm just across the road from it now." He hesitated again and then said, "It's a very odd feeling, you know. It's almost as if you'd marked the place for us."

There was silence for several seconds, and then Tom said, "I went there to look at it, you know. Goodman St. John, I mean. It's a pretty village, isn't it? Lots of ancient little houses clustered together up the High Street, then a square with the squire's mansion, a pub, a church, a vicarage with swifts nesting in the eaves. All that kind of thing."

"You didn't say you'd been here."

"No. I suppose I didn't."

William looked out across the square for a moment and then said, "The vicarage is where we're staying. I think we might be here for quite a bit. You're right, it's a pretty place."

"It's not far from here. I could easily pay you a visit."

"Yes," William said, "that's a very good idea. Come and see us as soon as you can. Come tomorrow, if you like."

"I can't. Maybe in a day or two, though. I'm due a day off."

"Good," William said. "We'll be expecting you."

⁓

"I HAVE OFFERED the post of vicarage gardener to Mr. Pasenik, and he has accepted it," John Vernon said.

"Good," Masterman said. "I gather he is a botanist by training. No doubt he will do great things. And of course, as a former teacher, he can contribute to the school when it is properly established here."

"Personally," John Vernon said, "I think a small school would be an excellent use for the building. But there will be one or two formalities, I'm afraid. I'll have to talk to the parish, and, of course, the church commissioners. They will take a view. They always do. It will be a lengthy process." He looked gloomy.

"Of course, my school isn't just any old school," Masterman said. "It's a quite remarkable school, in the vanguard of modern educational thinking."

"There's nothing wrong with modern thinking," the vicar said. "I feel I'm quite modern myself." He laughed and then looked serious again. "But we have to remember that this is church property. A school would have to conform to the principles that the church espouses."

"Goodness," Masterman said, "I can't see that being the slightest problem. We have absolutely nothing to hide."

"Hmm," the vicar said.

⌒

MOMENTS AFTER THE crash, a large quantity of leaves had fluttered down from the chestnut into the vicarage garden. Beneath the leaves lay shattered slates, baulks of timber, sheets of lead, fragments of glass, and substantial chunks of flint and limestone; and underneath all that debris lay the vegetables that Janosz Pasenik had decided were his first priority. The vicar had asked that everything that could possibly be reused should be kept for the day the rebuilding of the church began. For several days a group of volunteers from the village, bent over like policemen searching for clues, had been working their way across the garden, collecting, sieving, and sorting. In the potting shed Jan Pasenik was assembling piles of stained glass of various colors. They worked slowly and with intense concentration and were glad when, in the late evening, the sun came out and shone upon their labors.

When William, Matron, and Todger visited him, the new gardener appeared already at home. He had perceived the vicar's benevolence and accepted the nature of the bargain that had been offered; after all, despite his unsatisfactory faith, and indeed his youth, John Vernon appeared to possess some of the graces of a priest. There was nothing dishonorable about the arrangement. It was true that Janosz had once been a professional man of some standing, but he quite understood that sanctuary had a price.

"I've brought you a little something," Matron said, handing a small green book to Janosz. She stepped back, enjoying the sense of warmth that comes from doing good, and he turned the book over in his hands. He had not understood what Matron said, though it was clear that the book was a gift. On the dust jacket was a design in green; it depicted a small field, a greenhouse, and a basket containing five onions, four potatoes, several runner beans, two tomatoes, and a marrow. He opened the book and discovered a photograph of apples hanging from a branch. He pointed to the caption and said, "What is this?"

Matron put on her glasses. "It says: 'The Precious Fruit of the Earth,' " she said, and felt suddenly emotional. Later she told Polly about the way the melancholy man had held the little book in his battered hands, and how his face had gradually been illuminated with pleasure as he realized what it was about.

The content of *Brush Up Your Gardening,* by Stanley B. White-head, D.Sc., was immediately familiar to Janosz. He soon learned by heart the quotation from Genesis at the beginning of chapter 1, and many years later he was able to declaim it to visitors: "Let the earth bring forth grass, the herb yielding seed, and the fruit tree yielding fruit after its kind!"

Todger tugged at his sleeve, and Janosz looked up from the book. The boy was holding an open shoe box. "Ah," Janosz said, looking into it, *"Mustela putorius."*

"Actually," William said, "it's Todger's ferret."

Janosz nodded. "Todger's ferret," he said slowly, and thought for a moment. "Is kind of polecat."

"I'm sure you're right," William said. "She smells a bit, and bites like anything."

Janosz picked up the animal by the scruff of the neck, inspected it, and nodded, apparently in approval.

"We need a proper cage for that creature," William said. "She keeps escaping, and now she's got babies as well. A strong wooden box with wire netting across the front, that's what we want." With his hands he sketched a cage in the air.

"Good," Janosz said. "This boy make it. Come."

Todger went with him to the workbench, and the ferret's new home was made before teatime. Todger was proud of it. He sat before the cage, put his face close to the wire, and said to the animal, "That's fixed you, eh?" The young ferrets shoved fiercely at their mother's teats as she lay in the straw.

⁓

MASTERMAN STOPPED WILLIAM in the village square and said, "I'm beginning to think we're going to have trouble with that gardener chap."

"What, you mean Mr. Pasenik?"

"Yes. Did you know he was a schoolteacher?"

"Of course. He's a teacher of natural science. He knows an awful lot about animals and plants."

"I sent Irma to quiz him about his educational principles. He used to have his own school in a village in Poland, you know. He was a headmaster."

"That's jolly useful. He could be a great help."

"No, William, it's not useful at all. He's altogether the wrong type for Liberty Hall. Apparently, he thinks education is all about knowledge."

"Well," William said, "that's true to some extent, of course."

Masterman looked at him. "I don't think you've been listening, these past months."

"I don't mean that other things aren't important, too."

"William, you're heading for an ideological crisis. If you stand in the middle of the road, you'll get knocked over."

Masterman strode away. William went into the Crown, bought a pint of bitter, and sat on a bench outside. Masterman had a knack of putting things in a way that seemed incontrovertible, but he wasn't always right. It was a beautiful evening. He sipped his beer and watched the swallows gathering along the wires.

⁓

IN THE MIDDLE of that night there began the faintest of murmurs. It was nothing more than a slight reduction in the stillness. Janosz Pasenik woke immediately and looked up at his bedroom ceiling as if trying to stare through the plaster and thatch into the night sky. Matron woke, too, and lay listening. For several minutes the rest of the vicarage did not stir; the children went on sleeping in the abandoned way that children do, and so did William, Polly's arm lying across his chest. The vicar, John Vernon, turned over and muttered something but did not wake. Masterman and Irma lay side by side, and only a close inspection would have shown that Masterman's eyes had opened.

The murmuring grew. Matron got out of bed and put on her slippers. She walked through the darkness to the bedroom door and took her dressing gown off the hook. She put it on, secured the belt carefully, went to the window, and opened the curtains. There was no moon, but the night was clear and the stars bright. She opened the window and the sound was abruptly louder. No doubt about it: Aircraft were coming this way, lots of aircraft.

She went out of the bedroom, across the landing, and tapped on William's door. There was no reply. She tapped again and went in. "William," she said into the darkness, and again, "William."

"What? Is that you, Matron?"

"Yes. We must get up. Bombers are coming. We've got to move the children."

"All right. Just a minute." Bedsprings creaked and William said, "Polly? Polly, wake up. We've got to get up."

Polly groaned. "Oh God, have we really? It's the middle of the night."

"I know. But there's going to be an air raid."

"Give me a hand, then. I feel like a stranded whale."

Matron went downstairs to the first of the children's rooms, went in, and switched on the light. The O'Leary boys were all in one bed. She woke them, got them into outdoor clothes and wellingtons, and went on to the next room. Polly and William came down; together they organized the children and got them into the garden.

The sound of engines had become a growl, and there was a new sound, a distant wailing. "Sirens," William said. "Sirens on the coast somewhere."

"About time, too," Matron said. As she spoke, another siren began its quavering call, a siren that was much nearer and much louder.

William looked up and saw that aircraft were passing overhead, faint shadows flickering across the stars.

John Vernon came out of the house wearing a dressing gown and carrying a large key ring and a shopping basket. "The safest place is the crypt," he said. "It's quite undamaged. Come along."

The group of children and adults hurried through the gate into the churchyard. John Vernon unlocked the crypt and handed out candles and matches.

"This is good," Ian Lambert said.

"No, it isn't," Timothy Needham said. "It's absolutely horrid."

"It'll be all right," Matron said. "I'll sit next to you." She held up a candle and led the children down into the darkness. Polly arrived with Arthur Beckingsale and Lucy Standish. "That's the lot, I think. I'll count them again when we're all inside."

"All right. I'll see if anyone's left behind."

Janosz Pasenik was standing stock-still in the center of the garden, as if by effort of will he could defend it from further damage.

"Come on, Mr. Pasenik," William said. "Please come into the crypt. It's too dangerous out here."

Janosz gazed upward. "They are not coming," he said. "They go to London."

William looked up. The aircraft roared steadily overhead, heading northwest. "Of course they are," he said. "How stupid of me. They wouldn't bother with a little place like this, would they?"

He turned again to Janosz. "But it would be best to come inside, even so. There might be some stray bombs."

"Why are no guns shooting?"

"I don't know," William said. "Probably there aren't any guns round here." The two men stood in the garden, looking upward. "In the end, they'll be stopped," William said.

There was heavy gunfire in the distance, and a series of deeper explosions. "Come on," he said. "We really ought to shelter with the others."

Janosz was reluctant, but William was firm. They stooped through the door of the crypt and saw the children sitting in a circle, their pink faces illuminated by candlelight. Polly was counting them again.

William and Janosz went down the steps, and Polly said, "Oh, there you are. Everyone's here except Masterman. And where's Irma?" She flashed her torch around the crypt. "There's no sign of either of them."

"I'll go and look," William said.

"Be careful, won't you."

As he went across the garden there was a flicker of yellow light in the sky and a series of distant explosions. He went into the vicarage and called for Masterman, but there was no reply. He searched the building floor by floor until he reached the top of the house. When he pushed open the attic door, Masterman and Irma had their backs to him and were looking out the open window.

"Masterman," William said, "you and Irma ought to come down. We're all in the crypt."

"Have a look at this," Masterman said without turning around.

William stepped forward and Masterman passed him a pair of binoculars. At first he could see nothing but blackness, then he caught sight of a red spark. He fiddled with the focus while the spark trembled in the lenses. Abruptly the faraway glimmer sharpened into a roaring fire, yellow flames rising among billowing smoke.

"It's London," Masterman said. "London's on fire. Just look at that. Amazing!"

A string of flashes lit the smoke, and several seconds later William felt the concussion of the bombs as a curious flutter in the air. There was now a line of fire on the horizon, and the flames and smoke were easily visible to the naked eye. The orange light shimmered on a few wispy feathers of cirrus that lingered high up in the night sky.

Masterman put his arm around Irma and said, "The sunset of the capitalist age! Who would have thought we would witness it!"

William put down the binoculars and turned away from the window. He went down through the empty building, out into the garden, and through the gate into the churchyard. The ruined church was illuminated by flickers of light. He descended into the coolness of the crypt. "They're all right," he said to Polly. "They're upstairs, watching the fireworks."

Polly looked at him. "What's the matter?"

"Nothing," William said. He looked around. "We need to get organized. We need to get beds and bedding down here for next time. Food as well, and something to heat water and make drinks."

"All right," Matron said. "I'll make a list."

As she spoke there was an explosion nearby, and then another. Dust and fragments of plaster fell from the roof. Several children cried out. "It's all right," William called out. "We can't come to any harm in here. Just keep still and wait for them to go away."

He sat next to Polly and looked thoughtful. "Somehow we'll have to get a grip on this," he said.

"We'll start a singsong."

"I don't mean the air raid. I mean the whole Liberty Hall thing."

Polly laughed and put her arm around him. "All right," she said, "but first things first, don't you think?"

THE SQUADRON LEADER banged his pipe into his ashtray. "Anderson, I understand from the adjutant that you took a squadron motorcycle and used a tankful of petrol without the relevant chitty. He's threatening to put you on a charge."

"Well . . . I needed it urgently, sir."

"You'll have to do better than that."

"It was . . . well, squadron business, sir. Sort of."

"What kind of business?"

"Actually, sir . . ."

"Come on, Anderson. Out with it."

"I wanted to see the 109 I shot down."

"Oh, did you?"

"It fell on a church."

"I know it did. I won't hold you responsible for that, Anderson, though God may." The squadron leader laughed to himself. "Now, what am I going to tell the adj, for Christ's sake?"

"I don't know, sir."

"What did you do, exactly?"

"I followed the ambulance to a village called Goodman St. John, sir, and they were digging the Messerschmitt out of the church. They found the pilot and took him away."

Tapping his teeth with the mouthpiece of his pipe, the squadron leader said, "All right. So you just went there and looked at the wreckage, did you?"

"Well, no, sir. I followed the ambulance to the mortuary."

The squadron leader sat up. "What on earth did you do that for?"

"I wanted to know his name, sir. The name of the pilot."

"You wanted to know his name." The squadron leader took a penknife from his pocket and scraped at the bowl of his pipe, not looking at Tom. "And did you find it out?"

"Yes. I asked an orderly if they'd found his papers, and he told me—"

"Dammit, I don't want to know the name of the bloody Jerry, do I? I've never heard anything so bloody ridiculous in my life."

"Yes, sir."

The squadron leader stood up, walked over to the window, and looked out across the airfield. "For God's sake," he said, not turning round, "why on earth did you want to know his bloody name?"

"I caught his eye before he crashed. I flew alongside. He looked across at me, then he dived away. I just thought I'd like to know who he was."

"Jesus. You thought you'd like to know who he was, so you asked, and some bloody idiot told you."

"Yes, sir."

"For Christ's sake." The squadron leader turned around and walked back to his desk. "Stand up, Pilot Officer Anderson."

Tom stood up. It was hard to see why the man was so angry. Perhaps it was something to do with his age. He must be thirty at least.

"Very well. I'll square the adjutant, but you will not take squadron property without a chitty ever again."

"No, sir."

"More than that. If you do anything like this again, I will remove you from operational duties. You're a bloody fighter pilot. Your job is to shoot down fucking Germans. You don't have to know their fucking *names*. Do you understand, Anderson?"

"Yes, sir."

"Very well. Dismissed."

Tom saluted and left the room.

The squadron leader sat down and went on scraping at his pipe. "Jesus," he said.

After a while he pressed a bell and the WAAF clerk came in. "Doreen, be a love and get on the blower, would you? See if you can find out where they took the Jerry that Anderson shot down. The one that hit the church. An ambulance took him to a mortuary somewhere. The Red Cross ought to know. Then get me the name of whoever's in charge."

He scraped his pipe some more. A few minutes later he rang the bell again. When Doreen came in he said, "That business about Anderson's Jerry. On second thought, scrub it. Sleeping dogs and all that." He shook his head. "What are we running here, Doreen? A bloody kindergarten, or what?"

"I'm sure I don't know, sir," Doreen said.

There was the cough of an engine starting, and then another. The squadron leader got up and walked to the window. A ground crew was warming up the engines of a Blenheim night fighter.

"It's already getting darker in the evenings," the squadron leader said. "Let's hope this winter isn't as bad as last." He stuffed tobacco into his pipe and struck a match. A minute passed, and eventually Doreen said, "Will that be all, sir?"

He turned around in a cloud of smoke. "God, I'm sorry, old dear. I was forgetting. Off you go."

The squadron leader stood at the window until dusk had fallen. The Blenheim took off, its exhausts flaring yellow and blue. He watched it climbing steadily toward the upper air, whose clouds the setting sun had tinged with pinkish light.

In the mess, Nobby Clark nudged Tom with his elbow and said, "You're a very naughty boy, aren't you, Tommy? What did the CO say?"

"He just tore me off a strip, that's all."

"No guard duty, then?"

"No."

"Did you tell him about going to the morgue?"

"Yes, I did, actually."

"And about getting the Jerry's name?"

"Yes."

"And what did he say?"

"He was bloody cross."

"Was he?" Nobby lit a cigarette. "I suppose he thinks it's fraternizing with the enemy."

"It bloody well isn't."

"All right, Tom, I know that."

"It's got nothing to do with the war. It was just something I wanted to do." Tom picked up his glass, drank some beer, and wiped his lips. "I saw the bloke's face, and he saw me. I just wondered who he was. He was only a young chap, by the look of him. Just another bloody German fighter pilot. I suppose it was pretty silly, when you come to think of it, wanting to know who he was."

"Not silly to do it. Silly to tell anyone, maybe."

"I didn't think it would matter."

"But now you know different."

"Yes. The CO said I was to get on with killing fucking Germans and never mind about their fucking names."

Nobby laughed and slapped Tom's shoulder. "That's what we're here for, dear boy, and to hell with the comradeship of the air."

⌒

THAT NIGHT TOM found himself awake and searching for the faint square of the window to see if it was yet grayer than the rest of the darkness. Again and again he turned over, seeking for his hip a softer hollow in the hard pad of the mattress.

Three times during August he had spoken to Elizabeth on the telephone, but they had been unable to meet. He lay with his eyes open, remembered the moment in the rain when she had stepped down from the wing of the Spitfire and turned to face him. He turned over yet again, and eventually he slept.

At some later hour it seemed that he felt movement and warmth, and she was with him. He had not realized how thin she was. In the darkness he explored with his hands the long bones of her legs, the intricate mechanism of her feet, the warm, smooth skin between her thighs. She reached toward him and he felt her lips and the slippery pip of her tongue. He held her head in his hands, feeling her cheekbones under his palms, his fingers brushing her ears and her breath slow and warm against his neck. Across the dimpled hollow of her back he brushed his fingers. In his hands lay the bones and tendons of her hands, so much smaller than his own. There was something wonderfully slick about her skin, about the way it moved over her hips and her shoulder blades. He was moving his hands across the hollowness of her stomach, discovering her ribs and then her breasts, when someone shook his shoulder and she was gone into a dazzle of light.

"Are you all right, sir?"

He rolled over. The mess steward was shaking him. "Oh, no," he said. "For God's sake put that torch out."

"Sorry, sir."

"I was having a dream."

"Yes, sir. I could see that."

"Christ, I feel awful."

"Here's your tea, sir."

"Jenkins. It's really you, is it?"

"Yes, sir. I'm afraid it is. The CO said to call everyone, sir. There's a flap on again."

"What's the time?"

"Four-thirty, sir. It'll be light soon."

"Oh God. I'd better get up. Thanks for the tea."

"Thank you, sir."

⁓

FIRST LIGHT. AT the head of the estuary, where the Thames loops and twists out of the city, smoke rose from broken terraces, shattered quays, and wrecked warehouses. The All Clear had sounded and the worst of the fires had been conquered, but flames still gleamed here and there among the roofless buildings. Firemen's hoses twisted along the wet cobbles between heaps of bricks and tiles. Groups of blackened firemen sat around their pumps and ladders. The air-raid wardens took off their tin hats, scratched their heads, and rubbed their eyes. The gunners swabbed their barrels and slowly began to replenish their stocks of shells. Here and there a householder emerged, stepping warily, stopping now and then to gaze about. Along came a small gray van, lurching over the rubble. Two women got out, opened the doors of the van, took out a folding table, set it up on the pavement, and covered it with a piece of patterned oilcloth. From the van they took a tea urn and a tray of china mugs. A queue began to form. Each person was given a mug of sweet tea and two biscuits. They stood about in groups, not saying much, just sipping their tea and absorbing the tranquillity of the morning.

Farther east, the vast estuary was calm and empty of ships. The faintest skim of mist lay on the water. Gentle waves lifted and fell along the shore. The tide was ebbing, the mud flats uncovering, and in all the inlets and creeks of Essex and Kent the waders were at work: redshank, curlew, and oystercatchers, stepping in their mechanical way along the tideline, spearing the water and calling melodiously into the silence. Three miles offshore, out by the Whitaker Beacon, half a dozen seals elbowed themselves ashore on Foulness Sands.

IN THE CRYPT the children were still asleep, curled among a jumble of pillows and blankets. William went up the stone stairs, opened the door, and stepped outside. He stretched and yawned. It was going to be another beautiful day. He sniffed: There was a faint smell of burning. He sat on one of the piles of stones and looked at the remains of the church. After a while Polly appeared and sat beside him. For a minute or two they sat in silence.

"It's obvious how silly it was to bring the children over here," William said. "But we can't do anything about it unless Masterman agrees, and he certainly won't. He thinks he's found the new Liberty Hall."

"And perhaps he has."

"At times he makes me feel like an infant crying in the night," William said. He paused. "And there's another thing, too."

"What?"

William waved his arm at the ruin. "This church," he said. "It was Tom. I told you about the German aircraft he shot down. Well, this is where it crashed."

Polly looked at him for some seconds and then said, "Why on earth didn't you tell me that before?"

"I don't know," William said. "I really don't know."

"Bloody hell," Polly said.

"Yes."

"I don't mean bloody hell about Tom wrecking the church, I mean bloody hell about you not telling me. I really can't understand why you didn't tell me, William."

"Perhaps it wasn't all that important. There was a lot going on."

"Rubbish." Polly put her chin in her hands and stared out across the orchards and woods. "It's like you not telling Tom about the baby. I just can't understand it."

"I'm sorry," William said.

"I daresay you are. But I don't see why you keep things like that to yourself."

"Tom keeps coming into my head," William said. "I see him in his uniform sometimes, sitting in a deck chair or climbing into his aeroplane. Sometimes I remember how we were years ago. Things that happened at school. How we were always together. Once we were caught pinching a couple of Flake bars, and the shopkeeper followed us to the den we'd made in an old building site. That was a secret of ours."

Polly turned to look at him. "What happened?"

"We got away from him. We never went back to the shop, and we never told anyone about it."

"I'm sorry to be cross, but you ought to tell me things. Your family never gives anything away, does it? God knows how you managed to get yourself involved with Liberty Hall."

William was silent for some moments. Eventually he said, "I know people ought to speak out. It's obviously right for people to say what they think, isn't it? But now I see something else as well. People get things done by bottling up their feelings. They get things organized and they get things done, and that's quite right, too. You can't just let things drift, can you?"

"Is life about getting things done, then? Is that what you've decided?"

"What else is there? Otherwise you wouldn't be spending all this time becoming a doctor, would you?"

Polly laughed. "Oh, you've got it all worked out, have you?"

"It's something to do with wanting to succeed, isn't it?"

"Maybe I just want to mother people."

"Then you could have been a nurse or a housemaid."

Polly looked up at the sky. "Your Milly is more loyal to you than I could ever be. It would make no difference to her if you were a murderer. She'd stand by you, just the same. Somehow she's bound to your family forever, come hell or high water."

"That's another person who never lets on what she's feeling. Milly, I mean."

"So it isn't just the middle classes, then. It's the bloody English. All of them."

"I suppose so. But in her case . . ."

"What?"

"She wants to keep herself to herself, but it's because she's a private person, not a secretive one, don't you think?"

"Also, she's lonely."

"Is she?"

"Of course she is."

"It never occurred to me."

"Well, it should have. When you and Tom left home, her main purpose was gone."

"It's true she doesn't get on in the same way with Stella."

"Did you see Milly at the reception?"

"Of course I did."

"But did you see her standing at the back, all alone, and then slipping away early?"

"Did she?"

"Yes."

"She doesn't much like talking to people. She never has. She's worked for us for twenty-odd years, but she never said what she was thinking, even to Tom and me. She just got on with it."

"She's kept herself completely to herself for all that time. All those years. Just think of it, William."

"Yes."

"Whom did she learn it from?"

"I don't know. Maybe she did learn it from us." He stood up, walked a few paces toward the church, and stood looking at the ruined tower. "The question is," he said, "what are we going to do now?"

Polly got up and went across to him. "We're going to help the school get sorted out here, then we'll decide what we're going to do after that."

"Yes. We can't possibly walk out on everyone at the moment."

"That's settled, then."

THE SUN'S RIM edged above the horizon. Along the English coast, in the huts beneath the radar aerials, young women watched lines of light glimmering across cathode-ray tubes. All across the Home Counties the Observer Corps fidgeted in their sandbagged enclosures. Aircraftsmen began to wipe away the dew that lay on wings and fuselages. In the operations rooms the duty crews put on their headphones and stood ready; the controllers on their balcony talked quietly, their eyes turning, now and again, toward the empty map table.

ON THE FRENCH coast the invading soldiers awoke. They clapped one another on the back and began to talk about going home. In the end, it had taken only a few days, and now it was almost over. The pioneer battalions had been working all night, digging trenches, pouring concrete, and mining the sands toward Calais and the west. As it grew light they stopped work, lit cigarettes, and looked out at the calm water. Farther inland, on the captured airfields of Artois and Picardy, the Luftwaffe ground crews began to prepare their Heinkels and Messerschmitts. Soon the pilots assembled, received their briefings, and strolled toward their machines.

WHEN THE FIRST telephone rang in the operations room, everyone stopped talking and there was a tiny pause before one of the controllers picked it up. He listened and then said to one of the WAAFs, "Twenty plus, one nine five, angels twenty." She selected a red marker, gave it a numbered flag, and placed it in position on the map table.

A minute or two passed before another telephone rang and a second red marker was placed near the first. The controllers talked quietly to one another, and one picked up his telephone and gave an order; soon a black marker appeared on the English side of the table as the first of the defending squadrons became airborne.

More telephones rang. Teleprinters began to chatter. The girls worked their long rakes like croupiers, nudging the red and black markers this way and that, while the controllers spoke in their curt jargon, responding calmly to the urgent cries of the men in the air.

FROM THE AIRFIELDS of northern France, flying northwest at twenty thousand feet, came a formation of thirty Heinkels, and high above, an escort of Messerschmitts. From the Sussex coast came the first squadron of defending fighters, twelve aircraft flying in sections of three, the undersides of their wings illuminated by the low sun. They circled over Beachy Head in the smooth morning air, climbing strongly. To the east a second squadron had taken off and was also gaining height. The third squadron waited, its pilots lounging on the grass beside their aircraft.

IN GOODMAN ST. John, the children crowded into the vicarage kitchen and ate bacon and eggs. William and Polly were there, with Matron and John Vernon. Through the window William saw that Janosz was already working on the clearance of the last of the vegetable beds, tipping fragments of stone and glass from a sieve into a bucket. He picked up a rake and drew it with regular strokes through the soil.

William banged on the table with the back of a spoon, and when it grew quiet he said, "I've just been upstairs and Masterman's still asleep. So is Irma. I think we need to sort things out and decide what to do. We need to get organized."

"Yes," Matron said. "We certainly do."

"After last night, the first thing is to decide whether we should stay here."

"I don't see why not," Todger said. "No bombs fell on us."

"Not yet, they didn't," Susan said.

"Exactly," William said. "This is a risky place."

"If an invasion comes, Kent will certainly be in the front line," John Vernon said.

"Look," one of the O'Leary boys said. Several children went to the window. High up, a group of black specks crossed the sky toward the southeast. "Hurricanes," said Nigel O'Leary.

"Spitfires," Masterman said. Nobody had noticed him come in. He was wearing his straw hat and a blue dressing gown embroidered with yellow dragons.

"You can't possibly tell what they are from this distance," Susan said.

"I have excellent eyesight, Susan," Masterman said. "Is there any tea in the pot?"

"We're talking about what to do next," William said.

"Talk away, old chap," Masterman said. "It's a free country."

William said, "We've certainly gone far enough, and maybe too far. We're right in the line of fire. There could be an invasion any day, and this place will be a battlefield."

"You're unusually forceful this morning, dear boy," Masterman said. "Just remember that the same thing applies to the millions who live round here. They know about the risk, but you don't see them running away, do you? Even the evacuees are creeping back." He took a cigar from his top pocket and sniffed it.

There were footsteps on the stairs and Irma came into the kitchen.

"Hello, Irma," William said. "We're just talking about what we should do next. After all that bombing last night."

"Oh, I see," Irma said. She looked around the room and then went across to Masterman.

"It's not a question of running away," William said. "That's not the point. It's got nothing to do with the people who live here. The point is, we're responsible for our children, and we're putting them at risk."

"Risk is part of life, William." Masterman looked around the room and smiled in a benevolent way. "Risk is what makes life worth living."

William said, "We must ask everyone what they think. It's extremely kind of John Vernon to let us stay here for a bit, but perhaps we should move to somewhere safer."

Masterman lit a match, applied it to the end of his cigar, and puffed smoke upward. "Well, then," he said, "who thinks we ought to move away from here?"

"Oh, I like this house," Belinda said. "I think it's sweet."

"We shouldn't give in to the Jerries," said Arthur Beckingsale.

"Actually, I think I'd like to stay," Todger said. "I quite like it here."

Nobody else said anything.

"Good," Masterman said. "Best to get that sort of thing decided as soon as possible, I always think."

"All right," William said. "That's decided. We'll stay here. But we still need to take better precautions."

Matron said, "Oh yes. We really do, you know. That's absolutely right, William."

"I'd like to get the crypt organized into a proper shelter, for a start," William said. "I want some volunteers to help with that."

"Certainly," John Vernon said. "Count me in, my dear fellow."

"I'll help," Todger said. Several other children put their hands up, saying, "I will, I will."

"Good," William said. "We'll make a start after breakfast with a meeting for everyone who wants to help. Nine o'clock sharp."

OUTSIDE, JANOSZ PASENIK sank his spade into the soil, a blackbird sang, and pigeons fluttered in the eaves. After raking together the glass fragments and stones he had collected, Janosz shoveled them into the sieve and tipped them onto the growing heap in the corner. Here he planned to make a rock garden; the stony base would drain well and permit the planting of an interesting collection of alpines and other hardy perennials.

～

TOM SWUNG HIMSELF onto the wing and stepped across into the cockpit. He grasped the windscreen with both hands and lowered himself into the seat. Yawning, he stretched his arms upward; then, seeing Alan watching him, he laughed and said, "I'll be awake in a minute, Alan. I had a bad night."

The aircraftsman handed him a mug of tea, and he clasped it with both hands.

"She's warmed up and I've given her another good look over," Alan said. "I changed those fuses and checked the brakes again."

"Oh, did you? Good." Tom reached forward, tapped the face of the altimeter, and set it to zero. "Did you find anything?"

"No. She's fine."

Alan leaned against the side of the cockpit and sipped his tea. Tom watched the sun edging upward through a layer of mist. After a while he said, "You don't know if the armorers looked at that dodgy Browning, do you?"

"Yes, they did," Alan said. "I told you that yesterday."

"Of course you did. Sorry."

"They couldn't find anything wrong with it."

"I expect it'll be all right." He finished his tea and passed the mug to Alan. The aircraftsman stepped down from the wing and walked away toward the dispersal hut. Tom began to strap himself in.

～

THE SUN WAS up, the tide was at its lowest ebb, and the long shoals of the estuary lay exposed like the spines of great creatures. In the Dover Strait, off Dungeness and Beachy Head, and all along the

Normandy coast the sea remained calm. On the heights of Cap Gris-Nez, the Wehrmacht observers changed the watch, and the new men, as they always did, turned their binoculars across the narrows toward the gleam of the Dover cliffs.

⌐⌐

MOMENTS AFTER THE telephone rang in the dispersal hut, the airfield controller began shouting orders and the pilots ran to their aircraft. Tom was glad to be already strapped in and waiting. The warm engine started easily, Alan dragged the chocks away, and the aeroplane began rolling along in its ungainly way, like a duck walking, clouds of dust rising on either side as the rest of the squadron began to move.

He went through the takeoff checks, lowered the flaps, opened the radiator. The radio crackled and Nobby Clark asked him where he was. Tom leaned his head over the side of the cockpit, trying to identify the aircraft in front. It was Nobby all right. "I'm just behind you," he said. They taxied to the end of the airfield and lined up in sections. When it came to their turn, Nobby glanced sideways at Tom and Colin, the engines bellowed, and they were away across the grass, bouncing a little, lifting from the ground, and climbing away, suddenly graceful in the air.

⌐⌐

ALAN WILLIS KEPT on watching until the aircraft had vanished into the distance. He looked at his watch; it was eight o'clock. They'd be back in an hour or so. It was nice when they'd all gone. The place went quiet and you suddenly noticed the warm breeze that came steadily across the grass. He looked up, shading his eyes: Somewhere high up, a bird was singing, but he couldn't see it. He began to walk toward the aircraftsmen's mess. There was plenty of time for a bit of breakfast and a cup of tea before they came back.

⌐⌐

THE TWELVE SPITFIRES climbed steadily. At ten thousand feet they went through a layer of wispy cloud. At fifteen thousand their engines were still at full boost. Nothing could be seen in the southeast except the sun's glare. They passed twenty-five thousand and the pilots began to fly with particular care, their aircraft less stable in the thinning air. Below lay all the country from the North Foreland to Dungeness, sharp and clear. At twenty-six thousand feet the controller gave them a new vector. They turned south, still climbing, and at last saw the enemy two or three thousand feet below: thirty Heinkels on a northerly course. Tom looked in his mirror and then up into the blue; there was nothing above, nothing behind. The squadron leader's voice crackled in their headphones, telling Nobby Clark to attack with two sections while the rest stayed high.

Tom wriggled deeper into his seat and moved his body against the straps, testing their tightness. He put both hands on the stick. The aeroplane shimmered with the fine vibration of high speed, trembling occasionally as it nudged the slipstream of the leaders. Fifty feet to his left was Nobby, steady as a rock. Tom saw him turn his head left and right and then glance upward: He was a good man, Nobby, always checking, always looking.

The six aircraft broke away from the others in a diving turn that took them away in a wide sweep behind the bombers. Their speed built up quickly. The controls grew heavy and the aircraft began to shudder. "D section, take the back row," Nobby said. "We'll take the rest."

It was perfect: break left, line astern, echelon right. They came in from below, the enemy formation seemingly drawn toward them by some mysterious force until Tom's gunsight was filled with the pale underside of a Heinkel. He fired, the Heinkel swerved, there was an explosion, the sky went black, something struck Tom's aircraft with a violent impact, and then he was through the smoke and following Nobby as he pulled away in a steep turn.

Sweat ran down Tom's back. He wrenched the aeroplane around. He could hear shouts in his headphones but made no sense of them. He must stay with Nobby. He pushed the throttle through the emergency gate, and the force of the turn crushed him into his seat. For a moment his vision blacked out and then was clear again, but it was all right, he had caught up. Tom throttled back; but then the cock-

pit filled with dense white smoke and he could see nothing. The
noise was still in his headphones: It was Nobby, he realized, Nobby
was shouting his name, and at that instant he felt a wave of ferocious
heat from somewhere beneath the cockpit: The aeroplane was burning. He pushed back the hood and fumbled to undo the straps, the
oxygen supply, the radio leads. The smoke swirled, he looked ahead
and for a moment saw the sea below, then with a violent effort he
stood up and found himself out in the rushing air, tumbling over and
over.

He tugged at the parachute release and it came free in his hand—
for a moment he thought it had broken, and then he was jerked upright like a puppet and was hanging in midair, swinging in a wide
arc and gasping for breath.

WHEN HE LIFTED his head only the faint sound of engines lingered in the air. He looked around. No sign of his own aircraft, or of
any others. Nothing at all. There was a moment of fury and then
nothing, just as Uncle Oscar always said.

He was still high, perhaps ten thousand feet, and not far from the
coast: three or four miles out, five or six at the most, certainly near
enough to be seen. People at Hythe and Folkestone and Dover would
be watching from their windows and deck chairs; somebody would
see the parachute and reach for the telephone.

He lifted his hands and inspected them, peered down at his
dangling legs, turned his head one way and the other: He was un-
harmed. He reached for the tube of his Mae West and began to in-
flate it. The yellow collar swelled slowly. He squeezed it with one
hand until it felt firm enough. Suddenly feeling exhausted, he reached
up and grasped the straps above his head. As he did so he heard the
sound of an engine.

It was Nobby Clark, of course. Good old Nobby! Twisting awkwardly in the harness to look behind, Tom saw the Spitfire, and there
he was, circling steeply around him, hood flung back, waving like
mad. Tom shook both fists in mock rage, setting himself swinging
and bobbing beneath the parachute. "I'm all right," he shouted into

the din of the engine, grinning and waving, "I'm all right!" Nobby circled twice, three times, four times, waved once more, and then the aeroplane straightened up and flew away toward the land.

He looked down, kicked off his flying boots, and watched them fall toward the dark silver of the sea. It was late summer and the water would be warm. Nobby would tell them where he was, and soon he would be rescued. He could hear a dog barking somewhere across the water, and a bell was ringing; it sounded like a school bell, the kind that called the children in from the playground at the start of the day. He looked at his watch. It was nine o'clock, and at that moment he slid into the enfolding waters of the English Channel, the parachute settling lightly on the surface beside him like an enormous white flower.

⌒

"I'VE SPOKEN TO the children," William said. "I've also had an interesting conversation with Mr. Pasenik, who was a teacher until recently, and with John Vernon, Polly, and Matron. I've got a few suggestions for things we ought to do this week, and I'm working on some ideas for the rest of the autumn term."

"A timetable," Masterman said. "A curriculum."

"Irma," William said, "your drama show at Easter was so good that we thought we might do something similar just before Christmas, perhaps when the church commissioners come to talk to us. What do you think?"

"Well," Irma said. She looked sideways at Masterman. "I'd really like to do another show. Everybody gets such a lot out of it, and it's such fun."

"A timetable," Masterman said again. "Rules and regulations. Perhaps even uniforms. Have you thought of uniforms?"

"I know you don't like what I'm saying, Masterman," William said, "but we need to get better organized. We need more security. We need to know what we're doing. Everybody thinks so."

"Everybody?"

"Yes," William said. "Everybody." He turned to Masterman. "And there's one more thing," he said.

"You're frightfully decisive today, William," Masterman said.

"John Vernon has asked me to speak to you and Irma. He's had several complaints from villagers about your sunbathing."

Masterman laughed, but William took no notice. "They don't like you two sunbathing without any clothes."

"Nude," Masterman said. "Naked."

"Yes," William said. "Exactly. And you've simply got to stop doing it, particularly in the vicarage garden. They won't want the school here if you do that sort of thing."

Masterman considered the question and then looked at Irma. "Quite ludicrous, the attitudes of some people," he said. Irma said nothing.

———

THE SQUADRON RETURNED. Alan Willis watched them come over the hedge and settle on the airfield, and when he saw that two aircraft were missing he put down his cup and began to run across the grass. He reached the dispersal area as Nobby Clark was stepping down from the wing.

"Tom's in the water," Nobby said. "He's a few miles off Folkestone. He'll be all right. They'll fish him out in a minute." He looked around at the other aircraft. "I don't know where Colin is. I didn't see him after the attack. God knows what happened to him."

He opened his cigarette case, took out a cigarette, and tapped it on the lid. "I'm sorry, old chap. Put the word around the ground crews, would you? Not a lot we can do except wait."

———

HE COULD SEE almost nothing but the sky. Now and again, when a larger swell lifted him, he glimpsed something that might be land, away to the north. The sun was hot on his face. He kicked his legs and paddled a little with his hands. The life jacket was keeping him face up, but he could swim a clumsy kind of backstroke. Which way was the tide? Would it carry him inshore? There was no way of telling. He would swim north. He lay back and began to swim at a steady pace, steering by the sun. Occasionally a wave lapped his mouth. Nobby would have got his position and reported it. Someone would come. The sea was calm. It was a perfect summer's day. There was plenty of time. All he had to do was keep swimming and wait for someone to arrive.

⌒

THE PILOTS STOOD in a circle and the squadron leader told them that Group HQ had forbidden them to search for Tom and Colin; every squadron and every pilot was needed for operations.

The pilots murmured and shuffled their feet.

"However," the CO went on, "we'll fly the next operation, and on the way back I think we'll get a little disoriented." The pilots nodded as they took his meaning.

"Somehow we'll find ourselves coming back via Dover, and quite low, so keep a good lookout and give a shout if you see anything. All right?" They nodded. "I've told the adj to pester the navy and the coast guard. That's all, chaps. Carry on."

The squadron leader went over to Nobby Clark.

"Tom's perfectly all right," Nobby said. "He was waving like a maniac and grinning all over his silly face. He still had the right number of arms and legs. I don't know about Colin. I haven't a clue what happened to him. I'm sorry."

They walked toward the aircraft and the squadron leader put his arm around Nobby's shoulders. "It's not your fault, old chap," he said. "It's just one of those bloody things. The silly sods will be back in no time."

⌒

IN THE MIDDLE of the morning a sea breeze set in. The waves were small but occasionally slapped into Tom's eyes and mouth. He was still paddling steadily toward the coast because you couldn't know whether anyone would come out for you, so you had to keep going.

Actually, the water wasn't as warm as he'd thought, but it wasn't particularly cold, either. He ought to be able to stay afloat for hours yet. If he wasn't picked up, the squadron would surely come looking for him. They wouldn't just leave him there. Nobby and Colin certainly would come looking. Nobby knew where he was, and he'd remember about the tide. Nobby would know about that. He'd work it out. He worked everything out, Nobby did, even though he sometimes behaved like a complete ass. Tom laughed and a wave rolled over his head, making him splutter. The wind must be getting up a bit more. He stopped paddling and tried again to see where he was, but there was still no sign of the shore. This bloody wind was a nuisance. The waves were beginning to come over his face all the time. He began swimming again, more urgently. At least the wind was in the right direction, pushing him toward the shore. That was something, anyway.

"LINE ABREAST," THE squadron leader said. The ten aircraft spread out, flying westward at fifteen hundred feet. They made one run a mile off the shore, turned, and came back.

"Zulu leader," the controller was saying in their headphones, "Zulu leader, do you read me? Come in, Zulu leader."

The squadron leader took no notice. "All right, chaps," he said, "one more run and then we'll go home."

TOM HEARD THE Spitfires coming from the east and turned around to face them, waving and shouting. One of them went smack over his head and he went on waving, but in a few seconds they were out of sight. He stopped swimming and waited. Surely they had seen him, surely they would come back. He trod water. Five or six minutes passed and then he heard them returning. He began waving again, but this time they were too far to the south. He lay back and went on swimming. It was good of them to come looking for him. He had known they would. They were jolly good chaps, all of them.

AT MIDDAY THE squadron took off on its third operation of the day and was surprised by more than thirty enemy fighters. Two more aircraft were lost and four damaged, two of them seriously. No pilot was seen to bail out. When they returned, the squadron leader went into the dispersal hut to telephone Group. When he came out he said, "They've told us to stand by for the rest of today. They're sending us a couple more aircraft sometime this afternoon. We'll have another briefing later on."

"That's bloody silly," Nobby said. "We could put the rest of our aircraft up, surely? Don't they want us?"

"Of course they want us, Clark. But they want a proper bloody squadron, not a raggle-taggle army." He went back into the dispersal hut and banged the door.

⁓

IT WAS HARD to work out exactly what had happened. They had certainly made a good job of the attack. It had been copybook stuff. He'd got that Heinkel fair and square. Its bombs must have gone off, and then a piece of the wreckage, something big, had hit his aeroplane and split the fuel tank. That white smoke in the cockpit was probably glycol from the cooling system; the engine must have been hit as well. But it was such a bloody shambles and so quick that you couldn't sort it out, and that was two bloody Spitfires he'd lost, for Christ's sake.

Above him the sky was clear and blue, but away to the north, above the coast, the morning's puffy cumulus had fattened into substantial clouds with dark undersides. The clouds were very high; the cloud base was five or six thousand feet and the clouds surged upward for another six or seven thousand at least, brilliantly white in the sunshine and bursting with energy. He lay in the water and looked at them for a while, then began swimming again.

⁓

AS MASTERMAN HAD said, twelve was a convenient number. For an hour in the afternoon, a group of four children marked out their own patches of garden under the supervision of Janosz Pasenik. A second group of four worked with Irma on ideas for the November performance. William took the third group himself; he wanted to establish exactly how much mathematics each child knew, beginning with the multiplication tables. They seemed to like doing sums. At the end of an hour they had a break, and the groups changed over. It all worked rather well, and gave to the afternoon a definite sense of achievement.

The children's chanting drifted up through the open windows of the vicarage. Polly lay dozing in her room. On the top floor, Masterman had surrounded himself with books and begun writing a paper called "From Hegemony to Pedagogy" that was going to turn the educational world upside down. Matron, with the help of several villagers, had arranged proper beds and bedding in the crypt. A supply of electrical power was being installed by the church warden, Alvin Sutton.

Matron nodded to herself: Excellent progress was being made.

~~~~~

ALL AFTERNOON THE pilots waited, smoking, reading, and dozing on the dry grass. Three replacement aircraft were delivered in midafternoon, but still the squadron was not called into action.

At four o'clock Nobby Clark asked the squadron leader if they could make another search along the coast.

"I've been checking the tides, sir," Nobby said, "and I reckon I know exactly where Tom is. If we look properly, we're bound to find him. Colin must be nearby, too. We could borrow the Oxford, fill it with sharp-eyed bods, and fly a proper square search."

The squadron leader thought about it and then said, "All right, but I'll have to ask Group. They probably won't want an unarmed aeroplane messing about and confusing the picture."

A few minutes later he emerged from the dispersal hut shaking his head. "No can do," he said. "We've got to let the coast guard get on with it. They're the experts."

At nine o'clock the squadron was told to stand down. The pilots went into the mess and got Jenkins to open the bar.

"I'd just keep filling them up if I were you," the squadron leader said to Jenkins. "It's going to be one of those nights."

After an hour Jack Horner began crooning: "I put my finger in the

woodpecker's hole, and the woodpecker said, 'God bless my soul!' "
They sang a chorus and Jack Horner continued in his clear voice, "I
removed my finger from the woodpecker's hole, and the woodpecker
said, 'God bless my soul!' "

All the pilots joined in again, then someone suggested "Lydia
Pink," a song they always thought highly amusing:

> *We'll drink, a drink, a drink,*
> *To Lydia Pink, a Pink, a Pink,*
> *The savior of the human race,*
> *For she invented a medicinal comp-u-ound,*
> *Most efficacious in every case.*

They sang many more songs as darkness fell, including "She Was
Poor, but She Was Honest," "Sing Us Another One," "Did You Ever
See Such a Funny Thing Before?," "The Lobster," and a bawdy ver-
sion of "Christopher Robin."

Late in the evening, Nobby Clark buttonholed the squadron
leader and said, "What is particularly nice about these songs is their
complete absurdity, don't you agree, sir?"

"Absolutely, Nobby," the squadron leader said. "And their total
filthiness, of course. Is that an empty glass you've got there?"

"By God," Nobby said, waving it over his head. "A damned
empty glass! It's an offense to common decency."

"I'll get another for you, dear boy," the squadron leader said.

After the singing they held a lengthy and confused drinking con-
test, and finally, by popular request, Jack Horner sang in his clear
baritone the mournful verses of "Kathleen":

> *Oh, I will take you back, Kathleen,*
> *To where your heart will feel no pain*
> *And where the fields are fresh and green;*
> *I'll take you to your home, Kathleen.*

By this time several pilots had fallen asleep in the easy chairs or on
the grass outside, under the stars.

⌒

THE TIDE HAD taken Tom five miles along the coast and back
again. By nightfall he was no closer to the shore and he kept falling
asleep. After the second or third time, he woke and tears ran down
his face because all this was so silly, so silly. He wasn't hurt at all,
Nobby had spotted him, he was only a few miles offshore, and the
weather was perfectly all right. All he needed was for someone to
find him, but now it was dark and much colder.

Later the moon rose and the wind fell light. This wasn't so bad.
The sea was calm again, the water moved lazily about him like black
silk, and he could sleep more easily.

⌒

UNTIL LATE THAT night William worked on his plans for the
rest of the term, and at eleven-thirty the sirens began again. The new
arrangements worked well. Everybody got up and went in an orderly
fashion to the crypt. The lights that Alvin Sutton had rigged up made
a great difference; they sat around in a circle, singing "Early One
Morning," "The Foggy, Foggy Dew," "I Know Where I'm Going,"
and other favorites.

After the singing, Matron put out all the lights except a candle
beside the steps. The raid went on for more than two hours, but no
bombs fell nearby. At first, the children whispered and giggled, but
it was not long before they fell asleep. William lay awake until the
raid had ended, watching the steady flame of the candle and listening to the small sounds in the darkness around him.

⌒

JUST AFTER DAWN, the coxswain of the lifeboat glimpsed the
yellow of a life jacket, turned in a broad circle, and came slowly
alongside. The boat lay stopped, rolling slowly in the swell, while
the second coxswain snared the pilot with a boathook. They got a
rope around him, pulled him aboard as carefully as they could, and
laid him on the foredeck. Two of the crew set to work and got some
of the water out of him, but the coxswain soon told them to stop. It

was obviously no good. They wrapped the body in a tarpaulin and lashed it down beside the others. The coxswain lit a cigarette, leaned on the rail, and blew a spear of smoke out across the water. "That's enough for one bloody night," he said. He stepped up to the wheel and set course for the harbor.

At Dover the boat came alongside and the ambulance men came down the steps with stretchers. "Watch out," the coxswain said, "That one's a Jerry." He nudged one of the bodies with his foot. "Don't muddle him up with the RAF boys."

DOREEN GOT INTO the squadron office early. The airfield was quiet. Airmen were standing about, but nothing much was happening. She tapped on the squadron leader's door and went in. He was sitting at his desk.

"Good morning, sir," Doreen said. "Would you like some tea?"

He looked up. "You're a treasure, Doreen." He thought for a moment and then said, "See if you can find Nobby Clark, would you, and get him to come in and see me. Perhaps you could make a cup for him, too."

When Nobby came in, the squadron leader waved him to a chair. Nobby looked at him and said, "They've found Tom, have they?"

"I'm afraid they have. And Colin."

"Both of them."

"Yes. One of the lifeboats found them in the end, but they'd been in the water much too long by that time."

Doreen came in, put down their cups of tea, and went out again.

Nobby said, "Why didn't the bloody navy go and look for them?"

"They probably did. I don't know. Maybe the Channel's too dangerous to risk a ship for a couple of men."

"Tom was only four miles off the coast. I saw him. I know exactly where he was."

"I know that, Nobby, but it's no use saying that now, is it? I've sent the telegrams. We'll get their stuff collected up. Can you get Jenkins to do that? I'll talk to the ground crews later on."

Nobby Clark reached for his tea and sipped it slowly.

"Look, Nobby," the squadron leader said, "we've got to get operational again. That's the only thing that matters."

"All right, sir, I know," Nobby said, standing up. "The navy fished me out, you know. They could have had a decent look for Tom and Colin as well."

Alan Willis was hanging about on the grass outside the CO's office. Nobby Clark stopped and said, "I'm sorry, Willis. Bad news, I'm afraid."

"Oh, is it, sir?"

"Yes. I'm sorry."

"Oh, I see," Alan said. "Thank you, sir."

"He bailed out into the sea and nobody could find him in time. It was a dreadful thing. We could have gone out and found him, but they wouldn't let us, the bastards."

"Yes," Alan said. "Yes, I see, sir."

"It's an awful business."

Alan hesitated. "Do you think someone will tell his brother, sir?"

"The CO's sent a telegram to his parents."

"Yes, but they don't know where his brother is."

"Ah," Nobby said. "That's a thought. But we do."

"Yes, sir. That's what I meant."

⌒

JENKINS PACKED UP the belongings of the four pilot officers, stacked the suitcases on a handcart, and wheeled them round to the adjutant's office. "Leave them in the corner," the adjutant said. "I'm too busy to think about them at the moment."

"All right, sir," Jenkins said.

⌒

THE TRAIN RATTLED across Monckton Marshes, skirted the floodplain of the Great Stour, and turned southwest to Canterbury, where it rested for several minutes. Nobby Clark looked at his reflection in the window and straightened his tie.

At Bagham he left the train, walked for half a mile along the valley road into Goodman St. John, and turned into the High Street.

The houses clustered together, their upper stories overhanging the road. He climbed the hill to the square. When he saw the church he stopped and stared at it for several minutes.

Children were playing in the vicarage garden. "I'm looking for William Anderson," he said.

"Oh, we know him all right," one of the girls said. "He's inside." She jerked her thumb at the window behind her.

⁓

IN THE KITCHEN, William reached across the table and took Polly's hand. "It wasn't too bad," he said. "It worked out all right in the end, didn't it?"

"Yes," she said, laughing. "It was jolly good. No arguments. Everyone just got on with it. And in the end I'm not sure that Masterman minded all that much." She looked up and saw the young man in RAF uniform in the garden. "Oh, William," she said, putting her hand to her mouth.

William turned around. He thought it was Tom, but then he saw it was a stranger, a tall young man who was holding his cap in his hand and talking to Belinda.

William let go of Polly's hand and stood up.

⁓

BELINDA WATCHED WILLIAM and Polly go up to the young man. They took him through the gate into the churchyard and sat on one of the piles of stones. Belinda followed at a distance and stood in the shade of the archway.

When the young man had finished talking he sat still, turning his cap in his hands. William stood up and took a few steps toward the tall chestnut, then Polly went over and put her arms around him. They stood together for a long time. Belinda lay down in the long grass beside the wall of the churchyard and rested her chin in her hands. The young man was still sitting on the pile of stones. Polly and William stood together. The sun was hot, and Belinda could hear the regular ticking of a grasshopper nearby.

October

A FLY droned past, collided with the window, and fell to rotating on the linoleum. A heap of dismembered magazines and newspapers lay on a low table. William took Saturday's *Times* from the top of the pile and turned to the crossword. "An unprogressive, frequently apt description of a punt-pole" was obviously "Stick in the mud." He took a pencil from his pocket and wrote it in.

A nurse, dressed in a blue-and-white-checked uniform and a white cap, walked through the waiting room, not looking at him. In some ways nurses were like mothers, but in others they were not. They held your hand when it hurt and helped you on and off with your pajamas; meanwhile, on their left breast, a few inches from your eye, there ticked an inverted, inscrutable watch. Oh Tom, William said to himself.

Sixteen across was easy. "There has fallen a splendid——, From the passion-flower at the gate." Four letters. That was from "Maud." He shut his eyes and the lines came to him:

> There has fallen a splendid tear
> From the passion-flower at the gate.
> She is coming, my dove, my dear;

She is coming, my life, my fate;
The red rose cries, "She is near, she is near";
And the white rose weeps, "She is late";
The larkspur listens, "I hear, I hear";
And the lily whispers "I wait."

There was something slightly ridiculous about that poem, come to think of it. He wrote in "Tear." That gave an "a" for the Whittington one, which must be "Turn again."

The nurse came back. "Congratulations," she said. "You've got a little boy."

"What? A boy? Have I?"

"You can see your wife and the baby now. Come this way."

When he got to the ward, William saw Polly lying in the bed with the baby wrapped in white. He knelt beside the bed and the nurse pulled the curtains around them. William lifted his head and looked at the sunlit fabric. "It's like being in a tent," he said. "It's like a nomad's tent in the desert."

"No self-respecting nomad would have a tent with those awful roses on it," Polly said, and began to cry and laugh at the same time.

⌐⌐⌐

THE WAY LED along a lane beside the church, across the main road, and uphill through the stubble of a wheat field. Halfway up, William stopped and looked back across the valley. Goodman St. John presented itself to them: the High Street, the village square, the vicarage, the Crown Inn, the crumpled church.

Polly said, "What are you looking at?"

"It's funny, you know. If you look at the clouds, there's a definite pattern, a kind of regularity, even though they're all different. They come along in lines and groups, like musical notes. If you wrote them down, you'd probably get a symphony."

"Would you?"

"Oh yes. I've often noticed it."

"William, are you sure there isn't a touch of Masterman in that?"

"A touch of Masterman lurks in all of us."

"Not in me, it doesn't."

"Some of them may be too fast to detect. Or too slow, of course. The patterns and rhythms, I mean."

"No doubt."

"I'll go on talking, shall I, even if you're not listening?"

"I *am* listening, William. But someone has to push the pram."

"Do you remember I told you about that bit of verse about the airmen? The one that made Tom sit up?"

" 'Pilots of the purple twilight, dropping down with costly bales,' " Polly said, maneuvering the pram through a muddy patch.

"Yes. It's pretty, but it isn't very true, is it?"

At Old Wives Lees the road passed three oasthouses and ran through an orchard. They turned off the road and took a path between two lines of pollarded willows. It led into a shallow valley filled with hop poles. A row of beeches, their thinning leaves gleaming in the sun, marched up the far side of the valley and over the next crest. The path was steep. William turned the pram and pulled it backward up the slope. "It's easier this way," he said.

"That's all right, then," Polly said.

He looked at her. "You're laughing at me again," he said.

"What, me? Surely not."

At the top they stopped for a moment, and William looked up at the sky. Some of the clouds were darker now. Maybe rain was coming.

"Oh dear," he said, "I keep thinking about him. I can't stop doing it."

Polly said nothing.

"I think of him out at sea all that night, and nobody coming to him. I think of his beautiful aeroplane lying at the bottom of the Channel and slowly dissolving away."

Polly still said nothing. They walked across the top of the hill, pushing the pram side by side, and Polly put her arm through William's.

"I don't see how I can ever get used to him not being here," William said. "It's funny, you know. Whenever I think of him the same scene comes to mind. He's dashing off somewhere in a hurry and he's late. He's all dressed up and he's running his hand through his hair

like he often did when he was thinking about something complicated."

"You do that, too."

"What?"

"That thing with your hair."

Beside the path were several more oasthouses, their chimney cowls
swiveling this way and that in the breeze. They went on through
Chartham Hatch into No Man's Orchard, a sloping field full of
newly planted apple trees. Some of the young trees bore just a single fat apple. When they got to Golden Hill William stopped and
picked up a scallop shell.

"Proper pilgrims have been along here," he said.

The cathedral lay in the valley before them, a mile away.

"It's very fine," William said, "but I'm not going to believe a word
of it."

"We've almost done it. We've made a pilgrimage all the way to a
place we don't believe in."

"Yes," William said. "It seemed like a good idea at the time. Actually, it still is, because life doesn't have any particular purpose, you
know."

"Ah," Polly said. "I see."

"You have to make your own purpose. It can't be anything you
like, though. It has to fit in with other people. That's where Masterman gets it wrong."

Polly turned to look at the cathedral. "Those stonemasons made
themselves a bloody good purpose," she said.

William said, "If I wake in the night and hear bombers, I always think about Tom saying, 'If they're synchronized, they're ours.
If they're not, get under the table.' "

They reached the outskirts of the city. At St. Dunstan's church
Polly said, "Look at that." The rows of tapered stones looked like
wrapped mummies. One of the headstones was engraved with crossed
rifles and a military cap. Polly read out the inscription:

IN LOVING MEMORY OF ALBERT (BERT) COLDSACK,
LATE CPL OF THE 2ND BUFFS, DEARLY LOVED
HUSBAND OF GLADYS COLDSACK, DIED AT LENHAM

NOVEMBER 28TH 1918 AGED 27. ALSO OF COM
SGT I. L. FAIRCLOTH, 7TH SUSSEX BATTN, FIRST
HUSBAND OF THE ABOVE, KILLED IN ACTION
DECEMBER 28TH 1915 AGED 25, ERECTED BY THEIR
SORROWING WIFE.
THEIR COUNTRY CALLED THEM.

"The Coldsacks lying forever in their cold sacks," William said. "There's nothing new about any of this, is there?"

"Poor Gladys," Polly said. "She wasn't lucky, was she?"

In the cathedral, candles flickered here and there. The choir was practicing.

> We plow the fields and scatter
> The good seed on the land,
> But it is fed and watered
> By God's almighty hand.

From the guidebook Polly read out, " 'The latten tomb of Edward the Black Prince is surmounted by replicas of his surcoat, helmet, gauntlets, and accoutrements.' "

William looked at the gleaming yellow figure. "What does 'latten' mean?"

"Brass," Polly said. "Obviously."

"Why don't they call it that, then?"

"Because it doesn't sound so good, of course. Edward the Brass Prince? No good at all."

The choir began singing again:

> All good gifts about us
> Are sent from heaven above
> Then thank the Lord,
> O thank the Lord,
> For all His love.

In the undercroft, the candles flickered and shadows moved. A figure knelt on the flagstones beside a man in a cassock. It was Janosz

Pasenik. He had chosen this place to begin telling, for the first time, in a slow and hesitant fashion, the story of what had occurred in a small village far away in the middle of the great plain of Poland. The young cleric listened with care; he felt he might have a vocation for this kind of thing.

William and Polly stepped back into the shadows, but when the baby began to howl the noise echoed around the cavern of the nave. The choirmaster turned around and looked at them severely.

"Oh goodness," William said.

"I'll have to feed him."

"Can you feed a baby in here?"

"Of course I can. I'd like to see them stop me."

"Oh. All right, then."

Polly took the child from the pram and sat on a chair. William paced up and down. He looked at her and the child and was conscious of the beating of his heart; he sat down and put his arms around them.

"That's better," Polly said. "It's not very warm in here."

THEY WALKED BACK toward the station. At West Gate they met Janosz, who was sitting on a park bench and looking at the river. He stood up and said, "You are in the cathedral."

"Yes," Polly said. "We saw you in there, too."

"I am telling the priest about my family."

"Good," William said.

Janosz looked into the pram. "My son was called Thomas," he said.

"Oh," Polly said. "Was he?"

"Yes," Janosz said. "And the girl was Maria."

There was a pause.

"We're going to get a train back to Goodman St. John," William said. "Are you coming?"

"Yes," Janosz said. As he spoke, a heron lifted from the shallows of the river, climbed ten or fifteen feet, and curved downwind to alight twenty yards upstream.

"*Ardea cinerea,*" Janosz said. "I do not know the English."

"It's a gray heron," William said.

"Gray heron." Janosz repeated the name carefully. "Aeneas burns the city Ardea. This bird flies from the ashes. It is called *Ardea cinerea*. It is a hopeless sign."

"Hopeful," William said. "I think you mean hopeful."

ABOUT THE AUTHOR

A graduate of the creative writing MA at the University of East Anglia, MARTIN CORRICK was formerly a lecturer at the University of Southampton in England. Now a full-time writer, he lives in the rural county of Gloucestershire.

ABOUT THE TYPE

This book was set in Garamond, a typeface originally designed by the Parisian typecutter Claude Garamond (1480–1561). This version of Garamond was modeled on a 1592 specimen sheet from the Egenolff-Berner foundry, which was produced from types assumed to have been brought to Frankfurt by the punchcutter Jacques Sabon.

Claude Garamond's distinguished romans and italics first appeared in *Opera Ciceronis* in 1543–44. The Garamond types are clear, open, and elegant.